DREAMWALKER

ALLAN MICHAEL HARDIN

iUniverse, Inc.
New York   Bloomington

Dreamwalker

Copyright © 2008 by Allan Michael Hardin

iUniverse books may be ordered through booksellers or by contacting:

iUniverse
1663 Liberty Drive
Bloomington, IN 47403
www.iuniverse.com
1-800-Authors (1-800-288-4677)

ISBN: 978-0-595-52256-9 (pbk)
ISBN: 978-0-595-51147-1 (cloth)
ISBN: 978-0-595-62312-9 (ebk)

Printed in the United States of America

For my darling wife, Linda

Contents

Chapter 1 - Jail Break   1

Chapter 2 - Massacre   24

Chapter 3 - Little Fox   52

Chapter 4 – Into the Wilderness   60

Chapter 5 - The Hunters   74

Chapter 6 - Over the Passes   84

Chapter 7 – The Lake   104

Chapter 8 – The Necklace   122

Chapter 9 – The Beating of Sean McClaren   137

Chapter 10 – Everybody's Dreaming   147

Chapter 11- Fish for Dinner   168

Chapter 12 – Birds   181

Chapter 13 – Luke's Pain   197

Chapter 14 – Trouble with Beavers   216

Chapter 15 – Collin Makes Enemies   232

Chapter 16 – Collin's Fall   248

Chapter 17 – Chicken and Rabbit   280

Chapter 18 – Brimsby and the Bear   297

Chapter 19 – Maggots Galore   316

Chapter 20 – Sibling Rivalry   333

Chapter 21 – Talk of Destiny   347

Chapter 22 – Swamp   357

Chapter 23 – Gold   368

Chapter 1 - Jail Break

The ache in Andrew MacDonald's left arm was rapidly developing into an excruciating pain. He laid the short-barrel, 12 gauge shotgun across the saddle and held it in his left hand, while he massaged his throbbing left arm with his right hand. The pain intensified as it radiated up his arm and across his chest. His heart felt like it was going to explode. His body involuntarily jerked backwards and he dropped from the back of the horse like a sack of potatoes, dead before he hit the ground.

"Mac! Mac, what's wrong?" shouted Berger, as he spurred his horse towards his fallen comrade. He reined in and swung down off his mount, all in one swift motion. While he was checking MacDonald for any signs of life, the other two prison guards rode up, inquiring as to what happened.

Berger lifted his head up in time to see them dismount, when he suddenly realized no one was watching the inmates. It was too late. One of the prisoners nearest to the fallen MacDonald was approaching to investigate the commotion. Berger reached for his shotgun, but it was out of reach where he'd dropped it when he'd rushed to MacDonald's side. He pulled his revolver, cocked the hammer, stood, and walked towards the approaching prisoner. When he was close enough, he brought the pistol butt down hard across the man's ear. As the convict went down from the blow, a shotgun blast hit Berger like a battering ram and knocked him backwards. As he hit the ground, his navy blue jacket rapidly turning crimson, his two companions turned in the direction of the shot.

Clarence Whitney seized the opportunity presented to him when MacDonald suffered the heart attack. As his body jerked backwards, MacDonald flayed his arms and as his left arm came up, the shotgun flew from his hand, landing near Whitney. While the other three guards were occupied with MacDonald, Whitney picked up the shotgun, cocked both hammers, and advanced towards the three unsuspecting men. A prisoner, blocking Berger's line of sight, allowed Whitney to get even closer without being seen.

When Whitney caught the motion of Berger rising, he stopped and aimed the scatter gun. As the clubbed prisoner fell, Berger was exposed and Whitney fired one of the barrels. The shotgun was loaded heavy, meant to inflict maximum damage. Berger caught the full blast in the chest at short range.

At the sound of the shot, the other two guards turned and faced Whitney. One still had his shotgun and the other was reaching for his pistol, when Whitney said, "Not a smart move, boys. You see what the first shot did to your friend there? Which one of you wants the second one?"

Whitney could see their hesitation and before either man could react, he spoke again, "I know what you are thinking. He's only got one shot left and there are two of us. You have to ask yourself if you are willing to sacrifice your life in order to give the other one a chance to get me, or maybe, just maybe, at this range, I can get you both. Actually, you know what? I'll make it easy for you."

Whitney took three quick strides, bringing him to within a couple of feet of the two men. As he took the last step, he fired the second barrel at the guard holding the shotgun. Before the second man could pull his pistol, Whitney was beside him and butt- ended him across the nose as hard as he could. The guard slumped to the ground in an unconscious heap. Whitney drew the pistol from the guard's holster and fired a shot into the prone man's temple.

Whitney was one of twenty two prisoners put on a work gang, mainly to keep them busy. Occasionally, their labours served a useful purpose such as maintenance work on the Cariboo Trail that was built nearly a decade previous to handle the large volumes of traffic to the gold fields further north.

On this day, however, they were about five miles north of Lytton, on the west side of the Fraser River, cutting firewood from an area that was ravaged by a forest fire a few years back. Burnt out areas, such as this, where the fire had raced through the forest searing only the branches and the bark, but leaving the wood intact, were ideal for gathering dry, hot burning firewood. The fire-killed trees were all concentrated in one area, making it much easier to manage a large number of prisoners. The men were not shackled or chained together, so they could work more efficiently. They were scattered over half an acre, falling the trees, de-branching them, bucking them into eight foot lengths, scaling the burnt bark from them, and stacking the logs near the road, ready for hauling. Near the end of the day, the prepared logs would be loaded onto three wagons, the convicts would climb atop the logs, and the whole entourage would head back to the camp, where the logs were unloaded and stacked in the yard.

While the prisoners worked, four mounted guards, armed with sawed-off, 12 gauge, double barrel shotguns and Remington single action, .44 calibre revolvers, rode back and forth, through and around the men, ever vigilante for any signs of trouble. Disobedience or perceived infractions were dealt with harshly, usually a couple of good hard swings from a baton and where the baton landed was, usually, of no concern to the wielder.

Ian Berger was in charge of the wood cutting detail and he carried a little something extra, an eight foot bullwhip, with which he was quite proficient. He bragged he could knock a fly off a man's nose without touching the skin. Not many doubted him and, certainly, no one was going to willingly volunteer to be the target, so as to disprove his claim. Berger used his whip indiscriminately at the slightest provocation. Nearly every man in the work gang was marked with a little scar or welt somewhere on his body as a result of the bullwhip's bite. Not a single man, who looked down on Berger's mangled body, felt any sympathy.

As soon as Whitney disposed of the last guard, he walked back the few paces to where Berger lay, stared at him for a few seconds, and then spat on him. He turned back to face the rest of the prisoners. Using the pistol, he fired two shots into the air and shouted, "Everyone gather around and make it quick!" Eight of the men, working at the far end of the burnt area, had already scattered into the live forest and were well on their way to putting some distance between themselves and any trouble. The remaining prisoners quickly made their way to Whitney's location and formed a group a few feet in front of him. They stood looking at one another, waiting anxiously to see what was going to happen next. Some were curious, most were indifferent, and one or two were apprehensive.

Whitney looked them all over and then spoke directly to Sean McClaren, a young lad, barely sixteen years of age. "You, kid. Gather up all the guns and all the ammunition from the dead bulls and bring them here." Whitney prided himself in his ability to read people and his understanding of human nature. He was confident the kid was the safest bet to gather the firearms and ammunition without thoughts of keeping them for himself.

When the shooting began, three of the four guard's horses bolted and ran off as far as the edge of the road, where clumps of Foxtail Barley caught their attention and they stopped to graze. The fourth horse remained near its master, Ian Berger, as he lay bleeding out. Whitney said to the kid, as he began to walk away, "Boy, grab that horse, as well."

Whitney surveyed the group again, looking each man over carefully. His gaze settled upon Mathew Briscoe and his brother Luke. He said, "You two, go chase down those other horses," and after a momentary pause, he added "And boys, no thoughts of riding off yourself, eh? We wouldn't want to do anything as foolish as that, would we?" Whitney waved the pistol to emphasize the message. Mathew and Luke Briscoe were criminals of opportunity. They were not smart enough to plan ahead and Whitney knew this when he sent them out.

The gun-butted prisoner began to stir. He moaned, felt the side of his head, sat up and as awareness returned, he looked all around. He saw the bodies of the guards, the group of men behind him, and the towering image of Clarence Whitney standing over him with a cocked pistol aimed at his forehead. "Please, don't shoot. I won't cause you any trouble, I assure you," he pleaded.

Whitney lowered the pistol, extended his left arm, and helped the man to his feet. Harold Grant wasn't a violent man. He was a depot agent for a transport company when he was arrested for embezzlement. As he steadied himself and full consciousness returned, he walked to Berger's body and gave it a good swift kick in the ribs. Whitney watched in fascination. Grant, realizing what he'd done, looked to Whitney for a reaction. He didn't know what to expect. Whitney simply grinned and told him to join the rest of the men.

Whitney addressed the group, "Gentlemen, I have a proposition for you, a proposition that will make you all extremely rich."

His thoughts drifted back to the damp, eight by twelve foot cell he'd called home for the past twenty months. By the time he arrived in the gold fields in 1868, most of the good claims were filed and worked out. What was left, took a lot of hard work just to find enough color to pay for keep and a little extra for some whiskey.

He was drowning his sorrows in a tavern at 100 Mile House, when a couple of drunks decided he would be their evening's entertainment. They kept insisting they wanted to be friends and Whitney should buy them a drink. Whitney wanted to be left alone and when the drunks wouldn't stop, he broke a whiskey bottle on the bar rail and using the jagged edge, kept swinging until one of the drunks lay bleeding out on the floor and the other ran out the saloon door, cut up and fearing for his life. After coming out of the blind rage, Whitney tossed the broken bottle to the floor, searched the dying man's pockets for some money, and when he found some loose change, threw it on the counter and demanded another bottle.

Whiskey in hand, he returned to his claim, where several days later he was arrested for murder. At his trial, the proprietor of the roadhouse testified Whitney was provoked and had acted in self defence. The judge took this into consideration, reduced the charge to manslaughter, and sentenced Whitney to seven years hard labour.

His cellmate for the past two months was, what most people considered, a crazy old coot with no sense of reality, resulting from too much time spent alone in the hills, looking for the yellow curse. He called himself Diamond Jack and was serving ninety days for being drunk and disorderly. Two weeks into his sentence, he caught a bad cold that developed into pneumonia. As he lay wheezing and slowly drowning in his own fluids, he kept ranting on about a fortune in gold he'd found and how he needed to get back to it.

At first, Whitney didn't pay much attention to the old man's ramblings. In fact, he was about ready to strangle the old fool if he didn't stop his incessant whining. Perhaps to placate him, Whitney began to pay attention to him. He began to talk to the old man and tried to reassure him that he would be fine and then he could go find his gold again.

Somehow the old man knew he wasn't going to make it. He forced himself up on his elbows and begged Whitney to come closer. Whitney obliged and the old man looked him directly in the eyes and swore on his mother's grave that he was speaking the truth. He was going to give it all to Whitney and all he wanted in return was for Whitney to promise he would use some of the fortune to put a nice headstone on his grave and to find his daughter in Victoria and make sure she got enough of the gold to live comfortably for the rest of her life. Whitney began to believe him and he gave the old man his word. He would have said anything; after all, the man was dying.

Diamond Jack lasted another three weeks and several times a day Whitney would feed him what passed for food and pump him for information. They went over and over the route to the gold a dozen times a day until it was branded into Whitney's memory. After the old man passed away, Whitney would constantly review the route in his mind, sometimes speaking aloud to himself. The guards were beginning to think Whitney had been cooped up with the old prospector too long and had gone around the bend himself.

Whitney calculated, with time off for good behaviour, he could be out after serving five years, a little over three years from now, which didn't seem too long. But fate stepped in and here he was, presented with an opportunity to escape and he had taken it.

As he faced the group of convicts, he was already formulating a plan. He didn't need all these men to help him find the mine, but he felt there was safety in numbers and he was going to need some help hauling all the gold out. He could always ditch this collection of riff-raff when the time was right. He continued, "That's right, boys. I know where there is a treasure. Way I see it, you all have a choice to make."

"Ah, this is bullshit. I'm not standing here listening to this fool. I am getting the hell out of here," spat one of the men in front. "Anyone coming with me?"

As the man turned to leave, Whitney aimed the revolver and fired. It was a headshot and the man was killed instantly. Whitney addressed the group again as calmly as if he were chatting about the weather. "Now see, he didn't let me finish. As I was saying, it comes down to two choices. Option one, you come with me. Option two — " Whitney paused and his gazed shifted to the dead man in front of them. He continued, "Anybody else picking option two?"

Whitney studied their faces for a reaction. He had their attention for the moment, but he needed to act quickly. If he was to maintain control, he couldn't give them time enough to think. "Everyone have a seat and we'll wait for the rest of the men to come back with the horses and guns," he said.

Sean McClaren finished gathering all the fire arms and ammunition from the dead guards. He lost his stomach contents several times. He never saw anyone shot dead before, but he kept at his appointed task. He was much more concerned about annoying Whitney than about the blood and gore around him. He removed one of the guard's coats to use as a makeshift bag to carry the shotguns, revolvers, and spare ammunition.

Once everything was inside the coat, he did the buttons up and using the sleeves, he tied the whole bundle to the saddle horn of Berger's horse. Leading the horse, he was starting back towards Whitney when the shot rang out. He stood frozen for a moment and then continued on, as if nothing happened.

"Here ya go, Sir. I got all the guns and ammo and the horse, just like ya told me to," Sean said quietly.

Whitney turned and looked at the coat tied to the saddle horn and said, "Throw those guns down on the ground. Bring yourself and the horse around in front of me where I can see you."

The Briscoe brothers approached with the other three horses, each astride one and Mathew leading the third one. Whitney ordered them to dismount, hand the reins to Sean and then to join the group. "What's all the shootin'?" asked Mathew, as he looked at the body on the ground.

Whitney answered without hesitation, "We were voting on a couple of options on our next move. He disagreed with the majority."

Mathew seemed confused. Collin Pilkington, a storekeeper jailed for arson, put his hand on Mathew's shoulder and said, "Best keep your mouth shut and follow along."

Whitney caught the gesture and inquired, "What did you say to him?"

"I informed him it would be in his best interest to keep quiet and listen," replied Pilkington.

Whitney stared at the storekeeper for a moment and then smiled as he said, "That's good advice. You're a smart man." He turned his gaze back to the group and continued, "Now that we are all here, let us review our situation. I assume we have all chosen option one."

He paused for effect and then realized the three late arrivals hadn't heard the proposal. "For the three gentlemen who have just arrived, we voted on two choices. Option one was to come with me and get rich and option two was — not to." He nodded in the direction of the man he'd just shot and continued, "This man was the only one who chose option two. I am assuming you three are voting for option one."

Whitney checked for any signs of disapproval and continued. "Now, maybe you think I'm crazy. Maybe, I am and maybe, I'm not. I have seen a lot of this world and have done a lot of things in my time. I am not one to get taken in by silly notions or pipe dreams.

"As some of you probably know, I have been sharing a cell with a crazy old prospector, who has been telling me for over a month about the location of a mother lode he found and he willed it to me, boys. Fact of the matter is, I believed him and you fine gentlemen are going to help me find that gold and as a reward, you will become very rich men. There is enough for all of us."

He paused to arrange his thoughts and to let what he said sink in, then he continued, "About three hundred miles to the northwest is a large river valley with dozens of creeks running off the mountain sides. Up one of those creeks is a wall of gold. The old prospector told me he dug out enough free gold to fill two dozen flour sacks and it is all there just waiting for us."

Whitney was not lying when he told them about his worldly travels and experiences. He was on the streets of London at the age of twelve, thrown out by a drunken father and a spineless mother. He learned to survive through stealing, breaking and entry, pick pocketing, and the like. At the age of fifteen, he snuck on board a ship headed for the Americas. Not long out, he was found and the ship's captain made him work long hard hours to pay for his keep. Because he was a stowaway and likely, nobody would care, he was subjected to physical and sexual abuse almost daily. He endured it all by convincing himself it was the price of passage to America.

He jumped ship in New York City, where he took up his old criminal habits and he was not above cutting a throat, if necessary, to get a purse. In 1861 he joined the Union Army to fight in the American Civil War. He deserted in 1863 and headed west, where he wandered from place to place without purpose or goals, working at menial jobs to make enough money to get to the next spot up the road. He was cutting timber in Oregon when he heard about people finding gold in the Cariboo, but by the time he got there, the strike was over and the pickings were scarce.

Whitney directed his attention to young Sean and said, "Kid, open the coat and let's see what we have." Sean untied the sleeves and undid the coat buttons, exposing the contents. Including the one Whitney had emptied on the two guards, there were four sawed-off, double barrelled, 12 gauge shotguns with twenty two rounds. There were also three fully loaded pistols with no extra ammunition, a hunting knife, four batons, and Berger's bullwhip.

Whitney glanced at the contents. With one eye on the group, he knelt down and picked up two of the fully loaded pistols and stuck them in his waistband, with the butts facing inward. He emptied the cartridges from the third pistol, as well as the ones left in the pistol he was currently using and put them in his coat pocket. He picked up one of the shotguns, broke the breech to make sure it was loaded, selected four of the extra shells, and added them to the pistol cartridges in his pocket. He stuck the knife in his waistband in the small of his back and picked up the coiled bullwhip.

Whitney had developed the skill of assessing a man's character quickly and this played to his advantage. He decided the Briscoe brothers would make good henchmen. Not that they could be trusted, but they were the type of men who would follow orders if they thought there was something in it for them. He instructed them to come and get two of the remaining shotguns and to split the extra shells. He picked up the fourth shotgun, ordered the storekeeper to stand, and tossed the weapon to him.

Collin Pilkington was forty years old with rosy cheeks and a full head of curly black hair, interspersed with a touch of grey. He wore an endearing smile, which made most people like him as soon as they met him. He never wanted much out of life other than to earn a comfortable living and when the work for the day was done, to retire to the back room of the store, where he liked to lose himself in a book or to carve wooden birds and paint them, which he then sold in the store.

Unfortunately for him, his wife was very ambitious. She was never satisfied with their lot in life and continually wanted more. He always complied with her wishes because it was easier than having to live with her constant whining. They were married when they were both in their early twenties and had left England to come to the colonies, namely Victoria in British Columbia. Here, they tried business venture after business venture that were mostly successful to the point where they earned a comfortable living, but it never seemed to be enough for his wife.

In 1866 they headed for the Cariboo to try their luck. Nothing changed. They invested their capital in a mining supply store and were doing quite well until the gold began to peter out. They changed their operation to a general mercantile store, but business still didn't improve.

Nag, nag, nag — Collin wanted to go back to Victoria, but his wife insisted they pack up their bags and head east to the Kootenays and the new gold strike she'd gotten wind of. Collin burnt the store down and when questioned by the Constable, he immediately confessed to the crime of arson even though there was no concrete evidence to convict him of anything. Most people thought he confessed to get away from his wife.

Collin handed the shotgun back to Whitney and stammered, "No. No, I — I have no use for weapons. I don't think — No, I am sure — I have never fired a gun in my life."

Whitney took the shotgun from Pilkington. His first thought was to shoot this man, but his keen reasoning took over. The group wouldn't be bothered a great deal by the killing of sadistic guards, or the big blowhard who was planning to leave, but murdering this lovable weakling could incite some anger in the group and cause Whitney to lose the control he needed.

As Whitney was deciding who should have the shotgun, Frank Oakley stepped forward and said, "I'll take it, if you want. I'm pretty handy with a gun."

He wasn't exaggerating with this boast. He was young, cocky, and full of himself. He grew up in Texas and at the very young age of sixteen, began drifting north through Colorado and Wyoming as a working cowboy. As he was growing up, much to his parent's dismay, he spent all the money he was saving on an old navy colt and a beat up holster. He practised drawing the pistol for hours on end. Whenever he made a nickel working at the livery or grocery store, he would buy some cartridges. He'd set up tin cans on the rail of the backyard fence and he'd gotten to the point where he could hit six out of six at a distance of fifty feet and all dead center, quite remarkable marksmanship.

Because he was so young, he was usually the brunt of hazing or teasing by some of the older hands on the ranches where he worked. Frank took it all in stride until one night a cowhand pushed him too far and Frank challenged him to a shootout. The cowboy didn't stand a chance. In fact, he was trying to talk the kid out of it. When he saw Frank was not going to back down, he went for his pistol. It was a fatal mistake. He never even got his gun out of the holster before Frank's bullet hit him in the chest. Everyone said it was self defence, but the foreman sent Frank packing, anyway.

Several such incidents got him the same treatment. One night in Montana, he killed a likeable lad not much older than himself. There was some serious talk about a lynching and Frank lit out. His name got spread around and nobody wanted to hire him. He heard of a gold strike up in Canada and decided to try his luck. Like a lot of others, he came too late and ended up trying to eke out a living, doing whatever he could.

He beat a very drunk miner half to death with his gun butt in a road house one night. Frank didn't shoot him because he was unarmed. The Constables were summoned and were on the scene in time to save the miner's life. Frank gave up without a fight and was serving a sentence of three years hard labour for assault.

Whitney asked. "How do I know I can trust you?"

11

Oakley shrugged and replied, "I don't know. That's up to you, I guess. Your story of making me rich got my attention and I'll back your play. If I find out you're conning us, I can't promise anything."

Whitney tossed Frank the shotgun and instructed Mathew Briscoe to give him some ammunition.

Looking at the shotgun, Frank said, "This is nice, but I would much rather have a pistol. I'm much better with it than I am with this."

"That's what I'm afraid of," replied Whitney.

"Well, why arm me at all if you don't trust me?" asked Oakley.

Whitney thought for a moment. "You've got a point." He reached into his pocket and counted out six cartridges, handed them to Frank, and told him to pick up one of the pistols. Frank gave the shotgun back to Whitney, who in turn tossed it to Sean McClaren and said, "Don't shoot yourself."

"What about me?" asked Con Murdock, a gambler, serving a one-year sentence for fraud.

Whitney, recognizing him, said, "You? I wouldn't trust you as far as I could throw you."

"Just thought you could use another gun, is all," replied the gambler.

Whitney answered, with a definite tone of condescension, "I think the two hillbillies, the kid, and the cowpuncher will be sufficient, but thanks for the offer."

Whitney turned his attention back to the group. "So gentlemen, this brings us back to our travel plans. I have invited you all to come along with me because I can't have any of you getting caught and telling the law where the rest of us have gone. Once we have been on the trail for a couple of days, if some of you feel you don't want to be rich, we can come to some other arrangement."

The men all looked at each other and there was some mumbling and grumbling, but not one of them protested too loudly. No one was quite sure what Whitney meant by '*other arrangement*', but most of them had a gnawing feeling it wasn't good.

Whitney felt uncomfortable. He scanned the group once more and discovered the source of his unease; a stocky, very muscular man with shoulder length, jet black hair was looking at him defiantly. He was five foot, ten inches tall and his dark skin made his blue-grey eyes stand out even more. There were two scars on his face, which made you want to look at him a little longer than you should. One started below his left eye and ran diagonally down across his nose, stopping in the middle of his right cheek. The other one ran parallel to his jaw line, about an inch above it, from one side of his face to the other.

Whitney knew him simply as '*Breed*'. "You got a problem with our travel plans?" he asked.

The Métis hesitated and then said, "No, I am sure I'll be okay." He looked at each man around him and then added, "I ain't so sure about the rest of 'em."

Once again Whitney's first thought was to shoot the man, but his reasoning intervened once more. Here was an invaluable resource he could use. The man knew the country and most likely knew how to survive in the bush. The half breed was right. Some of these men would not do well on a three week journey through wild country.

"Well, Breed —" Whitney began.

The Métis interrupted, "My name is Michael George."

Whitney was annoyed. "Michael George? What, no last name?" he said, mockingly and then continued, "Well, Michael George, your job on this little expedition is to make sure they all *do* survive. You do whatever it takes and maybe, just maybe, I'll give you a share of the gold instead of putting a bullet between those adorable blue eyes of yours. Do we understand each other?"

Michael didn't answer. He simply looked away.

"Alright then, they are not going to miss us until dark, which gives us a good eight hours head start. Let's get moving!" commanded Whitney.

-2-

When the group was ready to depart, Josiah Morgan was assigned the task of driving one of the large wagons, used to transport supplies and prisoners to the work site and the cut logs back to the penal camp. Josiah never had any steady employment. He was a drunk and his only fixed address was the current jail where he was residing. He wasn't a criminal, as such, but he would seek out employment for menial jobs, get hired, and then give the employer some sad story about needing money immediately in order to feed his starving family. He was so good at this con job, the employer would feel sympathetic and usually give him a modest advance. Josiah would head for the nearest tavern and drink up the money, not bothering to show up for work.

His last little ploy got him arrested for fraud, when a liveryman bought his story and hired him to clean stables. The liveryman went to the local tavern for his daily lunchtime pint and much to his surprise, there was Josiah. The liveryman grabbed him by the scruff of the neck and dragged him to the Constable's office, a few doors down the street from the tavern and there he pressed charges. Josiah's sentence was six months at hard labour.

While serving his latest term, Josiah became a changed man. He found God. He never cared much for his appearance before incarceration, but a couple of months into his sentence he developed a fetish for cleanliness, which seemed to have begun with his new found faith. Like Lady Macbeth, he could never get his hands clean. He was constantly washing them, a dozen times a day when the opportunity presented itself. It was as if he were trying to wash his sins and self loathing away. Josiah stopped taking responsibility for his life; it was in God's hands. Whatever happened to him was the will of God and, of course, anytime he committed a sin, it was the Devil's doing.

He came with Whitney primarily because he was afraid of the consequences if he refused, but part of him was very curious about the hidden gold mine that Whitney kept going on about. He felt God must have given him this opportunity to become rich.

The troop travelled for about an hour down the road back toward civilization. Whitney, the Briscoe brothers, and Frank Oakley put on the dead guards' uniforms. Luke Briscoe barely fit into MacDonald's tunic, even though Mac was considered a large man. Whitney and Oakley rode in front and the two Briscoe brothers rode behind the three wagons. To the casual observer, the prisoners were being escorted back to the camp, perhaps a little earlier in the day than usual, but nothing out of the ordinary.

When they reached the Stein River, they veered right and headed west along the high ridge overlooking the stream. It would have easier to cross the river using the bridge and travel along the south shore. Two things aided Whitney in his decision; the old prospector instructed him to use the north shore and secondly and most important, if the authorities thought of looking for them up the river, they would most likely search the easier, more travelled south shore.

They turned onto a fairly wide, rocky path that could hardly be called a road. Two miles down the trail, the wagons could go no further. Whitney commanded the men to unhitch the mules and push the wagons far enough into the trees, so they could not be seen from the trail. They put together some makeshift riding halters out of the existing driving reins and some rope and put them on the six mules. Before hiding the wagons, they gathered up all the food there was; a slab of bacon, two pounds of beef jerky, about three pounds of white beans, a pound or so of coffee, and three large loaves of bread and put them all in a pack on one of the mules. They put a buck saw and a couple of axes, along with the pack containing all of the pots, plates, cups, and eating utensils onto a second mule.

Whitney assigned Sean McClaren his own mule to ride. He ordered Silas Davidson and Michael George to each ride the two mules carrying the packs and Nathaniel Brimsby to pair up with Con Murdock, Harold Grant with Collin Pilkington, and Josiah Morgan with Fredrick Guetch. He told them they would have to double up on the three remaining mules.

The entourage was forced to ride single file for the better part of three miles. They crossed over two talus slopes; the first was over three hundred yards wide and the second, about half the length of the first. Between the two rock slides was a small creek, full and overflowing in the spring, but waning all summer, until by late August there was barely a trickle, or on occasion, during drier years, there was no water at all. There were still several inches of cool, refreshing liquid gurgling around the rocks, enough to water all the stock and quench the men's thirst.

Whitney ordered a halt. He handed the reins of his horse to Sean and told the kid to water it. The Briscoe brothers and Frank Oakley dismounted and led their horses to the small creek while the rest of the men stood around, not sure what to do. Whitney, looking about, asked, "Is there a problem?"

Silas Davidson spoke up. "Not to bother you, Sir, but what are your orders — I mean, whom do you want to do what?"

Whitney seemed taken aback with the question. It never occurred to him grown men would need specific instructions to do everything.

"Who do you think I am?" spat Whitney. "You think my job is to spoon feed you your orders? Somebody take charge and get the stock watered!"

The men were still standing around when Silas Davidson finally barked out some orders. He directed two men, Nathaniel Brimsby and Harold Grant, to water the six mules. He turned back to Whitney and asked, "Would it be alright if we all had a little bite to eat?"

Whitney covered the few paces between them, reached upwards, set his hand on Silas's shoulder, and shouted, "Men! Could I have your attention?" He gave them a few minutes to gather around and then continued, "It appears the time has come to hand out the duty roster for this little excursion of ours. I, the Briscoe brothers, and Mr. Oakley will have the horses and the weapons. They will take orders from me. We will be responsible for the safety and discipline in the group and we will do the hunting to provide us with meat."

He paused long enough to let the thought sink in and then directed his attention back to Silas Davidson, "And this fine gentleman will be in charge of the rest of the menial labour I can't be bothered with — cooking, cleaning, care of the livestock, and so on, and so on. The rest of you will answer to him."

Con Murdoch asked Whitney why the kid had a shotgun. Whitney simply ignored him. He turned Silas so they were face to face and then spoke directly to him, although he said it loud enough for everyone to hear, "Anyone doesn't pull their weight, you let me know — uh — what is your name?"

"Silas — Silas Davidson," was the reply.

Silas looked like a stork. He was six feet, four inches tall, but weighed only one hundred and sixty pounds. He had a very sharp hawk's beak nose, a pair of bushy lamb chops, and a big handle bar moustache, which were a deeper red than the color of the hair on his head. His fingers were extremely long and thin and he annoyingly pointed and shook them at a person when he was trying to make a point. He considered himself a leader of men and felt he was destined for big things. He was very impatient with life; everyone and everything seemed to get in his way.

He was born in England to poor parents. His father worked as a clerk for a money lender and young Silas followed his father into the world of commerce when he was of age. He dreamed of riches and power while labouring over other people's ledgers. He'd saved enough money for passage to Canada and at the age of twenty four, he landed in Victoria with a letter of recommendation from a money house in England. He was hired by The British Bank of North America as a clerk. It was not exactly a step up and dissatisfaction soon set in again. This new situation was not much different from the one in England. He wasn't getting ahead, even in this supposed land of opportunity.

He caught gold fever and with excitement in his heart and a placer pan in his hand, he set out for the gold fields. He did find some yellow, not enough to make him a rich man, but enough to give him a good grubstake for a business. He set up a mercantile store in one of the larger mining camps.

Business boomed for a few years until most of the miners moved on to better prospects. Placer miners are a fickle breed. Unless they are making a big fortune at their current digs, the instant they hear gold is discovered elsewhere, they pack up and try their luck in the new place, looking for that one big strike. Silas's business steadily went down hill to the point where he looked forward to the visit and conversation from the one or two customers he received weekly.

Using his knowledge of the banking business, he easily obtained a loan with fictitious collateral. Of course, the bank foreclosed when the loan came due and the thousands of dollars of mining equipment, supposedly in stock, was nowhere to be found. Silas was arrested for fraud and was serving a five year sentence at the time of the jail break.

"Mr. Davidson, I am counting on you to run things smoothly. Do you think you can handle the job? Because if you can't I'll get some one else — but if I did that — I'm not sure what further use I would have for you," Whitney stated as a matter of fact, but with a definite threatening undertone.

After taking the time to eat a small chunk of jerky and a piece of bread each, the troop continued on. Whitney stated rather strongly how he did not want to take the time out to cook anything. The rest of the day took them through a variety of terrain. Parts of the trail were rocky ground with several talus slopes, while other sections wound through thick groves of Douglas fir mixed with spruce and pine trees. They crossed numerous creeks that roared downed the mountain sides into the river valley below. The trail followed one of these creeks down into the river's flood plain.

Twilight brought them to another creek. The Briscoe brothers, who were scouting ahead, returned with news of a good spot to camp. The men were a very weary and hungry bunch when they finally stopped. Most of them simply dismounted and found a comfortable spot to sit or lay down. Silas Davidson didn't let them get too comfortable. He started shouting out orders. He told Nathaniel Brimsby and Harold Grant to tend to the horses and mules. Fredrick Guetch and Josiah Morgan were to collect water and build a fire pit, while Collin Pilkington volunteered to do the cooking. Silas ordered Michael George and Con Murdock to gather up lots of firewood.

Whitney watched the whole business with amused interest, as Silas Davidson gave out his orders and the men grumbled and gave him dirty looks, but reluctantly got up when Silas would glance in Whitney's direction and then back at them. Davidson did not command any fear or even respect, but the imposing figure of Whitney, overseeing the proceedings, convinced the men it would be in their best interests to follow Davidson's orders.

Whitney walked to within earshot of Silas and said, "Not him!" pointing to Michael George. "He doesn't get out of my sight."

Whitney turned and shouted to the Briscoe brothers, "You two, tie our half breed friend very securely to a tree for the night. Tie him well because if he isn't here in the morning, you may not be either."

Luke Briscoe got a piece of rope while his brother, Mathew, escorted Michael to a nearby young pine tree, approximately six inches in diameter. Mathew directed Michael to sit with his back to the tree facing the camp. He told Michael to extend his arms behind his back and then Luke tied Michael's wrists securely around and behind the tree.

Michael watched as the rest of the men prepared the camp. There was a pot of beans boiling and some bacon frying. Collin Pilkington had already poured coffee all around and everyone was waiting for the beans to cook. A half hour later, Pilkington tested the beans. He remarked, "Good enough," then added the fried bacon to the mixture and began to dole it out. Each man tore off a piece of bread to go with the bacon and beans and found a spot to sit and eat.

Pilkington loaded up two plates and handed both to Josiah Morgan, indicating the other one was for Michael George. Josiah tore off a couple of pieces of bread from one of the loaves and carried the two plates to Michael. He set one plate down and was ready to feed Michael from the other one, when suddenly it was sent flying. Frank Oakley had kicked it out of Josiah's hands.

"No stinkin' breed is gonna eat our food. We got very little as — " Oakley never finished the sentence because Whitney's backhand slap caught him on the side of the head. He turned quickly with his hand on the butt of his pistol. When he saw it was Whitney, he eased his hand away from the gun and cried out, "What the hell did you do that for?"

Whitney responded as if he was reproaching a child, "I am only going to tell you this once. I decide what goes on in this group. Think about this, Mr. Oakley; I need the breed more than I do you on this little expedition. Now, get him something to eat — Oh, by the way, Mr. Oakley, if you wish to eat, your dinner is on the ground."

Oakley tromped away in a huff. Any other time, he would have pulled his pistol and filled the son-of-a-bitch full of holes. He didn't think himself a coward, but there was something about Whitney that was dangerous and Oakley's intuition told him this was neither the time nor the place. He took comfort in the thought there would be plenty of other opportunities.

He was still angry when he brought Josiah another helping of the bacon and beans and a hunk of bread. He handed the food to Josiah and then stared at Michael, who returned his gaze and then cracked a wry smile.

Josiah fed Michael and then got him a drink of water. "Don't have any blankets to offer you. You gonna be alright?" Josiah asked with genuine concern.

"I'll be fine, thank you — uh?"

"Oh, my name's Josiah."

"Well, thanks again, Josiah." Michael shifted positions to get comfortable and closed his eyes, hoping to get some much needed sleep.

Michael hardly spoke at all, but if asked his opinion, he was brutally honest and this often got him into trouble. He didn't trust a soul in this world. Being a half breed, Irish on his mother's side and Native American on his father's, he was shunned and abused by most members of both societies, native and white, alike. At this point in his life, he was not sure where he belonged. He was very angry at both sides and renounced any allegiance to either one.

In 1838 an Irish trapper traded his sixteen year old daughter to Michael's father for three horses and a winter's trapping of furs, probably because he had no desire to care for his daughter any longer and he saw an opportunity to get a huge cache of furs without having to do any work for them.

The young girl was in mortal fear when her father left her, but it wasn't long before she accepted her fate. Michael's father treated her gently and gave her nearly a year to get used to being his bride. The young girl, Mary McQuire by name, came to accept and eventually love her husband and became devoted to him and him to her.

Michael was born two years later. His father had picked a Salish name for him, but Mary pleaded to let the boy be called Michael. Her husband relented, stating that when he reached puberty, Michael would have to go on a vision quest and his guiding spirit would give him his adult name. Michael went on such a quest into the forest where he had a vision that showed him an old man who gave him a name, but he was mocked when he tried to tell anyone, so he stayed "Michael". If a white man asked his name, he was Michael *Stl'atl'imx*, which was what the native people called themselves, but very few white men knew this. Once, one of them even tried to pronounce it, but gave up. White men simply referred to him as "Breed".

Michael faced a hard life growing up. There was always an aura of distain towards him and his mother, as if they were simply being tolerated. As a young boy, he did not understand why he was different until, when he was about eight years of age, some fur traders came to the camp and his mother explained to him these people represented the other half of his heritage. He also saw how these white men reacted when they learned there was a white woman in the camp.

They offered to "rescue" her, but when she indicated she was there of her own free will, Michael saw the looks on their faces and heard the distain in their voices.

Michael had no siblings. Complications at his birth prevented his mother from bearing any other children. Michael never did fit in. He was always last to eat when community food was served and the last one picked to participate in games or hunts. He was constantly reminded he was different and the stock he came from were inferior beings, thus he was not worthy.

Michael's mother died of Pneumonia when he was twelve. The village Shaman took the boy under his wing and convinced Michael he should begin studies to become a Medicine Man. Michael liked the idea. It would give him some status and, perhaps, the respect he so badly wanted. He listened attentively and studied hard. He went on many vision quests and was well on his way to becoming a Healer, when several young men his own age began persecuting him again. They held him down and cut his face up, resulting in the scars on his face. For the first time in his life, Michael fought back, seriously injuring one of the young men and after the dust settled, Michael, barely sixteen, was asked to leave.

He spoke English well, as a result of his mother's teachings. He could even read and write somewhat. He used this skill to enter the white man's world. He found out there was a good living to be made in the guiding business. He escorted trappers and speculators and when gold was found in the Cariboo country, he spent several years leading the fortune seekers to the creeks and rivers. As the gold waned, he hired on as a teamster and drove freight wagons, until he beat a big miner half to death. The man made some demeaning remark about his ancestry. Michael was awaiting trial for assault at the time of the jail break.

-3-

About the same time the escapees were setting up camp for the night, Albert Corman, the newest member of the six man squad of prisoner guards assigned to oversee the men on the labour gang, was beginning to worry. Ian Berger and the other three guards should have been back to the main camp, with the prisoners, over an hour ago. Sometimes they were a few minutes late, but never this long.

Albert and another young guard, Simon Kinney, were responsible for the main camp; the cooking, cleaning, care of the animals, and any other menial jobs that needed doing. Although they were both Privates, Simon outranked Albert, based on their length of service.

"Guess you better ride out and see what's keepin' them fellas," Simon said, more as a suggestion than an order.

The scene that lay before Albert was so unexpected that he sat in the saddle, dazed and in shock for the longest time, before he dismounted and cautiously made his way to the bodies on the ground. After a loose examination of the corpses, consisting of several gentle nudging kicks to see if there were any signs of life, he actually turned the bodies over one by one on their backs and checked them more closely. He concluded there was nothing more he could do for his comrades.

He dragged each body by the arms and lined them up side by side in close proximity. He drew his revolver and began a sweep of the area. He did not know what had transpired, but he knew Berger and Mac would not have given up without a fight. He was looking for any clue that might indicate what took place and deep down he was hoping he would find the bodies of some of the pond scum, as Berger liked to call the prisoners. He found only the body of the convict Whitney had shot. "Well, at least they got one," he said to himself.

He was getting ready to remount, when he heard a rustling behind him. He quickly drew his revolver again, turned, and with a shaky hand, pointed it in the direction of the noise. One of the prisoners was advancing slowly towards Albert with his arms raised over his head.

"Stop! You stop right where you are!" shouted Albert, with a bit of quiver in his voice.

"Please don't shoot. I'm surrenderin'. I had no part in any of this I swear," pleaded the prisoner.

The four and a half miles back to the camp was slow going, because Albert did not have the courage to double up with the prisoner. Consequently, he made the convict jog ahead of him as he rode. Back at the camp, he locked the inmate to the shackling rail in the middle of the compound and went into the large tent that served as the central activity center.

Albert explained to Simon what he'd found and Simon was as shocked and disbelieving as Albert was.

"What should we do?" queried Albert.

"We have to let the Constables know right away. They will know what to do," answered Simon. Then he remembered the prisoner. "Bring that scum in here. Maybe he can tell us what happened."

Albert retrieved the prisoner, brought him into the tent, and sat him down roughly at one of the log tables. The inmate, Henry Enstrom by name, was one week away from finishing a ninety day stint for drunk and disorderly conduct. He was harmless, except when he was drunk and then he would fight anybody who ridiculed his Swedish heritage or poked fun at his heavy accent.

Simon didn't have to threaten the Swede to get him to talk. He was only too willing to tell all he knew. He was one of the eight prisoners who fled into the forest when the shooting started. He didn't want to escape, as he had only a week left to serve on his sentence and an escape attempt usually added six months. He found a large tree to hide behind and stayed there until Whitney had called everyone together.

He began slowly making his way to the group gathered near Whitney, but when Whitney shot the prisoner, Enstrom snuck back a few yards and hid. After Whitney and his entourage departed, he stayed in the work area until someone in authority showed up. He saw and heard everything and related it all to Simon and Albert.

"Any idea which way they might have gone?" asked Simon.

The Swede answered without hesitation, "No Sir. I heard this fella, what was doing all the shootin' and talkin', say something about goin' to find some gold mine."

Simon turned to Albert and said, "First light, you ride like the wind and get the Constables."

Chapter 2 - Massacre

Josiah Morgan was on his knees in the middle of the village, tears streaming down his cheeks, as he looked up to the heavens and cried out in anguish, "Where are you, oh Lord? Why are you letting this happen? Why? Why?" He hung his head in shame because he had begun to doubt his new found faith. From somewhere behind him, he could hear a woman screaming in terror amongst the excited hooting and hollering of the convicts as they scurried about, collecting spoils, like ants foraging after dropped cake crumbs at a church picnic.

A few hours before, as the sun was rising, Clarence Whitney made his way through the scattered array of sleeping men, shouting out orders and kicking slumbering bodies. Once he was sure everyone was awake and he had their full attention, he said, "Gentlemen, we need to get moving. By now, the authorities know we have escaped and they are looking for us. Mr. Davidson, get whatever food is left cooked up and while we are waiting for breakfast, the rest of you get your animals ready to ride."

Silas Davidson shouted his orders to the same crew who set up camp the night before. It was nearly half an hour before breakfast was called, which wasn't much; a spoonful of the beans and bacon mixture, a small piece of beef jerky, and a tiny piece of bread per man, was all that was left.

When Silas handed Whitney's share to him, Whitney gave him a questioning look. Silas said apologetically, "That's all there is, Sir. There are a lot of mouths to feed. We are out of food."

Whitney handed the plate back to him and said, "Here, you eat it. I'll make sure the hillbillies find some game before nightfall. You tell anyone who complains that I said there will be meat for the evening meal."

The trail started out fairly flat through a canopy of fir and pine trees and a long stretch of wet, swampy ground. Much to Whitney's chagrin, it took them upward and back out of the river valley. They travelled another three miles, crossing several creeks and another rock slide, before the trail went back down to the river, where it was flat and easy going. An hour later, they came to the confluence of a creek and the river. The creek flowed from the northwest, but about five hundred yards upstream from the river it split into two forks; one fork flowing in a south easterly direction and the other running almost due south. The result was a triangular shaped island, with the two forks of the creek forming two of the sides and the river making up the third.

As the men crossed the eastern branch of the creek and up the embankment to the island, a pungent fishy odour filled their nostrils. There were at least two dozen large smoke racks scattered about, all covered with salmon filets. As Whitney and the rest of the group approached, three women came to greet them. The women looked puzzled, even apprehensive. They seldom saw white men this far up river and they were curious as to why they were here.

Whitney approached the three women and asked in English, "Where is your camp?" Where are the men? I want to do some trading."

The women all looked at Whitney somewhat puzzled. One of them shook her head and kept repeating, "*Loot kin t'emshux na.*"

Whitney turned and shouted for Michael. Mathew Briscoe quickly appeared with Michael in tow, who was astride one of the mules with his hands tied behind his back. Whitney said to Michael, "Tell me what she is saying?"

Michael looked at the woman and asked her to repeat what she previously had said. He listened and then translated for Whitney, "She's saying she don't understand you."

Whitney looked at the woman and then back to Michael, "Tell her we are on a long journey and we would like to trade for some supplies. Tell her this and nothing else. You hear me, Breed?"

Michael thought quickly and told the woman, "Don't change your expression. Don't look worried. These are very bad men. You must do as they say. Take us to the village."

The women played along. The one who was doing the talking asked Michael why he was tied up.

"What did she say?" demanded Whitney.

"She asked me why I was tied."

"Tell her we are the law and we are chasing a gang of renegades and you are guiding us. We have you tied because you are one of them and we don't want you to escape."

Michael addressed the woman again, "As soon as we get to the camp, tell The People to be fearful of these men. Don't trust them."

The woman nodded assent and she and the others turned to go.

"What the hell did you say to her, Breed?" asked Whitney, suspiciously.

"Just like you said, I told her you were worried I'd run away."

Whitney withdrew one of the pistols from his waistband and cocked the hammer. He aimed it at Michael, held it there for a moment, lowered it, and said, "I don't trust you, but I need you. If I find out you are lying to me, I'll kill you anyway."

The women were already a fair distance ahead. Whitney galloped his horse to catch up and the rest of the group followed suit. They crossed the island and forded the west branch of the creek, which brought them to a broad, flat plateau where the main part of the village was situated. As Whiney looked ahead, he could see about a dozen huts in a haphazard circle around a central area where there was a fire pit, burning even in the heat of the day. Off to his right, past the dwellings, at the far end of the camp, he saw a large corral containing a number of horses.

The three women stopped near the entrance to the encampment, where they were met by four men; one was quite young and the other three were much older. Whitney reined in his horse and gave the rope tied to Michael's mule a good yank. When the mule was parallel with his own horse, he looked Michael in the eyes and said very slowly, "You are going to translate for me. We need horses and food. I don't have anything to trade, so you have to convince these heathens that I will keep killing them one by one until I get what I need. If they comply, no one needs to get hurt. If they don't — well —"

"I understand," answered Michael.

"Well you better. Any horseshit and I start shooting. You make it very clear," emphasized Whitney.

Michael looked at the closest man to him. As their eyes met, the old man asked, "Why are you tied up like an animal?" When Michael didn't answer, he continued, "What does this man want of us?"

"He wants your horses and food. You must give him what he asks for. He is an evil man and he will kill many if he doesn't get what he wants," replied Michael, with conviction in his voice.

The old man looked at Whiney and said something in a defiant tone.

Whitney asked, "What did he say?"

The old man had told Michael they couldn't have anything. Michael lied when he told Whitney, "He said they ain't got much food, but we're welcome to take a meal with 'em."

Michael knew Whitney didn't believe him, so he added his own thoughts. "He's probably telling the truth. It is only mid summer, so they can't be far into winter food storage, yet."

Whitney wasn't convinced. He said, "Fine, we'll take whatever food they do have, the horses, and any firearms and ammunition. Tell him!"

Michael translated and when he was finished, the young man, who had been listening quietly throughout the conversation, suddenly spoke to Whitney with animated anger. Whitney didn't ask for a translation. He drew one of his pistols and shot the young man in the forehead. He turned the weapon in the direction of the older man who had been doing all the talking and shot him through the heart. He waved the pistol in the direction of the remaining two older men and said to Michael, "Tell these two gentlemen I am through being pleasant. Someone better start telling me what I want to hear!"

"Tell this devil something before he kills the whole village," pleaded Michael.

The older of the two remaining men spoke, "I am the Medicine Man of The People. I am not afraid to die."

Michael responded in anger, "Think of the women and children."

The old man thought for a moment and then replied, "You are right. What should we do?

"Give this man the horses and the food and he will leave you in peace," replied Michael. He turned towards Whitney and said, "I believe I've convinced him to do what you want."

"Good," said Whitney. "Find out how many horses and weapons they have."

Michael translated the request. The old man told him there were five ponies, but only three saddles. As far as he knew, there was only one rifle in the compound somewhere. As to food, all they had was venison jerky, some dried serviceberry cakes from last season, and lots of Eulachon oil, if Whitney wanted it. He added there would be plenty of fresh meat when the hunters returned.

Whitney sighed and said, "Dried meat and fish oil. No thanks." Without stopping for a breath he added, "Guess I don't need you two any longer." He shot the old man nearest him and was turning the pistol on the Medicine Man, when Michael moved his body sideways and bumped Whitney.

Whitney turned the gun on Michael and was about to fire when Michael said without fear, "Don't kill him! We can use him. He probably knows the country better than anyone."

Whitney lowered the pistol and replied, "Don't need him. I got you."

Michael argued, "But he knows more than I do. He can tell you when bad weather is coming. He can find game."

"Then what do I need you for?"

"You still need a translator. One more thing, a Medicine Man is a revered individual in the village. He would make a valuable hostage. The hunters wouldn't attack us for fear of hurting him."

Whitney looked puzzled. "Attack us? Why would they attack us?"

"Because we have killed three of their people and they won't take kindly to it."

"Well then, we shall have to dissuade them from pursuing us, won't we?" He turned to the men and shouted, "Gather up the horses, any guns and ammo, food, and any blankets you can find and don't leave any witnesses. When you are done, burn the place to the ground!"

Michael shouted, "You bastard, you can't do this!"

"Oh can't I? Watch me," replied Whitney, with a wry grin on his face.

He turned back to the men, "What are you waiting for? I gave you an order."

Not one of them moved. Most of them sat in disbelief, unsure of how to start. After a lengthy pause, Mathew Briscoe took charge. He let out a rebel yell at the top of his lungs and spurred his horse into a gallop. His brother Luke was right behind him, Sean McClaren and Frank Oakley a moment later.

There was one young man in his late teens, about a dozen older men, the Medicine Man, eight women, including the three who had met the troop, and several small children left in the village. The rest of the inhabitants were away. Several of the younger men were out hunting for deer or elk and they wouldn't return until they had lots of meat. The rest of the women and children were several miles up river digging roots and picking berries.

The villagers had tentatively moved closer to where they could see what was going on. When Whitney shot the first two men, the women and children scattered, some to the perceived safety of the lodges and the rest headed for the river bank, where scrub brush and willows offered a place to hide. The older men ran to get their hunting bows. The teenager ran to his lodge to get his Spencer rifle. His father, who died of a fever two winter's before, gave it to him as a gift, along with a dozen cartridges. He'd traded two fine horses and twenty pounds of elk meat to a white man for it. From a deer hide pouch, the boy took out three shells. He didn't have time to load the rifle, using the cartridge tube which ran through the stock, so he loaded one of the shells into the breech, clenched the other two between his teeth, and stuffed the bag with the remaining ammunition into his waistband.

The timing was such that the boy emerged from the lodge as the four riders came galloping up. He raised the rifle and shot without aiming, thus not hitting anything. Frank Oakley, salivating at the thought of getting into some gunplay, shot the boy dead center, through the heart, killing him instantly. As the boy dropped to his knees and slumped down onto his haunches in a sitting position,

Oakley rode up and with a vicious kick, knocked the corpse over on its back. He was grinning from ear to ear as he rode to catch up to the Briscoe brothers and the kid.

The dozen or so lodges of the encampment were arranged in two semicircles centered by a common area. A well worn path ran through the center of the compound from east to west. There was a wooded area on the opposite side of the path from the horse corral, where the trail continued down to the river. Here, five men, with bows in hand, took up positions. They quickly discussed a plan of action. Two of them hid themselves on one side of the trail, while two others hid on the other side. The fifth man stood in the open, on the path, with bow drawn tight. The plan called for him to fire, then turn and run into the trees. Hopefully, the white men would follow and be caught in a crossfire.

They didn't have long to wait. A few seconds after they were in position, the Briscoe brothers and Sean McClaren appeared from the lodge area, thirty feet from the trees. The man with his bow poised, fired. He wasn't aiming to hit anything, but Luke Briscoe turned his horse at the sight of the man and he caught the arrow in his left buttock. As the man with the bow turned to run, Mathew Briscoe nearly cut him in half with both barrels of the shotgun.

When Mathew stopped to reload, it probably saved his life. As he was reloading, the two men on his left came out from cover prematurely. Luke Briscoe, a few feet behind Mathew, saw them step out from behind a large fir tree. Ignoring his pain, he fired both barrels of the shotgun, hitting them both. His peripheral vision caught movement on the other side of his brother and he hollered, "Mathew, to your right!"

Mathew only had time to load one shell into the shotgun. He closed the breech at lightning speed, pulled back the hammer and all in one motion, fired as his vision caught movement. He instinctively ducked at the same time. His shot caught the man at the knees, knocking him to the ground and the arrow he'd fired, whistled over Mathew's head. The second man momentarily glanced down at his fallen comrade before he drew back his bow. He was about to let the arrow fly into Mathew, when he was sent reeling backwards by the bullet that caught him right between the eyes. Frank Oakley had caught up just in time to save Mathew Briscoe's life.

The Briscoe brothers and Frank Oakley, with guns cocked and ready, scanned the area in a complete three hundred and sixty degree sweep. There was no further activity. They each let go the breath they were holding and relaxed.

"Hoo whee, sure gets the blood goin', don't it, Brother Luke?" bellowed Mathew.

"It sure 'nough do, Brother Mathew. It sure 'nough do," answered Luke. "What are we gonna to do about this?" he asked, pointing to the arrow in his rear.

Mathew looked at it and then let out a roar of laughter. Luke began to laugh boisterously, as well. This was a sign of permission for Oakley to join in without fear of reprisal. After the laughter stopped, Mathew rode over to Luke and told him to lift himself up from the saddle. He then gave the shaft of the arrow a quick strong jerk. It came out without hesitation, but still set Luke off in a howl of pain. Mathew said, "You oughta get that cleaned up when we're done here, but I don't know anyone who'll do it for you."

This brought another round of laughter and as the jocularity subsided, Mathew ran a dirty sleeve across his face to wipe the sweat off. His attention was drawn to Sean McClaren, stationed several yards behind them. "D'you get yourself lost, youngin'? Where was you when all the shootin' started?" he asked the boy.

Sean stammered, "No, I — well — well, you see — it — well, it all happened so fast, I didn't know what to do."

A painful groan from the man Mathew had shot in the legs, caught their attention. Mathew looked down at the wounded native and then addressed Sean, "Well lookee here. This 'un ain't quite dead. Here's your big chance, boy. Finish 'im off.

Sean looked into Mathew's grinning face and with shaky hand lifted the shotgun. He aimed the weapon at the man on the ground, who looked up at him, stopped moaning, and simply closed his eyes, waiting for the shot to come. Sean lowered the shotgun and shook his head. "I can't. I can't kill him in cold blood."

Mathew moved his horse closer to Sean's mule and jerked the shotgun from his grasp, turned, and fired both barrels into the man. He threw the empty shotgun back at Sean and shook his head as he turned his horse away. "Come on boys, let's go find us someone else to kill."

Sean McClaren was in shock from the slaughter he witnessed. He had let the reins go slack, so he had no control of the mule he was riding. Consequently, it simply wandered down the length of the compound and stopped to eat some scattered hay outside the corral.

Upon Mathew Briscoe's suggestion, he, his brother Luke, and Frank Oakley began circling in and out of the array of lodges, systematically searching each dwelling. Some of the lodges were winter pit houses, consisting of a circular, excavated pit protected by a conical roof of poles covered with brush and earth. Others were summer lodges, rectangular in shape with one end rounded and covered with woven tule-grass mats.

Luke Briscoe flung back the mat, which served as a door, to one of the huts. He stood for a moment letting his eyes adjust to the dim light. He was about to enter when someone came charging at him. His reflexes kicked in and he turned sideways, barely avoiding the knife in the woman's hand. As she went by him, Luke grabbed her from behind with one arm around her neck. At the same time, he grabbed hold of her knife hand with his free hand and gave it a nasty twist. He could hear the bones crack in the woman's wrist and she dropped the knife, screaming in pain. He thought he was in control of the situation when another woman came out of the lodge and jumped on his back. She was a younger, smaller woman than the one with the knife. She clamped her arms around his neck and sunk her teeth into his shoulder. Luke gave the woman he was holding a vicious punch, knocking her half unconscious. He reached behind his head and grabbed a fistful of the biting woman's hair with one hand and her garment with the other and pulled forward with all his strength, flipping the woman over his head and onto the ground. As she went over, Luke did not let go with either hand, so he ended up with a fist full of hair in one hand and a large chunk of her garment in the other.

"Looks like you've got your hands full there, Brother Luke," said Mathew, laughingly. He looked at the two women on the ground. The woman Luke punched was just getting her senses back, but what drew Mathew's attention were the exposed breasts of the younger one.

Luke followed his brother's gaze to see what had caught his attention. He covered the distance to the young woman in two long strides, picked her by the arms, and lifted her to her feet. "I think I'm gonna have me a little fun, if it's alright by you, Brother Mathew?" he said.

"You go right ahead, Brother Luke," replied Mathew. as he glanced at the older woman and added, "In fact, I might join ya."

Luke picked up the younger woman with one massive arm and held her close to his body while she kicked, punched, and screamed at him. He entered the lodge, threw her viciously to the ground, and kicked her twice in the solar plexus, knocking the wind completely out of her. He turned her over, tore the rest of her garment off, unbuttoned his pants, and mounted her. He held her arms down and all the while he was raping her, she spit and screamed and fought with all her might. Luke laughed and said, "That's right, girly. You fight. You fight hard. I like it like that."

Meanwhile, Mathew dragged the other woman into the lodge and immediately beat her into near unconsciousness. He then stripped the inert woman and violated her. When he was done, he stood and buttoned his pants. He was reaching for the shotgun when he caught a glimpse of a large knife by the fire. He set the shotgun down, picked up the knife, pinned the still unconscious woman with one knee on her chest, and in one strong sweeping motion, cut her throat from ear to ear.

He walked slowly to where Luke was still busy with the younger woman. He sat down on the ground, crossed his legs, and watched his brother. Finally, Luke climaxed and let out a loud, "Hoo whee!" The woman, by this time, had given up the fight and lay motionless. Luke rolled off to one side and was catching his breath when he noticed his brother sitting on the other side of the woman with the bloodied knife in his hand.

Mathew turned the knife and offered it to Luke, handle first. "Need to finish it. Boss said no witnesses."

Luke stood, did up his pants and went outside for his shotgun. Once he was back inside, he cocked the hammer on one of the chambers and aimed the weapon. Before he could pull the trigger, Mathew said, "No sense wasting a shell," as he plunged the knife deep into the woman's chest. He pulled the knife out and drove it in several more times for good measure.

"Jesus, Mathew!" remarked Luke.

Mathew looked up and said, "Sorry little brother. Got a little carried away, there."

"Why'd you have to go and kill those nice ladies for?" asked Luke, in all sincerity.

Mathew thought for a moment before answering, "Like I explained to ya before, little brother, Mr. Whitney don't want no witnesses and we gotta do like he says. He's the boss, don't ya see?"

Mathew was always able to control his younger brother even though Luke was nearly twice his size. Mathew was of average height and, although, not a big man, he was very muscular from years of hard manual labour. He had a weathered face and his eyes seemed to be in a permanent squint. He walked with a slight limp; the result of a fall from a barn roof that broke his leg in three places. It was never set correctly, so it never healed properly.

As a grown man, Mathew became basically lazy. Work to him was a four letter word. He did what he needed to do to fill his belly and he wasn't too fussy if it was legal or not, as long as it didn't involve a lot of effort. He was weak when it came to standing up for anything. He would never take sides until he saw which way the wind was blowing and then he would pick the most popular one.

The only responsibility he took seriously was his younger brother's welfare. Luke was mentally slow and Mathew was fanatical about protecting him from the cruel world, but at the same time he used his brother as an excuse for his own shortcomings and failures.

Mathew and Luke's parents were hardworking sharecroppers who left Tennessee for a better life in Oregon. They loaded a couple of wagons with all their worldly possessions and their five children and headed out. The three oldest children were girls, so Mark Briscoe was delighted when his last two children were boys. Mathew was fourteen and Luke twelve years old when they headed west. They were both expected to work as hard as their father in carving out a living from the wilderness.

Luke's father lost patience with his younger son's mental limitations when they were still back in Tennessee. Luke stuck to his older brother like glue and Mathew accepted the job of his brother's keeper. He would often get reprimanded by his father for not doing his work and he would use Luke's need for him as an excuse.

When Mathew was seventeen and Luke fifteen, Luke became enthralled with the workings of a coal oil lamp. He was inspecting it, burned himself, and knocked the lamp over. The resulting fire destroyed a work shed along with most of his father's tools. In a rage, their father began to beat Luke and after Mathew intervened, their father threw them both out.

The boys spent the next few years working as farm hands, general labourers, camp cooks for cattle outfits and mines, teamsters, and the list went on. They heard of untold riches in the Cariboo and came to seek their fortune. They dug out enough gold to buy a small farm back in Oregon. It didn't take long for it to go under, so back to the gold fields they went. This didn't work out, either, so it was back to scrounging for a living with any work they could find.

Mathew got the bright idea bounty hunting might be a lucrative trade. How hard could it be? Find a wanted man and bring him in for the money. At the time of the jail break, they were awaiting trial for shooting an innocent man, whom they mistook for someone on a wanted poster.

Luke had grown into a tall and very heavy set man. When he and Mathew stood together, they looked like a grizzly bear and her cub. Everything about Luke was big and powerful from a physical perspective. He could open walnuts with his fingers. He hadn't lost an arm wrestling match since he was fifteen. Mathew won many a night's free drinks on the strength of Luke's right arm.

As strong as he was physically, Luke was mentally a young child, totally dependent on his brother. In his eyes, his brother was God and Luke would do anything Mathew told him to, without question or hesitation.

He was nervous in the presence of others, never saying much. He needed to be reassured, usually by Mathew, that the people around him meant him no harm, before he felt at ease. When he was comfortable, or if Mathew allowed him a drink or two, he could be quite boisterous and loud. Often, not realizing his own strength, he would push, slap or hug somebody a little too hard. This would cause a fuss that Mathew would defuse by explaining Luke was slow and didn't mean anything by it. He would buy the offended party a drink and usually it all ended well. He kept trying to explain to Luke that he couldn't do these sorts of things, but he gave it up as a lost cause.

-2-

As the Briscoe brothers, Frank Oakley, and Sean McClaren headed off on their killing spree, Silas Davidson and the rest of the men remained where they were, unsure of what to do. Whitney picked up on the situation at once and said, "Mr. Davidson, get the rest of these men gathering up anything we can use and be quick about it."

Silas turned to the men and started yelling out orders. "Men, we need any food we can find, any weapons and ammunition, and blankets. Bring whatever you find back here and pile it up." As an afterthought, he said to no one in particular, "Yes, I think we need some blankets. I was awfully cold last night."

He did a mental headcount and then added, "Everyone dismount. You two come with me to the huts at this end of the camp," he said, pointing to Harold Grant and Collin Pilkington, "and the rest of you go do the other end," referring to Con Murdock, Josiah Morgan, Fredrick Guetch, and Nathaniel Brimsby.

Josiah Morgan was in front of his group as they entered the north end of the camp, just in time to see Mathew Briscoe dragging a woman back into a lodge. He thought about stopping Mathew from his intentions, but as he approached the hut he couldn't find the courage to go in. Instead, he turned around and began to wander aimlessly. At the end of the compound, he saw the bodies of the slain men. He felt so helpless. He turned and staggered back through the encampment and when he got to the common area, he sank to his knees in anguish and began berating God.

Silas Davidson, Harold Grant, and Collin Pilkington began a systematic search of each lodge on the south end of the encampment. Silas told Harold Grant to check the first hut, which he entered, and after letting his eyes adjust to the dim light, he scanned the interior. In the center of the floor, straddling a small fire pit, was a tripod with a pot hanging from the center. Arranged in a circle around the interior of the lodge were sleeping places for five people. In each spot there was a reed mat to lie on and covers made up of blankets mixed in with some hides. In one corner was a rack on which a buckskin shirt was hung.

Scattered about the hut were numerous reed baskets of various sizes. Harold began his search by checking to see what the baskets may contain. He selected one of the larger ones, turned it over and emptied the contents on the ground. It was full of rawhide strips of different widths and lengths, used to tie things together. Harold sat on one of the mats and picked up a strip to examine it.

As he felt the texture of the buckskin strip, his mind drifted back to his home in England. "Why did I ever leave?" he had asked himself many times in the last few months.

Harold Grant was a fair-haired, balding man in his early forties, of average build and height. He was soft, almost feminine in manner. Although he could beat few men physically, he believed he was smarter than anyone else and he could talk his way out of any situation. He was very manipulative and could persuade a person to give him the shirt off their back and afterwards they would wonder how it happened. Harold would keep pressing an issue until he aggravated a listener to the point where he would want to slap Harold and tell him to be quiet.

He was a bookkeeper for a large textile firm in London. He headed for the "Colonies" when he was twenty three, boasting about how he would be returning soon with a fortune. He landed in Victoria and was hired by a transport company as a clerk. It wasn't long before he had his eye on a management position. He never got the job mainly because he wasn't there long enough and a clerk with more seniority was promoted ahead of him. As the years passed, Harold never did advance. His brash manner, his constant bickering and self pity, when others were promoted ahead of him, held him back. To get rid of him, he was finally promoted to Depot Manager. The only catch — the depot was in Barkerville, at the north end of the Cariboo Country.

Harold realized he was never going to make a fortune honestly, so he began shorting shipments, claiming the goods were either lost or damaged. He was caught when he sold some supposedly lost goods to an undercover agent. He was convicted of embezzlement and was only a year into a seven year sentence. Josiah Morgan's loud wailing brought Harold's attention back to the present and he continued his search.

Con Murdock was in his mid thirties. He was sneaky, underhanded, and an opportunist of the highest order. He was a very handsome man with black wavy hair, dark ebony eyes, a pencil thin moustache, and bright white teeth. His smile and sweet talk could melt any young lady's heart. He grew up in eastern Missouri on the banks of the Mississippi River. He was fascinated by the big sternwheelers and would sit and watch them go by for hours.

Con's father was a very good gambler and he applied his skills well enough to make a good living. Con started learning the tricks of the trade from his father at a very young age, so when he was ready to strike out on his own, he was quite skilled as a card sharp. At the age of nineteen, he headed for California, where he plied his trade in the gambling houses and saloons along the Barbary Coast. He had a keen awareness for when he was wearing out his welcome in any particular saloon or town and he would move on before he was either shot or lynched.

He followed the gold rush to the Cariboo and plied his trade in the numerous camps where the miners and other hard working stiffs were only too happy to part with their gold. He was serving a one year stint for fraud when he honestly (how ironic) cleaned out a judge of all his money. The judge had him arrested and sent him off to prison for one year. He was almost finished the sentence at the time of the outbreak and likely wouldn't have come along with Whitney, if he hadn't feared for his life. Now, here he was in the wilds of Canada, reduced to robbing natives of what little they possessed.

Con followed Josiah to the north end of the camp and when Josiah turned to go back the way they had come, Con waited until he was far enough away, then he began a systematic search of the bodies and finding nothing of value, he began rifling the lodges. In one of the dwellings, he emptied a small reed basket on the floor. As he knelt down to examine the contents, his excitement grew. There was a collection of necklaces, some made of beads, others of animal teeth and claws, but the one made of small gold nuggets, got his attention. He carried it to the lodge opening and looked at the necklace in the sunlight. Sure enough, it was gold! He folded it over and put it in his pocket.

Anticipating other treasures, he began sprinting from lodge to lodge. Inside, he was a whirling dervish, throwing things about, frantically dumping out baskets, and scrutinizing the contents. His fever pitched frenzy ended when he opened the flap of the lodge where the Briscoe brothers were busy with the women. They didn't see him, so he gently closed the flap and backed away. He was headed for the next hut when he heard his name being called. He turned in the direction of the sound and saw Silas Davidson motioning to him. He was torn between continuing on his own or helping Silas. He decided going with Silas was the better option. He did not want to incur the wrath of Whitney for not following orders and now that he knew precious things were kept in the little baskets, he could search with Silas near by and still be able to pocket any treasures he might find without him noticing.

As Nathaniel Brimsby entered one of the lodges, he was bombarded by a tirade of shouts that sounded like curses, coming from a woman standing at the far wall. There was a knife in her hand and she was uttering threats through her clenched teeth, while making stabbing motions with the knife.

Nathaniel stood as if mesmerized. His eyes were seeing a native woman, in fear for her life, waving a knife in his direction; his mind saw his dead wife shaking a mirror at him, as she chastised him.

Nathaniel was in his mid thirties. He was an average looking man, taller than most, with a medium build, fair hair, and blue eyes. He was quiet and unassuming. He was an honest hard worker and very devoted to those he loved and that's what got him into trouble.

He came to the Cariboo with a group of fellow gold seekers using the Overland Route. It was a very difficult journey and they ran out of supplies long before they reached their destination. Somehow, he made it and for the past seven years he was working one claim after another. He didn't make a fortune, but he did save a tidy little nest egg. His plan was to go to the west coast and open a business of some sort. He wasn't sure what kind, perhaps a men's haberdashery.

But life has a way of intervening in a man's plans. He met and fell in love with a young woman named Anna, who was working as a waitress in an eatery in Barkerville. He married her not long after meeting her. There was a strong feeling Anna married him for his money, but such was the plan of many of the young women who came to the Cariboo. Their intent was to find a rich man and get married.

Things went well for the first couple of years and then Nathaniel filed another claim that turned out to have real promise of some serious gold, so he was working long hard hours. If he found some good color, this would be the last of the hard work and he and his wife could head to Victoria or perhaps New Westminster to start a new life together.

Nathaniel refused to believe the rumours about his wife's unfaithfulness, but the rumours persisted, so he set a trap. He told Anna he would be working the claim for a few days and then hid himself in a grove of trees near their cabin. The rumours, much to Nathaniel's dismay, were true. Anna received a male visitor.

Nathaniel waited for a few minutes until the visitor was well inside, then he entered, carrying a pick-axe. The amorous couple were already in bed and they both sat up startled when Nathaniel entered. Before either one could react, Nathaniel strode to the bedside and with all his might, drove the pick-axe into the man's skull. He pulled the pick-axe out and advanced on his wife. Instead of cowering in fear, she picked up a hand mirror from the bureau beside the bed and began waving it at him, all the time berating him for being something less than a good husband, saying if he was more of a man and was able to satisfy her, she would not need to resort to infidelity.

It was said he hit her so many times with the pick-axe she was totally unrecognizable. For some unknown reason, the judge was compassionate and gave Nathaniel a life sentence instead of the death penalty. He justified the lighter sentence by calling the murder a crime of extreme passion and a man should not lose his life over some whore who couldn't keep her legs together.

As Nathaniel stood in the lodge, his mind was back in his cabin on that fateful night. He moved forward, wrestled the knife from the woman, and used it to stab her over and over again. The first two thrusts were enough to kill her, but Nathaniel was venting his hatred for his wife and he didn't stop until he made mincemeat of the woman's body. He stood as if in shock for several moments, then left the lodge covered in blood, with the knife still in his hand.

At about the same time Nathaniel Brimsby was immersed in his stabbing rage, Fredrick Guetch was involved in some debauchery of his own. He was tall, solidly built, balding and whiskered. He had a constant unkempt appearance all of the time, as if he had been on a five day drunk. He never smiled. He detested himself and the rest of the world. He was strong and confident around men, but couldn't function well around women. He didn't know how to interact with them and became frustrated and then sullen and angry. In the presence of young girls, he would get a sickly smile on his face. One knew he was not thinking about giving them candy.

Fredrick was of German descent. His parents immigrated to the United States when he was four years old. They never seemed to stay in one place for very long, continually moving westward as the country opened up. He was eight years old when his father died of cholera. He was raised by a domineering mother, an aunt, and four older sisters, who were all man haters and as a result, his masculinity was severely trampled.

When he was fifteen, his mother remarried. Her new husband took them to a homestead in western Kansas. Even though his new found father witnessed the verbal and physical abuse he suffered at the hands of all the women, he would not stand up for Fredrick, saying it was none of his business.

At the age of nineteen, Fredrick left the homestead and struck out on his own. Always on the move, he started drifting further and further west, as if he were running away from himself. Every time he lost a fight or an argument with a man, he would find some woman to take it out on, usually a whore. One night he went too far and actually killed the young woman.

His life was full of debauchery and self-hatred. Sex was never the issue; it was always the control over the women. It usually started with a beating and then when the woman was helpless, he would rape her, all the while calling her all sorts of defiling names. If the woman fought back at all, such as the first one he killed in Abilene, he would continue to beat them, in a lot of cases, to death. He would then go into a long period of depression and self loathing and when the guilt passed, he would find another poor soul on whom to vent his wrath.

He made his way to the west coast and his penchant for rape went relatively undetected in the city of San Francisco until he left a rather feisty whore alive and she gave the law a good description. It was time to move on. What better place to get lost than in the wilds of British Columbia. He heard they were finding gold in some place called the Cariboo.

Totally focused on his new found venture, he left the girls alone until after a few months of not finding any glitter, he decided to take his frustrations out on a young lady. He beat her severely, but she survived to identify him. The Constables arrested him and he was sentenced to six years hard labour.

Fredrick entered one of the lodges on the opposite side of the encampment from where Silas Davidson and the others were searching. Two women, an older one and a much younger one, were huddled at the far end of the lodge, under a blanket. They were trying to be very quiet, but Frederick heard the muffled sobs coming from the younger one. A sinister grin came over his face. He licked his lips and then wiped them off with the back of his hand, as he crossed the floor of the lodge with anticipation and tore the blanket back, exposing both the women. The older woman was holding the younger one, who was frantic with fear. "My, oh my, what do we have here?" Fredrick remarked.

He grabbed the older woman by the hair and lifted to her feet. She swung at him with a fist and followed with an attempted kick to the groin. The fist caught him in the forehead and the kick glanced off the front of his thigh. Unhurt, but enraged, he held her at bay with one hand and beat her with the other one, putting all his strength into each blow. He threw punch after punch to her head and abdomen and when she lost consciousness, he let her fall to the ground and delivered dozens of vicious, crushing kicks to her inert body.

As his rage subsided, he turned to the young girl. She had watched in terror while this animal beat her mother to death. She didn't move as Guetch advanced. She sat in a catatonic state, not caring what happened. Guetch hit her with a powerful, well placed backhand, knocking her flat on her back. He tore her shirt and skirt off, dropped his trousers, and mounted the young girl, just as Collin Pilkington entered the lodge. "Oh, I didn't know someone else was searching this one," said Collin, apologetically.

He began to back out and then he noticed the battered body on the ground and he heard the muffled cries coming from the young woman. "Here now, what do you think you are doing?" he asked.

Frederick jumped up, startled. He quickly pulled up his pants and was trying to button them up as he ran past Collin, out into the compound. Collin knelt beside the girl to see if he could be of assistance. The occasional sob followed by an involuntary jerk, was the only reaction he got from her. He gathered her clothing and indicated to her she should put them on. She was still unresponsive, so he gently lifted her to a sitting position and with great difficulty, got her shirt over her head. He tried to get her skirt back on, but it was almost impossible with her in a sitting position, so he stood her up and coaxed her to put it on herself. He then walked her out into the sun light, where he ushered her through the row of lodges, across an open area, and into the safety of the trees.

Collin knew the river was to the south and he tried to tell the woman to run towards it. She was unresponsive, so he shoved her several times. On the third push, she seemed to come to her senses, but it took her a moment to process what was happening. Collin pushed her once more and made a motion with his hand, indicating she should go. She suddenly realized what Collin meant and she ran off through the trees as fast as she could go.

She ran for several hundred yards through the forest, down an embankment to the rivers edge, and headed upstream. As she passed a thick growth of willows, someone called out her name. She recognized the voice of her aunt. She stopped and parted the bushes, where she saw the old woman and two children huddled together. She crouched down next to them and helped calm the frightened youngsters.

Her aunt asked her if she had seen a third child. She was trying to get three young children down to the river to hide them. They were in the relative safety of the woods, when the five year old girl insisted on going back for a flute her father made for her. She broke free of the aunt's grasp and ran back to the camp. The young woman said she had not seen the child and they both feared the worst for her.

-3-

A s Collin Pilkington was ushering the young woman to safety, the ravaging of the camp was waning. Sean McClaren was riding his mule aimlessly back and forth through the compound. He felt like he was in a nightmare and he desperately wanted to wake up. It had to be a dream. Men didn't do the terrible things he was seeing, did they?

Sean was barely sixteen years old. He was a tall, yet a very thin boy, whose clothes hung on him. He had very greasy and matted black hair, dark ebony eyes, and he seemed to have an unnatural naivety about everything. He was always furtive, like he was afraid of something most of the time. He would never initiate a conversation with anyone, but would answer politely, when spoken to. To others, he seemed confused, not sure what to do or say.

Inwardly, he tried not to think about what would happen next. He feared the future. He was afraid of life and what it had done to him so far. Hence, he thought if he stayed inside himself, avoiding human interaction, the less likely bad things could happen to him.

When he was eight years old, Sean, his parents, his older brother, and younger sister were on their way to California when they were attacked by marauders, who preyed on small groups travelling in the wilderness. Everyone else in his family was murdered, but he survived because his mother pulled him under her body as she lie dying. He was found several days later, sitting in the middle of the carnage, by a priest and three nuns, who took the boy in. They treated him worse than any slave and when he'd finally had enough, he ran away at the age of fourteen to find work in the gold fields. No one would hire him, partly because of his age, but mostly because he looked so frail. He resorted to petty crime just to get enough to eat. A Constable caught him stealing several times and through what the policeman thought was an act of kindness, persuaded a judge to jail the boy, so he would, at least, have a roof over his head and some food in his belly.

Sean was being used and abused in the jail until Mathew Briscoe stepped in and told the other prisoners to leave the boy alone. The convicts knew how protective Mathew was of his brother Luke and they assumed he would apply the same vigour in defending Sean, so they complied with his wish.

Sean found himself back at the entrance to the encampment, where Whitney had remained with Michael and the old man. Whitney waited until Sean was within earshot and then he said, "I am going to check and see what this bunch of misfits is up to. You keep an eye on these two." He paused for a moment and then added for emphasis, "Don't you mess up, boy! I'm not a patient man, as you probably have already noticed and I don't tolerate incompetence."

"I don't have any bullets left," replied Sean.

Whitney seemed mildly surprised. "Well, well. You've got more sand than I gave you credit for, boy. Good work."

He manoeuvred his horse next to Sean's mule and handed him two shot gun shells and the end of the rope to Michael's mule. He spurred his mount into a canter and rode to the far end of the compound, turned, and rode back to the central meeting area. He looked like a Civil War general, riding through the aftermath of a big battle, taking stock of all the carnage.

He nearly rode over Josiah Morgan, still on his knees wailing and sobbing. Josiah stopped his blubbering and looked up at Whitney who simply said, "Don't have any use for weak, gutless men in this outfit. Pull yourself together."

As soon as Whitney was out of range, Michael said to Sean, "You little shit. You're killing these people?"

"I — me — no. No sir," stammered Sean.

"Why are you out of shells?" continued Michael.

"Mr. Briscoe, he fired them shots."

"He used your gun? I don't understand."

"He — he — uhh — he told me to shoot this wounded Indian. I couldn't do it, so he took my shotgun and killed him and threw the gun back to me."

Michael seemed satisfied with the answer. He didn't think the kid was a cold blooded killer. Then a thought crossed his mind; this could be the opportune time to get away. He mulled it over momentarily and then decided against it. He wasn't a hundred percent sure the kid wouldn't shoot if he did try to escape. He had already surmised the kid wasn't a killer, but that's not to say he wouldn't shoot as instructed, because of his fear of reprisal from Whitney.

The old man spoke to Michael, "I fear the worst. I have heard shots and women screaming. My spirit eyes show me much pain and death. Who are these devils and why are they doing this to The People?"

There was no Salish word for '*jail*', but Michael told the old man these men had done bad things and were captives of the Constables. They lived in lodges with steel bars as a punishment.

Sean interrupted, "What's he saying?"

Michael made eye contact with Sean and waited a few seconds before answering in a subdued tone, "He wants to know why you are killing his people." Sean didn't respond. "Well?" asked Michael, still waiting for an answer.

Sean blurted out in anger, "I'm just doing what I'm told."

"And that makes it alright?" said Michael, also irritated.

Sean was upset by the third degree. He pointed the shotgun at Michael and ordered him to be quiet.

In the center of the compound, Whitney drew a pistol, fired two shots into the air, and shouted loudly, "Alright, you riffraff, gather around and bring whatever you have with you."

When Sean heard Whitney calling, he jerked on the rope tied to Michael's mule and as he started off, he realized he'd forgotten something. He stopped and told Michael that the old man must come with them.

Michael translated Sean's instructions. The Medicine Man, who was sitting, said as he rose, "When he turns his back again, I shall run for the river. I do not believe he will shoot me."

Michael asked, "What is your name?"

"I am called Dancing Crow."

"Dancing Crow, listen to me. You could get away from the boy, but the one called Whitney won't rest until he finds you. While he is looking for you, he may find more of your people. It is best if we wait for a better time, away from the village," explained Michael.

Dancing Crow thought for a moment and then nodded in agreement.

"What was all that about?" asked Sean.

"He said he was too tired to walk and I explained to him he shouldn't make Whitney angry," replied Michael.

Heeding Whitney's call, the convicts made their way to his location. Silas Davidson and Harold Grant were the first to arrive, laden down with blankets, clothing, and a few cooking utensils, which they dropped in a heap on the ground. They hurried back to the front of a nearby lodge where they had left several large baskets and brought them back, adding them to the existing pile. Josiah Morgan wasn't far behind. He looked much more composed than he had been a few moments before. He was still unsure as to whose wrath he feared the most; Whitney's or God's.

The Briscoe brothers and Nathaniel Brimsby came back together. Whitney saw all the blood on Mathew and Nathaniel and was about to ask them what happened, then thought better of it. Maybe it was better if he didn't know. Brimsby's head hung down low and he wouldn't make eye contact. Somewhere along the way, he had tossed the knife he was carrying.

Frederick Guetch emerged from between two lodges and as he made his way to Whitney's position, Collin Pilkington caught sight of him and hurried to catch up. They arrived at the gathering spot at the same time. Collin began shouting at Whitney, "Sir, this animal beat a woman to death." He was about to add how he had seen Guetch violating another woman, but his gut told him to let sleeping dogs lie. He didn't want it to come out how he'd helped her escape.

Whitney replied without any emotion, "None of my business."

Guetch stared at Pilkington and then a wry smile crossed his lips and he winked. Collin wished he'd kept his mouth shut.

Con Murdoch came into view carrying a Spencer rifle and a bag containing eleven shells, which he laid atop the pile of blankets. Con, who didn't miss a thing that might be valuable, found the two cartridges in the dirt beside the body of the teenager and put them back in the cartridge bag with the rest. Frank Oakley arrived from the far end of the compound just as Sean, Michael, and Dancing Crow came in from the other direction. Whitney acknowledged Sean's presence and then looked at Oakley, who saw an opportunity to get into Whitney's good books.

"There's five horses and three beat up old saddles in the corral," Oakley stated, as if he'd made the discovery of the century.

"Good work," replied Whitney. "What else have we got?"

After taking inventory, they had gathered half a dozen woollen blankets, five deer hides and one black bear hide; three baskets containing what appeared to be meat jerky of some kind and one basket full of pressed service berry biscuits. There was the Spencer rifle with the bag of shells that Whitney instructed Oakley to take for his use.

"Did any of you find anything interesting?" inquired Whitney, as he surveyed the faces of the gathered men.

Con Murdock was very adept at looking a man in the eyes and lying through his teeth. He was not about to give up the necklace of nuggets, so he merely shook his head "*no*".

"That was hardly worth the trouble," commented Whitney. He barked out orders, "Hillbillies, you get the horses and saddles and whatever ropes you can find." He searched out Silas Davidson and said to him, "Stork, you and some of the others get this gear packed on a couple of the mules."

Whitney sat very erect in the saddle as he watched Silas Davidson, Collin Pilkington, and Harold Grant tie the gear to the mules. Before they were done, the Briscoe brother's returned with the horses, three of which were saddled and ready to ride. The other two were bridled, but would have to be ridden bareback.

Whitney made eye contact with Michael and said, "Breed, ask the old man if he knows where we can find a trail heading northwest that will lead to us to a high mountain pass."

Michael said to Dancing Crow, "He wants to know about a pass to the northwest."

Dancing Crow thought for a moment before answering, "There is such a pass, but why would I show him?"

"Because he will kill you if you don't," replied Michael.

"I am not afraid to die," said Dancing Crow, haughtily.

"But I am," retorted Michael. "He may kill me if you don't help. We must do as he says for now. We'll find an opportunity to escape later."

"For you, I will do this. The hunters will be back in a few days and they will catch up with us."

Whitney interrupted, "Alright, alright, enough. A simple 'yes' or 'no' will do."

"He says he knows about a pass," answered Michael.

"Then what was the rest of that horse shit about?" asked Whitney.

Michael decided he would give Whitney something to worry about. "He was telling me how he's looking forward to the time when the hunting party catches up with you."

"Hunting party?" asked Whitney.

"Yes, most of the men in the village are out on a hunting trip."

Whitney hesitated and then asked, "How many?"

"I don't know," replied Michael. "I'll ask him."

Michael translated Whitney's question, "He wants to know how many men in the hunting party."

"There are six, but tell him there are twenty," Dancing Crow replied, holding all his fingers up, folding them and then opening them again. The physical display was for Whitney's benefit.

Michael turned to Whitney and said, "He says twenty."

Whitney didn't respond for the longest time. He looked them both in the eyes and said, "I don't believe a word of it. This camp isn't big enough for that many heathens."

Michael interjected quickly, "These people don't live like white men, one family to a house. They'll have two or sometimes three families in the same lodge."

Whitney was evil incarnate, but he was also very intelligent. "So answer me this, Breed. Where are all the women and children who go with twenty men?"

Michael spoke to Dancing Crow, "He thinks we are lying. He wants to know where all the women and children are."

"Tell him they are scattered in the hills digging roots and gathering medicines. They could be anywhere," Dancing Crow replied and then he smiled and gave his head a single nod as if to say, "and that's all there is".

The gesture hadn't escaped Whitney's eye. As Michael translated, Whitney drew his pistol and took aim at Dancing Crow's forehead.

Michael said without emotion in his voice, "If you kill him, you'll lose any bargaining power if the hunters catch up to us. This man is the spiritual leader of these people and he is very valuable to them."

Whitney mulled the idea over, uncocked the pistol, and put it back in his waistband. "You two are on the very edge. Keep pushing and I will shoot you both and damn the consequences. One more thing," added Whitney, "are there other villages between here and the big lake to the northwest?"

Michael translated Whitney's request to Dancing Crow, who was reluctant to tell Whitney anything more. Michael convinced him if Whitney knew where The People were, he would avoid them rather than risk a confrontation. Dancing Crow told him there was a large settlement at the southeast end of the lake. The branch of the trail they would be using would take them to the opposite end and as far as he knew, there were no people living there. Michael passed this onto Whitney, who seemed satisfied with the information.

Mathew Briscoe moved in close enough to hear everything. He asked, "Think we should wait on them hunters and take care of them when they get here?"

Whitney usually didn't explain himself to anyone, but he was warming up to Briscoe like the most despicable of men could warm up to a friendly dog. He said in explanation, "I don't believe there are twenty heathens out there, but I can't take the chance, so let's get out of here." He shouted orders for everyone to mount up.

Silas Davidson posed the question, "With the addition of the extra horses, whom do you wish to ride what?"

Whitney sighed and said, "Mr. Davidson, you take a horse with a saddle. The hillbillies and the gunfighter keep their mounts and the kid gets a horse and saddle. The rest, I really don't give a damn about, but get it sorted out, quickly." As an after thought he added, "Put these two together on one horse, so I can keep an eye on them," indicating Michael and Dancing Crow. "You, Hillbillies, make sure the breed's wrists are tied tight and once they are mounted, throw a rope around them both."

To Sean McClaren he said, "Kid, you take the rope. It is your job to look after these two heathens. Don't let me down."

As the Briscoe brothers set about their assigned task, Luke asked Mathew, "Why does he call us Hillbillies?"

Mathew replied, "'Cause he likes us."

Luke was confused by the answer, but it came from Mathew, so he smiled and accepted it without question.

Silas Davidson quickly designated riding assignments. He gave the two remaining horses to Brimsby and Guetch, not through any logically thinking. He merely surmised it would cause the least amount of complaining. Murdock, Grant, Pilkington, and Josiah Morgan ended up with the mules. The only one complaining was Con Murdock, who thought ridding a mule was beneath him.

Just before they were ready to leave, Whitney ordered the Briscoe brothers and Frank Oakley to tear one of the old blankets into strips and wrap them around several fair sized sticks. They set the makeshift torches ablaze from the still burning fire. Shouting and hurrahing, they rode about setting all the lodges on fire. As the dwellings were burning, two large white haired, growling dogs, with teeth bared, charged at them. Mathew shot one and Luke took care of the other one before the dogs could reach the horses.

Dancing Crow said to Michael, "They seem to enjoy the killing of living things for no reason."

Michael replied, "Yes, they do."

Whitney asked Michael what was said.

Michael lied and told him the old man had said something about it being a waste of two good dogs

Whitney replied, "Yes, it is too bad. I, for one, like dogs."

Packed, saddled, and mounted, with Whitney in the lead, the troop headed to the north end of the compound, where as indicated by Dancing Crow, they found a trail heading to the northwest. As they started out, Whitney turned back to look at the burning camp. The hair on the back of his neck stood up and he felt the strongest sensation that he was being watched. As he turned his attention back to the trail, a five year old girl stepped out of the trees, directly into his path. She was convulsing with sobs and crying for her mother. Whitney could have avoided her, but he deliberately rode over the child, trampling her under the horse's hoofs.

Dancing Crow could feel the intense anger swell up in Michael. He was seated behind the young Métis, which enabled him to put his arms around him. As he embraced Michael, he whispered in his ear, "Do not act now. His time will come. I know it."

Chapter 3 - Little Fox

The Lynx had just shown him a terrifying vision that filled his very soul with absolute horror. His eyes snapped open as he jolted back into the physical realm. As an awareness of his earthly environment returned, he involuntarily shivered. It was raining lightly, a cold rain; the droplets running down his naked back. He retrieved his shirt and vest from a nearby deer-hide bag and quickly put them on. He stood, stretched his cold, stiff muscles, draped a buckskin poncho over his shoulders, and started back to his village on a dead run.

As he ran, his body began to warm and he was able to focus his thoughts on this latest vision. Was it a depiction of something which had already taken place, was going to take place, or was it a trickster spirit that had come to him and was playing a prank on him? He didn't want to believe the vision to be true.

This was one of a few vision quests he'd gone on alone. He'd been on dozens of such outings before, but he was always accompanied by his grandfather, Dancing Crow, the village Medicine Man. He was on this current quest to fast, meditate, and seek answers to questions about his future. He was not quite sure if he wanted to follow the path of the Shaman. His grandfather was training him in the ways of a spiritual leader, a healer, a seer, but he was still inwardly fighting the choice. He felt he did not want the responsibility of looking after an entire community's medicinal and spiritual needs. He wanted his time to himself, to explore the magic of Shamanism for his own pleasure of discovery.

Recently, Little Fox had completed his long wander, a rite of passage where a young man goes for a lengthy walk in the wilderness without food or water. During the wander, which can take several days, the intent was to receive a vision that would point him to his life's path. Little Fox was given several visions. In one, he was indeed a very powerful Medicine Man, revered and loved by all who knew him. However, another image disturbed him greatly. This vision was confusing and he wasn't sure what the spirits were trying to tell him. In it, he was pursuing some white men with anger and hatred in his heart. He saw himself surrounded by animal spirits, but he did not sense they were there to guide him. It felt more like they were part of him, or he was part of them; he wasn't sure which. When he asked his grandfather what the vision might mean, Dancing Crow told him he would be able to call on the power of any animal spirit to help him.

From a very early age, Little Fox exhibited abilities never found in one so young. One such talent was to foretell the weather with uncanny accuracy. He was barely five years old when he astounded a group of women, gathering grasses and reeds for basket making. It was mid afternoon on a bright sunny day in early October, around mid afternoon. Five of the women were cutting and collecting the plant material, while two others were watching a group of young children.

Suddenly, Little Fox became increasingly agitated and began to make a fuss. One of the women noticed and came to see what might be the matter. He hugged her ever so tightly and said they should all go back to the safety of the village. When the woman asked why, he told her a very bad storm was coming. The woman looked up and seeing nothing but blue sky didn't pay any attention to him. An hour later a massive cold front moved in from the northwest. The temperature plummeted and rain mixed with snow came pelting down, soaking women and children, alike. It was a very cold and wet two mile walk back to the village.

When his grandfather heard of the incident, he took the boy aside and asked him how he knew it was going to storm. Little Fox told him he was laying on the hillside with his eyes closed, enjoying the warm sunlight. He was almost asleep, at the state where one is no longer conscious of their surroundings anymore, but not quite in slumber. In his mind, he saw a red fox coming towards him. When the fox was very close, it stood on its hind legs and its form changed to a man with the head of a fox. When it told him to look to the northern sky, he obeyed and saw a dark purple, almost black, swirling cloud appear. He sat upright, fully awake and much shaken by his vision. He was still visibly upset when the storm hit and as they all hurried back to the safety of the village, one of the women asked him how he knew bad weather was coming. Little Fox told her a fox man had shown him a vision of the impending storm. The woman looked all around and seeing no signs of any such creature, told him it was only his imagination and to stop being so silly.

On that day, Dancing Crow told him the fox was his power animal and he gave the boy his spirit name; Little Fox. It was a great honour to receive a spiritual name at such a young age. It usually didn't happen until young boys were well into puberty. Dancing Crow didn't receive his name until he was in his twentieth summer. He too, was trained in the magic arts. His totem animal was the crow, a very magical and spiritual creature. He would often come out of a sweat lodge in a trance-like state and hop about like a crow, hence his name.

As time passed, Little Fox continued to astound those in his village. He would tell pregnant women the gender of their unborn children. He would tell the hunters where to find game. He would take the gatherers to places where roots, or at other times, berries were plentiful. Every year he would know, to the day, when the salmon would arrive. He possessed an uncanny knowledge of medicinal herbs and healing rituals. When pressured to explain how he knew all these things, Little Fox would say, matter-of-factually, that his friend Fox Man had told him.

While his abilities awed some of The People, it frightened others. He could find lost objects and was once accused of stealing a knife and hiding it in the bush so he could later pretend he found it. The elder, who lost the knife, when told by Little Fox where the knife could be found, began to berate the boy. Little Fox was confused and frightened. He thought he was doing a good thing and yet, the elder was very upset.

Dancing Crow quickly stepped in, calmed the elder down, and then asked the man if he recalled having the knife at that location. The elder thought for a moment and then completely embarrassed, apologized to Little Fox. He, indeed, was using the knife to cut some willow, had set it down, and then left without it.

Fear of the unknown and of things out of the realm of their understanding caused most people of the village to avoid Little Fox. One of his greatest gifts was the ability to make a person see things that in reality weren't there. He discovered he could do this when he was nine years old. His were the best of intentions and he didn't mean to cause anyone any harm. A little girl, about his age, found a dead robin and was visibly upset at the bird's demise. Little Fox told her to throw the bird into the air. She obeyed and in her eyes, the bird came back to life and flew away. In reality, the dead robin merely fell to the ground, but Little Fox made her see the bird fly away. It would not have been such a big issue except an older man was watching. He questioned the girl as to what happened and when he found out, he spread the news to the rest of the village. Dancing Crow was absolutely delighted when he heard, but he didn't want to show his amazement to rest of the villagers. They were in the presence of a truly remarkable young Shaman with extremely powerful magic.

At times, Little Fox felt isolated, alone, like he didn't belong. Even his parents were often approached with caution for having produced this strange child. His father didn't mind. He was a hunter and Little Fox told him where to find the deer and elk, where to set his pit falls, and where to set his snares for rabbit and mink. His father contributed more than his share to the well being and wealth of the village and was greatly respected. Many people thought his success could be attributed to his odd son, but no one dared suggest such a thing. It would have been very disrespectful.

In Little Fox's eleventh winter, Dancing Crow found him huddled in a dark corner of his pit house. His parents were concerned because the boy had not eaten for two days and would not speak. They asked his grandfather to see if he could help the boy. After much cajoling, Little Fox confided that in early winter, Fox Man had shown him a vision in which a man named Skywatcher would have an accident and would die, if Little Fox didn't warn him. He went to Skywatcher to tell him of his vision, but the man grabbed the boy and shook him violently, calling him a demon and warning him to stay away. Several days later, Skywatcher fell through some thin ice and was swept down the frigid river, never to be seen again.

Fox Man showed him another vision in which a young woman had a bad fall. After the treatment he received at the hands of Skywatcher, Little Fox did not warn the woman and a short time later she slipped down an embankment and broke her leg in two places. He felt guilty and confused about what he should have done.

His parent's did not know how to help him. Dancing Crow offered a solution and after a lengthy discussion, they agreed to let him take their son under his care, to guide and train him in the ways of a Shaman. From then on, whenever Little Fox's spirit animal brought him visions, he passed them on to his grandfather, who dealt with the issue with the results often adding to Dancing Crow's celebrity.

A year later, a Smallpox epidemic swept through the village. The sick and dying were everywhere. Even with all his knowledge and skills, Dancing Crow could not fight the white man's disease. He managed to save a few lives, but by the time the worst had passed, more than half of the villagers had died, including Little Fox's parents. Little Fox was very ill himself, but his youthful strength and will to survive saw him through. Dancing Crow never took ill. It seemed he was protected.

Over the next few years, Little Fox was an avid student, eager to learn anything his grandfather could teach him and in turn Dancing Crow was delighted in passing on his vast knowledge to such an enthusiastic pupil. He learned all there was about the art of healing; the medicines and causes of illness, including those brought on by evil spirits. He learned all the religious ceremonies, all the rites and all the magic rituals, including the blessing of the first salmon of the season, breathing through the feather, protection against enemies, and countless others. He learned all the legends and stories that were passed on down from generation to generation to be told around winter fires. He studied the fine art of prophecy, including weather prediction, both short and long term.

Now, a young man in his late teens, Little Fox was slowly taking over most of the duties of the village Shaman, under his grandfather's watchful eye, of course. He learned, during meditation, to travel back and forth between the physical and the spiritual realms. A new personal totem entered his life, the Lynx, who teaches one to know the inner workings of others, such as their fears and tendencies. Because of this ability, people around a Lynx person feel uncomfortable. They sense that he sees what they are not showing and hears what they are not saying. Lynx teaches one how to be alone without being lonely and how to project and utilize the life force in powerful ways.

Four days prior to this latest vision quest, Little Fox had spent the morning in a sweat lodge with Dancing Crow, performing a cleansing ceremony. This was usually done before one went into the forest for a time of solitude and meditation. He left the village and walked upstream for several miles where the river was the shallowest. He crossed the river to the south shore and climbed the embankment to the top, where he pick up a trail he knew well. Almost twenty miles to the south there was a small, heavily wooded plateau that was considered a sacred place where spirits often came to visit. Little Fox, on his last meditation there, received a very vivid vision of Lynx changing forms very rapidly; first to wolf, then bear, eagle, crane, and then back to Lynx. Little Fox intuitively knew it had something to do with the magic of shape shifting and after sharing his vision with Dancing Crow, his hunch was confirmed.

There was a small, flat, moss covered area, encircled by large fir trees that provided shade from the hot sun and some shelter during inclement weather. A six foot circle made of fist-sized stones was in the center of the small clearing. Inside the circle were four arrows, formed from smaller pebbles, each one pointing to one of the four directions. Little Fox stripped off his shirt and vest, put them in a deer-skin pouch and with only a water bag beside him, he sat cross-legged in the middle of the circle. He said a prayer to the four directions, closed his eyes, and began to breathe deeply.

Because of his extensive training and practice, he was quickly into a dream-like state of mind. Thus he stayed for four days, without food, or the comfort of a fire, and only an occasional sip of water. His intent was to extent his relationship with his new totem, Lynx. For most of the meditation, his mind wandered. He couldn't seem to focus like he usually did. He saw past events and past lessons he had learned, almost like a review.

On the fourth day, Lynx took him back to his village. It was a ghastly vision. Pit houses and grass matted huts were ablaze. Dead and dying people were everywhere. He could hear the cries for help and screams of anguish in his mind. The last thing he saw before he returned to the physical world was an image of Dancing Crow, tethered around the waist to another man. They were both atop one of the village ponies. He saw a large group of white men and he focused on the leader. The man looked up at him as if he knew Little Fox was watching. He felt a chill and a great wave of revulsion growing inside him. He felt he was in the presence of a vile demon. The white man dropped his gaze, spurred his horse, and rode off.

Little Fox seldom used a horse for travel. He preferred to walk, or if he was in a hurry, he would run. A wolf spirit taught him a loping gait he used to travel great distances rapidly, without expending a lot of energy.

He was almost to the village by nightfall. When darkness fell, the sky was still overcast, with no moonlight. He still had to cross the river and cover the last few miles in pitch black darkness. After stumbling and falling for the third time, he sat to rest for a moment. His common sense told him to stay put for the night and at the first sign of light, he could be on his way again. The urge was too strong to get back home and he decided to keep going in spite of the limited visibility. As he began to rise, he saw in his mind's eye an owl flying towards him. He sat back down, anxious to see how the vision might unfold.

He closed his eyes, relaxed, and gave himself over to the dream state. In his imagination, he held out his arm for the owl to perch. The owl landed and turned its head, so they were face to face. The owl blinked several times and said, "You may use my eyes until your own can guide you."

Little Fox gave his thanks, the bird flew off and Little Fox opened his eyes and stood up. He looked from side to side and then down the trail. He could see everything, not quite as clearly as if it were daylight, but in the way things appear in the few minutes of twilight before darkness takes over.

He set out again using his loping pace and it seemed like little time had passed, before he crossed the river and he found himself near his village. He couldn't see anything of the compound or any of his people, but he heard the mournful wailing and chanting from the women.

As he made his way through the trees to where he could see the camp, he felt a wave of despair envelope him. He was hoping his vision was wrong, but he knew deep down it wasn't. His visions never were. It was as he'd foreseen; the burnt out lodges, the bodies on the ground, and the death songs filling the night air.

Chapter 4 – Into the Wilderness

Clarence Whitney turned in the saddle and gazed at the valley stretching to the distant horizon far behind him. The trail rose gradually until, from this high vantage point, the creek they were following looked like a silver ribbon on the valley floor below. He reflected on the events earlier in the day that had left some questions unanswered. Whitney didn't like unfinished business. He hadn't seen many young men in the village and there didn't seem to be enough people to occupy all the lodges they had burnt. How many men actually were there? Would they come after him? The old heathen said there were twenty, but Whitney didn't believe it. He concluded the number was more like eight or ten, at most, and they probably would pursue him, but he was also confident they could handle the situation, if and when the time came.

He seemed less concerned about the Constables finding them. It would be, at the very least, two or three days before they could get to the prison camp. They would most likely come to the conclusion the convicts had headed southwest, back to the coast and freedom, using the Old Wagon Road and there was nobody around to tell them any different. Even if, by some miracle, they did figure it all out, he would be so far ahead of them that they couldn't possibly catch up. All he needed to do was get past the big lake ahead of the law and he was very confident they would do so. There could be other native encampments by the lake, but Whitney thought he would cross that bridge when he came to it.

As he watched the men slowly making their way up to his position, his thoughts centered on the collection of rabble he was leading. They reminded him of the men he had fought with in the Battle of Sharpsburg in September of 1862, one of the bloodiest battles of the American Civil War. That motley collection of humanity had enlisted for various reasons; some for a sense of adventure, some to escape their dreary lives, and some because they truly believed what they were doing was right.

As the battle escalated, the two armies jockeyed back and forth for position. The Union troops pushed back the Confederates, who would then rally and charge, forcing the Yankees into retreat. The Union commanders moved troops from their flanks and with a big surge up the middle drove the Confederates back again.

Whitney served in the division under General John Sedgwick's command which was ordered to go through a corn field of full grown corn stocks in an attempt to outflank the enemy. He shuddered as his memory took him back to that fateful day. He relived the feeling of helplessness and terror as he recalled running across the corn field while heavy fire hit them from both sides. He remembered hearing the "whiz" of the rifle balls as they passed close to him and the dull thud of the lead as it hit his comrades beside him. He could hear the screams of the men as they fell and he could smell the odour of gunpowder smoke mixed with that of blood.

The Southerners closed in on them through the tall corn and the fighting was reduced to hand to hand combat with bayonets and rifle butts. Whitney did not want to die. He shut out his fear and turned into a whirling dervish, slashing and clubbing at anything in a grey uniform. After what seemed an eternity, the battle was over, but still Whitney continued to thrust his bayonet in all directions, as if he were surrounded by enemy soldiers.

Someone shouting loudly brought him out of his stupor. One of the platoon's sergeants was hollering at him, "Soldier, they are all dead! You can stop now!"

According to eyewitness accounts, Whitney had killed seven of the enemy single handed, for which he was awarded a field commendation. However, what was left out of the records, is how in a trance-like fit of rage, Whitney kept bayoneting the lifeless bodies over and over again.

Whitney was in two more skirmishes before he deserted in the early part of 1863. In the second of those two battles, the Union forces had overwhelmed the Southerners and Whitney's platoon was more or less "mopping up", which entailed collecting rifles, pistols, and ammunition found on the battle field, taking prisoners, and assisting the enemy wounded. Not to Whitney's liking! He was bayoneting the wounded Confederates and when one of his comrades witnessed this act of atrocity and threatened to report him, Whitney stabbed the man through the heart and ran.

-2-

Earlier in the day, after they left the native village, everyone in the troop was sullen and silent. The only conversation was between Michael George and Dancing Crow. It bothered Whitney that he could not understand what was being said and he knew damn well they were lying to him when he asked for a translation.

"Get ready, old man. I am going to try and escape if the chance comes up," Michael told Dancing Crow.

"I will help you anyway I can," offered the old man.

"No! You stay outta this. Don't put yourself in harm's way. He won't kill you. He needs one of us as a guide," replied Michael, putting as much authority in his voice as he could.

"Do not take any foolish chances. My people will come and save us from this devil," answered Dancing Crow, with equal emphasis.

"You two, cut the gab," ordered Whitney.

After leaving the devastated village, the group followed the northwest branch of the creek to its headwaters. The trail was an easy one to read. It followed the creek, crossing back and forth across the water frequently to avoid climbing up large embankments or any sudden rise in the terrain.

Late in the day, Whitney ordered a short stop to let the animals blow and drink. Silas Davidson tried to manoeuvre his horse next to Whitney's. Mathew Briscoe saw the move as a threat and quickly spurred his mount between them. "For God's sake, I just want to talk to the man," snorted Davidson.

"It's alright, Mathew," said Whitney.

Briscoe backed his horse out and allowed Davidson access to Whitney. He felt good inside, real good. The boss had called him by his first name. With that small gesture, Whitney had bought himself a huge pile of loyalty, but then he knew that when he said it.

"What is it, Mr. Davidson?" Whitney asked with a hint of irritation.

"I know it is not my place to say, but do you think we could stop for the night, or at least for something to eat. The men are complaining they are hungry," replied Silas.

"Let them complain. We keep going until it's too dark to see," said Whitney, firmly.

"But Sir, could you possibly stop some time before dark? I mean just enough time for me and my crew to set up camp and get a meal going before it gets to dark to see," pleaded Silas.

Whitney thought for a moment. It was a reasonable request and it made sense, but he did not want to back down from his original order because it would show a sign of weakness and the last thing he wanted to do was show a chink in his armour to this band of ruffians.

They had been travelling northwest, but for the last three miles the creek was making a wide turn to the southwest and as they neared the headwaters, the terrain was also changing. It became flat and the creek valley widened considerably. The creek changed into a narrower, slower running version of itself. Whitney studied the area ahead of them and his memory took him back to the dank jail cell and the dying prospector. Recognition quickly dispelled the momentary anxiety he felt. The mountain looming directly in front of them was exactly like the old miner described. They would have to go over a pass on the left side of the mountain, but the trail was relatively easy going. On the other side of the pass was a deep, narrow valley where they would become boxed in on all sides. Roughly five miles of travel would bring them to a second, but a much steeper pass than the first one. Another ten miles would bring them to the head waters of a creek that headed northeast, back toward civilization, certainly not the direction Whitney wanted to go. They were to continue in a north-westerly direction, up and over a third pass. After that, it was smooth sailing with no more mountains to climb.

"Some pretty rough terrain coming up. I think the horses and the mules could use a rest, so we'll call it a day," he said with enough conviction so anyone within earshot would have no doubt it was his decision and not anything Silas Davidson may have said.

The loud rapport of a gunshot surprised the horses and mules and it took a bit of work to settle some of them down. The shot came from downstream and all eyes turned in that direction. Frank Oakley had fired the Spencer at the far bank. Anticipating an outburst from Whitney, Oakley spoke up quickly, "I think we are going to have some fresh meat for supper, boys." He turned and spurred his horse to the spot where he'd seen the deer go down.

Mathew Briscoe wasn't far behind him. As he came up next to Oakley, he saw the wounded deer. Oakley had drawn his pistol and was about to put the poor creature out of its torment, when Briscoe stopped him. "Save the bullets! We may need them," he said as he dismounted, withdrew the big knife he'd found in the lodge, made his way to the dying deer, and all in one swift motion, lifted its head and cut its throat.

By this time, Whitney was on the scene, as well. "Mr. Briscoe, can you gut and skin this thing?" he asked.

"I can sure give it a try, Boss."

Whitney looked back to the group and then again at Mathew. "What is your brother's name?" he asked.

"Luke, Boss. His name is Luke."

Whitney turned back and shouted, "Luke, bring the breed and the old man."

When Luke arrived with Michael and Dancing Crow in tow, Whitney said, "Breed, you and the old man skin out this deer. Mathew, you and Luke make sure he doesn't try anything funny with that knife."

Michael, with Dancing Crow's assistance, deftly gutted, skinned, and quartered the deer. As he rinsed the blood from the meat, he looked up at Mathew and asked for something to cover it. As Mathew turned to go, Michael suggested one of the deer hides they had brought from the camp.

Dancing Crow had cut a small piece of flesh from the flank and now on his knees, was chanting a prayer of thanks to the spirit of the deer. Luke, not sure what the old man was doing, dismounted and approached. Michael was finishing with one of the hind quarters as Luke drew near and with Luke's attention fully on Dancing Crow, Michael saw an opportunity. He stood up with a hind quarter of the deer in his hands and lobbed it in Luke's direction. With a shotgun in one hand, Luke instinctively reached out with his free hand to catch the object coming towards him, but he wasn't very successful. He didn't fully grasp the hunk of meat and as it started to slip from his grip, he tried to pin it against his knees. He was in the midst of trying to get his balance, so he could heft the meat up to his chest where he could control it, when Michael kicked his feet out from under him. With one quick, hard punch to Luke's jaw, Michael dazed him enough to give himself the few seconds he needed to grab the shotgun and make it to the heavy willows a few feet away.

Mathew was on his way back when he saw Michael disappear into the bushes. He spurred his horse and was at the scene in seconds. He dismounted on the fly and was beside Luke as he was getting back to his feet. Mathew grabbed a fistful of Luke's shirt front and screamed in his face, "What the hell did you do, you dumb sack of shit? How'd the breed get away?"

Luke was twice the size of Mathew, but he dared not resist. Over the years, there were many other such instances when Luke had totally messed things up and had to face Mathew's wrath. He knew Mathew would get really angry, call him a bunch of nasty names, cool off in a few minutes, and then try to set things right again.

Whitney's angry tone got both of their attention. "Jesus Christ, don't tell me you two hillbillies let the breed get away."

It was a cross between a question and a statement of fact. Mathew let loose of Luke and faced Whitney. "I was trying to figure out what happened, Boss." He turned back to Luke, "Well, explain it to me, you dumb ox."

Luke took a deep breath and said, "He threw a chunk of that deer at me. It all happened so fast, Mathew. I didn't have no time to think."

Whitney gave them both a long nasty look and then rode to the edge of the willows and shouted, "Breed, I know you can hear me, so listen up. You have one minute to get your sorry ass out here. One minute, Breed — One minute and then I kill the old man."

Michael was quite surprised that Whitney knew he would still be within earshot. It was a common trick young Salish boys learned when they were playing pursuit games. The concept was to run for dense cover and then once you were well hidden from view, make a ninety degree turn either to the right or the left, run a short distance, and then make another ninety degree turn, back in the direction you started from. While your pursuers chased you one way, you were going in the opposite direction. Michael planned to do exactly that. He ran deep into the dense bushes, turned to his left, headed twenty yards downstream, and then turned back in the direction of the creek, where he would hide and wait in the willows until it was safe for him to cross the stream and get behind the troop.

Michael could see Whitney, the Briscoe Brothers, and Dancing Crow quite clearly from his vantage point. Some of the other men, curious as to what was occurring, wandered downstream to get a look. Whitney dismounted, handed the reins to Luke, grabbed Dancing Crow by the scruff of his shirt, and walked him into the middle of the creek. He put pressure on the old man's shoulders and forced him to his knees in the icy stream.

"Time's up, Breed," Whitney shouted as he forced Dancing Crow's face into the water and held him there. He lifted the old man's head up long enough for him to catch a breath and then forced him back under. He repeated the process twice before he let the old man back up to his knees. Dancing Crow was gasping for every breath and it was clear he couldn't take much more of this treatment.

"While this is a whole lot of fun, I am getting tired of it and I will drown him," said Whitney.

Mathew Briscoe interjected, "Boss, what if he can't hear you?"

"Then I guess we'll be two short for supper," Whitney replied with a smile, as he pushed Dancing Crow's face back into the water.

Michael had fended for himself his entire life. He cared little for anyone else with the exception of his dear mother and his childhood mentor, Blue Elk. Dancing Crow reminded him greatly of the only man he'd grown to love and respect and he felt a strange affinity towards this elder he barely knew.

His mind drifted back to a time when he was about fourteen years old. It was the only happy time he could recall. His mother passed away when he was eleven. His father was devoted to his mother, but for some unknown reason, he never bonded with Michael. Perhaps, it was because his mother was over protective of him, or it might have been the fact Michael was half white, which degraded his father's status in the community and he resented Michael for it.

The village Medicine Man, Blue Elk, needed a student helper and asked Michael's father if he could take the boy under his wing. His father gave him up, only too willingly. For a long time Michael was devastated. Not only did his beloved mother die, but in addition, his father did not want him. In time, he learned to forget, shutting out all his emotional pain and he began to enjoy his life as a student of the spiritual arts.

Blue Elk would take young Michael on regular excursions into the forest, where he would pass on his knowledge of plants and herbs and how they should be used in healing and ceremonial rites. Blue Elk taught him how to meditate and how to communicate with the spirit world. Michael learned about the animal totems and used a ritual exercise to call his own animal spirit, a beautiful white crane, which Blue Elk explained represented solitude and independence.

Michael rose and stepped out of the willows into the open with both arms extended over his head. Whitney drew his pistol, headed straight for Michael, and when he was within an arm's length, he cocked the pistol and aimed it at Michael's forehead. "Give me one good reason why I shouldn't shoot you where you stand," Whitney said.

Michael didn't show any signs of fear or even concern. He thought for a moment before answering, "None that I can think of, other than I think you like me."

Whitney was certainly not expecting that answer and it set him back somewhat. He chuckled and replied, "Not good enough. Try again."

Michael remained calm and answered almost condescendingly, "Because you still need me as a translator."

"I'm getting tired of having to worry about you two. I'm thinking I'll kill you both and take my chances on getting where I need to be."

"Another thing," said Michael, "when the hunters catch up to us, you are going to need a negotiator to save your hide."

Once more Whitney was surprised by Michael's response. He chuckled again and changing the subject, he asked, "The shotgun, where is it?"

Michael lowered his right arm and pointed to the willow clump he'd just emerged from.

"Mr. Briscoe," Whitney shouted, "front and center!"

Mathew rushed over and was ordered to retrieve the shotgun. Whitney then addressed Michael. "Alright Breed, you got one more chance, which is more than I give most men." He paused and then added with a smile, "Because I like you." He turned away, took two steps, stopped, turned back towards Michael, and said as an afterthought, "Next time either one of you gets out of line, I will kill you both. Pass that on the old man."

-3-

Whitney was amused at the way the majority of his band of misfits was gravitating towards two distinct classes. The Briscoe brothers, Frank Oakley, and Sean McClaren were his soldiers and followed his orders directly. Con Murdock, the gambler, hung around them, wanting desperately to be included. Gradually, he was accepted, but only to the extent that his presence was tolerated. Whitney didn't trust him with a firearm and gave him the more menial jobs, such as care of their horses.

Silas Davidson was in charge of a group which consisted of himself, Harold Grant, Collin Pilkington, and Josiah Morgan. They had assumed the necessary menial duties associated with a trek through the wilderness. They gathered the wood and water and did all the cooking and cleanup. In the evening after the meal was over and everyone was sitting about, they sat away from the 'soldier' faction.

Nathaniel Brimsby and Fredrick Guetch didn't fit into either circle. They each liked to be alone and seldom interacted with anyone else. Occasionally, Silas saw them loafing about and tried to put them to work, to no avail.

Silas Davidson and his three assistants were sitting on a small knoll a few yards back of the campfire. With the evening meal over, the cleanup done, and enough wood stacked for the morning fire, they had some time to rest and socialize.

Harold Grant addressed Silas Davidson, "Mr. Davidson, you seem to have taken charge of our little gang of peons. Yes sir, you just jumped right in there. You seem to be a born leader. What did you do for a living?" Harold was a manipulator of the highest order and he got great joy out of putting people on the spot and getting them to embarrass themselves. He thought it made him look clever in the eyes of onlookers he was trying to impress.

Silas took the bait. "I suppose leadership comes natural to me. I ran several very successful businesses. I understand men like Mr. Whitney. I know how they —"

Harold interrupted, "Leadership? You don't know a thing about Whitney other than the fact you need to bow and scrap and answer his every beck and call."

"No, that's not true — I know how he thinks and I give him no reason to be angry at me. That is pretty clever on my part, if you ask me," replied Davidson, proudly.

Grant kept pushing, "You are just a tall skinny coward, Mr. Davidson and nothing more."

"Now see here!" Davidson spat as he stood and approached Grant, who rose to meet his challenge. They stood with faces six inches apart for the longest time.

"Gentlemen! Gentlemen, if you please. Let us not fight amongst ourselves," Collin Pilkington pleaded, as he stepped between the two potential combatants.

Silas Davidson stepped back and said with a touch of superiority in his voice, "Why don't we see what Mr. Whitney might have to say with regard to your attitude, Mr. Grant. Hmmmm, what do you think of that?"

As Silas turned to go, Josiah Morgan stopped him and while clutching Davidson's arm with both of his hands, he begged, "Please, Mr. Davidson, don't bring the wrath of that devil upon us. Mr. Grant was pulling your leg. Weren't you, Mr. Grant? Tell him. Tell him you were just joking about, please."

Davidson looked at Grant, half expecting him to back down and offer some sort of apology. Grant simply smiled and said, "No, I meant every word."

Davidson turned and set out for the other side of the night fire, where Whitney stood, sipping on the last of his coffee. When Davidson was within a few feet of Whitney, the Briscoe brothers stepped between him and their leader.

Whitney lowered his cup and asked, "What can I do for you, Mr. Davidson?"

Silas stammered, "Well, you see — I — I mean we — you see we are having a problem with one of the men."

"Mr. Davidson, I believe I told you once before, those men are your responsibility, not mine. If you want me to solve your problem, I will." He touched one of the pistols in his belt and added, "But I will do it my way."

Silas reconsidered his options. If he let Whitney interfere, Harold Grant could easily wind up dead and at the same time any power Silas commanded over his little group would be diminished. "No, you are right, Mr. Whitney. I should handle my own problems," Silas replied as he turned to go.

As Silas walked past the firewood pile, he selected a thick, sturdy stick which he carried half hidden behind his back. When he was within a few feet of Harold Grant, Silas swung the stick with all his might and caught the surprised Grant full force across his left ear, knocking him to the ground. Dazed, Grant felt his bloodied ear and started to say, "What the h —" but he never got it all out, because a second blow across his back knocked the wind out of him.

Josiah Morgan stepped between Silas and the prone Grant and cried out, "Stop it! Stop it! You're killing him!"

Silas pushed him aside and moved in for another swing at Grant. Josiah's interference gave Grant enough time to get his wind back and as Davidson raised his arm for another swing, Grant rose up and charged him, hitting him square in the midsection with both shoulders. Silas went over backwards with Grant on top of him.

By this time, everyone in camp was gathered around to watch the fight, with the exception of Whitney, who stood several feet back of the crowd observing with contented amusement. As the onlookers cheered and jeered and gave instructions, Davidson and Grant rolled over and over several times before Davidson got his stick arm free and gave Grant another good whack on the back of the head, ending the fight.

Silas struggled to his feet, wiped his face with the back of his hand, and said through gasps for air, "Anyone else have difficulty taking orders from me?"

Mathew Briscoe stepped forward and was about to issue a challenge when Whitney said, "Let it go, Mathew."

Whitney made his way through the circle of men and confronted Davidson. He put one arm around Silas and said, "You see, Mr. Davidson, I knew you had it in you." He squeezed Silas's shoulder and added, "Good job."

The men all dispersed while Josiah Morgan helped Harold Grant back to the knoll and using a corner of his shirt, he began to tend to Harold's torn ear. Davidson approached them with stick in hand and remarked, "Maybe tall and skinny, but a coward, I think not. I demand an apology from you, Sir."

Collin Pilkington interjected, "Mr. Davidson, you beat the man half to death. Isn't that enough?"

Silas turned his attention to Collin. "Are you looking for a lesson in obedience as well, Mr. Storekeeper?"

Collin backed away and Silas turned his attention back to Harold Grant. "I am still waiting for that apology, Mr. Grant."

Harold mumbled something quite unintelligible under his breath. Davidson responded with, "Louder, Mr. Grant. I can't hear you."

"I said, I'm sorry. Now, leave me be," Harold snarled.

Silas decided not to push it any further. He was shaking from the adrenalin rush. He felt frightened, but very much exhilarated at the same time. As he turned towards the fire, Nathaniel Brimsby was waiting for him. He approached Silas until they were almost nose to nose. Nathaniel said very deliberately, "Try that with me and I will kill you." He turned and walked away, leaving Silas feeling deflated.

-4-

Nathaniel Brimsby had always been independent, never relying on anyone else for anything. He looked after himself and his own and pity the man who tried to take anything from him. Nathaniel resolved himself to life in prison. He minded his own business, kept to himself, and was always polite to the guards.

The warden, who liked to get acquainted with all of his 'guests' as he called them, saw Nathaniel as a victim of circumstance and like the judge who sentenced him, had sympathy for him. He allowed Nathaniel to carry a very small pocket knife that Nathaniel used to carve wooden penny whistles.

Most of the inmates honoured his privacy and left him alone, but as is true in most walks of life, there is always someone who doesn't like you for some reason and finds it necessary to prove it to you. Nathaniel had one such nemesis, a large obese man with a mean streak as big as his girth. He was a bully, who elevated his self esteem by crushing that of others. He would watch Nathaniel carve his whistles and when he thought Nathaniel was close to finishing one, he would take it from him and smash it under his boot heel.

Nathaniel let it go the first two times, but the third time, he waited until the fat man turned his back and then he acted. He kicked the man behind the left knee as hard as he could. The man went down in a heap and Nathaniel was on top of him, pummelling him relentlessly. Nathaniel would have beaten the man to death, if the guards hadn't pulled him off. He was sentenced to three years at hard labour for the beating, but from then on, the rest of the inmates avoided him. It became a lonely existence for Nathaniel, but most of the time he preferred it that way.

He had no recollection of the murder of his wife and her lover. He knew he'd perpetrated an act of horrific violence with tragic consequences, but he remembered no details, nor felt any emotion. He merely accepted it when they told him what he'd done. It was the same with the fat man and the woman back at the encampment. All he remembered in both cases was he'd snapped and blanked out. He'd had a very strong impulse to take the stick away from Silas Davidson and beat him with it. However, he took control of the urge and let Davidson off with a warning.

He made his way to the creek bank a few yards away from the camp and found a comfortable grassy spot where he sat and dangled his legs over the edge, put his hands on the ground behind him, leaned back and tilted his head so he could feel the night breeze gently blow across his face.

"Nice night, wouldn't you say?" Whitney's voice startled Nathaniel. He jerked his shoulders ever so slightly and then slowly opened his eyes, nonchalantly turning his head in Whitney's direction. He didn't want Whitney to have the satisfaction of knowing he'd been caught unaware.

"Sure is," Nathaniel replied, courteously.

Whitney moved to Nathaniel's left and sat down with his legs also hanging over the embankment. Nathaniel watched the movement and he noticed, as Whitney sat down, that he had one hand on the butt of one of his pistols.

"What's on your mind, Mr. Whitney?"

"You have the advantage over me, Sir. You know me, but I don't even know your name," stated Whitney.

"Brimsby, Nathaniel Brimsby."

There was an uneasy silence for a brief moment and when Whitney realized there was no more information forthcoming, he asked, "What were in you in for, Mr. Brimsby?"

"They say I killed my wife and her lover."

"They say? You mean you didn't do it?"

"I did it, sure enough. I just don't remember it." He paused and shifted his upper body so he could look directly at Whitney and then said, "I know you didn't come over here to chat about the nice evening. What do you want?"

"To the point," said Whitney. "I like that in a man. Alright then, I need to know two things, Mr. Brimsby; one, what is the trouble between you and Mr. Davidson and secondly, do I have to watch my back when you are around?"

"A little misunderstanding between Mr. Davidson and myself. Let's just say, I disapprove of his methods. As to the second part of your question, I have a feeling my answer will determine whether I am still on the bank here enjoying the night air, or lying face down in the creek below with a bullet in my brain."

Whitney grinned and replied, "You are a smart man, Mr. Brimsby. What I need to decide right now, is if a smart man like you is a benefit or a threat to me."

Brimsby answered without emotion, "I believe I am of no real benefit to you, and I have no thoughts of malice towards you. That's my word and that's about all I can say on the subject."

"Fair enough," concluded Whitney as he extended his right arm. They shook hands and then Whitney got to his feet and headed back to the warmth of the campfire, leaving Nathaniel to his solitude.

Chapter 5 - The Hunters

Wounded Hawk was very pleased with the hunt. He and five others had come to the secluded valley on Little Fox's advice. Although it was many miles up river from the village, Little Fox assured them they would find an abundance of game. They had bagged six whitetail deer in a little over three days and were headed home much earlier than anticipated.

Wounded Hawk came by his name the hard way. When he was eleven years old, he thought it might be fun to climb a tree and have a look at some owl fledglings in the nest. Mother Owl did not appreciate him being so close and took a dive at his head, with talons extended. Startled, Wounded Hawk lost his balance and fell out of the tree from a considerable height. When he hit the ground, his left elbow took the brunt of the force, shattering the bones in the joint. Dancing Crow did all he could, but the arm was so badly broken the bones never did heal properly, leaving Wounded Hawk with a useless left arm.

His handicap didn't prevent him from becoming one of the best hunters in the clan. At a very early age, he insisted he go on hunts with the men. He watched everything the hunters did and became an expert at tracking game. He developed the skill to see things at a distance others could not, thus the "Hawk" part of his name. The only drawback was that he could not participate in the kill because he did not have the strength to pull back a bow.

Walking Spear was the marksman of the group. Although there was a rifle in the village, he preferred the bow. When he was a young boy, his father made him a bow a six year old could handle. He also gave the youngster several arrows, but ended up having to teach Walking Spear how to make his own arrows because the boy kept losing them.

Walking Spear would wander the woods around the camp, firing at anything that moved. He was chided never to shoot at any people, horses, or dogs in the camp. Anything else was fair game. For years, he practised sneaking up on squirrels and rabbits. He became so skillful that he was supplying the village with virtually all the rabbit meat they could eat, leaving the older hunters to find bigger game. The men nicknamed him "Rabbit Killer".

When he reached puberty, he'd gone on his first vision quest, a rite where a young man might receive an insight to his future calling, such as a hunter or a healer. In Walking Spear's case, a white heron showed him a vision of himself as an expert with the bow. He received images of all his people admiring and honouring him for his expertise as a hunter.

He did not receive his adult name from his vision quests. He got it from a man in the village. When he was fourteen, he went into an unusual growth spurt. In a matter of months, he shot up to six foot, two inches tall, but his weight did not increase at the same rate. He was the tallest, thinnest person the villagers had ever seen. One of the older men said he looked like a walking spear and the name stuck. Now, at the age of twenty three, he'd filled out considerably, but the name was still with him. Walking Spear grew used to it. In fact, he accepted his name because it was unique and everyone used it with respect.

On the third day out, shortly after dawn, Wounded Hawk found a well worn game trail descending into a narrow gully with a small creek running through it. The hunting party dismounted at the top of the ravine, tied their horses up securely, and climbed down the steep hill to the bottom of the gully. They made their way stealthily through the thick willow growths on the banks of the small brook, all the while following the game trail.

The gully took a sharp turn to the left and Wounded Hawk, who was in the lead, held his hand up to indicate they should all stop and be still. He motioned to Walking Spear to join him. The narrow gully widened out considerably for a short distance and then narrowed again. In the small open area, there were four deer; one stag and three females. They weren't grazing, but were engrossed in a salt lick, a natural mineral deposit that attracted all sorts of animal life.

Wounded Hawk waved at Laughing Coyote to come forward. When he was very close, Wounded Hawk whispered to him, telling him to climb back out of the ravine, circle around the deer, and come back down into the gully, downstream of them. Once he was in position, they would have the deer in a cross fire. There was one possible flaw in the plan; Laughing Coyote would be upwind of the deer and they might smell him, but there was virtually no breeze at all, so they decided to take the chance.

Laughing Coyote was a well deserved name. He was a jokester and he laughed hilariously at his own pranks. When his laughter accelerated, it changed to a chorus of several high pitched yelps, not unlike a coyote. He started at a very young age by putting worms and snails into his mother's and sisters' moccasins and then laughing with glee as he watched them scream when they put their feet into the midst of the slimy crawlers. By his teens, his pranks became more sophisticated. On one occasion, he took the time and trouble to make an unusual ball for the upcoming stick-ball game. His ball was not made of the usual moss filled deer hide, but instead he filled it with the brownish powdery pollen found in the white puff-ball mushrooms, which he spent days gathering.

He carefully switched the real ball for his new one without anyone seeing and then sat back to watch the fun. The game, similar to field hockey, consisted of a playing field, with an occupied goal at each end. The objective was to get the ball to the opponent's goal and try to put it in. This was accomplished by stick handling, passing the ball, and body checking. Once the attacking team had the ball in a position to take a shot on the goal, some of the more adept players would flip the ball onto their stick, toss the ball into the air, and then smash it like a baseball, driving it toward the goal.

Laughing Coyote couldn't have planned it better. One of the best players got the ball in front of his opposition's goal, tossed it up, and gave it a mighty smash. There was an explosion of brown dust that enveloped the player and the deflated ball fell to the ground at his feet. Everyone stood about, stunned, not sure what had happened. At the sound of Laughing Coyote's yipping laugh, everyone knew he had something to do with it. The dust covered player and several others grabbed Laughing Coyote by his arms and legs, dragged him to the river, and threw him in. Cold and wet, he stood up and was still laughing, which was extremely contagious and soon everyone was in a fit of hysterics.

Once Laughing Coyote was in position, he imitated an owl's call. This startled the deer and they lifted their heads simultaneously, looking around in all directions. They stood motionless for a few seconds, listening for the sound to repeat itself. The stag, satisfied there was no danger, lowered its head and continued to lick up minerals and the three females followed his lead.

Wounded Hawk directed Bear Chaser to line up directly behind Walking Spear with his bow at the ready. As soon as Walking Spear took his shot, he would quickly duck down and Bear Chaser would rise and fire.

Bear Chaser was a young man of eighteen and was already becoming a proficient hunter. He'd earned his name by deed when in his fourteenth year, he was assigned sentry duty. There were six elders and only two women left back at the encampment. They were looking after seven small children while the rest of the village were at the river catching, gutting, and cutting salmon into fillets, to be hung on the drying racks.

He was taking his duties quite seriously as the camp guardian, patrolling from one end of the compound to the other with a long wooden staff as a weapon. As he neared the horse corral, he saw the horses were very agitated. The cause of their anxiety, a young black bear, emerged from the grove of trees next to the corral, scrounging for something to eat. It paused near the corral, took a sniff of the horses, decided they weren't on the menu, and began lumbering towards Bear Chaser.

Unafraid, Bear Chaser extended his arms over his head and holding the pole in both hands, waved it back and forth from side to side, all the while talking to the bear in a very deep and commanding voice. The bear stood on its hind legs, sniffed at Bear Chaser, dropped down, and charged. It stopped after a few feet and stood up again. Bear Chaser knew this had been the bear's false charge. Black bears will often do this to see what the adversary will do. If the opposition runs, the bear knows it has the upper hand and will give chase. If the adversary stands its ground, the bear will rise up a second time and when it comes down, it has made its decision; it will either turn and run or advance on the perceived threat.

Bear Chaser didn't give it the opportunity to decide. As soon as the bear stood up the second time, he advanced slowly towards it, waving the staff. The young bear was intimidated. It dropped down, turned tail, and began meandering away. Bear Chaser ran after it until he was within striking distance and using the pole, he gave the bear a good whack in the hind quarters. The frightened bear took off as fast as it could run into the trees.

One of the elders witnessed the entire event and around the evening fire, he told everyone what he had seen. Of course, in the telling, the bear was three times larger and very ferocious and according to the witness, the young lad barely got away with his life. The boy was known as Bear Chaser from that day forth.

When Bear Chaser was in place, Wounded Hawk repeated the owl hoot and the deer raised their heads. Simultaneously, after a silent count of three, Laughing Coyote shot at the stag because it was the closest to him and Walking Spear shot at the doe nearest to him. As soon as his arrow was gone, he ducked down and Bear Chaser shot another one of the does. At almost the same instant, Laughing Coyote shot the remaining doe before it could run. It was a very successful hunt. They killed three of the deer with heart shots. Bear Chaser's aim was a little high and his doe was lung shot. It ran, trying to climb out of the gully, but its lung filled up with blood and it fell, sliding back down the embankment to where it had started.

Magpie was the youngest of the group, not quite sixteen years old. His name had something to do with him constantly chattering about everything and nothing. He tied a large loop at one end of a long rawhide rope, selected a strong overhanging branch on a nearby tree and threw the rope over it.

Son of Tsiatko, the final member of the hunting party, picked up one of the deer, hoisted it over his shoulder and carried it to where

Magpie was waiting. He laid the deer down and held up the hind legs while Magpie slipped the loop around its hind ankles and together they pulled it into the air. Son of Tsiatko held the deer up while Magpie tied off the loose end of the rope.

Son of Tsiatko was a very large man. He was six foot three and weighed two hundred and twenty pounds, much larger than the average genetic size for the men in his tribe. When he was born, he was a huge baby and rumours began to spread that his mother had slept with a Tsiatko, a giant of legend, who roamed the forests. Dancing Crow came to the poor woman's rescue and quickly dispelled any of the rumours by telling the villagers that normal people could not mate with the Tsiatko, so it was not possible the child was the son of one. He lied, of course, but no one knew the difference and it preserved harmony in the clan.

However, the name stuck. As a youngster, the older boys would constantly harass him even though he was their size or in some cases larger. A few wrestling matches, where Son of Tsiatko pinned his opponents and pinched the skin on their chest until they promised to stop the teasing, earned him a measure of respect. From then on, he was proud of his name and since he showed pride in himself, he earned the approval of everyone else in the village.

The six of them worked in harmony. Son of Tsiatko carried the deer to the hanging tree. Magpie, Walking Spear, and Bear Chaser disembowelled, skinned, and quartered the animals while Laughing Coyote and Wounded Hawk collected the quarters of meat and put them in the small creek to cool, washed the blood from the hides, folded them and set them aside. If they had been closer to the village, they would have merely gutted the animals and taken them back, but because they were some distance from camp, the fact that it was a very hot day, and the proximity of cold water to cool the meat, led to the decision to dress the carcasses where they were.

When the first deer was hoisted, Waking Spear cut the jugular vein to bleed it out. He called Magpie closer and stroked the boy's face with his blood soaked hands and then he marked his own cheeks, looked skyward and thanked the Great Spirit for the bounty. He asked the spirit of the deer for forgiveness for having taken its life, assuring it that its death was not in vain and the meat would be well received by The People and the hide would keep someone warm in the winter. The repentant ritual was repeated for each of the other three deer.

With the four animals skinned out and cooling in the creek, Walking Spear cut one of the livers into six equal pieces and passed them around. The liver was still warm, as they had not put it in the water to cool. Each man relished his piece, for it was a rite of the hunt and it tasted like candy might to a white child.

Each man shouldered a quarter of the venison, with the exception of Son of Tsiatko, who carried two and then made their way back up to the top of the ravine, where the horses were tied. Magpie and Wounded Hawk remained to wrap the meat in buckskin blankets and tied the parcels securely to the two pack horses, while the others returned to the gully floor and carried out the rest of the venison and hides.

With everything secure, they set out for the village. They hadn't travelled for more than a couple of hours, along the ridge above the river, when Wounded Hawk halted them. They had come to a small alpine meadow and there in the middle were five more deer. The men all dismounted and quietly discussed their plan of attack. Bear Chaser was excited. Never before had he seen such generosity from the Great Spirit. Magpie was chattering about how pleased everyone would be when they came home with nine deer. Wounded Hawk put a damper on their enthusiasm when he suggested it was still a very long way back to the village and the pack horses couldn't carry much more.

He suggested they take only two of the deer and leave the rest. They wouldn't go far and would still be around for the next hunt. Walking Spear and Laughing Coyote made their way just inside the trees that encircled the meadow. Wounded Hawk kept them in sight and when they were in position, he exposed himself to the deer and shouted. They all bolted for the nearest trees, where the two hunters lay in wait. It was an easy shot for both the men. This time, they just bled and gutted the deer, leaving the hide on, because there was no running water nearby to cool the meat.

By mid afternoon, the hunting party was on the last part of the trail leading to the encampment. As they followed the well worn path up the embankment and onto the small plateau on which the village sat, Wounded Hawk had an uneasy feeling, a knot in his stomach, and he knew something was wrong. As they came out of the trees, they stopped in shock. Every lodge was a smoky, smouldering pile of burnt poles and mats.

Wounded Hawk spurred his pony hard. He was in the middle of the compound in a matter of seconds, with the others not far behind. The women and older children, who had returned from berry picking and root gathering, sat cross-legged in front of the bodies of the dead villagers, which had been laid side by side in a row on the ground. The women were all chanting death songs while the children watched, confused and unsure of what was occurring.

Little Fox stood behind them and he turned when he heard Wounded Hawk approaching. As he dismounted, Wounded Hawk could see the tears streaming down Little Fox's cheeks. He ran up to the young Shaman, gave him a hug, and then asked what had happened.

"I had a vision in the sacred place," replied Little Fox. "It was many white men." He paused momentarily and then added, "I came as quickly as I could. I arrived late last night."

By this time the others in the hunting party had arrived and dismounted. "How many?" asked Walking Spear.

"Little Fox gave him the numbers, by holding up the fingers of his hands, "Nine men, four women, and a child." As soon as he finished, he walked to Son of Tsiatko and took the man's hands in his and told him the child and one of the women were his wife and daughter.

Son of Tsiatko dropped to his knees and let out a heart wrenching cry of utter anguish. He pulled hard at his hair, tore his shirt front to expose his torso, and ran his skinning knife twice across his chest at an angle from his left shoulder to his lower ribs on his right side. The cuts were not deep enough to be life threatening. The self mutilation was a vehicle for venting the pain he felt.

Wounded Hawk remained composed. "How long ago?" he asked Little Fox.

"Yesterday, as the sun was at its highest," Little Fox replied.

They all stood in an uncomfortable silence for what seemed an eternity, when Little Fox spoke again. "Morning Light was in the village when the white men came. One of them helped her to hide in the reeds by the river. She has told me of all the things she has seen."

Magpie didn't understand. "What did they want? If it was a raid, why didn't they just take what they needed? Why did they have to kill everyone?"

"That's the way of the white man," answered Laughing Coyote. "He destroys."

Walking Spear threw his arms skyward and shouted, "We will find these white men and kill them all!"

Little Fox walked to him and with a hand on his shoulder, calmed him down. "I know there is vengeance in your heart, Walking Spear, but we must be patient. They have taken Dancing Crow and I want to get him back alive. I am afraid they will kill him if we attack them."

Walking Spear waved his arm across the laid out bodies of the villagers and went on, "Our people's spirits cry out for vengeance."

"I know my brother. I know," replied Little Fox, trying to be comforting.

Wounded Hawk shot a direct question at Little Fox. "Dancing Crow is not here. You are the adviser now. What do the spirits want us to do?"

Little Fox answered as directly as Wounded Hawk had asked, "I will go after these men and get my grandfather back. You will see to the dead, and rebuilding of the village. That is very important. If in three days I have not returned, you will come and find me. I will leave a trail of three cuts on the trees."

"Then we shall kill them all?" asked Bear Chaser.

"The spirits will guide us," was Little Fox's answer.

"The spirits tell me they want vengeance!" retorted Walking Spear.

"That is your heart speaking," said Little Fox. These white men will get what they deserve. The spirits of our loved ones will be satisfied. My brother, you must not let your anger lead you. It will only get more of our people killed for no reason. Do as I say and all will be well."

Walking Spear thought for a long time before he sighed and relaxed. "I will trust you, Little Fox." He spoke with the respect and trust the men of the village had for their spiritual leaders.

"When do you go?" asked Wounded Hawk.

"We will sing our mourning songs and dance our spirit dances. I shall pray for our loved ones and guide them to the Land of the Dead and then I shall go."

The men hugged each other and then, under Little Fox's guidance, set about the gruesome task of preparing the bodies for burial. The dead were dressed in their best garments and small personal belongings were gathered to be buried with each one. Graves were dug on a sandy plateau west of the compound, above the river where their spirits would have a magnificent view of the entire valley that had been their earthly home. They were buried sitting up in a grave lined with grasses and marked with a circle of stones.

It was well into the night before the task was complete. Some women still sang their mourning songs and cried into the darkness, while most fell asleep from exhaustion.

Chapter 6 - Over the Passes

Little Fox took several deep breaths, relaxing his entire body. He spent the hour before daybreak in a deep meditation in which he envisioned his grandfather. Once there was a clear image of Dancing Crow in his mind, he used his imagination to remove his grandfather's face as if it were a mask and place it over his own. In this way, he could see through his grandfather's eyes.

Dancing Crow was asleep when Little Fox made mental contact and he awoke with a start. As soon as he sensed his grandson's presence, he knew what was happening. He stood and turning slowly in a full circle, he surveyed the entire camp. He said under his breath, "I am well. It is dark and not much for you to see. We shall do this again with the coming of the sun."

Michael, a very light sleeper, was wakened by Dancing Crow's movement. "What's wrong?" he asked.

Caught off guard, Dancing Crow answered, "Me? Uh — it was my grandson paying a visit."

Michael, looking all around, tried in vain to see something in the penetrating darkness. Unable to see or hear anything, he said, "I don't see him. Where is he?"

Dancing Crow laughed quietly and said as he pointed to his head, "He's in here." He could see Michael did not fully understand, so he continued, "My grandson is a very powerful Medicine Man. He can send his spirit out from his own body. He is here with us now."

Michael had heard of such things when he was being schooled in mystical matters by Blue Elk. Michael didn't believe any of the stories passed on to him, but now, having heard it from another Medicine Man, he felt a connection, as he remembered his own teacher.

"Hey, you two! What the hell do you think you're doin'?" Frank Oakley demanded to know as he approached.

Michael, thinking quickly, replied, "The old man is having some bad dreams."

"About what?" asked Oakley, almost surprised. Because of his low regard for any indigenous people, the thought of them dreaming or performing any other natural human function, never occurred to him.

"You massacred his whole village. What the hell do you think?" Michael replied with indignation.

"Ya well, you quiet down. You wake up any of the other men and there will be hell to pay," Oakley said as he turned and walked back to the fire.

Frank Oakley was a man who carried a grudge for a long time. He couldn't decide whom he was going to enjoy killing more; this insolent half breed or Whitney. Thinking of Whitney brought on a strong feeling of anger. Whitney made him look small in front of all the other men and for what; a stinking old Indian and a half breed.

During his cow punching days, Frank didn't let the usual teasing and harassing,

doled out in most cattle camps, affect him. No one took it too seriously and when someone did, apologies were issued, hands were shaken, and all was forgotten. However, Frank would become instantly enraged whenever someone questioned his manhood, or made him look small in front of others. On such occasions, he was like a coyote with a bone; he just wouldn't let it go.

He recalled the last place, a small ranch in eastern Montana, he worked before he headed for the gold fields. It was spring roundup and Frank, like a lot of other drifting cowboys, landed a few weeks' work. He was enjoying the job, minding his own business, and felt comfortable with the rest of the eight-man crew.

Frank followed a daily ritual. After work, he would wash up and while waiting for dinner, he would sit on his bunk and take out his pistol. With a clean rag, he would wipe it down, checking both the cylinder by spinning it and the hammer by cocking it and easing it back down several times. Then he would put the pistol back in the black leather holster and carefully slide the whole rig back under his pillow.

Randy Pearce, a young lad only a year or two younger than Frank, was the outfit's wrangler. He was a fun loving prankster, but at times he went a little too far. This usually got him a backhand across the cheek or a kick in the pants from the irate victim. The other men always intervened before it went too far and saved Randy from any further physical abuse. Randy would apologize and it would end there, with a pat on a shoulder and a "*Don't you ever do that again,*" from the injured party.

As Frank was cleaning his pistol one night, Randy snatched the gun out of his hand and began to twirl and twist it and then pretended to holster it in a mock fashion. He lost control of the pistol as he was twirling it and it hit the floor. In the blink of an eye, Frank picked up the pistol, aimed it at Randy, and fired. The gun was empty, but the act itself brought an eerie quiet throughout the bunkhouse.

"You got a gun, Mister?" Frank snarled at Randy.

Randy considered himself quite handy with a pistol. He spent a lot of time practising fancy twists and turns and fast draws. He was an excellent marksman, as well, but he had never shot at a man. In fact, it never crossed his mind to do so. "Yeah, I got a gun. So what?" he answered.

"Then get it. I'll be outside," spat Frank, as he buckled on his rig and stepped out of the bunkhouse.

Randy didn't know what to do. He was a very frightened young man. The other men convinced him to stay inside while they dealt with Frank. Several of the older, wiser cowhands went outside and finally convinced Frank that Randy didn't mean any harm and to let it go. Frank relented and it seemed it would all blow over until several days later when Frank overheard Randy bragging to one of the other hands how he wouldn't have backed down from a bunch of old men, like Frank had.

Frank crossed the few feet to the group and looking directly at Randy, he remarked, "I didn't back down. I wasn't the one hiding in the bunkhouse, pissing in my britches." He went back to the chuck wagon for his noon meal. He loaded up on some beef and beans and a couple of biscuits and found a comfortable spot to sit. Feeling really hungry, he was engrossed in the meal, so he never noticed Randy approach.

"Hey Big Man, I got me a gun," Randy said with challenge in his voice.

Frank looked up to see the young wrangler with a cocked pistol in his hand. He careful set his plate on the ground and stood with his hands raised. "I ain't armed, as you can plainly see. Let me get my gun and I'll give you the fight you're looking for."

Randy wasn't listening. "Let's see who pisses their pants now," he said, as he fired two shots into the dirt between Frank's feet.

Before he could do any more damage, one man blindsided Randy, knocking him to the ground, while another picked up the pistol. Frank didn't say a word. He simply mounted his horse and rode off.

Everyone, including Randy, thought the incident was over. They couldn't have been further from the truth. About an hour later, Frank returned. He dismounted, tied off his horse, and approached the group with hate in his eyes. Everybody could see the polished pistol in Frank's hand.

Frank didn't waste time or mince words. He strode into the middle of the camp and said with conviction, "I'm back, you sack of shit. Get your gun and let's settle this." He quickly glanced at all the men and added, "Anyone else moves a muscle and I'll put a bullet in your kneecap."

Randy stood and explained, "Now, it's me who ain't got a gun."

Frank fired two shots into the ground, extremely close to Randy's toes and then ordered. "Someone give him a gun."

No one moved. Frank shot the closet man to Randy in the knee. As the man cried out in pain, Frank said slowly and deliberately, "I said, someone give him a gun!"

The cowhand, who had taken Randy's gun, rose very cautiously, handed it to him, and sat back down, never taking his eyes off Frank.

Randy was thinking of turning and firing, but he changed his mind and with shaking hand, he set the pistol in his empty holster and turned to face Frank. He pleaded, "Listen Frank, I lost my head. I didn't mean nothin', honest."

Frank wasn't listening. "Shut your mouth and draw."

"No, I ain't gonna draw against you. You go to Hell," snapped Randy.

"I can wait while you have another piss, if you like," goaded Frank, as he holstered his pistol.

Randy became enraged and clawed clumsily for his gun. Frank's shot was through Randy's heart before he could even get his pistol out of the holster.

The men rose as one and began to advance on Frank with some mention that a hanging was in order. Frank cocked the pistol and said, "Still two left. Two of you will die to hang me. Who is it going to be?"

The statement halted the cowpunchers, allowing Frank to mount his horse and ride out of their lives forever.

-2-

The switchback, crossing back and forth up the side of the mountain to the pass at the top, was very narrow and quite steep. All the men dismounted and led their horses and mules, respectively, in single file. Much to Whitney's dismay, this was slowing them down far more than he cared for.

For the most part, the first pass they negotiated earlier in the morning was a straight line over a saddleback between two mountains. The climb up was gradual and easy, but on the down side they went slowly through a slag pile, consisting of a loose mixture of broken shale and crushed sandstone. Although Whitney seemed to be in a hurry, the last thing he wanted was for one of the horses or mules to twist or break a leg.

The narrow, streamless valley headed northwest, in the direction Whitney wanted to go. It was set between two rows of quickly rising, steep hills. The trail was easy to follow and quite distinct in most places, but occasionally it would disappear for a few yards where it veered to the left or right to go around fallen trees or other obstacles, but it was easily located again a short distance on the other side of the obstruction. Just as the dying miner had indicated, five more miles brought them to the end of the valley, where the mountains surrounded them on three sides. It appeared the only way out of the valley was in the direction they had come. Again, Whitney felt a hint of doubt, but it quickly dissipated when he recalled what the old prospector told him. "It'll look like ya got nowheres to go, but there is a good trail to the right of the big mountain in front of ya that'll take ya over."

Whitney scrutinized the right side of the mountain and couldn't see any signs of a trail. "Alright, rest the animals," he commanded. "Bring me the breed and the old man."

Con Murdoch, who was leading the horse carrying Michael and Dancing Crow, pulled them up alongside Whitney's mount.

"Breed, ask the old man where the trail over the pass might be," he ordered. "He wants to know where the pass is," Michael translated for Dancing Crow.

"Why are you asking me? I believe you know where it is as well as I," was Dancing Crow's curt reply.

Michael grinned, "Yeah. Yeah, I do. Just keep talking and he'll think the information came from you."

"What did you want to talk about?"

"How was the salmon run last year? Lots of fish?"

"Yes, the spirits were very kind. Many fish and big ones."

They were interrupted by Whitney, "Enough! Where is the pass?"

Michael turned his attention to Whitney, "He says you can't see the pass from here. You gotta stay on the trail and the way to the pass will come clear."

"What was all the other gibberish about?" asked Whitney, suspiciously.

"I wanted to be sure I understood what the old man was saying," answered Michael.

Whitney glared at him for a moment and then decided not to push the issue. He knew damn well they were talking about more than the subject at hand and the minute he didn't need either of them, he was going to enjoy putting a bullet between the old man's eyes. As for the breed, he was going to choke him with his bare hands and take pleasure in watching that goddamn smirk disappear from his face as he struggled to breathe.

"He does not seem pleased with us," remarked Dancing Crow.

Michael winked and said, "Yeah, I think we're getting under his skin."

As Michael had told Whitney, the trail disappeared into the thick trees then rose sharply to the top of a knoll, from where they could see the northeast slope of the mountain more clearly. The faint outline of a trail cutting back and forth across the mountainside could be seen. The route continued up and over two more small hills and as the troop reached the bottom of the second one, the trail widened out into a meadow centered by a large alga covered pond. Whitney called a break to let the animals water.

As Fredrick Guetch watched his horse drink, his thoughts drifted off to his stepfather's homestead in Kansas, where he lived for four years before he set out on his own, at the age of fifteen. Near the north end of the property was a spring-fed creek that emerged seemingly out of nowhere and cascaded down a small rock outcrop. Over the centuries, the falling water had gouged out a fair sized pool at the bottom of the crag.

Fredrick would come to the pool whenever he needed to escape from his mother, his aunt, his four sisters, and a stepfather, who never came to his aid when the women were on him. He would sit gazing into the crystal clear water. The reflected sunlight from the misty spray looked like little diamonds and the constant rhythmic beat of the running water was very soothing. It was the one and only place where he felt at peace, but there was always a price to pay. Because he would spend so much time at the pool, he would often neglect his chores and the nagging and name calling he got from the women when he got back was even worse.

He would daydream for hours on end at the sanctity of the pool. His fantasies always centered on obtaining his mother's, aunt's and sisters' respect and approval, something he knew would never happen in real life. Usually, he would see himself committing some heroic deed, such as giving some imagined ruffians a well deserved beating because they had insulted one of the women while they were in the nearby town.

At times, his fantasy was on a much grander scale. He would see himself as a cavalry officer leading heroic charges against marauding Indians. He would save the day for many a homesteader and rescue many a damsel from the clutches of the savages, winning the respect and gratitude of all.

The snorting of his horse bought him back to reality. As he looked over at the rest of the men watering their mounts, his usual feelings of inadequacy returned. He tried to fit in, but the men seemed to sense something about him and avoided him. Whether it was his own fear or the stigma of a rapist, he couldn't be sure what made them shy away.

In any prison, the most detestable crime, according to the prisoners' standards, was rape or sexual molestation, especially of children. There seemed to be a double standard, however. It seemed it was acceptable, even applauded, to have your way with any woman who wasn't considered a '*lady*' in the eyes of society. This included native women, women of mixed race, and white women who were considered fair game because of their occupation, such as prostitutes and saloon girls.

The campfire conversation from the previous night was a good example of this double standard. Mathew and Luke were bragging of their exploits with the native women. As they boasted, they laughed and treated it all like a big joke and nobody seemed to mind. Fredrick dared not say a word about what he had done. He knew deep down it was foolhardy to mention it. At one point, he glanced at Collin Pilkington, who met his look and Pilkington's returning glare reinforced his feeling that it would be best to keep his mouth shut. Wanting to get away form the rest of the men, he got up and walked to the edge of the camp area, pretending to relieve himself.

It was past noon when the troop was over the second pass and down the other side to the valley below. According to the old prospector, there would be one more pass to go over and then easy going from there on. The men were starting to grumble. The bacon, beans, beef jerky, and the bread were gone. Silas, finding no use for the large pot anymore, left it behind. Breakfast consisted of burnt deer meat and those damn dry berry cakes from the village with no coffee to wash them down. There was enough coffee to make a small pot full, about five cups worth. Whitney had taken the lion's share for himself and gave the rest to the Briscoe Brothers.

Once on the valley floor, the troop found themselves at the head waters of a creek that flowed down the center of the valley. The trail was not difficult to pick up. It followed the creek for the most part, diverting up and around large rock outcrops, occasionally. Whitney insisted, in the interest of saving time, they travel in the water rather than follow the trail.

Sean McClaren was in the lead when they went into the water on one such occasion. As he cautiously entered the stream, he could see the bank dropped sharply into a deep pool. He backed his horse out to go around the deeper water and as he did so a school of small trout darted across the pool and hid themselves behind some rocks on the far side.

Sean rode around the pool and downstream far enough to get past the rock outcrop. He could see the spot where the trail began again on the other side of the obstruction. He rode up the embankment and waited for the rest of the group to catch up. Mathew Briscoe wasn't far behind him and once he was alongside Sean, he said, "You scout pretty darn good for a youngin'. Good job, boy."

The praise from Mathew made Sean feel good. It boosted his self esteem, which was pretty low after the massacre. He felt useless because he couldn't bring himself to shoot the wounded Indian and Mathew was forced to do it. He felt the men all thought he was a coward for not being able to kill someone. If he could do it over, he knew he would pull the trigger. Whatever moral fibre was holding him back from murder would be overcome by his need to please the men, especially Mathew, who had looked after him in prison.

He recalled having felt he could have killed once before. It was a few years after the priest and the two nuns took him in. Day after day, he endured long hours of hard labour, stopping only long enough to be given very little to eat and then a bed of straw and an old blanket in the barn with the horses. Then it was up at dawn of the next day to repeat the process. The only reprieve was on Sunday mornings during mass.

If he was seen taking a breather by Father Barkley or one of the two nuns, Bertha or Margaret, he could expect a couple of good whacks across the back with a willow and it usually meant going without the next meal, justified by a sermon about sloth and laziness. "*Good people work for what they get!*" was drilled into him.

He endured this existence until he was thirteen. For nearly five years he ploughed fields, hoed weeds, shovelled manure, cut firewood, and any other chore the holy trinity could find for him to do, with "*Idle hands are the hands of the devil,*" ringing in his ears.

Although he was wan and sickly now, the hard work had toughened him up physically and by the age of thirteen he was as tall and as strong as Father Barkley. He remembered the day of reckoning between him and the priest. It was very hot and humid and he'd spent the entire morning digging around a huge stump that was interfering with Sister Margaret's plans for a flower garden.

He stopped digging momentarily, took a drink of water, and leaned on the end of the shovel to catch his breath. Of course, the timing was terrible. Father Barkley emerged around the corner of the woodshed just in time to see him resting. He promptly marched to Sean and said, "Lazy, that's what you are. God does not abide sloth and laziness."

The priest raised his right arm and swung down with all of his might with a thick willow stick. Sean usually turned his back to the impending blow, but this time he stood his ground, grabbed the willow stick as it came down, and with one quick yank, pulled it from the priest's hand. Father Barkley was completely surprised and before he could gain his composure, Sean's face was within inches of his. Sean said with seething anger and conviction, "No more! You will not hit me anymore!"

Father Barkley was convinced Sean meant it. He also knew they had come to a crossroads in their relationship. Father Barkley realized he'd lost any control he previously held over Sean.

For the next year and a half, there were no more beatings. Sean still worked hard because he believed he needed to earn his keep, but he ate as much as he wanted, not the meagre portions previously doled out. Father Barkley and the two beloved Sisters began a campaign of constant ridicule and scripture quotes. Close to his fifteenth birthday, Sean decided he'd had enough and left.

"Hey Kid, move it along," barked Mathew.

Sean turned his horse and took up the lead position again. It was relatively easy going for the rest of the day. The trail, which wasn't difficult to follow, ran parallel to the creek down the entire length of the valley. At one point it cut a path through the middle of a small grassy meadow. Before Sean rode out of the cover of the trees, Mathew stopped him, then dismounted and told Sean to do the same. By the time they tied off their horses, Luke Briscoe and Frank Oakley had reached them.

"What's happening, Brother Mathew?" asked Luke.

"Caught sight of somethin' movin' on the other side, there," replied Mathew as he pointed to the far side of the meadow. "Might be a deer. I'm gonna circle 'round and chase him your way. Don't you miss, Brother Luke."

Mathew disappeared into the trees encircling the meadow. It wasn't long before they heard him hooting and hollering and two whitetail deer came bounding right towards them. Luke shouted, "You take the one on the left and I'll take the other." Oakley raised the Spencer and fired almost simultaneously with Luke. The deer were only thirty feet away, so they could hardly miss. Oakley's was a head shot while Luke's blast, with the heavily loaded shotgun, nearly beheaded the second deer.

The rest of the troop caught up and Whitney was making his way to the front to see what the delay was, when the two shots rang out. He spurred his horse and was beside Sean before the echo of the gunshots died down. "What the hell's all the shooting?" demanded Whitney.

Sean answered, "Just fetching supper, Sir," as he pointed to Luke and Frank, who were inspecting their handy work. Whitney surveyed the scene and said, "Good work, men. Davidson, bring your crew. There's work to do."

Silas Davidson, Harold Grant, Collin Pilkington, and Josiah Morgan came forward, dismounted, and made their way to the two carcasses. Mathew Briscoe handed Silas his knife, who took it reluctantly, inspected it briefly, and then looked up at Whitney with a pleading look. "Please Mr. Whitney, amongst the four of us there is not one who has any experience in this sort of business."

Whitney hollered, "Bring me the breed."

Con Murdoch promptly arrived with Michael and Dancing Crow in tow.

Whiney ordered, "Breed, show this bunch of women, how to eviscerate a deer. Mr. Davidson, I suggest you and your friends pay close attention. There will be no more lessons."

Murdoch untied Michael's hands and he dismounted. He took the knife from Silas and in a few minutes had the first deer bled out, disembowelled, and head and hoofs removed. He handed the knife back to Silas and said, "Your turn."

Silas passed the knife to Collin Pilkington, who stared at it as if he'd never seen one before. He glanced at the deer and then shifted his gaze back to Silas and said, "Me? Oh, no thanks. I couldn't possibly."

Silas glanced up at Whitney, but he already knew he was expected to deal with Collin and that Whitney was watching intently to see how he would handle it. Silas said to Collin, "You have to do your part, Mr. Pilkington. If you can't, you don't eat." He paused for effect and then added, "In fact, I'm not sure it would be necessary for you to travel any further with the rest of us."

Silas's implied threat took Collin by complete surprise. With shaking hand, he started to sever the jugular vein the same way he had observed Michael do it. Michael

interrupted, "Raise the hind end of the deer so the blood can flow out," he suggested.

Collin had an idea. He wanted to use the dressed carcass as a work surface, and as he was trying to pull it into position, Silas realized what he was attempting to do and ordered Harold Grant and Josiah Morgan to assist him.

Whitney, satisfied the situation was under control, turned to the rest of the troop and ordered a rest stop while Silas's group finished cleaning and packing the two deer. Collin did fine once he convinced himself it wasn't that difficult. Michael stood near and watched, offering advice when it looked like Collin might need it.

Collin finished with the deer after vomiting twice. Harold and Josiah cut the two deer into quarters, leaving the hide on to protect the meat. They wrapped the chunks in a couple of the buckskin blankets and secured the packages to one of the mules.

Harold Grant went to the creek and plunged his hands in the cold water to wash off the deer blood. As he sat on the bank, soaking in the noonday sun, he remembered how full of hope and excitement he had been about coming to this godforsaken country. He was very confident he would make his fortune in no time at all and return to England a rich and respected man.

That dream was shattered. He thought being sent to prison was the worst thing that had ever happened to him, but here he was in the middle of nowhere, smelling of deer dung and following a madman to some supposed 'Eldorado'. "How did it all go down hill so fast?" he asked himself. Harold didn't realize that men who make fortunes are usually very lucky, or they work very hard and sometimes it takes a combination of both. Harold was neither lucky nor hard working, but he never blamed himself for his misfortunes. Someone else was always responsible for his troubles and if he couldn't find a human being to point a finger at, then it was fate or God, but certainly not his own fault.

He held onto a delusional idea that if he made his opponents or superiors look small or weak in the eyes of his peers, he, in turn, would be elevated in stature. He had tried the concept with Silas Davidson and received a beating for it. Harold's other major personality flaw began to surface. He felt incredibly sorry for himself and he began fantasizing different revenge scenarios involving Silas Davidson.

-3-

With an easy trail and visions of a forthcoming fresh venison feast, the troop was in fine spirits as they made their way down the valley. Con Murdock, who was still leading the horse carrying Michael and Dancing Crow, rode at the back end of the string of single file riders, with Whitney behind them. Con undid two buttons on his shirt, reached inside, and pulled out the gold nugget necklace he'd looted from the village. As he admired it, he looked back at Whitney and when their eyes met, Whitney's cold stare bothered him. It was as if those piercing green eyes looked right into your soul and when he smiled at you, it was like the man knew what you were thinking. Con turned back, quickly tucked the necklace back in his shirt, and did the buttons back up.

Although he made his living as a gambler, Con was not adverse to thievery. He was not a hold-up man or a burglar, but a thief of opportunity. If something of value such as a wallet or jewellery was left unattended, it ended up in his pocket. The necklace inside his shirt brought back a memory of another necklace that once came into his possession.

Con was in a casino called '*Seven Come Eleven*', a dive on the San Francisco waterfront, frequented by ruffians from various walks of society. On any given night, there would be a gold miner or two, who came in to throw his money away on whiskey, women, or the turn of a card.

Con was having a shot of cheap whiskey at the bar, when opportunity came knocking. A regular patron, a miner who'd struck it rich, took a shine to one of the girls. In fact, he was in love with her. He wanted to marry her and take her away from the sinful life she was leading. To entice her, he purchased a diamond necklace worth a small fortune and presented it to the young damsel, in the middle of the casino floor. The girl was enthralled. After her suitor put the jewellery on her neck, she began to twirl around the casino floor showing it off to everyone.

Another of the establishment's beauties expressed her jealousy by attempting to tear the necklace from the first girl's neck and a pushing and shoving match ensued that took the combatants from one side of the huge room to the other. As they came close to where Con was leaning against the bar, the necklace clasp broke free and it landed right at his feet. The entangled girls moved their struggle towards the end of the bar and all eyes in the room followed them except Con's, who casually, yet quickly, reached down, picked up, and pocketed the necklace.

It wasn't long before the fight stopped and the young lady realized her necklace was missing. Con knew in a moment no one would be allowed to leave the bar and a systematic search for the missing necklace would begin. Con thought quickly. Catching site of a man leaving, he pointed and shouted, "It's him! He's got her necklace!"

The result was a mass exodus out the doors and while the mob followed the innocent man, Con headed in the other direction. He sold the necklace to a fence for a third of its value, but it was enough to pay his expenses for a few months.

It was late afternoon when Whitney called a halt for the day. For the last three miles, they could see a row of peaks crossing perpendicular to their path. As they continued to descend, the valley opened up and connected to another watershed flowing from the southwest to the northeast. Whitney recalled the dying prospector's words, "When ya come to the place where the valleys meet, don't go left or right. Ya cross the creek and keep going straight for about two miles to the base of the mountain in front of ya. Ya'll see a trail up to the pass. This'll be the last pass, but it is the worst one, real slow goin'."

Whitney concluded it would be best to tackle the tough pass in the morning with rested animals. They crossed the creek and found a nice flat spot to make camp, close to the water. Silas's crew, working like a well oiled machine, had the camp set up in a matter of minutes. Silas enlisted Michael's help in preparing a hind quarter of venison, while Frank Oakley stood by with rifle in hand and a watchful eye. Dancing Crow sat leaning against a large fir tree, close to the action.

"I saw some onion on the creek bank. It would go good with the meat," Dancing Crow commented.

"Why do you want to do anything you don't have to for these bastards?" asked Michael.

"It is not for the white men. I like onion with my meat."

"Then onion you shall have," promised Michael. He turned to Oakley and said, "The old man says there is some onion at the edge of the bank."

Oakley didn't change his stern expression when he said, "So?"

"The onion would make the deer meat a lot tastier. I am sure Whitney would like that," replied Michael.

The mention of Whitney got Oakley's attention. He thought for a moment and then said, "Tell the old man to go get some. Tell him not to get any ideas, if he knows what's good for him."

Michael said to Dancing Crow, "He says you can go get some onion."

"You should go get the onion. I am an old man," was Dancing Crow's response.

"I don't think he'll let me get the onion. Besides, I am busy with the meat," replied Michael, amused at Dancing Crow's attempt to have him do the work.

Dancing Crow, with embellished groans and moans, got to his feet and walked the fifty feet to the edge of the bank, muttering to himself all the way. Oakley alternated his gaze between Dancing Crow picking the onion and Silas and Michael preparing the venison.

Dancing Crow picked the green tops of some of the onions and pulled some of the bulbs out of the ground, as well. His intention was to go down the bank to the water and wash the bulbs off. Oakley thought it was an attempt to escape. He cocked the hammer of the Spencer and started towards the embankment, raising the rifle to his shoulder. He didn't know what hit him. He was focused on Dancing Crow and had forgotten all about Michael.

As soon as Michael caught sight of Oakley's movement, he reacted with the speed of a mountain lion. He drove his fist to the side of Oakley's head, knocking him to the ground. As Oakley fell, the rifle came up and Michael snatched it out of his hand. His foot was planted on Oakley's chest and the cocked rifle under his chin, before Oakley even realized what had happened.

"I wouldn't kill him if I were you," boomed Whitney.

Michael looked up and made eye contact with Whitney. "Why not? Will you miss him?" he asked.

"Hmmm," replied Whitney, "good point. Alright then shoot him."

Oakley turned his head in Whitney's direction. "Mr. Whitney, Sir, don't let him kill me!" he pleaded.

Whitney stated, emphatically, "Mr. Oakley, I told you once before, I make the decisions about actions to be taken in this group. Killing the old savage would have caused me some consternation and I don't like consternation."

Oakley didn't know what *consternation* meant, but he was sure it wasn't a good thing. He turned his head back and looked Michael in the eyes. He saw the anger there and he knew he was walking a tight rope. "I wasn't going to shoot the old man, I swear. I was just making sure he wasn't trying to run away."

Michael didn't believe him and he couldn't make up his mind on whether to pull the trigger or not. Dancing Crow's gentle voice calmed him when he said, "Let him live. It is not worth having his blood on your hands."

Michael took a step backwards, let the hammer down on the rifle, and threw it on the ground. As soon as Oakley was sure he was no longer in danger, he took out his pistol, cocked it, and aimed it at Michael.

"I need him, too," said Whitney.

Oakley let the hammer down and put the pistol back in his waistband. He got to his feet and while dusting himself off, he issued a warning to Michael. "There'll come a time, Breed. There'll come a time."

With bellies full of venison and onion, most of the men lay about digesting and enjoying the time away from the saddle. Collin Pilkington finished cleaning up and was looking forward to enjoying some quiet time alone. Earlier, as he was gathering firewood, he'd seen a sheltered spot where he could hunker down and wiggle in under the extended branches of a couple of spruce trees. The two trees had grown so close together, their overlapping branches formed a small alcove.

He crawled in, got himself comfortable, closed his eyes, and let his thoughts drift. Collin was a quiet man, but not a timid one. He would often intervene in a matter of injustice or wrong doing that he was witness to, as he did by interrupting Fredrick Guetch back at the encampment and then helping the young woman to escape to the river. He had stuck his nose into the disagreement between Davidson and Grant and suffered Davidson's wrath as a result.

Collin was one of those rare or perhaps even strange people who didn't mind prison life. He actually felt secure, protected from life and most of all, he was free of his nagging wife. Little did he know, two weeks after his arrest, she'd already latched on to another man, a rather obese gentleman, who made a small fortune in the hardware business. He was up the Cariboo Trail looking for business opportunities when Collin's wife set her sights on him and before long, she and the fat man were strolling down the streets of Victoria, arm in arm, with poor Collin all but forgotten.

He felt a sense of brotherhood with this group of men, as if for the first time in his life he belonged to something. He wasn't afraid of Whitney. To Collin, Whitney was someone whom you were very careful with, not unlike approaching a growling mongrel dog in an alley. The murder and mayhem in the village should have made him despise these men, but he went into a state of denial and told himself it was not his place to judge them.

He could not understand why some of the men hated the native people so. He was observing the Medicine Man and found him fascinating. He thought if only he could speak the language, he could learn more about the old man's people and their way of life. "Ah well, maybe some other time," he said to himself and drifted off to sleep.

Michael and Dancing Crow were bound up for the night with their hands behind their backs and tied tightly at the wrists. As an extra measure, the Briscoe brothers wrapped a rope around their midsections and secured them to a pine tree. When they were finished, Luke gave Dancing Crow a kick in the leg, not hard enough to inflict any damage, but enough to cause a bit of pain. When Mathew Briscoe saw Michael scowl at Luke, he grabbed a handful of Michael's hair, pulled his head back and asked him if he wanted some, too.

A short time after the Briscoes departed, Josiah Morgan approached with a blanket. He was crouched and moving very quietly, not wanting to be seen or heard. He draped the blanket over the two men, nodded, and vanished as quickly and as quietly as he'd come.

Michael was having a difficult time understanding. He nudged Dancing Crow with his elbow and assured that he had the old man's attention, he said, "As long as I live, I won't understand the white man. Why are some so evil and yet others show kindness?"

"It is the same for all men. Not only the white man," replied Dancing Crow.

Michael pondered this for a moment and then asked, "What makes a man chose between kindness and cruelty."

Dancing Crow did not answer right away. He thought for a moment and then spoke, "There is a battle between two wolves which live in every man. One is evil and has anger, hate, greed, self-pity, and sorrow. The other wolf is good and has joy, love, peace, honour, and courage. The wolf that wins out, my son, is the one we feed the most."

Josiah Morgan made it back to his sleeping spot without being seen. He removed his prison issue ankle boots and set them neatly at edge of his blanket. He got up onto his knees and with hands held in prayer, he looked heavenwards and began to pray aloud. Josiah didn't pray in a conventional sense; he whined to God. He felt like life offered him nothing and he complained about every little thing that befell him. He was a man in complete despair, who saw no joy in living. He likened himself to Job and he equated the world he lived in to the belly of the whale. Everybody and everything was put on this earth to torment him.

He wasn't a healthy man. He suffered from malnutrition, not because of a lack of food, but because he would rather drink than eat. He always walked bent over slightly and when anyone approached him he would tense up as if he was expecting to get hit. He appeared so pathetic the other prisoners left him alone. It wasn't sporting to pick on Josiah. It was like kicking a kitten.

Josiah was as terrified on the inside as he appeared on the outside. The only time he interacted with other human beings was when he needed money to get his alcohol for the day and he had to run one of his begging scams to get the price of a drink or two. He was two weeks away from finishing his six month sentence and the thought of having to deal with his addiction panicked him. He wanted to die the first two weeks in prison as he was going through withdrawal and he would have done absolutely anything for a drink. He turned to God and became intoxicated with the joy he felt. He looked forward to a new life where God would keep him from harm and chase away his fears. It didn't happen. His paranoia returned and his prayers changed from those of joy and love to ones of blame and blasphemy. He was obsessive about praying. When he wasn't breaking rocks or cutting trees on the work crews, he was on his knees berating God for all that was happening to him.

He was in the middle of a rant when a hard shove in the back sent him face first into the ground. Harold Grant stood over Josiah and said, "Enough nonsense. I'm trying to get some sleep."

Josiah turned his body, so he could see who was harassing him. "Brother, why do you torment me? Did the Lord send you to test me?" he asked.

Harold shook his head and replied, "You pathetic son-of-a-bitch, how can you believe God exists? Do you think God would allow all the murder and misery we have seen in the last couple of days?" Josiah didn't answer and Harold finished up with, "Well, do ya?"

"God tests us all. We have to live our lives to be worthy of his love," was Josiah's reply.

Harold laughed and said, "And you consider yourself worthy?"

Harold's question made Josiah think. He felt undeserving, even despised by God because of his lust for the drink, but he held a faint hope that he was on the road to redemption. He looked up at Harold and didn't answer the bully's question.

Harold returned the look, turned to go and as he walked away, he had a final word, "Like I said, you're pathetic."

"Trouble?" Whitney asked.

Whitney's presence, a few feet away, took Harold totally by surprise. He stammered, "No — uh — you see — no. No trouble at all."

"Why did you kick the little preacher?" asked Whitney.

Harold didn't have an answer. Whitney, sensing Harold was not going to say anything, continued, "You know what I think? I think you are a big bully. I don't like bullies. You received a good beating for your trouble last night. You'd think you would learn. This will be the last time I talk to you about this."

"Yes, Sir," Harold answered, with a telltale quiver in his voice.

Chapter 7 – The Lake

Little Fox's eyelids opened in unison with the first light of dawn. He rose, stretched, and quickly began filling a deer-hide bag with the things he would need; a small fishing net, a snare rope, several different herbs, and some pouches of various concoctions only a learned Medicine Man would find useful. He tied the flap of the bag down and using the long attached strap, he slipped it over his head and positioned the bag so it sat across his back, the strap resting on his right shoulder.

Little Fox had anxiously wanted to leave the previous day, but he felt a strong urge to stay a little longer and council his friends, especially Son of Tsiatko. Now, the big man didn't seem much better. He was still sitting in the middle of the burnt out compound, engaged in his mourning chant. Occasionally, he would stop, rise, and walk about the encampment to release some of his pent up energy. As Son of Tsiatko approached Little Fox, the young Shaman looked into his tear filled eyes. He'd never seen his friend in such pain and agony and his heart went out to the man.

Seeing the travelling bag around Little Fox's shoulder, Son of Tsiatko asked, "Little Fox, are you leaving us?"

"I must," replied Little Fox.

"Little Fox, please, tell me the spirits of my wife and child are at peace," Son of Tsiatko said and then added, "Their spirits will not rest until they are avenged."

"Not many can tell you if your family is at peace, my friend, but I can tell you they will be much more content if they can see you are not suffering any more," Little Fox told him with complete sincerity.

"Thank you, Little Fox."

Little Fox continued, "I don't believe your wife and child are seeking vengeance. Some spirits, who have been greatly wronged just before their death, have that need, but I do not see it in your family. I shall tell you what I do know. There is balance in all things. For the evil a man does in the world of the living, he will have to answer for in the land of the spirit. He can turn to the good in himself and with kind heart and deed he can reduce the evil debt he has created, while he is still in the land of the living."

Son of Tsiatko looked puzzled, confused, as if he did not understand.

Little Fox reached down into the dust of the compound and using his hands he created a small pile of dirt. He said, "This represents the evil a man commits in his life." He scooped up a hand full of soil with his left hand and slowly poured it onto the pile, adding to its size. As he poured, he said, "If a man continues with evil heart and evil deed, the pile continues to grow."

He scooped some dirt into another small pile and began pouring onto this new pile with his right hand. "And this represents the good things a man does."

He paused long enough to see if Son of Tsiatko understood. Assured the big man was following his logic, he continued, "It is the Great Spirit's wish that our good pile is always so much larger than our evil pile. The man of good heart and deed will have good things and happiness in his life and he will find the pathway to the spirit world well lit and easy to follow when he dies. The man of evil heart and deed will have sadness and misery in his life and he will find the path to the spirit world dark and frightening and he may not want to go. It is said some never find the way."

He motioned to the two small heaps of earth again and continued, "If a man's evil pile is very large, he can make it smaller by becoming a man of good heart and deed and his evil pile will grow smaller while his good pile grows larger." He illustrated this by taking some dirt from the evil pile and pouring it onto the good one.

Little Fox put his hand on Son of Tsiatko's shoulder and concluded his teaching session, "The belief is, my friend, what a man creates in thought and deed is added to his evil or his good pile. This is how the balance is reached." Little Fox could see Son of Tsiatko didn't fully understand, so he added, "The evil will be punished and the good will be rewarded."

"Is this true for the white men?" asked Son of Tsiatko.

"It is true for all men, my friend. The white men just don't know it," answered Little Fox, with a touch of sarcasm.

"But who will punish these white men?" asked Son of Tsiatko.

Little Fox thought carefully before answering. He came to the conclusion any more attempts at a simplistic explanation of good and evil would only add to his friend's confusion. He simply said, "They will punish themselves — with a little help from me."

Son of Tsiatko did not understand what Little Fox meant, but he trusted his friend, so in his mind there was no need for understanding. He said, "Thank you, Little Fox," and turned back in the direction of the burial grounds and began to wail as he walked away, but there didn't seem to be as much anguish in his voice.

Little Fox closed his eyes and in his mind's eye he envisioned Son of Tsiatko smiling and enjoying life again. He said a short prayer, turned, and ran off in a loping wolf stride. As he ran, in his mind, he brought Dancing Crow's face into focus and said, "I'm coming, Grandfather. I am coming."

-2-

It was an hour before dawn and it had been raining heavily for some time. Silas Davidson woke up cold and shivering. He threw off his soaked blanket and made for the cover of a nearby large spruce tree, with branches very low to the ground. He struggled and fought his way under the branches and although he felt cramped, he discovered it was relatively dry.

The thing he hated the most about being out in the rain was the way his spectacles dotted up with droplets until seeing anything clearly was impossible. As Silas removed his glasses, he did a mental search for something dry to wipe them with, but the only thing he could think of was his shirt tail. It would have to do, even though it was quite damp.

Well sheltered from the downpour, Silas began to feel better. To comfort himself, he began to fantasize about what he would do with his share of the gold. He envisioned himself back in England, where he would either buy or build a very successful business with at least a dozen employees. He would be respected and admired and everyone would call him *Sir*. If there was enough money, he might even start up a bank. Then he realized he couldn't go to England. He would be a wanted fugitive and he could be easily extradited back to Canada. Well, perhaps, the United States or even Mexico would be a better idea.

Silas's thoughts steered him back to his present situation. He was doing all he could to please Whitney and to show their leader he was an integral part of what it would take to get to the gold and perhaps Whitney would give him a share equal to his worth.

"Hey Stork! Where are you?"

Silas didn't have to see the man who spoke. He knew by the mocking tone it was Mathew Briscoe. "What do you want at this ungodly hour?" Silas asked, as he crawled out from the sanctuary of the big spruce tree.

"Boss says you and your boys get a good fire goin' and vitals cookin', pronto," Briscoe replied.

Silas rousted Josiah Morgan, Harold Grant, and Fredrick Guetch. He couldn't find Collin Pilkington. He was still nestled under the two spruce trees on the outskirts of the camp. Silas's group had developed a modicum of efficiency with the morning routine, so it wasn't long before there was a blazing fire, with dozens of strips of meat hung on green willow sticks, roasting over the flames.

The rain had stopped, but the air was very wet and the dampness seemed to go through to the bone. The men all moved in closer to the fire to get some warmth which made it difficult for Fredrick and Josiah to do the cooking without bumping into someone. Josiah was hurriedly adjusting the willow sticks, so the venison wouldn't burn. As he turned sharply, he hit Luke Briscoe in the face with one of the meat sticks.

"Jesus Christ almighty, watch what you're doin'," Luke bellowed as he instinctively back handed Josiah and knocked him to the ground. Josiah hadn't shaken off the effects of the first blow, when Luke lifted him up and backhanded him as hard as he could again. He was all set to do it a third time, when a tight grip on his right arm stopped him.

Nathaniel Brimsby said firmly, "I think he's had enough," as he looked into Luke's eyes.

Usually, in a similar circumstance, Luke would have started swinging, but there was an aura about Nathaniel that made him hesitate.

"Hey, little brother, what's goin' on?" Mathew Briscoe inquired? He was tending to the horses and mules when the commotion started.

"It's alright, Mathew. The crazy man hit me and I hit him back, and this man stopped me," Luke said, indicating Nathaniel.

Mathew addressed Nathaniel, "Lay a hand on my brother again and I'll —"

Nathaniel moved in closer to Mathew and interrupted, "You'll what?"

Mathew pulled the knife from his waistband and showed it to Nathaniel. Nathaniel didn't even flinch, which surprised Mathew. He wasn't sure what to do next. He'd never seen a man so cold and fearless as Brimsby.

Silas's timely appearance diffused the situation. He and Harold Grant had just returned, each with an arm full of firewood. As soon as Silas saw Josiah on the ground and Mathew with his knife out, he jumped to the wrong conclusion. "Mr. Briscoe, what have you done to Mr. Morgan?" he asked.

Mathew put the knife back in his waistband, gave Nathaniel a stern look, and then answered Silas, "Not a thing, Stork. I didn't touch the crazy bastard." He helped himself to some of the venison, stood glaring at Brimsby for a moment, and then headed back in the direction of the picket lines.

As he walked and ate, he thought back to another time, one of many, when he came to Luke's rescue. After a short stint in the gold fields, the boys found a little color. It was enough to put a down payment on a small farm in northeast Oregon. They tried their best, but they soon ran the farm into the ground and with the bank foreclosing, they just left it all and came back to the Cariboo.

While they were still on the homestead, they were invited to a barn dance and social at one of the more affluent farmer's place. The evening was progressing well. Mathew and Luke met most of their neighbours, drank some punch, and even danced a little. One very pretty young lady, feeling sorry for Luke, asked him to dance. Unfortunately, it was a slow waltz and Luke mistook the girl's proximity and her warm smile, as a genuine interest in him. He tried to kiss her and as she pulled away, her dress was torn at the shoulder. Several men came to the young lady's rescue and pushed Luke away.

Mathew stepped in quickly and tried to explain that Luke wasn't the sharpest knife in the drawer and it was all probably a big misunderstanding. The crowd would have no part of it. They asked Mathew and Luke to leave and none of them would have anything to do with the brothers from then on.

When these things happened, Mathew felt the urge to head out on his own and leave Luke to his own devices, but he would cool down and then things would go back to normal. At times he wished he was shed of the responsibility of looking after Luke, so he could live his own life and other times he felt looking after his younger brother was his life and he seemed satisfied with it.

Clarence Whitney was observing all the activity around the fire, adding to his knowledge of the nature of his motley crew. He determined Nathaniel Brimsby was the strongest of the group, maybe not in physical strength, but in character. Whitney concluded Brimsby wasn't as cold hearted as he made out to be. After all, he came to the aid of the crazy preacher.

He learned something new about Mathew Briscoe, as well. Mathew did have a bit of common sense. He backed off from a fight with Brimsby and Whitney thought it was a smart move. Maybe, the hillbilly wasn't so dumb after all.

By the time it was light enough to see clearly, the meal was over and just about everyone was gathering what relatively dry wood they could find for the fire. Whitney gave permission to spend an hour or so to get things somewhat dried out before departure.

The noise made by the men trampling about woke Collin Pilkington. He lifted one of the thick branches and saw Sean McClaren breaking off some deadwood from the tree next to him. He put two and two together and began to break branches from his little den and when he had a good armful, he carried them back to the fire.

Silas approached him and began giving him the third degree about his whereabouts, wanting to know why he missed the morning chores. Collin hastily explained where he had been. Silas studied him for a moment and then said, "Well, breakfast is over."

Collin helped the others in getting the animals packed and ready for travel. Josiah Morgan came close and tapped him on the shoulder. Collin turned to acknowledge him and Josiah attempted to hand him a cold greasy strip of deer meat.

"Oh no, thank you, Josiah, but I don't need it. I'll be fine," said Collin.

Josiah reached inside his shirt and pulled out two more strips, "For a snack," he said, as he snickered and then put all three pieces back.

Sean McClaren stood watch over Michael and Dancing Crow as they ate their breakfast. Dancing Crow was complaining about the lack of wild onion, when he suddenly stopped in the middle of a sentence, closed his eyes and his head slumped forward onto his chest. Michael thought something was seriously wrong. He raised his tied hands and began prodding Dancing Crow, asking him if needed help. He was about to call for Sean, when Dancing Crow took a deep breath, lifted his head, and opened his eyes.

"Are you alright?" asked Michael.

Dancing Crow smiled and replied, "I am well. I was talking to my grandson. He says he has left the village and is on his way."

Sean wandered within ear shot and asked, "What's the matter with the old man?"

"Breakfast disagreed with him," replied Michael.

"Then why is he smiling?"

"I'll ask him," said Michael. He turned to Dancing Crow and said, "He wants to know why you're smiling."

"Tell him I always smile when I have visitors."

Michael looked back at Sean and said, "He says it is a beautiful morning."

Sean looked around at the dense, damp mist enveloping everything and remarked, "Ah, you're both crazy," as he stomped away.

-3-

It was early afternoon when Albert Corman and four other Constables, led by Corporal Ian Ferguson, arrived at the work camp. Both men and horses looked exhausted as they had been travelling since sunrise and had covered the forty miles from Lillooet with a minimum of stops.

Simon Kinney was anxiously waiting for them and as he approached the group, he began chattering before the squad had time to set foot on solid ground. "In a moment, my good man. In a moment. Calm yourself," said Ian Ferguson in a commanding tone.

Simon backed off, while the Corporal dismounted and ordered the three Constables to tend to the mounts. He then addressed Simon and instructed him to get his men some food. He asked Albert Corman to show him the dead men. The Corporal pulled back the canvas tarp covering the bodies and examined each one carefully before ordering Albert to cover them back up.

"You say you have recaptured a prisoner?" he asked.

"It's more like he turned himself in, Sir," replied Albert.

"Then let's go talk to him," said Ferguson.

Albert escorted the Corporal to the large tent that served as sleeping quarters for all the convicts. Henry Enstrom, the prisoner, was lying on the bottom half of a set of bunk beds, shackled to the bed post.

"Sit up," commanded Ferguson. He waited while Enstrom rose to a sitting position on the edge of the bunk and then continued, "Tell me all you know about the murder of those fine men."

Enstrom was only too willing to cooperate. He described in great detail the events as he witnessed them. He explained how one man was responsible for all the killing, including the death of the prisoner. He told Corporal Ferguson how he thought a lot of the men were forced to go with the one who assumed leadership. The dead prisoner questioned the man's authority and died for it.

Ferguson grilled Enstrom for every detail. Lastly, he asked him if knew which way the prisoners had gone. Enstrom told him how he overheard the one who was in charge promise them all untold riches because he knew of a huge gold strike to the northwest somewhere.

After the interrogation, Ferguson told Albert that after something to eat, he wanted to go to the scene of the crime. When the two of them arrived at the cook tent, Simon Kinney and the three Constables were sitting down to a plate of elk stew, which had been simmering on the back of the stove in anticipation of their arrival. They ate quickly, resaddled with fresh horses, and rode to the escape site.

After spending the better part of an hour going over every square foot of the area, Corporal Ferguson gathered his men together, including Simon Kinney. Albert Corman had been left behind to guard Enstrom. Ferguson summarized, "It appears it is as the Swedish prisoner told it. A large group of convicts have commandeered the wagons. I believe their destination is Anderson Lake where they will take the Old Wagon Road to Port Douglas on Harrison Lake and then freedom. I suggest we head for the south end of Harrison Lake where we can stop and inspect anyone coming down the waterway. We should be able to get there before them. They may have a head start, but we can travel a lot faster down the Yale Road."

Simon Kinney spoke up when the Corporal stopped to take a breath. "But the Swede said they were headed northwest to look for some gold mine."

"I believe it was a ruse to throw us off their trail. They would certainly have time to make their way to the coast or the American border if we are occupied searching for them in the mountains to the northwest. No, I know how these people think and I truly believe we will find them on some Harrison Lake riverboat headed for the coast," concluded the Corporal.

"What about the others who aren't with this group?" asked Kinney.

Ferguson thought for a moment before replying. "We'll worry about them when we get this bunch. I want the bastards who murdered my friends." He paused and then said, "We shall return to camp, get provisioned, and head out tonight."

-4-

Con Murdock wished he was anywhere but here; someplace, anyplace dry and warm. They had been climbing up the mountain for most of the morning and he still couldn't see the top of the pass. Mind you, the moisture laden mist was at ground level and you couldn't see more than twenty feet ahead, anyway. Mathew Briscoe told him the clouds were actually touching the ground, which he really didn't care about. What concerned him most was how cold and uncomfortable he was.

Con hated the rain. It made everything so damn wet. He would often stand on the boardwalk under the cover of a veranda of some casino or saloon for the longest time rather than walk across the street in the rain to his hotel or some eating establishment.

On one such occasion, he was smoking a fine cigar, watching the rain pelt down into the street, when he heard the sound of approaching footsteps. He turned and immediately recognized two of the men with whom he had been playing cards, a short time before.

"Hey lookee, Sam. If it ain't Mr. Fancypants, himself. Fella what took all our money," said one of the men to his friend.

"Evenin', gamblin' man," remarked the second man, as he mockingly tipped his hat.

"Evening," Con returned the greeting. He was right about his gut feeling that this encounter was headed for trouble. The man in the lead stopped in front of him under the pretence of striking up a conversation, while the other continued to walk past. While Con's attention was on the first man, the second one turned and with a big roundhouse punch, hit Con on the side of the head and knocked him face first into the muddy street.

He was dazed for a moment and when his senses returned, he picked himself up and he realized he was soaked and covered with mud and horse dung. This infuriated him more than the fact that he had been attacked.

The two men were laughing boisterously and one said, "Oooooh, did you get your fancy duds all muddy?"

Con carried a Colt Pocket .41 with a 2 ¼ inch barrel. He pulled the Derringer out and cocked the hammer.

The two drunks stopped laughing and Con said, "Why don't you gentlemen join me down here?"

The two men raised their hands and stepped down into the street and slowly made their way towards Con. When they were within a few feet of him, Con ordered one of the men down on his belly in the muddy street. When he was prone, Con gave him two well placed kicks in the ribs and then ordered the other man to lie down as well.

The man hesitated and then said, "You go to hell." He lowered his head and charged Con like a bull, hitting him square in the mid section and knocking him flat on his back. Before the man on top of him could inflict any damage, Con began pummelling his head with the butt of the small pistol, knocking the man senseless. He was rolling the unconscious man to the side, when he saw the first man had regained his wind and was rushing at him with a knife in his hand, Con fired, putting a round right between the drunk's eyes. He stood quickly, ready to defend himself, should others come running to the sound of the shot. No one did.

Most anyone would have beat a hasty retreat out of the area, but not Con Murdock. He searched the two bodies for any valuables and the only thing he got for his trouble was two dollars and a cheap pocket watch. He spent the next day in his hotel room. He sent his clothes out for cleaning and his boots for a shining. When he came down for supper, the hotel clerk asked him if he knew anything about the killing in the street the previous night. Of course, Con said he didn't. The clerk went on to say the authorities were questioning men who wore fancy clothes and whom they thought might be gamblers. Apparently one of the men had lived and had given the Marshal a good description of his assailant. Con wolfed down some fried chicken and biscuits and then immediately checked out of the hotel and left town. Yes sir, Con Murdock did not like to be uncomfortable, but he told himself that for a fortune in gold he could tolerate all this misery.

The men were almost to the summit of what Whitney assured them was the last pass they would have to negotiate and once they were over the mountain, it was a gentle slope down to a long narrow lake. From there it was an easy ride to the gold.

By mid morning, the sun was out and the clouds had gone back up into the sky where they belonged. It was very difficult to make good time. The men were all afoot, leading their mounts up the rocky trail that, for the most part, consisted of small pieces of loose shale with very sharp edges that twisted ankles and cut boots and hooves alike. At regular intervals, they would cross solid rock that was several yards wide and ran across the trail. In dry conditions it was difficult enough for the horses and mules to traverse, but the heavy rain made the exposed bands of solid granite very slippery, causing both men and horses to slide and dance on the wet surface.

Whitney manoeuvred his horse onto a small flat area off to the side of the trail. He sat erect in the saddle, watching the men go by as they slowly and laboriously worked their way up the steep and narrow pathway, which cut back and forth across the moraine. Although he was very pleased that the route was exactly as his dying cellmate described, he was becoming somewhat agitated at all the incessant grumbling coming from this bunch of rag-tags. He thought when they got down the other side, he was going to give a stern lecture about all the whining and crying. Maybe it was time to set an example of someone. He hadn't decided whom that would be, yet.

It took them well past midday to make it over the pass and start down the other side. From the top of the pass, they could see a wide ribbon of blue directly ahead. Whitney pointed out that the lake was their objective for the day, which seemed to lift the men's spirits. Now, there was a tangible destination in sight.

Whitney shook his head and thought, *the human being is a strange creature, indeed. He is curious, even fascinated, by the unknown, but when obstacles and unforeseen circumstances hinder an objective, the unknown becomes aggravating rather than exciting.*

As Silas Davidson passed by, Whitney stopped him and asked, "What is the status of the food supply?"

"We have a small amount of one deer and the entire carcass of the other one," answered Silas.

"So, we have sufficient provisions for at least another day," summarized Whitney.

"Yes Sir, that is correct," replied Davidson.

The rest of the day's travel was uneventful. As they came down the mountain, they found a well used game trail that followed the creek as it made its journey to the valley floor. They passed an open meadow in which a half dozen elk were grazing at the far end. Mathew Briscoe asked if they should go bag one. Whitney said '*no*' for two reasons; there was enough meat for now and because it had taken so long to get over the pass, he wanted to make up some time.

The old prospector told Whitney he might see a large native village at the southwest end of the lake. To avoid contact, he suggested Whitney should stay on the south shore and head to the northeast end of the lake, where there would be another trail. When they arrived at the lake, Whitney sent the Briscoe brothers and Frank Oakley to see if there was, indeed, an encampment at the southwest end. He emphasized his concern about remaining unseen and to that end, he instructed them to avoid all contact with the people in the village.

Whitney ordered a rest while he three men were gone. A couple of hours later, the scouts were back and Mathew Briscoe reported on their findings. He said there was an easy crossing of the outlet stream at the southwest end of the lake and there was a large village on the other shore. They'd gotten close enough to have a good look and there didn't seem to be many people — half a dozen old men, a few women and a lot of children.

Whitney called for Michael and Dancing Crow and when they arrived he said to Michael, "Ask the old man, about the village. I need to know, specifically, if these people are a threat to us."

"So you can slaughter them all. Do you really believe the old man would tell you anything if he believes you will harm them?" retorted Michael.

"Why don't you put it to him in a way so he won't have reason to think I will," suggested Whitney.

Michael said to Dancing Crow, "He knows about a village at the other end of the lake and he wants to know if he should fear them. Old man, we must make him believe they are no threat or he will kill them as he did the others."

Dancing Crow replied, "What is in his heart to do, he will do, whether they are a threat or not. Make up a good story and let him follow the path he must."

Michael gave Dancing Crow a long hard look and then said, 'I don't understand you, old man. You sound like you don't care."

Dancing Crow spoke as if he were trying to make a child understand something beyond its grasp, "My son, I care very much. However, it is not in my hands. It is in yours — and his," his gaze indicating Whitney.

Michael turned to Whitney and said, "I asked him what you wanted to know. He says they might be a threat if they knew about the murders at the other village, but he believes they could not have found out so soon. Most of the adults will be out of camp catching and drying fish for the winter."

Michael knew the territory. When he was a boy, he had accompanied his father to do some trading in the area. Using that knowledge, he added, "The old man says, if we stay on the south side of the lake, there is another crossing at the north end and we can avoid the village."

This fit in with what Whitney already knew, so he bought the story.

His cellmate told Whitney the lake was about twelve miles long and at the northeast end of it, a short stream connected it to another lake. They were to cross this stream, continue in a northeast direction for a few miles where they would see the trail split off; one branch continued to follow the other lake and the other headed back northwest, the direction they should go.

Something of interest had caught Whitney's attention an hour or so prior to them reaching the lake shore. They were making their way down a gentle sloping embankment. Whitney stepped off the trail to assume his accustomed position of sitting tall in the saddle and watching the rest of the men ride by. The screeching of a hawk caught his attention. It came out of the sky and headed directly to a very old, burnt out tree trunk overlooking the trail. It settled on one of the larger branches and sat silent with its eyes focused on the line of riders. When Michael and Dancing Crow rode under the tree, the hawk became very agitated. It danced about on the tree limb and screeched several times before flying off in the direction it had come.

The antics of the hawk were unusual, but it was Dancing Crow's reaction to the bird of prey that aroused Whitney's curiosity. The old man acted like he'd seen a long lost friend. His face lit up in a radiant smile and he repeatedly patted the breed's shoulder with excitement and pointed to the hawk.

When Michael and Dancing Crow were parallel to Whitney's position, he motioned them to pull off the trail. He took one of the pistols from his waistband, checked the load, and put it back before he asked, "What was all that about?"

"What do you mean?" countered Michael.

"The business with the goddamn bird! And for your sake don't tell me again that you don't know what the hell I'm talking about."

Michael knew it would not be a good idea to push Whitney and he conveyed those thoughts to Dancing Crow. "He is furious. We shouldn't make him any more angry. He wants to know about the hawk."

Dancing Crow said, "He is not angry. He is afraid. What he does not understand frightens him. Tell him my grandson has sent a messenger to tell me he is near. Tell the Evil One the time for punishment is coming. Tell him!"

Michael addressed Whitney without the usual mockery in his voice and he maintained a serious tone when he said, "The old man is a Medicine Man. Animal sightings all have some meaning to him. I asked him what the hawk meant and he said it was an omen of good things to come."

"Explain to me why he was so excited when he saw the hawk and now he sounds angry," demanded Whitney.

Michael turned his attention back to Dancing Crow, "He wants to know why you were so happy to see the hawk?"

"I told you! Little Fox is here!"

Michael showed some concern and continued, "When you answer this time, old man, you gotta laugh and smile like you're very happy. You gotta do this or I believe he will shoot one of us."

Dancing Crow looked at Whitney than back to Michael. He was grinning from ear to ear when he said, "It is my hope this man doesn't shit for a week and dies in a pile of his own excrement when he explodes."

Michael fought hard to suppress the urge to laugh. He needed to come up with something believable or Whitney would suspect Dancing Crow's true feelings. He said, "He strongly believes the hawk came to deliver a message. To him, the hawk is bringer of good fortune. He believes we will be rescued soon by hunters from the village."

Whitney believed Michael's explanation, but then as a test, he told Michael to ask the old man how long the lake was and how to get across it. Michael translated for Dancing Crow and added, "I think he already knows the answer. I think he is testing us."

Dancing Crow said, "You know the answer to his questions as well as I do."

Michael smiled at the old man and turning to Whitney, said, "It is about a half day's ride to a creek between the two lakes, where we can cross."

Whitney grinned and said "Good decision."

-5-

Although it was early evening and a good time to stop for the night, Whitney's orders were to continue along the lake shore for a mile or two until they were well beyond the point where there was not the slightest chance anyone from the village would see their campfire light or smoke.

Silas Davidson and his crew soon had a roaring fire going and some of the men had taken off still damp clothing and were drying them out over the fire. Their bellies were full of venison and most of them were contented. Luke Briscoe decided Sean needed a bath, so he gave the kid a choice of going in fully dressed, or he could save himself the inconvenience of having to dry all his clothes over the fire, by stripping down.

Whitney saw the playful antics and suggested everyone was wise to do a little washing up. After several days on the trail, they were all getting a little rank. Whitney set the example. He undressed slowly and cautiously near a large boulder upon which he laid his folded clothes. He lifted one of the pistols high into the air, so anyone watching could see it and laid it atop his clothing. He eased into the water, got himself all wet, scooped up some of the sand from the lake bottom, used it as a scouring agent, and then rinsed it all off.

The rest of the men grumbled, but they all followed suit and after warming themselves by the big fire, it was mostly everyone's opinion it was a refreshing and rejuvenating experience. Mathew Briscoe mentioned Luke still didn't smell any better and a friendly wrestling match ensued.

The men all had different night time habits. Josiah Morgan and Collin Pilkington were usually one of the first ones to head for their sleeping spots, while Whitney and Silas were always the last ones to call it a night.

Silas, Frank Oakley, and Whitney were the only ones standing around the dying campfire. They were making small talk about the weather, the ride thus far, and the trail ahead. Frank Oakley was going on about one of his exploits with his revolver, something to do with a shooting contest where they shot at nails sticking out of the top of a fence rail, from a distance of twenty yards. Whitney wasn't buying it and Silas could have cared less, but they let Oakley ramble on.

As Silas looked across the fire to the edge of the trees, a few yards away, he thought he saw a shadow go by at extraordinary speed. Whitney caught the startled look on Davidson's face and asked him what was wrong. Silas told him it was nothing. He said he thought he saw something, most likely an animal running by.

They thought nothing of it and continued the small talk. A few minutes later, Frank Oakley saw the same shadow dash across his field of vision, only in the opposite direction from the one Silas witnessed. "There! There," he pointed, "I saw it, too. Something is moving near the trees."

Frank drew his pistol and headed for the tree line, with Whitney close behind. When they got to within a few feet of the trees, they walked a short distance in one direction and then turned and walked the opposite way, stopping every few feet to peer into the dark spaces between the trees. A deep throated growl that sounded like it was coming from a short distance into the grove, attracted their attention.

Oakley fired two shots in rapid succession in the direction of the noise. Whitney sounded irritated when he said, "Hold your fire! You are wasting precious ammunition. Wait until you see a target."

Oakley tucked his pistol away and they both headed back to the presumed safety of the camp. Awakened by the shots, some of the men were milling about the camp fire. As Whitney and Oakley approached, Mathew Briscoe asked, "Everything alright, Boss? What was it? Wasn't them heathens from the village, was it?"

Briscoe's question stirred up the others and there was a lot of mumbling and speculation. Whitney said, "Nothing to worry about, gentlemen. Just some animal, wolf or two most likely. Now, go back to your beds. Morning comes early."

After the men departed, Oakley said to Whitney, "That didn't sound like any wolf I ever heard."

"Think what you like, Mr. Oakley, but keep it to yourself. Consider it an order," commanded Whitney.

Oakley saw Whitney was dead serious. He replied, "Yes Sir, I will."

Silas, who'd heard the exchange, wasn't sure what to make of Whitney's reaction. Personally, he thought it was some animal. The natives, if there really were any, couldn't have possibly caught up to them. He reassured himself it was, indeed, some forest creature, but it sure seemed a lot larger and moved a lot faster than any animal he'd ever seen. He was going to argue the point with Whitney, but after hearing Whitney's exchange with Oakley, Silas kept quiet.

Chapter 8 – The Necklace

Josiah Morgan slowly opened his eyes and like every other morning, he went through a habitual ritual of licking his parched lips, wiping the dried crud from his eyes, and rubbing his stiff shoulders. As he rose to his feet, he remembered his dream from the night before. It was very vivid and he recalled every detail, which was very unusual because Josiah dreamt every night, but he seldom remembered even fragments of them. More often than not, his dreams left him with a feeling of apprehension, as if they were trying to tell him something, but when he woke up he couldn't recall any details, try as he might. Last night's dream, however, left him feeling elated and filled with joy. An angel had appeared and gave him a gift of a golden necklace. The angel said it was a reward for his faith in God.

Con Murdock had a very vivid dream, as well. He recalled making love to a beautiful, alluring saloon girl, which was an extremely pleasant experience until he remembered the end of the dream; the bitch had reached inside his shirt while they were embraced and stole his gold nugget necklace. His hand went quickly to his shirt even though he knew it was a dream and he was sure the necklace was still there. A look of astonishment came over his face. The necklace was gone. He frantically pulled his shirt out of his pants and while on his knees, he took hold of the shirt front with both hands and pulling it away from his body, he gave it a good shake, fully expecting the necklace to fall out. He checked the ground all around him and found nothing. He knelt down on all fours and carefully searched every square inch of his sleeping area. The necklace simply wasn't there.

He forgot about the dream and thought of a more practical solution to the mystery; one of those bastards had taken it. The question was who? He thought about each man in the troop and by the process of elimination he decided it was either Sean McClaren, or one or both of those damn Briscoe brothers. He formulated a plan to watch the three men closely and when he found out who had it, he would act accordingly. If it was the kid, he would threaten him and get his necklace back. If it was the Briscoes, he would have to wait for the opportune moment and steal it back.

Silas and crew had the morning fire going and were preparing strips of venison for cooking. Con Murdock rolled up his blanket and tied it up. He was making his way to the warmth of the fire, when a shouting Josiah Morgan got everyone's attention.

"Praise be to the Lord! Praise him in all his glory!" he shouted as he ran towards them.

Collin Pilkington stood and stopped the advancing Josiah. He put his hands on the little preacher's shoulders and asked, "What is all the excitement, Josiah?"

Josiah backed away and waved the necklace about. "A gift from God! An angel came to me last night and gave me this gold necklace saying, for being a good servant of God, this was my reward. Halleluiah! Halleluiah!"

It happened so suddenly, no one saw it coming. Even Con Murdock wasn't sure what had driven him. Con arrived at the fire just as Josiah was flaunting the necklace about. A wave of rage like he had never felt before surged up in him. He picked up Mathew Briscoe's big knife from the log where Silas had put it when he was done cutting venison strips for breakfast, charged Josiah, and buried the knife up to the hilt in his chest. Josiah went down like a rock and as he fell, Con snatched the necklace from his hand and turned to face the men gathered at the fire.

"Have you gone stark raving mad?" screamed Silas Davidson.

Con held up the necklace for everyone to see. His eyes were open wide and he had a crazed look on his face. "This is mine! I found it! It's mine!" Pointing to Josiah, he continued, "That bastard stole it from me while I was sleeping last night."

Collin Pilkington rushed to tend to the fatally wounded Josiah and said, "And for this you kill him?"

Sanity crawled its way slowly back into Con's mind. The enormity of the atrocity he'd just committed sank in. Inside, he was at a loss to explain what came over him. He had never in his life felt such anger and hatred. He'd never before let violence play a part in his life, except in self defence.

Outwardly, he needed to come up with some sort of reason for his actions. This is where Con Murdock was at his best. "I had to do it. Don't you see? He is a crazy man. Last night he steals from me in my sleep. What if he decides some night to bash someone's head in with a rock, because some goddamn angel told him to? No sir, I for one, have had enough. You should thank me. Every one of you sons-of-bitches thought the man was loco. Not one of you would do anything about it. Well, I did!"

Con thought he had them. His little speech got them all thinking. The rest of the men gathered around and some of the late comers were inquiring as to what had happened. Whitney broke through the crowd with Mathew Briscoe on one flank and Frank Oakley on the other and said, "Someone want to tell me what is going on?"

Silas Davidson cleared his throat and spoke, "It would appear Mr. Murdock has murdered Mr. Morgan. The cause of the dispute centers around a gold necklace Mr. Murdock claims Mr. Morgan took from his possession while he slept last night."

Whitney scrutinized the scene before speaking again, "Mr. Murdock, is this true?"

"Yes, it is, but let me exp —"

Whitney interrupted him. "Show me the necklace."

Murdock covered the short distance between himself and Whitney in two strides and handed him the necklace. Whitney examined it closely and then asked, "Where did you get this?"

Murdock lied and explained that as he had walked past one of the slain villagers, the necklace glinted in the sun, catching his eye and he took it off the body. He thought it would be a better story than the truth; how he was searching for valuables and kept the find from Whitney. He paused for a breath and then went on to recount the events leading up to the stabbing.

Whitney listened intently and then looked over at the dying Josiah. The knife missed Josiah's heart, but punctured a lung that was filling up with blood. The man was dying a slow, painful death, bleeding out internally.

Whitney had an important decision to make. He was about ready to get rid of Josiah himself. The man was a liability and a detriment to the mission. He was glad someone had taken care of the task for him, but what to do about Murdock? He surmised Murdock wasn't liked all that much, so if he took Murdock's life in retribution, not many of the men would care. On the other hand, he wanted to maintain a position of autonomy where his focus was the finding the gold. He wanted the men to see he didn't care about their personal squabbles as long as they did not interfere with the mission.

"Fine," Whitney said as he tossed the necklace back to Murdock, "finish the job."

Murdock wasn't sure what Whitney meant and the confused look on his face conveyed his lack of understanding.

"Put the man out of his misery, Mr. Murdock," was all the explanation Whitney offered.

Con felt like he was the center attraction at a three ring circus. All eyes were upon him, waiting to see what he would do. He turned back to face Josiah, who was coughing and spitting blood. Collin Pilkington was still holding Josiah's hand and trying to offer him some comfort. Murdock knelt down and pulled the knife from Josiah's chest. He looked at the knife as if in disbelief, threw it to the ground, and stood up.

"I can't kill him in cold blood. I just can't," he cried.

Whitney took him off the hook. "Mr. Briscoe, if you would be so kind as to put the poor wretch out of his misery, I would appreciate it."

Mathew walked toward Josiah and picked up the knife. Collin let go of Josiah's hand and stood. He positioned himself between Mathew and the dying preacher and said, "What are you going to do?" Realizing Briscoe's intent, he added, "You can't." He turned back to the men and pleaded, "Somebody please stop him."

Silas Davidson came forward and putting his arm around Collin's shoulders, pulled him away, saying, "There, there, Mr. Pilkington. I am afraid there is nothing we can do for poor Mr. Morgan. It is a good thing to end his suffering. Come along now."

As they walked away, Mathew had already slit Josiah's throat from ear to ear, nearly severing his head. There was one last sigh from Josiah and he was gone.

Dancing Crow and Michael George had a front row seat for the whole event. They were tied to a sapling pine tree that was on a small rise about twenty feet from the fire area. Michael had seen a few killings, but he was still shocked by the swiftness and sheer brutality of the attack and he expressed his thoughts to Dancing Crow. "I never thought a man like Murdock would kill with such rage."

"What kind of a man is the one called Murdock?" asked Dancing Crow.

"He is a snake. He will cheat and rob you of what you have, but not kill you for it," explained Michael.

"A mouse will attack a weasel if it is driven to do so," was Dancing Crow's answer.

"Yes," agreed Michael, "if it is defending its life or its young."

"Ah, but a man is so much more than a mouse. Other things drive him. Perhaps this young man was overcome by his anger at having been wronged or perhaps he was overcome by greed. Who knows?" Dancing Crow gave an '*I know the answer, but I'm not telling you*' look and then smiled.

"Don't you two every stop yammering?" Sean McClaren asked as he approached. "Looks like I am your nanny for the day, so let's get some grub and get going."

It was deathly quiet around the fire as everyone filled up on venison. Although some of the men wanted to say something, no one mentioned the killing. Collin asked Whitney about the possibility of a burial for Josiah. Whitney, in his usual manner, said he didn't care if Collin wanted to spend precious time burying Mr. Morgan, but he didn't see how Collin was going to manage it without a shovel and looking around he didn't see any suitable stones to cover the poor soul. He told Collin he was welcome to do what he liked, but his mule was coming with the rest of the troop and Collin would have to catch up on foot.

Silas came up with a compromise. He told Collin, Harold Grant, and Frank Guetch to carry the body a few feet into the woods, where they quickly covered it with moss and loose branches. It wasn't a proper grave and most likely wouldn't keep the animals out, but it was the best they could do. The gesture seemed to pacify Collin.

-2-

The morning ride was like a funeral march. Most of the men rode in complete silence without the chatter or small talk of previous days. They were all still trying to get their minds around the events of early morning. The killing of Josiah surprised even Whitney. He thought he had a good insight into the character of all the men in the group, but he didn't anticipated Murdock's actions. Mulling it over, he couldn't find any justification for Murdock to lash out so violently. He said to himself, "I'd have killed the son-of-a-bitch myself, if he stole from me, but then that's me, not Murdock."

Con Murdock rode at the rear of the procession, not because the other men put him there, but by his own choice. He needed time to think. Was he going crazy? Why did he snap? He tried to recall what he was thinking just before he grabbed the knife and ran at Josiah. He remembered he wasn't thinking about anything. It was as if he was no longer in control of his thoughts or actions for the short time it took to fatally wound the crazy preacher. He retrieved the gold necklace from inside his shirt, looked at it for a moment, and then threw it as far as he could into the bush.

The trail was exactly like Whitney promised; easy going for the most part, with level ground and a nice wide path to follow. In places, for a short distance, the men could even ride two by two, not that anyone was inclined to do so. For the entire morning they followed the lake shore. At midday, Whitney sent the Briscoe brothers on their back trail to see if they had been spotted and were being followed.

"Why did that fella kill the little preacher, Mathew?" asked Luke as they rode along.

"I don't rightly know, Brother Luke. Seems he just went crazy like people sometimes do." Mathew paused briefly to think and then continued "I figure he was pretty mad at the preacher for stealing his necklace. You remember when you was little and a store lady gave you a little itty bitty toy horse and Pa took it away. You remember how mad you got at him? You put mud inside his boots."

Luke laughed as he recalled the incident. "Boy, I was sure mad. You reckon he was that mad at the preacher?"

"I reckon so, Brother Luke, I reckon so."

They went about two miles, stopped and waited for an hour for any signs of activity. There was no one following, so they quickly headed back and reported to Whitney, who was pleased with the news.

Late afternoon brought them to the end of the lake. According to the old prospector, the stream at the end of the lake connected it to another body of water a few miles away. The plan was to cross the stream and continue to the northeast until the trail split, where they would take the northwest fork.

Whitney was trying to decide on whether to camp for the night or push on for a few more miles. The Old Wagon Road, once used to get to the Cariboo, lay just ahead. Though it was seldom used since the Cariboo Trail was built, Whitney still wanted to be careful not to be seen. He was concerned about what the authorities might be doing. Based on his military experience, he concluded the Constables would assume they were headed for the coast or the American border and would deploy all forces to watch the roads and waterways. They probably didn't even know Whitney and company had headed west. He was partly right. The authorities knew he headed west, but they assumed he was going to take the Old Wagon Road south and eventually get to the coast or the border and had ridden south to intercept him.

The stream crossing was an adventure, to say the least. The inexperience of a lot of the riders in crossing fast water led to a few precarious moments. Collin Pilkington was atop one of the more stubborn mules. It refused to go into the water and Collin was a loss at what to do. Mathew Briscoe gave the mule a hard slap on the rump which prompted it to bolt into the water and go dashing across to the other bank. The sudden leap threw Collin into the cold water, but the only thing hurt was his pride. Silas Davidson teased him about how he probably needed a bath anyway.

Fredrick Guetch's horse didn't like the water, either and refused to go in. Fredrick dismounted and began striking the horse with the ends of the reins. The horse reared which only spurred a more intense lashing from Fredrick. Frank Oakley intervened and stopped the abuse, telling Guetch to walk and lead the horse across, assuring him the water was only hip deep.

Michael suggested to Sean they should string the mounts, mules and horses alike, together, putting the unruly ones in the middle. The animals would feel less agitated, making the crossing much easier. Sean passed this information onto Whitney, who commended the boy for his good thinking and then ordered the rest of the stock to be strung together. Looking back at Michael, Sean smiled with embarrassment at having taken credit for the idea. Michael grinned back at him and didn't say anything.

With everyone safely across the stream, Whitney held a meeting with the Briscoe Brothers and Oakley. He told them of the Old Wagon Road and the circumstances surrounding it. He emphasized the importance of not being seen by anyone who might be on the road. This would be the last time they would have to worry about contact with any white men. The plan was to get close to the road and ascertain if there had been any recent traffic and then report back to Whitney.

While the Briscoe Brothers and Frank Oakley were gone, Whitney told the troop there would be a rest stop, but not to set up camp, as he wanted to go a little further before dark. His intention was to put a few miles between them and the Old Wagon Road and the possibility of human contact.

Con Murdock was one of the first to cross the stream. When Whitney called a rest, he dismounted and went into a large grove of fir trees. He found a thick bed of moss and collapsed from exhaustion. Josiah's murder and the emotions surrounding it had taken its toll on him.

He fell asleep instantly and soon found himself back at the village and in the lodge where he found the gold nugget necklace. It was a different reality. There were no sounds and his vision was in black and white, except for the necklace. It was the only thing in color which made it appear even brighter and shinier. As he looked about the lodge, he could not make out anything with any amount of clarity. Everything was a shade of grey or black and objects blended together.

The door flap opened and a shadowy figure came in and stood just inside the entrance. It beckoned Con to come nearer with a wave of its right arm. Con approached hesitantly and when he was within a few feet of the figure, it raised its head. It was Josiah Morgan! The knife was still in his chest!

Josiah didn't speak. Instead, he put his hands together and let his arms drop loosely in front of him. He turned his head sideways for Con to see the expression on his face. It was the saddest look Con had ever seen. It was as if Josiah was asking, "Why, oh why did you do this to me? What did I ever do to you to deserve this?"

As Con took another step closer, the figure stepped back through the doorway. Con lifted the flap and went through into the bright light of the compound. When he straightened up and looked around, his heart sank and his knees buckled to the point where he almost collapsed. There were over a dozen native people standing in the open area in front of the lodge. They were alive, but they shouldn't be. All their bodies were covered with ghastly gunshot and stab wounds, still oozing blood. They held out their arms in a questioning gesture. They all wore the same woeful expression as Josiah and they said in unison, "Why? Why, did you do this?" The odd thing was, they said it in English.

Con woke up and bolted upright into a sitting position. He glanced around and a feeling of great relief came over him as he realized it was all a dream. As he rose, the feeling of relief changed to one of sheer terror. There on the ground at his feet was the gold nugget necklace! He picked it and sprinted from the grove. His horse was not where he left it because, while he slept, Silas's crew had gathered all the horses and took saddles and blankets off to give them a breather. Most of the men were either seated or lying on the ground getting some valuable rest. Con stood for the longest time not knowing what to do. He heard a noise coming from the trees behind him, so he turned and there was Josiah posed with outstretched arms and blood spurting from his severed throat. Con knew he was awake and he surmised the spectre in the trees was a remnant of his dream. To test his theory, he turned back to face the camp and after a three count, he turned his gaze back to the trees, expecting Josiah to be gone, but he was still there with the same pitiful look on his face.

Silas Davidson was busy wiping his spectacles clean, when a wild eyed, frantic Con Murdock grabbed him by the shoulder to get his attention. Silas saw how distraught Con was and he began to talk to him quietly, trying to calm him down enough, so he could determine what the trouble might be.

Con kept mumbling something about Josiah being alive and hiding in the trees. He was begging Silas to come and see for himself and to humour him, Silas followed him to the edge of the dense grove. Con tentatively let his eyes fall on the spot where he last saw Josiah. He wasn't there. Con looked disappointed. He thought if Silas saw him too, it would verify he wasn't going insane. He turned back to the open area, still not able to grasp what was happening. Some internal urge pulled his gaze to the trail. There was Josiah again, this time motioning for him to follow.

Con pulled Silas around to face Josiah, all the while shouting, "There he is! Don't you see him? There he is!"

Silas looked down the trail. He didn't see Josiah Morgan, but he thought for a fleeting second he saw a shadow or figure or something disappear around the nearest corner. "No," he told himself, "I didn't see anything. It was my imagination playing tricks on me, no doubt greatly influenced by Mr. Murdock's hysteria."

Con continued his outburst, "See, he just went around the corner!" He let go of Silas's sleeve and went running after the apparition.

Silas stood for a moment and then decided it was his responsibility to see to the poor tortured man, even though he had no use for Con Murdock. He walked quickly down the trail leading back to the stream they had crossed a short time before.

When Silas got to the creek, he saw Murdock in the middle of the stream. It was a pitiful sight to watch. Con would run a few feet, stumble and fall into the water, get up, fall again, and rise only to stumble and fall once more. As he struggled through the water, he was shouting, "I'm sorry! I'm sorry!" between heart wrenching sobs. Finally, he reached the other shore and without looking back, he ran up the other bank and disappeared from view. Silas returned to the rest area, never to see Murdock again.

It is not known what became of Con Murdock, but years later there was a story told around native night fires about a crazy white man who came to the village trying to get someone to take a gold necklace from him. No one would accept it because they believed it was cursed and they chased the white man away. It is also said he still walks the pathways and some night if you meet a sobbing white man who offers you a gold necklace, don't take it, just run!

Whitney was waiting for Silas when he got back to the rest area. "What's going on?" he asked.

"It appears we have lost another man, Mr. Whitney," answered Silas.

"Who would that be, Mr. Davidson and under what circumstances?"

"Mr. Murdock has left our gracious company. It appears as though he was suffering from extreme bouts of guilt, fostered by his murder of Mr. Morgan, no doubt. I would also venture to say the theft of the gold necklace may have played a part as well. He claimed Josiah Morgan was haunting him. I last observed him running off into the distance, screaming with remorse."

Whitney thought for a moment and then remarked, "Ah well, no big loss."

-3-

A short time later, the Briscoe brothers and Frank Oakley returned and immediately reported to Whitney. Frank Oakley said the wagon road was up the trail about a half a mile and they had ridden up the road in both directions for a good distance and hadn't seen any tracks or sign of any kind that would indicate any recent human activity. He felt quite confident they would not be seen crossing the road.

Whitney ordered the men to be ready to leave in ten minutes. His plan was to cross the road and ride up the trail a couple of miles before setting up camp for the night. Silas approached Whitney and informed him there was just enough meat for the evening meal and perhaps breakfast. Whitney passed this information on to Mathew Briscoe and suggested they keep their eyes open for any game. After a short pause, he changed his mind and said the hunting should be left for the next day. He didn't want to run the risk of a gunshot being heard this close to the road.

The men quickly saddled up and were ready to ride in a matter of minutes. It was as if every one of them was anxious to be on their way, to put some distance between themselves and this place. Most of them witnessed Con Murdock running off, screaming like a banshee. They didn't know the circumstances surrounding the event and quite frankly, most of them could have cared less.

When they came to the road, Whitney ordered Mathew Briscoe to cut some full grown willow branches which they used to wipe out their tracks after they all crossed the road. The timing could not have been better. Darkness was starting to fall as the troop came to an open area wide enough to camp for the night and far enough up the trail from the road so as their night fire could not be seen.

As the men milled around the large campfire, finishing their venison and making conversation, there seemed to be an aura of apprehension; a general feeling something was out of place, that not everything was right with their world. Small talk started regarding the Con Murdock incident. Frank Oakley overheard bits and pieces about something happening to Murdock. He looked around the camp and not seeing Con anywhere, asked a group consisting of Collin Pilkington, Fredrick Guetch, and Nathaniel Brimsby as to what had transpired. Collin, acting as spokesman for the trio, told Oakley that Murdock claimed he'd seen Josiah Morgan, alive and well, heading back down the trail from whence they had come and ran off after him before anybody could stop him.

Oakley approached Whitney and asked him his version of the event. Whitney stated that according to Silas Davidson, who had a first hand account of the episode, Murdock had suffered from an attack of conscience over killing the crazy preacher and it drove him out of his mind.

Oakley suggested, perhaps, they should go after him and either bring him back or kill him to eliminate any possible chance of Murdock running into the authorities and divulging their location. Whitney said, in his opinion, Murdock was wandering about in the wilderness somewhere and he would, most likely, not live very long. Therefore, he posed no threat.

Most of the men slept soundly that night. If you asked any of them what they dreamt of, they wouldn't remember their dreams. In fact, they would tell you they didn't even recall dreaming at all. Luke

Briscoe, however, had a very vivid dream in which he went back in time to when he was eleven or twelve years old.

Elizabeth was the daughter of another sharecropper family, who worked the same farms as did Luke's family. Luke couldn't recall her surname, but he remembered what she looked like. She was the same age as Luke with long rusty coloured hair, hanging to the middle of her back. Her unusually white face, centered by two very deep blue eyes, was covered in freckles.

Luke and Elizabeth were having a picnic by one of the many spring fed ponds in the area. It was a very hot summer day and just as children, not only in Tennessee, but the world over, would do, they took their clothes off and went for a swim, only to be caught by Elizabeth's father. The children didn't think they had done anything wrong, but Elizabeth's father started slapping her and calling her a whore. Luke tried in vain to stop him and took a couple of nasty blows for his trouble. He dressed and ran home crying. His father was very upset and went to see Elizabeth's father. When he came back he gave Luke a beating. Elizabeth's father had told him that Luke had attacked his daughter and he better keep his perverted son away from her.

Luke never saw Elizabeth again, but in his dream he was with her by the same pond. This time, however, he was full grown, but Elizabeth was still the same little girl. He asked her if she wanted to go swimming again. Once they were naked and in the pond, Luke forced her under the water and held her there, face up. The look of absolute terror on Elizabeth's face as she drowned woke Luke up with a start.

As he became fully awake, he realized he was aroused and sporting an erection. The horror of what he'd done in his dream and the shame he felt from his physical condition sent him off into a fit of sobbing.

Mathew, who slept close by, was awakened by his brother's crying. He'd seen this several times in the past. When Luke's emotions got the better of him, he would have a crying fit. It was good for Luke, a relief of sorts. He always felt better after such a session. Mathew got next to Luke, put his arm around his brother's shoulder and tried to comfort him. "What's the matter, Luke?" he asked.

"I had this terrible dream, Mathew. I killed Elizabeth." He looked up into Mathew's face and then asked, "You remember Elizabeth, don't you?"

Mathew vaguely recalled a red headed girl by that name, but he told Luke, "Sure, sure, I remember her."

"Well, I kilt her Mathew and it made me feel good." He took his still erect penis in his hand and continued, "Just like I feel good when we has pecker fun with the ladies."

Mathew felt embarrassed and looked around to make sure no one else was stirring. He looked Luke in the eyes and said, "It was just a dream, Luke, just a dream. Do you understand? It didn't really happen. Elizabeth is not dead! She's probably married with a bunch of red headed kids runnin' around."

Luke still did not seem convinced. Mathew continued, "And you are not a bad man when it comes to havin' fun with women. Hell, you never bothered any little girls. You only had growed ladies or squaws and that ain't a bad thing. Buck up, Luke. It's alright."

All of the men slept through Luke's late night outburst except for Whitney, who never seemed to sleep and Dancing Crow, who was always aware of what went on around him. Whitney didn't give it a second thought, but he put it in the back of his mind to ask Mathew about it in the morning.

Dancing Crow nudged a sleeping Michael. "What is it?" Michael asked, groggily.

"My grandson is with us. I can feel him."

"You woke me up to tell me this. It couldn't have waited until morning?"

"Things are beginning to happen. Two are gone and many more will follow soon," said Dancing Crow with excitement in his voice.

Michael paused before saying anything more. He wanted to fully understand what Dancing Crow was saying. It sounded like the old man believed the younger, very powerful Shaman of his village was responsible for the events of the last few days. He didn't see how, but he wanted to hear the old man out.

"How is this possible? We haven't seen any sign of your grandson," Michael asked, not meaning to offend.

Dancing Crow couldn't face Michael because they were tied on opposite sides of a small sapling, so he put a condescending inflection in his voice when he said, "You do not look with your eyes to see what can not be seen. You do not listen with your ears to hear what cannot be heard. You just feel it and you know it is there."

Although Michael's own grandfather talked about the unseen in a similar fashion, he had no clear-cut comprehension of what Dancing Crow was talking about. Ghosts? Spirits? He couldn't be sure, but he thought it was something of the sort.

Sensing Michael still didn't understand, Dancing Crow tried a different approach. "There are other worlds beyond the one we as people live in. One of these is the world we go to when we dream at night. Think of the power one would have if they could freely go between both worlds?"

"And your grandson can do this?" asked Michael.

"Oh yes, and much more," replied Dancing Crow with pride.

Michael was not finished. "You can do this as well?"

"I can, but if you compare my power to Little Fox's, it is like comparing the pebble to the mountain."

Chapter 9 – The Beating of Sean McClaren

Sunrise found Son of Tsiatko and the other hunters making preparations for a long journey. They held a deep respect, sprinkled with a bit of awe, for Little Fox and so they would do as he asked. Wounded Hawk gathered the party together and explained once more what they were to do; find and follow the white men at a distance, but under no circumstances were they to engage them unless instructed by Little Fox to do so. Wounded Hawk was not sure how the message would be delivered if Little Fox got himself into trouble, but his faith in the powerful young Shaman quickly eliminated any doubts he may have had.

After goodbyes, hugs, and kisses from family members, they set out. Each one of them still harboured deep feelings of loss and sorrow, some more than others, but now there was a sense of purpose, a feeling that at last they were going to do something about the atrocities these white men had perpetrated on their families. There was a deep seeded knowing that their loved ones, who had gone to the spirit world, would be avenged.

Silas had miscalculated and there was only a small piece of venison left per man. Luke Briscoe was still not in control of his emotions as he sat and ate his meagre breakfast. The rest of the men noticed something was wrong, but they learned it didn't pay to ask questions and besides, they would, most likely, find out eventually. Sean McClaren asked the big man in all sincerity what the problem was, but before Luke could answer, Mathew stepped in and told him to mind his own business, thus setting the parameters for anyone else who had designs on any inquiries.

The death of Josiah Morgan, Con Murdock running off in a crazed state, the strange shadows and noises most of them saw or heard in the night, and now, seeing Luke Briscoe obviously very distraught, created an atmosphere of apprehension. Whitney could sense the anxiety, but he didn't know what he could say or do to alleviate it. There was a familiar feeling in Whitney's gut. He often felt this way before engaging the enemy at Sharpsburg. It was a persistent feeling, a sense you knew something was about to happen, and you wished whatever it was would hurry up and come to pass.

Whitney called the men together and spoke to them like a commander would to a group of battle weary soldiers. "Listen up men. Being out in the wilderness for a long time with only each other for company can take its toll. You feel isolated and alone and pretty soon you start seeing and hearing things. You start imagining there is a predator behind every tree and every noise in the bush is an enemy ready to pounce on you the first chance he gets." He paused for a moment to let what he said sink in and then continued, "I don't know what set our friend Mr. Murdock off and frankly I don't give a damn. It was one of those things that just happen. Maybe the killings in the heathens' village got to him or maybe he was just as crazy as Mr. Morgan, I don't know. But what I do know — this nonsense stops here and now.

"There are bears and mountain lions and wolves out there, but look around. Do you really believe they would bother this many men? There are no heathens following us. We made sure of it. No law either. They are most likely waiting for us to show up in the south somewhere.

"We still have the better part of two weeks and maybe more to our destination. Let's keep our heads on straight and maybe, just maybe, we'll all get there to split the gold."

He stood for a moment looking at each of the men in turn, letting them digest what they heard and then he began issuing orders. Since Silas lost two of his men, (not that Con Murdock ever did any work) Whitney ordered Sean McClaren to work with Silas. Sean didn't seem too pleased. To him, it was like a demotion.

Whitney wanted the Briscoes and Oakley to ride ahead of the troop by about a half mile or so. The old prospector told him he'd seen many Indians coming and going along the way and Whitney didn't want any surprises on the trail. He informed them the troop was out of food and they best scare something up, preferably not deer.

Even though the heat was becoming unbearable, the troop morale, which was boosted somewhat by Whitney's little pep talk, was still high. The trail was wide enough in places for the men to ride two or three a breast and carry on a conversation, if they chose to do so. Sean McClaren was still in a snit. Not only did the boss demote him to the "*washer woman*" crew, but now it was his job to baby sit the heathens, as Whitney called them.

Michael said to Dancing Crow, "He's not happy with his place in the order of things."

Dancing Crow replied, "As are most young men his age. He will grow out of it, if he lives long enough."

Michael's interest peaked. It seemed Dancing Crow knew something no one else did and Michael was dying to know what it was. He was about to ask the old man what he meant when a loud shot rang out followed by another one a few seconds later. It sounded like the Spencer rifle Oakley was carrying.

The riders all stopped in unison and stood waiting to see what had happened. A few minutes later Mathew Briscoe came trotting into view. He approached Whitney and said something to him, then rode back in the direction from where he'd come, while Whiney turned and rode the short distance back to the troop.

"Looks like elk meat for supper, boys. Mr. Davidson, you and your men take the extra mules and assist Mr. Briscoe."

Silas secured the two extra animals, courtesy of the departure of Josiah Morgan and Con Murdoch and he, Collin Pilkington, and Fredrick Guetch rode out to catch up to Mathew Briscoe.

The troop had been slowly going uphill all morning and they were pretty high up when they came to the summit of a natural pass between two rows of thickly wooded hills. For the past hour, they had been going downhill towards a river valley below.

Mathew, Luke, and Frank Oakley, who were scouting ahead, spotted the river. Thinking only of the cool water, they ran their horses down the embankment to the stream, surprising and scattering a herd of elk, which had come to the river's edge for a drink. The elk responded quickly, but not as fast as Frank Oakley. He had the rifle out, sighted, and dropped a large cow before she got to the safety of the brush. As the three of them rode up to claim their prize, they saw a young calf standing near its dead mother. Oakley chambered another shell and shot it.

While the elk were being gutted and quartered, the rest of the troop watered the stock and enjoyed the reprieve from the heat. As Sean was helping Michael and Dancing Crow dismount, Michael said to Sean, "Tell the boss man to put the meat in the water."

Sean studied Michael to see if he was joking or if he was telling the truth. Michael continued, "The meat will last longer in this heat if it is cooled in the water. Go tell him."

Sean tentatively approached Whitney, who was watering his horse, and said, "Mr. Whitney, one of the heathens says we should put the meat in the water to cool off. He says it will make it last longer."

"It is a sound idea, Mr. McClaren. See to it then," Whitney replied.

Sean felt elated, proud that Whitney showed him respect by addressing him as Mr. McClaren. He strutted to where Silas and crew were finishing with the carcasses and with a commanding tone instructed them to put the meat in the water.

"Who died and left him boss?" asked Fredrick Guetch of no one in particular.

Silas answered, "Just ignore the young pup. I'm sure the order came from Mr. Whitney."

With Mathew and Luke's assistance, Silas and his two helpers loaded the quartered carcasses on the two mules, took them to the river where they tied the legs of each quarter to bank willows and let the meat lay in the ice cold water for a few minutes.

The temperature continued to climb rapidly as the morning passed into afternoon. Yesterday, they were glad to be rid of the rain, but now, as the day wore on, they prayed for some relief from the heat. The trail crossed the river and went diagonally up a huge sandstone and shale embankment and onto a plateau. The route followed the river for a few miles and then turned northwest away from it.

The plateau was at the base of a row of tree covered hills, the symmetry of which was broken by the occasional mountain peak. From a high vantage point, one could see the row of hills go on and on, seemingly forever into the horizon. Whitney remembered his cellmate's description of the embankment coming out of the river valley, but he didn't recall anything about the plateau and the long row of hills. The dying man simple stated there was only one trail to follow and the next landmark of any consequence would be another large lake five or six days up the trail.

Luckily, there was an abundance of creeks in a variety of sizes flowing from the hills, across the plateau and on toward the river. It was late in the afternoon and the troop could have covered a few more miles before settling down for the night, but Whitney's horse was showing signs of fatigue from the heat. Based on his concern for the animals, Whitney called a halt near one of the creeks. The men shared the horses' and mules' sense of relief.

Some of the men asked Silas if they could use up the calf meat before starting on the older cow, to which he heartily agreed and everyone was waiting in anticipation of the tender young elk. Dancing Crow was pestering Michael to get him some chives, which he had seen in a nearby open area. He also mentioned there was, what the white man called, 'horseradish' growing along the creek bank. Michael reluctantly got Sean McClaren's attention.

"What do you want, heathen?" Sean asked. He started calling Michael and Dancing Crow 'heathens' as of late, emulating Whitney.

"The old man says there are lots of chives and horseradish growing around us. He thinks it would be a good thing if we could get some to eat with the elk meat. He says the rest of the men might even enjoy some."

"And who is going to pick them?" asked Sean in a defiant tone.

"Cut us loose. We can pick enough for everybody. The old man knows where to find them and I can do all the digging and picking. What do you say?" Michael said as he held out his bound wrists, indicating Sean should untie them.

Sean cocked the hammers of the shotgun, pointed it at Michael and told him to rise. Nathaniel Brimsby was the closest man to them. One of his boots was off and he was checking something inside of it. Sean ordered him to watch Dancing Crow while he took Michael to see Whitney.

"The heathen wants me to untie him and the old man so they can pick some vegetables or something," said Sean.

Michael interrupted, "Chives and horseradish. They'll go nice with the elk meat."

"Fine," said Whitney, "make sure we don't have a repeat of the incident similar to the last time the old heathen went onion picking."

Sean walked Michael back to where Dancing Crow should have been waiting. The old man was gone! A surge of panic ran through Sean. Nathaniel Brimsby was still fixing his boot. Sean crossed the few steps between them and jabbed Nathaniel with the barrel of the shotgun, "I thought I told you to watch the old man," he said with reproach.

Nathaniel set the boot down and stood up. With his face right in Sean's, he said through clenched teeth, "I don't take orders from no man, especially a piss ant like you. Now, beat it before I shove that shotgun up your ass and pull both triggers."

Sean's new found confidence was visibly shaken. He turned the shotgun on Michael and shouted, "You planned this! You planned this, so the old heathen could escape."

Michael talked slowly trying to calm Sean down. "Look, kid. The old man didn't go anywhere." He pointed to Dancing Crow, a few yards away on his knees gathering the chive tops, even though his wrists were still tied.

Sean felt a wave of relief and he lowered the shotgun. Regaining his composure, he ordered Michael to join Dancing Crow. While they gathered the chives, Michael said to the old man "This is the second time you have gotten me into trouble."

"Trouble? What trouble? I went to pick some onion. A man needs onion with his meat. What trouble can that be?" asked Dancing Crow with a slight smile.

The elk meat wasn't much different from the venison, but the chives and horseradish and the fact they were eating something other than deer meat, made the evening meal more palatable. Collin Pilkington had another surprise for them. While looking for firewood, he found a large raspberry patch. He came back to the camp, collected one of the large baskets and with Fredrick Guetch's help, the two of them picked enough raspberries for everyone to have a good helping.

Near dusk, Sean McClaren was making small talk with Luke Briscoe, near the fire. Luke mentioned he needed to empty his bladder and out of courtesy he walked several yards to the edge of the trees to do his business, accompanied by Sean. Luke was buttoning up his trousers, when he paused and looked into the darkening spaces between the trees.

"Elizabeth? Elizabeth, is that you?" he cried out.

Sean stood closer to Luke, trying to make out what the big man was looking at. He couldn't see anything but the black outline of the trees looking back at him. He thought he heard some movement as Luke spoke again. "I'm sorry, Elizabeth I didn't mean to hurt you. I'm so sorry."

Sean, still not seeing anything, asked, "What do you see, Luke? Who are you talking to?"

Luke pointed to an open spot directly in front of them, "My friend, Elizabeth. Don't ya see her?"

Sean took another long look. To his eyes, there was nothing there. "There's nobody there, ya big dummy."

Sean said it in the spirit of teasing and without malice. Luke did not take it that way. All his life he had been called stupid and a dummy and it made his blood boil. Many was the time Mathew pulled Luke off some big mouth who had referenced his degree of intelligence. Without warning, Luke turned and with the full force of his powerful muscles behind it, he backhanded Sean, lifting him off of his feet and knocking him flat on his back. No sooner did Sean hit the ground, when Luke was sitting on top of him, smashing the boy in the face with alternating left and rights.

Frank Oakley was the first one on the scene. He tried to grab Luke by the shoulder to stop him and got a back hand in the chest for his trouble. He pleaded several times for Luke to stop. It was like the big man was in a trance, oblivious to anything around him, except the task at hand. Oakley pulled his pistol and gun-butted Luke on the side of the head. Luke merely shook it off like a wet dog would to get rid of water, so Frank Oakley put a bullet high into his shoulder, knocking Luke off the unconscious, severely beaten Sean.

Mathew Briscoe, with his big knife drawn, shouted at Oakley, "You son-of-a-bitch, you shot my brother."

Oakley turned in the direction of Briscoe's voice. Seeing the knife in Mathew's hand, he cocked the pistol and issued a warning, "Don't come any closer, Hillbilly. I only winged your brother, but I'll put this one between your eyes."

Mathew stopped his advance. He stood in a crouch, tossing the knife from one hand to the other, ready to spring at Oakley. Frank Oakley deliberately raised the pistol and took aim as he said, "I mean it, Briscoe. I'll kill you."

Mathew was poised and ready for battle. He was not backing down and to the onlookers, it appeared as if he was waiting for the right moment to strike.

"Enough!" Whitney's forceful command caught everyone's attention, except Mathew's. He was still determined to get at the man who shot his brother. Oakley wasn't foolish enough to be distracted by the shout, so the two of them remained at an impasse until Whitney actually stepped between them.

"Somebody best tell me quickly what is going on here!" Whitney demanded.

Mathew spoke up immediately, "The son-of-a-bitch shot poor ole Luke!"

Whitney turned to Oakley and said rather sarcastically, "Pray tell, Mr. Oakley, why did you shoot poor old Luke?"

Taking Whitney's lead, Oakley replied with the same disdain in his voice, "Poor old Luke was killin' the kid and he wouldn't stop, so I winged him in the shoulder. No serious damage."

Whitney looked back at Mathew and with a hand gesture indicated he should put the knife away. With the same gesture, he suggested Oakley lower his gun, as well. He made his way to where Sean McClaren lay half dead and Luke Briscoe lay moaning and groaning, clutching his right shoulder. He got Luke's attention, demanding to know what happened.

Luke said, "He — he called me a dummy."

Whitney replied, "Well you are a dummy and for this you beat the kid to death."

Collin Pilkington, who was tending to Sean, spoke up, "He's not dead, Sir, but very close to it."

"You know something about doctoring, do you?" asked Whitney.

"Enough to be dangerous," replied Pilkington, forcing a small laugh.

Whitney almost cracked a smile and then told Collin to examine Luke Briscoe's wound. Oakley aimed well. The bullet hit Luke near the top of his right shoulder, just above the collar bone, angled in a downward trajectory, penetrating the muscles and tendons of the upper shoulder and finally lodging in Luke's thick back muscle. As Collin examined Luke's back, he could feel the bullet just under the skin. It had almost made it through. There was a lot of bleeding that could easily be stopped, but Collin felt, intuitively, the bullet needed to come out or the danger of infection and poisoning from the lead would set in. He passed on his diagnosis to Whitney, who didn't hesitate in ordering Collin to take the bullet out.

Collin was whining how he'd never done anything like this before and he was not sure of what he was doing. Whitney countered by telling him, "You're just lacking confidence, Mr. Pilkington. You can do it. Now, get on with it."

With Silas Davidson's help, they moved Luke near the fire for better lighting. Collin asked Mathew to explain to Luke what was about to happen and told him to hold his brother down. Collin heated Mathew's knife in the fire and let it cool. He felt for the bullet with his left hand and then made a quick deep cut above it. Luke screamed and tried to fight, but Mathew held him as tight as he could, reassuring him the procedure was necessary. Collin slid the tip of the knife blade into the wound and under the bullet and using the knife as a lever, forced the bullet up and out through the incision.

Luke let out a blood curdling scream. Mathew told him it was all over and the bullet was out. Collin reheated the knife to red hot and showed it to Mathew, who understood what was coming next. He held on to Luke as tight as he could and nodded to Collin to go ahead. When Collin put the hot knife blade to the crude incision, Luke passed out. This made it much easier to cauterize the entry wound.

Collin asked Silas to find something to bandage the wounds, while he tended to Sean. Silas couldn't find anything to use for bandages, so he tore several strips from the bottom of Luke's own shirt and used them as makeshift dressings.

Whitney, who had been watching the entire proceedings with interest said to Collin, "Good job, Mr. Pilkington. I knew you had it in you. What is the prognosis?"

Collin wasn't sure what Whitney meant, but he answered anyway. "Luke will be fine. I don't know about the boy, though."

"Can they travel?"

"I'm sure Luke will be able to sit a horse, but the boy certainly can not."

Whitney shook his head and said, "That is unfortunate."

Collin caught Whitney's meaning and protested, "You can't just leave him. It's inhuman."

"Don't worry yourself, Mr. Pilkington. We'll do the humane thing and kill him, so the animals don't get to him while he's still alive."

Collin did not know how to respond. He pleaded, "Isn't there anything we can do?"

Michael interjected, "You could build a travois."

Whitney turned to face Michael, his displeasure showing. He didn't say anything, which Michael mistook for Whitney not understanding, so he added, "It is two long poles with some blankets or hides laced to them so you can put things on and have a horse or a mule pull it along. We could make one to take the boy."

Whitney retorted, "I know what a goddamn travois is!" He paused and then in a controlled voice he added, "Alright, we'll try it in the morning. Someone needs to lead the mule and it better not slow us down. If it does, we'll hold services for young Mr. McClaren tomorrow evening."

Chapter 10 – Everybody's Dreaming

It was already sweltering hot even though the sun was barely over the eastern horizon. Dancing Crow knew from experience it was going to be a scorcher. On days like this, he liked to go deep into the coolness of the forest and spend the day in meditation and contemplation.

Dancing Crow had a talent for looking inside a person's soul and seeing their state of mind. He focused on Michael and sensed he was like the elusive mountain lion — solitary, independent, and dangerous. He felt Michael had neither a sense of belonging, nor any connection or ties to any group or even family. He was, indeed, a loner.

He had grown fond of Michael over the last few days and he thought once they were out of this current situation, he would offer his assistance to the young man in helping him find his place. Dancing Crow hoped it would be with his native roots.

Michael stirred and opened his eyes, as if he knew Dancing Crow was thinking about him. He yawned and took in a couple of deep breaths. The air was hot and dry. "Going to be hot today," he commented.

"Yes, it is going to be very hot," repeated Dancing Crow.

Michael looked around the camp. Collin Pilkington, Fredrick Guetch, and Silas Davidson already had a fire going and were absorbed in preparing breakfast. Whitney stood on a small knoll overlooking the trail ahead. Michael called out, "Hey, someone cut me loose. I'm going to piss myself."

No one moved, so Michael shouted once more. Again, no reaction. He thought for a moment and then laid his head back and howled like a wolf. This time there was a resounding response. Whitney turned towards him with his pistol drawn. Frank Oakley stood up from where he was sitting with the Spencer rifle in hand and advanced in the direction of the sound, with Mathew Briscoe not far behind.

Michael howled again. Whitney was the first to arrive on the scene and he quickly deduced it was either Michael or Dancing Crow making the noise. He sounded extremely short tempered when he said, "What the hell are you heathens up to?"

Michael sensed the anger and intolerance and answered accordingly, "I am sorry. I didn't mean to scare anyone. I gotta piss awful badly and I wasn't having much success getting anybody's attention. Didn't mean to cause a ruckus."

By this time, Oakley and Briscoe were beside Whitney and some of the other men were milling around, curious as to what the fuss was about. Michael's apologetic response saved him from a potential rage induced reaction from Whitney. Instead, Whitney scanned the men and said, "Mr. Brimsby, as Mr. McClaren is incapacitated and we don't have any other suitable candidates, I would like you to take charge of the heathens. Tied or untied, it is up to you. Handle it however you like, but they are your responsibility." He paused briefly and then as an after thought, he added, "Take Mr. McClaren's shotgun." He waited for Nathaniel's response. Brimsby merely nodded slightly as an acknowledgement of acceptance of the assignment.

Mathew Briscoe spoke up, "You gonna let him have a gun?"

Whiney didn't answer Mathew directly. Instead, he addressed Brimsby again, "Apparently, Mr. Briscoe is having some difficulty with you being armed. Do you think it will be a problem?"

Nathaniel gave Mathew a menacing look and then answered Whitney, "Won't be any trouble, unless someone else starts it."

"Does that meet with your approval, Mr. Briscoe?" asked Whitney.

It didn't, but Mathew wasn't going to let Whitney know it, so he didn't say anything.

Whitney ended the session, "Fine. Now, everyone go about your business."

Dancing Crow asked Michael about what had taken place. Michael explained Nathaniel Brimsby was now their caretaker. Dancing Crow, using his penchant of comparing a person's character to an animal's, told Michael he saw Nathaniel Brimsby as a poised rattlesnake waiting to strike.

Breakfast was eaten in an aura of quiet apprehension. Everyone felt on edge, unsure of what was happening. Their focus had changed. A couple of days ago they were brothers in arms with a common cause; the fortune of gold waiting for them at the end of their journey. Now, most of their thoughts centered on their own vulnerability; threats not only from the wilderness and unseen forces, but also from their fellow travelers.

Nathaniel Brimsby untied Michael and Dancing Crow and ordered them to build the travois to carry Sean McClaren. He asked Mathew Briscoe for the knife, which Mathew gave up reluctantly. They tied the travois to a makeshift harness made from ropes and moved the battered Sean onto it.

The boy was unrecognizable. His entire face had ballooned to nearly twice its normal size. Luke's vicious blows broke his nose, shattered his left cheek bone, and caved in his right eye socket. His swollen, purple coloured lips were cut through in several places where one punch drove them hard into his teeth. Several of the teeth were broken off and had to be cleaned out of Sean's mouth, so he wouldn't choke on them.

Several of the men asked Collin Pilkington, who was tending to Sean, if he thought the boy was going to make it. Collin told them he didn't think so, but not to give up hope because Sean was young and strong and had a great will to live. There was an undercurrent of resentment towards Luke Briscoe, although no one dared say anything aloud.

Michael saw the look of sympathy in Dancing Crow's eyes as they loaded Sean onto the travois. "You feel pity for the boy?" he asked in a surprised tone.

Dancing Crow responded with his usual manner of answering a question with a question. "What man, with a good heart, would not feel his pain?"

Michael didn't feel sorry for the boy. In his opinion, Sean had made his bed with these men and he had paid the price. "He brought this on himself," he said with conviction.

Dancing Crow covered Sean with a blanket, paused, sighed, and then said, "Think of a young wolf cub trying to learn its place in the pack. He desperately wants to fit in, so he does what he is told. He starts to feel good and he has a sense of power, but because he is young and inexperienced, he lets the power go to his head and he oversteps his boundaries. He is scolded and maybe even gently bitten by the others to humble him, so he remembers his place. A person looks at this and feels sympathy for the wolf cub and we hope he has learned his lesson. We would mourn him if the others killed him. The boy is not any different than the wolf cub."

Nathaniel Brimsby, who was listening, said, "What is all this talk of wolves?"

It took Michael by complete surprise. He stared at Brimsby for a moment and then said, "You speak our language."

"No, not really. I recognize some words and can get the gist of most chitchat, but to carry on a complete conversation, no," answered Brimsby.

"Where did you learn?" continued Michael.

"For nearly two years, I had an Indian partner and he was teaching me."

Dancing Crow asked Michael what was being said. Michael told him and Dancing Crow looked at Brimsby and said, "We shall have to be careful what we say around him, won't we?"

"Still need to know what you two were saying about wolves," said Brimsby.

Michael told him the truth and Brimsby looked at Sean, back at Michael and concluded, "The old man is pretty smart. Interesting — a pack of wolves. Yeah, he might be right."

All predictions of the weather for the day were accurate. It was scorching hot, not unusual for August. Fortunately, the trail was an easy one even though it rose rapidly in elevation and then went quickly downhill again. Roughly, every couple of miles there was a cool, spring-fed creek. Some were barely a foot across and others eight to ten feet wide in places. The cold, refreshing water was a welcome relief to both animals and men. The journey took on a new perspective in the minds of the men. The focus was no longer on some place far off in the distance, but on the next creek where they could get a respite from the heat for a few minutes.

Luke Briscoe was getting worse. Despite all of Collin Pilkington's efforts to the contrary, the shoulder wound was infected and Luke was running a high fever. He was barely conscious and was having great difficulty staying in the saddle. At one creek stop, Mathew watered Luke down and then tied his wrists to the saddle horn and his legs to each other with a rope under the horse's belly. In this way, even if Luke passed out, he would not fall off the horse, which would not sit well with Whitney.

Whitney ordered Mathew and Oakley to scout a few miles ahead and report back. It appeared this type of terrain went on forever, the thickly wooded rolling hills, broken by small gorges and canyons, which held the many creeks pouring out of the hills. The trail was far enough down the slope, so the troop was downstream from the canyons and crossing the streams was not difficult.

Cracks were appearing in Whitney's fortress of mental discipline. He prided himself in always being in control, not just when the occasion called for it, but every moment of every day. There wasn't a man alive who could rattle him, or cause any doubt about himself or his judgement, to enter his mind. He decided to take all these men along rather than a select few. He based this decision on the fact the old prospector told him that for the first week or so, he could possibly run into Indians. The old man didn't know if they were hostile or not. They hadn't bothered him at all, but you never know. Safety in numbers was Whitney's reasoning.

Now, because of the events of the last few days, he was having second thoughts. He didn't need these extra headaches. *The hell with it*, he thought, *I'll just let them kill each other*. He never intended to share the gold with this many men and maybe it was a good thing the numbers were depleting. It could save him some difficult decisions when they did reach their destination.

Having convinced himself his universe was indeed unfolding as it should, he smiled to himself and halted his horse. He looked behind him and saw the hills blending into one another like in a water color painting he'd seen once. As his line of sight travelled to the far horizon, the color of the hills changed from bright to darker shades of green, to darkening tones of blue and where earth and sky met they became purple mounds clouded in a shimmering haze. He turned his gaze to the way ahead. It was the same as the scene behind him. He felt as if he was on an ocean and each row of hills were waves.

He felt challenged. A man could lose himself in this country and forget all about civilization and all its trappings. Here, you felt your vulnerability. Here, you didn't hold any more status than the flowers or the mushrooms and if it wasn't for a man's superior brain power, he might even be considered low on the food chain. Here, you had no control over the things affecting you, such as the weather and the environment.

No, thought Whitney, *I can handle anything comes my way; always have, always will.*

"How will you fight the spirits of the ones you have murdered?" Although the voice was in his head, it was so sudden and so intense, it startled Whitney. To him, it was as if someone shouted in his right ear. He reacted so suddenly, it agitated his horse and it was fighting the bit. With anger swelling up inside him, he turned, fully expecting to see that either Michael George or Dancing Crow or both had somehow ridden up beside him. He was equally taken aback when he realized there was no one there. In fact, Michael and the old man were with Nathaniel Brimsby, thirty yards back down the trail. The closest man to him was Silas Davidson and even he was three horse lengths back.

He felt a sudden surge of fear; not terror or dread, but an unnerving anxiety that often came with situations he didn't readily comprehend. To Whitney, not understanding meant not being in control, which did not sit well with him.

As Silas approached, Whitney's sudden movements caught his attention. He looked into Whitney's face and saw something he'd never seen before. Whitney appeared confused, perhaps even frightened. "Something the matter, Mr. Whitney?" asked Silas when he was close enough.

Whitney thought quickly then answered with regained composure, "Just a bee, Mr. Davidson. A wayward bee has frightened my horse, is all."

Although Silas saw through the alibi, he was not about to push the issue any further. Still, he couldn't help wonder what had alarmed the stone hearted Clarence Whitney so badly.

The day continued to get even hotter as the sun climbed higher. By noon, the heat was almost unbearable. The troop came to a small area of flat, densely wooded terrain. Collin Pilkington suggested to Silas Davidson that a short rest in the woods would be soothing to both man and beast and perhaps he should ask Whitney if they could stop for a little while. Whitney was actually thinking the same thing, so he readily agreed an hour or so in the coolness of the thick grove would be beneficial to all, including the stock.

It was at least ten degrees cooler amongst the trees. Whitney gave orders for the animals to be taken care of before anyone rested. Those who had saddles took them off. Everyone found a shady spot to tie their own mounts and then they all pitched in to help Silas and Collin with the pack animals.

Mathew untied Luke's wrists and the rope connecting his ankles, lowered him to the ground, and helped his semiconscious brother to a spot under a large tree with a cool, green, thick carpet of moss beneath it. Luke groaned in pain as Mathew gently laid him down. Some paternal instinct guided Mathew to feel Luke's forehead and look under the crude bandage at the bullet wound, front and back. Luke was very hot to the touch and it wasn't from the heat. The tissue around the gash on his back looked very red and sore. A brackish yellow liquid was oozing out of the entry wound and had already saturated the bandage.

Mathew summoned Collin Pilkington, "Storekeep, get your ass over here!"

Collin hurried over to Mathew and when he was close enough for a normal level of conversation, Mathew began to give him the third degree. "What kind of doctor are you? He's sicker than a dog. Got himself a fever and the wound is all festered up. Thought you said you knowed what you was doin'?"

"I didn't say that. Look, I did the very best I could," said Collin in his own defence. He bent down to have a first hand look at the wound, but before he could get himself completely positioned, Mathew placed his hand on Collin's chest and pushed him away. He stumbled backwards a few steps, lost his balance, and landed on his rump. He picked himself up and walked away, indignant.

Mathew shouted after him, "My brother dies, so do you, Storekeep."

Collin stopped dead in his tracks, clenched his fists, and gritted his teeth. He did an about face and with definite purpose marched back to Mathew, who was tending to his brother. He was bent over with his back to Collin and never saw the well placed boot of Collin Pilkington before it caught him square in the seat of the pants. The force of the kick knocked him completely over, his face hitting the ground.

Mathew shook his head to clear the effects of the blow and focused on Collin. He half rose and grinned as if in amusement, with blood trickling out of his left nostril. He straightened up and drew out his big knife. He said in a haughty tone, "Well now, looks like Storekeep wants to play with the big boys, don't it." He switched the knife from hand to hand, as he did when he had confronted Frank Oakley and continued with his taunting, "I'm gonna gut you and skin you out just like we done to them elk. You remember don't ya, Storekeep? All the blood and guts and shit that come spillin' out when I gutted it. In a minute it's gonna be you. Maybe we can have roast leg of storekeep for supper?" He thought that part was funny and he laughed aloud, almost manically.

Luke's body lay between Mathew and Collin. Mathew had to either step over Luke or go around him. While he was making up his mind, Frank Oakley stepped next to Collin and handed him the Spencer. Collin took the rifle and looked back at Frank. "It's loaded and cocked," said Frank. "Just point and pull the trigger."

The sound of Oakley's voice caught Mathew's attention. He assessed the situation; the storekeeper had a loaded rifle pointed at his midsection and Frank Oakley had his pistol drawn as well. His own shotgun was out of reach, leaning against the tree near his horse. Mathew spoke slowly and deliberately, "So, if the storekeep misses, you gonna do the job for him, Gunfighter?"

Oakley looked at the pistol and stuck it back in his waistband. "Nope. Between you and him. Just evenin' out the odds a little."

Mathew turned his attention back to Collin. "You gonna shoot me, Storekeep?"

Collin stood cemented in place. He raised the rifle to his shoulder and was taking careful aim at Mathew. "I don't want to, but I will if you force me to," he replied.

Mathew believed him, which probably saved his life. It wasn't anger driving Collin; it was fear and Mathew knew it. He could sense Collin was afraid for his life, which made him a dangerous foe. He put the knife away and changing his tone, he asked, "Do ya think ya can do anythin' for him?" indicating his brother on the ground between them.

Collin didn't lower the rifle as he answered, "I will do the best I can with what I have and what I know. You can't ask any more of me. I will not be held responsible if your brother dies in spite of my efforts. Do I have your word, Mr. Briscoe?"

Mathew thought for a moment and agreed. Collin lowered the still cocked rifle and handed it to Frank Oakley, who set the hammer down gently and turned to walk away when Mathew addressed him, "Best sleep with one eye open from now on, Gunfighter."

Frank turned and walked back to his original position. He threw the Spencer in the dirt at Mathew's feet. "Let's settle it here, Hillbilly," he spat.

Mathew stared down at the rifle for a few seconds. Emotion ruled over common sense and he started to reach for it. He was bent over with one hand on the rifle when he heard the distinctive click of Oakley's pistol being cocked. He knew if he looked up he would see Frank with the pistol in his hand, so he let go of the rifle and slowly straightened up with his hands and arms raised.

"I see you anywhere near me when I'm bedded down and I will kill you, Hillbilly," Frank said as he let the hammer down on the pistol and put it back in his waistband. He picked up the Spencer and walked away. As he turned, he noticed Whitney was close by and had probably seen the entire incident. When Oakley made eye contact with him, Whitney asked, "Why didn't you shoot him?"

"Didn't see the need," replied Oakley.

"Should have killed him, son. You've made yourself a bad enemy. I would heed his warning and sleep with one eye open," Whitney advised.

Collin Pilkington took on the responsibility of nursemaid to the two injured men. He had both of his patients laid out side by side. He checked their wounds and then tried to get them both to drink some water. Luke was in and out of consciousness and managed to get some water down. Sean, on the other hand, was in a coma. Collin lifted his head and tried to force some water into him, but Sean was not responsive.

Nathaniel Brimsby stood by watching. When he saw Collin wasn't having much success, he suggested to Collin perhaps he should get the old Indian to help. "He is a Medicine Man and I'm sure he might have some ideas," Nathaniel said.

Collin thought for a moment and replied, "It wouldn't hurt. That's for sure."

Brimsby approached Michael and asked him to enlist Dancing Crow's help.

Michael translated the request, but Dancing Crow was indignant. He said bitterly, "Why would I help them live? I want them to die."

Michael seemed somewhat surprised at Dancing Crow's response. He said, "Only this morning you felt sorry for the boy."

"Ah, the coyote speaks. Tell me trickster, would not the spirits of our slain loved ones be angry with me, if I helped the white men," replied Dancing Crow.

"You call me, coyote — trickster. I am not trying to trick you, old man. Think about this. If you can keep these two alive, it will slow down Whitney and his plans," argued Michael.

After considering Michael's point, Dancing Crow said, "Your words make sense. I will do what I can."

Michael told Nathaniel that Dancing Crow was willing to help. Nathaniel untied them both and took them to the injured men, where Dancing Crow examined both Luke and Sean. He lifted Sean's head, whispered something in his ear and then turned his own ear to the boy's lips to listen for any response.

He addressed Michael, "Tell this white man," indicating Collin, "I cannot wake the young one. I will have to talk to his spirit and see if it wants to come back to the world of the living. We can help the big man by drawing the poison from his body."

Michael said to Collin, "He says you need to make some poultices for Briscoe and there is nothing you can do for the kid."

Collin didn't fully accept the answer, "I know there is nothing *I* can do. Is there something *he* can do?"

Michael replied, "He'll go to the dream world. He'll talk to the kid's spirit and try to convince it to come back to the world of the living."

He anticipated Collin would scoff and denounce the idea, but much to his surprise, Collin said, "If he thinks it will help, why not?"

Michael translated Collin's response and relayed Dancing Crow's requirements for Luke's poultices back to Collin, who went into the nearby trees to find the black lichen and moss Michael had described.

When Collin returned with the needed ingredients, Dancing Crow wanted to know if Luke had an infection before he was wounded. Collin did not know for sure, but Nathaniel Brimsby, who was still keeping a close eye on his two charges, stated he thought Luke had been shot with an arrow in the posterior. Michael turned Luke's unconscious body over while Collin checked and found a putrefied, festered, oozing gash on Luke's left buttock. After he pulled the arrow out, neither Luke nor anyone else ever tended the wound, so it was no wonder he was full of infection.

Dancing Crow was putting the finishing touches on the last poultice, when Mathew Briscoe rushed in and pushing the Medicine Man aside, tore the makeshift bandages from Luke's shoulder and back and threw them aside. He did not know about the one on Luke's buttock. As he turned to face all of them, he issued a warning, "Keep these goddamn savages away from my brother!"

Nathaniel escorted Michael and Dancing Crow away from the Briscoes. Michael asked Dancing Crow if he was still going to help the boy. Dancing Crow said he would try, but if the boy's spirit did not want to return, there was nothing he could do.

After his tirade, Mathew went back to his night spot and lay down. Collin waited a short time and then gathered the moss and black lichen poultices and reapplied them to Luke's wounds. As Collin was tending to him, Luke opened his eyes and began ranting about how sorry he was for having hurt someone named Elizabeth.

Dancing Crow sat cross-legged with his eyes closed and began a soft rhythmic chant. In his mind he saw himself sitting beside a large pool formed by a beautiful cascading waterfall. He called to the forest around him for Sean to appear. After several moments, Sean came out of the trees, approached Dancing Crow and sat next to him. Dancing Crow asked him, "Why do you stay in the shadow between life and death? Come back to the land of the living."

Language was not a barrier in the dream world, so Sean looked up at the old Medicine Man with a woe begotten look and answered, "I don't know about that. It is so peaceful here."

"You cannot stay here. You must pass into spirit or come back to the world of the living," said Dancing Crow.

"I will, in a while," said Sean, softly.

Dancing Crow opened his eyes and told Michael what Sean had said and Michael relayed the information to Collin.

Again, Michael expected Collin to scoff, but he merely said, "Well, that's good to know."

Several hours later, Harold Grant's shouting got everyone's attention, "I seen it! I seen it! There, running through the trees!"

Mathew Briscoe, who was tending his brother near the fire, was the closest one to the excited Harold Grant. With shotgun in hand, he quickly covered the short distance between himself and the edge of the trees where Harold stood, still shouting. He focused his eyes on the spot Harold was pointing to and saw something moving quickly back and forth, approximately thirty feet into the trees.

It was moving far too fast for Mathew to tell exactly what it might be, but it looked like a huge dog or a wolf running upright on its hind legs. The strange thing was, although the trees were very clear in the bright moonlight and Mathew could easily distinguish one from the other, the creature in question appeared as a blur, like a bad photograph where the subject is very fuzzy, but the background is perfectly clear.

Following his habit of shooting first and asking questions later, Mathew discharged both barrels of the shotgun, loaded his last shell and fired it in the general direction of the shadowy figure. Remembering Luke's shotgun, he sprinted back to his brother's side, picked up the double barrel, and searched Luke's pockets for extra shells, of which he found one. He raced back to the edge of the trees and spent all three shots in the general direction of the speedy spectre.

Harold's shouting and Briscoe's barrage brought mostly everyone running and they all wanted to know what was going on. Harold and Mathew both tried to talk at the same time. Whitney told Harold to shut up and then instructed Mathew to take a couple of deep breaths and explain the situation.

Mathew said, between pauses to catch his breath, "I don't know what it was. It looked like a real skinny bear walkin' upright, but no bear can move near as fast. It might be a wolf on its hind legs, but a wolf don't run on its hind legs. I just don't know, Mr. Whitney."

Whitney was about to ask Harold for his opinion when Oakley fired a pistol shot at something he'd seen. Whitney watched as Oakley cocked the hammer of the pistol for another shot and he heard the distinct thud of the firing pin hitting an empty shell. Oakley cocked and fired several more times, only to have the hammer fall on spent cartridges. Realizing the pistol was empty, he turned to Whitney and asked him for more ammunition.

"Sorry, Mr. Oakley. I told you once before to save ammunition and not shoot at ghosts," was Whitney's reply.

Oakley was enraged. He tossed the useless pistol into the bush, but before he could do something else rash, reason took over. He concluded he still had the Spencer rifle and seven shots and he would keep it close, real close, for self protection against Mathew Briscoe or whatever was running about in the woods.

The rest of the men began to peer into the trees. They saw nothing, as whatever it was had disappeared.

-2-

Frank Oakley was not afraid of Mathew Briscoe, but what Whitney said earlier, about sleeping with one eye open, stuck in his mind as he tossed and turned, trying to get to sleep. When he finally did doze off, he started dreaming. It was hard to tell if he was awake or not, because in the dream he was asleep on the ground and he awoke to someone at the edge of the trees calling his name. He rose and as he slowly walked in the direction of the voice, the outline of a man began to appear. As he cautiously inched his way closer, he recognized a young cowboy named Randy Pearce, someone he'd killed in a fit of anger, back in Montana. Legally, it was a fair fight, but Frank knew in his heart it wasn't. Randy had never drawn on a man before. Frank goaded him and the advantage was all his.

Frank stopped just short of Randy. "No, this can't be. You're dead. I'm dreaming. Yes that's it, I'm dreaming."

"There is a special place in hell for you, Oakley. We are all waiting for you, you murdering bastard," Randy said in response.

Frank reached for the gun in his holster, but when he looked down he wasn't wearing a holster. He was in his prison garb. He reached to the back of his waist band. Again he was disappointed. His pistol wasn't there.

"What's the matter, Gunfighter? Cat got your gun?" mocked Randy. Then he laughed out loud and vanished into thin air.

As the dream continued, Frank found himself back on the ground, asleep. Something pressing against his throat woke him up. He opened his eyes to see Mathew Briscoe kneeling beside him and the pressure he felt on his neck was the knife Mathew carried. He felt the blade cutting into his throat and he began to choke on his own blood.

He bolted upright into a sitting position, holding his throat. He was no longer choking and as he slowly took his hand away from his throat, he realized it wasn't cut at all. He quickly picked up the Spencer rifle and looked about. Everything was quiet in the camp. Mathew Briscoe was sound asleep beside his moaning brother. Frank was relieved. "It was a dream," he said to himself. "Nothing but a dream. But it seemed so real." Frank Oakley did not go back to sleep for the rest of the night.

Oakley wasn't the only one having bad dreams. Harold Grant found himself on the bank of a fair sized creek. He was on his haunches cleaning out some pots, when he looked up to see a figure shrouded in mist standing in the middle of the creek. The mist dissipated and there was Josiah Morgan, not *in* the water but standing *on* it. It was like a picture Harold had once seen of Jesus Christ standing on the waves, talking to his disciples in their boat.

Josiah pointed an accusing figure at him and said, "Harold Grant, you are a bully and a coward and you shall pay for your sins."

Suddenly, Harold was face down in the water. Something was holding him under. Panic set in. He began thrashing and kicking with every ounce of strength he possessed. Just as suddenly, the pressure was released.

He picked up the pots and hurried back to the camp area. As soon as the rest of the men saw him coming, they formed a circle around him and began pushing him from one man to another. Each time he came face to face with one of the troop, the man would give him orders to do some menial job. Fredrick Guetch wanted his socks and underwear washed, Frank Oakley wanted his boots shined, and on and on it went.

The scene changed and Harold found himself tending the animals. One of the mules, sensing his presence, turned and said to him, "How about a nice back rub?"

One of the horses, upon hearing the mule's request, asked Harold to scratch him behind the ears. It was all Harold could take. He screamed and opened his eyes. Like Frank Oakley, he was relieved it was only a dream, but like Oakley, he didn't dare go back to sleep.

Silas Davidson was having the worst nightmare of his life. Whitney had gathered everyone together. He singled out Silas and told him to strip naked. Silas did so and being very modest, he felt very vulnerable and exposed. Whitney offered him a deal; if Silas would consent to Whitney riding him like a horse around the camp, he would give Silas command for one day.

Silas agreed. Whitney tied a rope around his neck and ordered him down on all fours. Whitney sat astride Silas and rode him like a small pony around the camp several times, all the while pulling on the rope and slapping him on his bare buttocks.

Whitney dismounted and Silas put his clothing back on. Whitney gave him command of the troop. Silas's chest expanded with pride, but it quickly dissipated. Every order he gave was met with laughter and jeers. Nobody listened to a thing he said. No one even spoke to him; they would laugh and turn away.

He became more and more frustrated and finally went to Whitney and demanded he do something about the situation. Of course, Whitney refused. He looked at Silas and told him he just didn't look like a leader. Silas looked at himself and realized he was dressed like a court jester, complete with the pointed hat and clown shoes with the little bells on the toes. He was extremely relieved when he awoke and realized it was a dream.

Collin Pilkington found himself stuck in a pool of quicksand on the river bank where he had helped the native woman hide from the rest of the troop. While he was in up to his waist and unable to move, all of the murdered people from the village paraded past him with out stretched arms and forlorn looks on their faces. They moaned and wailed and as each one passed they would ask Collin why he hadn't helped them, as well.

Collin found himself screaming back at them, "I did what I could. What do you want from me?"

The more he screamed and the more he shifted his weight, the deeper he sank into the quicksand. He stopped moving and kept quiet. The people kept passing by and pleading with outstretched arms. Collin began to sob and he kept saying over and over, "It's not my fault. It's not my fault." He awoke with tears in his eyes. He had never experienced such an overwhelming sense of despair and sadness in his life.

Fredrick Guetch was enjoying the beginning of his dream in which he saw himself beating and then savagely raping his mother, aunt, and four sisters. This all took place in his quiet spot by the spring-fed pool where he used to go for solitude and to escape the ball breaking women. Each woman would come up in turn to belittle him. He would beat them unconscious with his fists and vicious kicks, violate their inert bodies, and then throw them into the water. Each body would sink to the bottom of the pool, turn belly up and look up at Fredrick.

After he ravaged all six of them, he thought it was over and he was filled with a great sense of gratification. He looked into the pool, but the bodies weren't there. They were back on solid ground, behind him. They approached him again, only this time as a group, not one at a time, as before. He began punching and kicking each one in turn. As he hit one, she would fall to the ground. He would turn to face another, only to have the first one stand again, apparently unhurt from the savage blows she had just received.

It seemed as if it would never end. No matter how hard he hit or kicked one of the women, she would get right up again and join the others in belittling his manhood. As time passed, the nagging and chattering from the women grew louder and faster. He was punching and kicking as quickly as he could, without effect.

Fredrick saw the pool as the only refuge from the horde of banshees. He dove in and swam to the bottom, where he sat holding his breath. Looking up at the surface, he could see refracted distortions of the women gathered around the pool. Unable to hold his breath any longer, he made for the surface. His head broke the water, where he took a gulp of air and dove for the bottom again. One of his sister's shouted, "There he is!" and the six of them jumped into the pool and swam to the bottom, where they encircled the beleaguered Fredrick and began berating him again.

Once more, Fredrick headed for the surface and climbed out of the pool, only to find the women waiting for him on the bank. This time the female entourage included the two native women from the village. They surrounded him, wrestled him to the ground and held him down while the native girl he had beaten to death unbuttoned his trousers, exposing his privates. She then took hold of his penis with one hand and wielding a large sharp knife in the other hand, took a swing, intending to cut it off. Fredrick awoke short of breath and sweating profusely.

Nathaniel Brimsby had no conscious recollection of killing his beloved Anna and her lover, nor did he remember slaying the woman in the village. He knew he committed the murders because everyone told him he had and he himself saw the aftermath of his handiwork, but he had no memory of actual participation in the gruesome killings.

In his dream he saw every strike, every blow of the pickaxe he wielded as if time had slowed down. He saw with vivid detail the weapon as it hit Anna's lover's head and sank deep into his brain. He felt every thud of the pickaxe as it struck Anna over and over again. He saw the blood spatter on his face and clothes with each blow and he witnessed how each successive swing demolished Anna's head, changing her face into an unrecognizable, pulverized pulp.

The scene shifted to the lodge where again he saw in great detail every stab of the knife and its result on the native woman. He heard the soft squish as the blade went into the woman's body time after time. He saw the blood spray in slow motion, covering his face and soaking his clothes until one couldn't tell who had wielded the knife or who had been cut.

Nathaniel sat up fully awake and immediately vomited all over himself. He got to his feet, stumbled the thirty yards to the creek, and threw himself into the ice cold water.

Mathew Briscoe's dream was one filled with rage. He saw himself shooting Frank Oakley over and over with the shotgun. He would let go with both barrels and Oakley's body would be lifted up by the tremendous blast and sent flying backwards, where he would land flat on his back. He would groan and get to his feet and begin to advance on Mathew, showing no signs of having been shot. Mathew would blast him again and as before, Oakley would go flying backwards, only to get up unscathed and come again.

After a dozen cycles, Oakley stood up. He was panting and short of breath. He held up one hand as a gesture to stop the proceedings and said, "Phew, boy this is tiring work. I need a bit of a rest before we carry on, but so you don't get bored with the whole thing, here are some friends of mine."

Oakley gestured to a spot behind him, where one of the native people Mathew had shot in the village appeared and took Frank's place. Nothing changed; Mathew would shoot the man and he would fly backwards, hit the ground hard, moan and get up, only to run the cycle again. Just as Frank Oakley did, he stopped after awhile and someone else took his place.

This continued on and on until there were half a dozen men grouped around Frank Oakley with hands on their knees, breathing hard. When the last one stopped the proceedings to catch his breath, no one appeared to take his place. Mathew felt relieved, but the feeling was short lived. His heart sank when he heard Frank Oakley say, "Guess it's my turn again," and the whole cycle started over again.

Mathew was not smart enough to think about what might happen if he didn't shoot, or maybe he didn't want to take the chance. He thought this was what hell would be like, where you relived a punishment over and over for all eternity. His screams of anguish woke him up.

Even the unflappable Whitney was having a restless night. In his dream, the entire troop, including the newly departed Josiah Morgan and Con Murdock were in a long line. Everyone was dressed in a Confederate uniform, with the exception of himself; he was in Union garb. Whitney was at the end of the line and when he poked his head out sideways to get a better view, to his astonishment the line seemed to be a mile long. He could barely make out the front of it.

He moved back into position and tried to make sense of it. What was everyone lined up for? What was at the end of the queue? He tapped the person in front of him and when the man turned around, to Whitney's surprise, it was Michael.

Whitney asked, "Why are we lined up?"

Michael appeared surprised that Whitney would ask that question. He replied, "We're here to get our share of the gold. We made it, Mr. Whitney. We made it!"

Whitney was still confused, "What gold? You don't mean the lost mine? Who are these other people?"

Michael answered, "These are people you owe. They get to take their share first. Sure hope there is something left when we get to the front."

Whitney had the strongest urge to run up to the front of the line to claim what was rightfully his, but he couldn't move from his spot. No matter how hard he tried, he could only move ahead as the line moved.

Finally, after what seemed an eternity, he was at the front of the line. There was Robert E. Lee in all his glory, sitting behind a table, in front of which was a huge steamer trunk with the lid wide open. Whitney looked inside and it was empty.

"Clarence Milford Whitney," read General Lee from a sheet of paper in front of him.

"Yes," replied Whitney.

"Take your share, Sir," commanded Lee.

Whitney hesitated and looked into the trunk once more before he said, "It's empty! There is nothing in it."

Lee stood up and after looking into the trunk for himself, said, "Looks like you're out of luck, Mr. Whitney. The gold is all gone."

Whitney woke up screaming, "But it's mine! It's mine!"

It was still very dark, about an hour before sunup, when Michael awoke to find Dancing Crow wide awake, as well. Dancing Crow remarked, "It appears all of the men are not sleeping very well. Perhaps, the Dreamwalker is about tonight."

Michael thought about what Dancing Crow had said. He wanted to ask the old man what he meant, but another thought vetoed the first one. "I had a very strange dream myself," he confessed.

Dancing Crow seemed very interested. "What did you see?" he asked.

Michael related his dream, "I was standing at the entrance to a very beautiful meadow which was completely surrounded by a high rock wall except for the gate where I stood. A deer and a coyote stood before me wanting passage to the meadow, but I could only let one of them in.

"They both pleaded and begged for me to let them enter. The deer claimed it needed to go in because it was hungry and the meadow was full of luscious grasses and young willow shoots it could eat. The coyote also argued it was very hungry, and the meadow was full of mice and ground squirrels for it to catch. I thought and thought and I could not decide, so I sent them both away."

Dancing Crow listened intently until Michael was done. He sat in silence with his head down for a moment. It appeared as if he was asleep, but then he lifted his head, smiled at Michael, and said, "I believe I know the meaning of your dream. The deer represents one side of you and the coyote represents the other. Both sides are pulling at you, but you do not know which side to chose or maybe you do not want to choose either, so you deny both sides."

"Which side is which?" asked Michael.

"I believe the deer symbolizes your native side and the coyote your white side."

"How do you know?" asked Michael, wanting to know more.

"The deer is the one who is gentle and lives off the land. It is connected to Mother Earth and she looks after the deer as she does my people.

"The coyote symbolizes your white side. He is an opportunist. He is filled with a paradox of wisdom and foolishness. He often makes things more complicated than they need to be. He is very skillful, but he will often let others do the work for him instead of using his own talents.

"By chasing them both away, the dream has shown you that you are having trouble making up your mind. You must meditate on the spirit of the deer and of the coyote and make a choice."

"Why do I have to choose? Why can't I be both or neither?" asked Michael.

"You can let both into the meadow, but you will have to be on a constant vigil to ensure the deer does not frighten away the mice and ground squirrels so the coyote cannot eat or the coyote will become angry and kill the deer. You must make sure the coyote accepts the deer and he lets the deer have its opportunity to flourish. If you are strong enough to do so, than choose both. If you are not, chose one, but you cannot chase them both away, one or both will always try to sneak into the meadow and you will be chasing them away forever."

Michael thought about what the old man told him and said, "I'll think on it."

Dancing Crow looked skyward and said, "There is a big storm coming."

Chapter 11- Fish for Dinner

The deluge began a short time after Dancing Crow's prediction. Brilliant streaks of lightning lit up the early morning sky every few seconds. The flashes were so frequent it was as though someone had hung a strobe light in the middle of the camp. The thunder was one continuous chorus of bangs and rumblings.

When the storm hit, the men quickly went into action as most of them were already wide awake. The cherry sized hail sent everyone scurrying to find a nearby tree to hide under. Whitney barked out orders, sending Mathew Briscoe and Frank Oakley to make sure the horses and mules were secure and Silas Davidson and Collin Pilkington to tend to the wounded men.

Silas Davidson tried to roust the unconscious Luke Briscoe, but he was not responding. He enlisted Collin's help and they moved Sean under a large spruce tree that offered some protection. Silas left Collin with Sean and then braved the pounding rain and hail to attend to Luke, who was positioned on his side to keep pressure off his wounded shoulder. Silas turned Luke on his back to allow the rain to hit his face and, perhaps, wake him up, but it didn't have any effect.

Silas called out to Collin for assistance. Mathew Briscoe heard the shouting and came out from his cozy spot he'd found under a fir tree. When he got to Luke, he saw his brother was not moving.

Feeling somewhat sheepish that he'd forgotten about Luke, he pushed Collin Pilkington, who was kneeling over Luke, out of the way and examined his brother closely.

Mathew stood up and grabbed Collin's shirt front with both hands. He asked through gritted teeth, "What did you do to my brother? He was fine last night."

Silas intervened, "He wasn't fine last night. The wound was infected and he had a high fever."

Mathew was confused. It was a minor shoulder wound that shouldn't have been a serious problem. He needed to lash out at someone and lay the blame somewhere. He knelt down and opened his brother's shirt to look for himself. The wounds were covered in lichen and moss, which, in turn, were covered and tied down with a strip from one of the blankets. Mathew tore the dressing off and turned to face Silas, demanding to know who had put the bandages back on Luke.

Silas indicated Collin tended to his brother and in Collin's defence, he was only following the Medicine Man's advice. Mathew stood up, seething in anger, looking around for Dancing Crow. Michael and Dancing Crow were still tied to the sapling where they had been put for the night. No one bothered to free them, so they could seek shelter from the storm.

When Michael saw Mathew approaching, he assumed they were going to be untied so they could find cover. He wondered why Mathew Briscoe was sent to perform the task. Perhaps, he was ordered to. Mathew stood in front of Dancing Crow and backhanded him with a vicious, full-force blow across the face. Michael, with his back to Dancing Crow, could not see what was transpiring, but he knew something was wrong when he heard the impact of hand on face and Dancing Crow's cry of surprise and pain.

"What did you do to my brother, you goddamn savage?" shouted Mathew.

Dancing Crow lifted his head and said something to Briscoe, who then took two steps to his left so he was facing Michael. "What did he say to me?" he demanded.

Michael said, "I don't know. With all this wind and rain, I didn't hear what he said."

Mathew took out his big knife and cut the rope holding Michael and Dancing Crow to the tree and to each other. Michael stood up, helped Dancing Crow to his feet and they both turned and headed for the shelter of the larger trees. Mathew stopped their progress by putting his hand on Michael's shoulder and spinning him around. He reminded Michael they still had some unfinished business.

Michael let Dancing Crow continue to the shelter of the trees while he addressed Mathew, "What is it you want?"

"I want to know what the savage did to make my brother so sick," demanded Briscoe.

"He didn't do anything. He's a healer. He used moss and lichen as a poultice to draw out the poison that was already there."

"I don't believe you," Mathew said as he turned and started after Dancing Crow. Mathew didn't get far as Michael kicked his legs out from under him with a sweeping leg motion from behind.

Mathew fell headfirst into the saturated ground. As surprised as he was by the attack, he still reacted with lightning speed. He was up on his feet with knife in hand, facing Michael before Michael could get to him. Mathew stood glaring at Michael. The mixture of mud and blood from his cut lip, embellishing a menacing grin, all added to a lunatic look. The heavy rain pouring on his face quickly washed away the grime. Briscoe said with malice, "Well Breed, I hope you know a short little prayer, 'cause you are about to go to the happy huntin' ground, or whatever you call it."

Briscoe was a skilled street fighter and he knew how to use a knife. Michael was not as experienced. However, he was much quicker on his feet than Briscoe and he was not without a few tricks of his own.

"I'm gonna start by giving you some more scars on your face to add to the big ones you already have, you ugly bastard," Mathew threatened.

"You going to keep talking or fight?" Michael baited him.

Mathew lunged forward with his head down, at the same time swinging the knife in a large sweeping arc. His intent was to hit Michael in the midsection with his head, knocking the wind out of him, while at the same time, his knife would find its mark in the middle of Michael's back. Michael saw it coming, took one big step to his right and as Mathew came charging by, Michael dipped down into a crouching position and again, with the same sweeping motion he used before, he knocked Briscoe's legs out from under him.

This time Michael reacted a lot quicker and he was atop Briscoe before he could regain his senses. He jammed his knee between Briscoe's shoulder blades. With both hands, he grabbed Briscoe's right arm and gave it a tremendous twist, nearly dislocating it at the elbow. Briscoe's arm went limp, making it easy for Michael to retrieve the knife. Once he had possession of the knife, he increased the pressure of his knee and then with all this strength, he shoved Briscoe's face into the ground. His intention was to kill the man by suffocating him.

Most of the group became aware of two men fighting out in the rain, but they didn't know who was involved or how it was progressing and not one of them wanted to leave their relatively dry shelters to go out in the downpour to have a closer look. Michael kept applying pressure, holding Briscoe's face down. Briscoe couldn't get any air and the panic of a drowning man set in, causing him to kick and flail his arms. Michael wouldn't ease up and Mathew's movements slowed down and then stopped entirely.

Michael would have killed him if Dancing Crow hadn't intervened. He came out into the rain, which seemed to get even more intense. He got close to Michael and shouted. "Do not kill him!"

Michael heard the old man's shout and relaxed the pressure on Briscoe. He got up and turned Briscoe over. As soon as the pounding rain hit Mathew's face, he coughed several times. His breathing sputtered and he coughed several more times before he was able to breathe normally. He looked up at Michael standing over him and said. "I'm gonna kill you, Heathen!"

Michael sat down on Mathew's chest and pinned his shoulders down with his knees and put the knife to his throat. "Well then I better finish this," he said.

Whitney's commanding voice drew Michael's attention. "What is all this about? It's pouring rain for God's sake." When he saw it was Michael holding the knife at Briscoe's throat, he paused before speaking again. "If you kill him, I'll be forced to do the same to you."

Michael did not ease the pressure on the knife. He turned his head slightly in Whitney's direction and said, "It doesn't appear you've left me any choice. If I kill him, you say you'll kill me. If I don't kill him, he says he'll kill me. He'll do that."

Whitney mulled over what Michael said then he spoke to Briscoe, "Mr. Briscoe, it appears we have a dilemma here. I see only one solution to saving your life. I will have the breed let you live, but you must promise me you won't kill him until I don't need him any more. When the time comes, you can do what you want."

Before Briscoe could answer, Michael spoke, "That solution does not solve my problem. In either case, I am a dead man."

"Let me sweeten the pot," replied Whitney. "When the time comes, I'll make sure it's a fair fight. You have my word."

Michael was still hesitant. "What do you need me for? You seem to know where you're going."

As I told you before, I need an interpreter."

"What do you need the old man for, then?"

"He is my insurance in case we meet any more heathens before we reach our destination." Whitney smiled because an idea came to him. He continued, "Think about this, Mr. George; if I have to kill you than I won't be able to negotiate for the old man's release with any heathens we run across, so why keep him around?"

With that thought in mind, Michael relaxed his grip on the knife, threw it at Whitney's feet and stood up. Briscoe stood up, still wanting to continue the fight. Whitney reminded him he'd just made a peace pact and he should honour it or there would be dire consequences. Briscoe believed Whitney meant it and he ended the affair by saying to Michael as he picked up his knife "Oh, I am going to enjoy carving you like Sunday's chicken, when the time comes."

Whitney wasn't done yet. He addressed Michael, "What started all this?"

Michael replied, "Does it matter?"

"Quite frankly, Mr. George, there are a lot of strange things happening lately and I think it would be in my best interest to know all that goes on. I won't ask you again. What started the fight?"

Michael believed Whitney was sincere in his quest for understanding. He said, "Briscoe starting beating on Dancing Crow, because he thinks the old man is responsible for this brother's condition."

"And what condition might that be?" asked Whitney.

"I really don't know," replied Michael.

Whitney looked around, but because the rain was so dense, he couldn't make out faces. "Mr. Pilkington, front and center," he shouted.

Collin rushed forward and stood before Whitney, who asked, "How are the wounded men?"

"No change in the young lad, Sir. Luke Briscoe has succumbed to infection and fever and I fear he may not make it either." Collin could see Whitney was giving this matter a lot of thought. Thinking Whitney might come to some decision that would entail leaving the two men behind or even killing them, he added, "They still won't slow us down. It won't take but a few minutes to build another travois, or they could even lay together on the one we do have."

Whitney simply stared at Collin for a moment and as he turned away, he said, "Fine — for now."

An hour later the rain stopped completely. The clouds vanished as if some sky god had taken a deep breath and with a mighty exhale blew them all away. Everything was soaking wet. The men were chilled to the bone, so they did not pay any attention to the breath taking array of colors forming in the eastern sky. Dancing Crow was the only one appreciating the bright pinks and oranges bordering the dark purples of the few clouds left over from the storm.

Silas Davidson, Fredrick Guetch, and a reluctant Harold Grant somehow managed to find enough dry twigs and witch's whiskers to get a fire going. Michael told Silas to look on the leeward side of thickly branched trees, near the ground for the dead, dry twigs and on the branches of the trees for the lichen, which actually looked like a beard. When dry, the lichen was the best fire starting material around. It was amazing even after the deluge, there were still some dry twigs and lichen to be found under the thick canopy of some of the larger spruce trees.

Silas was very careful to keep their meagre supply of matches dry. He wrapped them in a piece of deer hide and then wrapped them again in another larger piece of hide. He kept them inside his waistband for further protection. It wasn't long before there was a roaring fire going and they began to dry themselves out as well as everything else in camp.

No one thought of tying Dancing Crow and Michael back up, but any thoughts by Michael about making a break were put to rest by two things; the thought of leaving Dancing Crow to these vermin and the sight of Nathaniel Brimsby, shotgun in hand, watching his every move.

Dancing Crow was quite intrigued with the matches. He only ever saw them twice before in his life time and never this close. He kept asking Silas to light another one. He was so insistent, Silas, in desperation, summoned Michael and asked him to see what the old man wanted.

"He wants to know what you want." Michael translated.

"Tell the one who walks like a stork I would like to see the fire stick set ablaze again."

Michael told Silas the old man wanted him to light another match. Silas explained their supply was limited and he could not waste one to satisfy some old man's curiosity.

Michael said to Dancing Crow, "He says he can't burn another stick as they don't have very many. I'll persuade him to let you light the next fire with one of the sticks." Michael passed on the request to Silas, who merely grunted, shook his head, and reluctantly agreed.

Nathaniel Brimsby approached Michael and wanted to know what was going on. Michael explained it to him, after which he ordered Michael and Dancing Crow back to the small sapling and tied them back up. Michael pleaded his case, promising he wasn't going to run, but to no avail.

Silas and Harold Grant proceeded to retrieve some of the elk meat, which had been wrapped in a hide and pulled up into the air with a rope thrown over a branch of a large spruce tree. To their surprise and dismay, the meat was gone. It seemed something or someone pulled on the rope hard enough to break the branch, bringing the whole package to the ground. Whoever or whatever it was had removed the meat from its elk hide cover and absconded with it. The only thing left was a small portion of the hind quarter of the calf, which Silas had tied and hung up separately from the cow meat.

Whitney's reaction to the news of the missing meat mildly surprised Silas and Harold. He asked if Silas had determined what had taken it. Silas informed him he could not, mostly because the rain wiped out any sign. Whitney told him not to worry about it, saying there was plenty of game around. This seemed unusually pleasant coming from Whitney, but unknown to Silas, Whitney did not react to the theft because he did not want anymore speculations or rumours about things going bump in the night.

Silas divided the remaining meat into two equal halves; one for breakfast and one for their evening meal. Although there wasn't enough breakfast to satisfy some bigger appetites, the men felt sated and with things mostly dry, the troop set out. The vivid dreams everyone was experiencing the night before, combined with the present atmosphere, left an eerie sensation in most of them. The air was already hot and the rising mists from the drying trees and rocks added to the supernatural aura. All was quiet. No one spoke. Their thoughts were centered on their sleepless, dream filled night.

For most of the morning, they rode as if in a funeral march. Luke Briscoe was conscious and Mathew, fearing what Whitney might do if he discovered Luke couldn't ride, tied his brother to his horse again. Some of the men fell asleep in the saddle only to be jarred awake by the reoccurrence of the nightmares that had befallen them the night before. Every caw of a raven flying overhead or the scream of a golden eagle sitting atop a towering fir tree was greeted with anxiety. It was as if they all felt they were being watched, as if there was something laying in wait for them and it could pounce at any time.

The first time they stopped to water the animals at a small brook, not one man spoke to another. When anyone made eye contact, they would divert their gaze as if ashamed to look at the other man or to have the other man look at them. The only dialogue taking place was when Whitney inquired of Collin Pilkington as to the state of Sean McClaren and Collin replying there was no change in his condition.

For the rest of the day, they rode as they had in the morning, a slow methodical pace, lumbering along as if they had no direction or any destination. If viewed from a distance, they looked like an aimless herd of cattle, trudging along in single file, one behind the other. They were oblivious to where the trail might lead, but follow it, they must.

It was mid afternoon. Frank Oakley was leading the troop when a cougar darted across the trail, not twenty yards away. It spooked his horse, which reared on its hind legs and nearly threw him to the ground. The other horses and mules, reacting to the action of Oakley's horse and the smell of the mountain lion, became agitated and hard to handle.

The break in the monotony shook the troop out of their zombie-like stupor. Whitney came alive and seemed to be his old self when he started throwing orders around. He sent Frank Oakley and Mathew Briscoe ahead to find some game, with a warning to set their differences aside and if they both didn't come back, he would shoot the one who did. He called a short rest stop, mostly for the animals' sake, not the men's.

Early evening found them crossing a fair sized creek, running through a flat area between the two rows of hills that paralleled their route. Whitney ordered a halt for the night. Silas and his crew picketed the horses and were cooking the last of the elk meat over the coals of a fire, when Mathew Briscoe and Frank Oakley returned, empty handed. They claimed they sighted a deer three different times, but when they were in range of the Spencer, an eagle swooped down at the deer, chasing it away on all three occasions. As they listened, the energy went out of all the men in one large collective sigh. They all had one thought, "What next?"

Silas gave everyone their share of the meat, a couple of mouthfuls each. The men grumbled and shot nasty glances in the direction of Briscoe and Oakley because of their failure to bring back anything. Michael gave his share to Dancing Crow, who refused to accept it, out of pride. Michael left it on the ground near him, hoping he would eat it when Michael wasn't looking.

Nathaniel Brimsby decided he had enough guard duty for the day, so he instructed Michael and Dancing Crow to empty their bladders as he was going to tie them up for the night even though it was early evening and there was still a couple of hours of daylight left. No amount of arguing on Michael's part would dissuade Brimsby, so he accepted it and lowered his head into his lap and went to sleep. He wasn't sure how long he was out, perhaps a few minutes, when Fredrick Guetch's excited shouts woke him.

From what Michael could make of it, Guetch had seen some big fish in the creek when he went down to wash the few plates and cutlery the troop possessed. Whitney quickly dampened his enthusiasm when he asked Guetch how he expected to catch these fish. Partly from hunger and partly from wanting to be free of rope shackles for a little while, Michael spoke up, "I know a way to catch the fish."

The statement not only caught Whitney's attention, but aroused everyone else's interest. They all congregated around Michael like children gathered around an elder, waiting to hear a story. Michael went on to describe the procedure, "It will take a lot of us to pull it off. We dam up the downstream end of a pool where the fish like to gather. We then go upstream a fair distance and walk four or five abreast driving the fish downstream to the dammed end of the hole. We then plug up the upstream side and we have the fish trapped."

"Do you realize how long it will take to build a dam, remarked a sceptical Silas Davidson.

Michael explained, "Not long at all. All we need to do is to cut a few strong saplings. We tie some blankets to the poles, one at each end and a couple in the middle, stretch the whole thing across the downstream end of the creek and weight it down with rocks so the fish can't swim under. We build two of these; the first one we set in place at the end of the pool and the second one we hold out in front of us as we walk downstream, driving the fish in front of us. When we have the trout cornered, we go swimming."

"I still don't see how we can catch them?" remarked Silas.

"You bend over, grab one, and throw it on shore." Michael saw an opportunity for some humour, so he added, "One would think a stork would know how to fish."

This brought a sneer from Silas and a round of laughter and jeers from the rest of the men. Even Whitney smiled ever so slightly. He consented to the plan and under Michael's direction, they quickly assembled the two portable dams. Guetch showed Michael where he had seen the fish. Michael approached the spot slowly and stood far enough back from the edge of the bank so the trout would not see him. He let his eyes adjust and squinting, he searched the bottom of the creek bed. Sure enough, he could count seven or eight large fish, what the white men called Dollies. They were in a natural pool created by the water flowing over a rock shelf that crossed the creek. It was a two foot drop from the shelf to the pool.

This changed Michael's plan. It was going to be easier than he thought. He directed the men to string one of the blanket dams across the creek just downstream of the rock shelf. They weighed the bottom of the blankets down with rocks and Harold Grant and Nathaniel Brimsby were posted at each end with Fredrick Guetch in the middle of the damn to hold the saplings in place.

Michael instructed four other men, Mathew Briscoe, Collin Pilkington, Frank Oakley, and Silas Davidson to go to the downstream end of the pool and after making sure the blanket dam was hitting the bottom of the pool, to walk it upstream, forcing the fish to crowd against the upstream dam. Michael waded into the waist deep water and stood in the middle. He instructed the men to walk the dam forward until there were only a few feet between the two dams for the trout to manoeuvre. Michael motioned Whitney to join him in the water, who refused, but ordered Silas to go in.

Silas waded into the pool and awaited instructions. Michael told him to stand still, look, and feel. In the fading daylight, Silas could barely see the frantic fish swimming about, but he could feel them bumping his legs. Suddenly, Michael went into a crouch. He clasped his hands together to form a scoop, reached under one of the fish and with a big upward sweeping motion, tossed the fish on the rocky shore, far enough from the creek, so it couldn't flop back into the water.

Silas attempted the same manoeuvre and ended up falling into the water. A chorus of shouts and laughter greeted him as he surfaced, gasping for air. Michael threw three more fish on the shore, one of them quite large, roughly three pounds. Silas kept trying and missing. Finally, he got the hang of it and actually managed to toss a fish on to the creek bank.

By the time they were done, there were seven fair sized fish on the shore, more than enough to give everyone a good feed. Mathew Briscoe stepped up with his knife and gutted and cleaned all the fish and then cut thick willow sticks on which to hang them over the fire.

The trout were delicious, although at this point, anything would have tasted better than elk or venison. Michael brought Dancing Crow some of the trout with some chives he had found. Dancing Crow readily accepted the food and wolfed it down. When he was finished, he asked, "Why did you help the white men?"

The question surprised, as well as perplexed Michael. He wasn't sure what Dancing Crow meant. He answered hesitantly, "I didn't think of it as helping the white man so much as I was hungry and so were you."

"Who do you think I am that I need you to watch over me?" asked Dancing Crow, again surprising Michael with the question and the tone of it.

Michael clambered for an answer, "I — I mean — I just — Well, you don't understand how evil some of these men are. If there was nothing stopping them, they would kill you without hesitation."

"I know much more than you think I do, young pup!" retorted Dancing Crow.

"If it wasn't for you I could have escaped long ago," Michael said, regretting it the minute the words came out of his mouth.

Dancing Crow looked up with a hurt expression on his face, "Then go. Do not use me as an excuse to stay."

"I'm sorry. I said those words in anger. Of course, I wouldn't leave you to these vicious animals," replied Michael.

The old man smiled. It was a momentary test of wills. "Perhaps, the spirits of our loved ones will forgive us for this belly full of fish," Dancing Crow concluded as he patted his stomach.

The others in the troop were sated by the meal. Conversations centered on how delicious the fish tasted and what a nice change it was from the wild meat. Silas, Harold, and Fredrick went on wood gathering missions several more times. Nobody wanted to go to sleep. As the men sat or lay sprawled out by the fire, they took turns nodding off for a few seconds, only to jerk themselves awake, guiltily looking around at the other faces to see if anyone noticed.

It was well past midnight, when Whitney entered the circle around the fire. He had tried to get some rest, but like the others, the moment he feel asleep the nightmare would start all over again. It was as if he was watching a movie that was paused while he was awake and then resumed and repeated the minute he dozed off. He noticed, with the exception of the two heathens, no one else was entertaining any notion of going to sleep.

He approached the group under the pretence of checking on the condition of the two wounded men. Collin Pilkington answered his inquiries by stating Luke Briscoe's fever had dissipated and the infection appeared in recess thanks to the poultice Dancing Crow suggested. Sean McClaren, on the other hand, had not regained consciousness. He would not take food or drink and Collin feared if he did not show any signs of recovery soon, then the boy would die.

Whitney asked a rhetorical question, "Then why are we dragging him all over the countryside?"

Chapter 12 – Birds

The gunshot, in the still of early morning, startled everyone. The sun had been up for nearly half an hour, but no one was in any particular hurry to get up and start the day. Other than Michael and Dancing Crow, no one had slept at all. They all looked in the direction of the shot to see Whitney holding a smoking revolver. He was standing next to Sean McClaren, but no one suspected Whitney had done anything but fire into the air, until Collin Pilkington's outburst suggested something more sinister. "You murdering bastard! He's just a boy! You son-of-a-bitch! You will roast in hell for this!"

Whitney looked at the hole in the center of Sean McClaren's forehead, which was starting to ooze a trickle of blood. "The locale of my afterlife was determined a long time ago, Mr. Pilkington," he said with resignation.

Luke Briscoe reacted to the gunshot, as well. He was fully conscious and propped himself up, using his good arm. Whitney observed the movement and remarked to him, "And as for you, Mr. Briscoe, I am truly relieved to see you are among the land of the useful once more." Turning to face the rest of the men, he shouted, "Twenty minutes. Be ready to go."

As the men scrambled to their feet, Whitney ordered Brimsby to bring Michael and Dancing Crow to him. When they were front and center, Whitney addressed Michael, "I am going to promote you to scout and hunter for the outfit. We are out of food. You will find game and Mr. Brimsby will shoot it." He paused and then added, "Mr. Brimsby, if he gives you the slightest indication he is trying to escape, shoot him. Mr. George, should Mr. Brimsby be forced to shoot you or come back without you, the old heathen dies and I assure you he will suffer greatly before he begs me to kill him. One last thing, Mr. George, make sure you tell the old heathen that if he should somehow escape, he signs your death warrant when he leaves."

Nathaniel Brimsby traded weapons with Frank Oakley, his shotgun for Oakley's Spencer and he and Michael rode out immediately. Michael was given enough time to explain the situation to Dancing Crow, who assured him he would not jeopardize Michael's life by causing any trouble.

At first, the forced trade of fire arms did not sit well with Frank Oakley, but then he convinced himself a loaded shotgun would be much more effective at close range than the Spencer. Against what adversary, he wasn't sure.

Fredrick Guetch hurried down to the creek. Even though their tyrant of a leader wanted to leave immediately, he was not going to forego his morning ritual of washing his hands and face. It was as if the cold stream contained holy water which not only stimulated him physically, but it made him feel as if he were washing his sins away. As he splashed the icy water on his face and rubbed it in with his hands for the third time, he noticed a figure standing on the far bank of the creek.

He wiped the water from his eyes, ran his fingers through his hair, and focused on the figure. It was a beautiful Indian maiden washing herself in the stream. She removed her one piece garment from her shoulders and let it fall to her waist, which she kept from falling all the way down with one arm, while she washed her breasts and neck with the other.

Fredrick stood mesmerized. Never before had he seen such loveliness. The maiden noticed him watching as she turned and stepped out of the water onto the shore. She didn't bother to pull her garment back up, as she turned to face him and beckoned to him with a finger of her free hand. Fredrick didn't need to be asked twice. Dashing across the creek, he fell several times, his boots sliding on the slippery rocks of the streambed. As he looked up after his second stumble, the young woman was standing several feet up a small game trail leading from the water's edge, still beckoning for him to follow. When he reached the far shore, he saw her disappear around a corner, several yards up the trail. Fredrick began to run, but no matter how fast he went, the elusive maiden stayed just ahead of him. Several times he stopped, having decided he'd gone far enough, but when he did, she would come back to wait for him and keeping a safe distance, would beckon to him again.

Roughly a hundred yards from the creek, the path spread out into a small meadow centered by a towering pine tree and under it was the vision of beauty. Her garment was spread out on the ground and she lay on it completely naked, posed in an alluring posture. Fredrick couldn't believe his luck. He licked his lips, rubbed his hands together in anticipation and approached her cautiously.

When he was within a few feet of her, everything changed. Her image shimmered, like heat waves from a paved road on a very hot day. The maiden began to fade away and when she vanished completely, a huge Silverback Grizzly was in her place. It hadn't noticed Fredrick as it was entirely focused on digging out the ground squirrel it had discovered.

Fredrick's sudden gasp was his downfall. The startled bear spun around and charged immediately. Fredrick didn't have time to react. The bear hit him like a runaway locomotive, knocking him flat on his back. The bear then exhibited some very unusual behaviour. It placed one paw on Fredrick's chest to hold him down and then proceeded to swat him full force with its other front paw, not a raking blow with long sharp claws as a bear is apt do, but more of a punch.

With Fredrick barely conscious, the bear released the hold on his chest and began raking his inert body with its razor sharp claws, not deep enough to disembowel him, but with enough depth to cause great pain and cut his clothes and skin to shreds. He felt every swipe. It was as if someone was running a hot poker up and down his body. To his tortured mind it seemed like an eternity before the beast finally stopped its carnage and stood back as if to admire its handy work. There were claw marks on every square inch of the front of Fredrick's body, all oozing blood.

The bear moved so its head was directly over Fredrick's face. It stood for the longest time staring into his terror filled eyes, as if in judgement. Then it took a couple of steps backward, sank its teeth into Fredrick's genitals and with one shake of its massive head, tore them from his body.

As the troop was about to head out, Collin Pilkington mentioned that Fredrick Guetch was not with them. Whitney ordered Oakley to see what was keeping him. Oakley tracked Fredrick to the creek. He crossed the stream and picked up his trail on the other bank. The sign was easy to follow and in a few minutes he was in the meadow where the body of Fredrick Guetch lay, with the ravens and magpies already gathering in anticipation of a meal.

Oakley looked the body over and to him it was obvious Guetch had been viciously mauled by some animal. However, the torn out crotch didn't seem to fit. It seemed too deliberate an act for some creature to have committed. Oakley smiled a bit when he thought how this was a fitting demise for a rapist, a form of poetic justice. It was as if the creature knew about Guetch's sins and doled out an appropriate punishment.

Oakley raced his horse back to the troop. He felt an intense desire not to be left alone out here. He reported what he found and the news not only shocked but heightened the air of apprehension among the men. Whitney should have said something positive, using his powerful confident leadership skills to restore morale, but he didn't. He simply ignored the news and callously pointed out that due to the death of Fredrick Guetch and the untimely demise of young Sean McClaren, there were two more horses available. He assigned them to Harold Grant and Collin Pilkington and since Michael was out hunting with Brimsby, he ordered Dancing Crow be put on a manageable mule.

The day's travel was a carbon copy of the day before. The trail continued in a northwest direction, paralleling the mountain range to the west. Although they went up and down in elevation as they rode up one foothill and down another, the ascents and descents were relatively gradual and not very taxing on man or beast.

As they rode along, the only sound heard was the clip clop of hooves on rocks, the occasional scream of an eagle flying overhead, and the chatter of a group of birds that seemed to be following them.

There was still an abundance of creeks crossing their trail where they would stop in solemn silence and water themselves and the stock. It was becoming apparent, every time they halted, more and more jays, magpies, and ravens were gathering. They would fly and light on the trees close to the men and would chirp, squawk, and croak in a chorus of disconnected clatter that played on the men's already frazzled nerves, like a set of finger nails running down a slate chalkboard.

Luke Briscoe, who seemed to be getting his strength back rapidly and was capable of keeping himself upright in the saddle, lost it. "Shut them up! They are driving me crazy!" He charged his horse towards the trees hoping to scare the birds off. Not only did they not fly away, but directed all their attention towards him instead. A magpie and a jay left the safety of their perch and swooped down upon him, missing his head by inches. For the rest of the day, the beleaguered troop enjoyed the company of the multitude of screeching and scolding fine feathered friends, flitting from tree to tree, taunting them.

Michael George and Nathaniel Brimsby were a couple of miles ahead of the slower moving troop. On two occasions, they found a game trail crossing the main path. They followed the first such path several hundred yards into the bush where, in a sunny opening, they saw a doe and her fawn browsing on willow buds. Nathaniel dismounted and was in position, ready to fire, when a loud snapping noise startled the deer and they bounded off into the cover of the trees.

Michael, still mounted, searched the area in a full circle. He didn't see anything, especially something large enough to have snapped a twig loud enough to scare the deer off. Nathaniel was scanning the area surrounding the small clearing. He saw nothing, as well and when his eyes met Michael's, they each noticed the other's expression of bewilderment.

"What do think it was?" asked Nathaniel.

"I didn't see a thing," replied Michael.

"Neither did I, but that's not what I asked you. I want to know what you think it was," snapped Brimsby.

Michael hesitated before answering. He wasn't trying to deceive Brimsby. He really wasn't sure what it might be. His senses told him he should have caught sight of something big enough to snap a large twig. He also had an uneasy feeling in the pit of his gut. He couldn't put his finger on it, but he felt apprehensive, as if he was being watched. "I really don't know. If I had to guess, I would say it was a moose. We may have startled it and a moose on the run can make a loud noise."

"Why didn't we see it?" continued Brimsby.

"Exactly where the sound comes from can fool you sometimes. Who knows where the moose was. Could have been out of our sight to begin with," explained Michael. Nathaniel seemed satisfied with Michael's theory, but he also felt an unexplainable sense of unease.

An hour or so later they came across another well worn path and decided to follow it. They were barely on the game trail when Michael spotted some movement in the trees a short distance ahead. He halted his horse and signalled Brimsby to approach and when Nathaniel was abreast, Michael pointed down the trail. A large Whitetail buck was ambling down the path. It would walk a few steps, nibble at something on the ground, lift its head, look all about, sniff the air, and then repeat the whole process.

Michael and Nathaniel dismounted and began to sneak up on the stag. Again, as Nathaniel was about to shoot, a very loud wolf howl startled the deer and it was gone in a flash.

Nathaniel stood and faced Michael. His first thought was that Michael had made the howl, but the thought quickly dissipated when he saw Michael was as surprised as he was.

Nathaniel opened his arms in a what-the-hell gesture and asked Michael, "What is going on?"

"It seems someone or something, doesn't want us to be successful," concluded Michael.

Nathaniel couldn't wrap his mind around the idea. "I think it's a coincidence. Let's move on."

Back on the main trail, Michael tried to be encouraging to the disappointed Nathaniel, when he said, "Don't worry. We will find other game."

As if in answer, a pair of ravens cawed overhead. Michael and Nathaniel watched as the ravens flew to the top of a tall spruce tree a short distance ahead and began to squawk in unison. As the hunters made their way down the trail, the ravens would take flight and land on another tree a short distance ahead of them and begin their guttural caws once more.

It was well into the afternoon and it appeared the ravens were not going to let up with the game they were playing. Nathaniel stopped his horse and said, "This is useless. We are not going to see any game with these two following us every step of the way."

"What do you want to do?" asked Michael.

"Go back, I guess."

"Whitney won't be pleased if we come back empty handed," argued Michael.

"I ain't afraid of him," retorted Nathaniel. "We'll explain what happened."

"You're the boss," said Michael.

Nathaniel detected a hint of condescendence in Michael's tone. "Well, what do you suggest we do?" he asked.

"I would simply tell him we didn't see anything. I wouldn't tell him the rest," said Michael.

Nathaniel looked at Michael with scepticism. "Why not?" he asked.

"Whitney doesn't like failure, but I think he likes excuses even less," replied Michael.

"What do you make of what is going on?" asked Nathaniel, as if he expected Michael to have some understanding he lacked.

"What do you mean?" asked Michael, wanting more specifics.

"You know, the gambler killing the preacher and then running off like a madman and Luke Briscoe beating the kid half to death. That ain't natural." He stopped to catch his breath and to let Michael digest what he was saying and then continued, "What is with all this spook stuff; creatures running around the camp all night, everyone having nightmares, and these damn ravens following us all day? It's like they are doing it on purpose, trying to scare off any game we might find."

Michael mentally sorted through all of Brimsby's questions. He couldn't decide whether to offer his theories or to play dumb. He replied, "I don't know. Perhaps, it's the spirits of the dead people from the village."

Brimsby seemed annoyed with the answer. This was the first time in years he'd opened up to anyone and he was expecting Michael to share his thoughts on all he had mentioned, but instead all he got was some comment about ghosts.

"That's all you got to say?" he asked with annoyance.

"That is all I have to say," was Michael's curt reply.

After Michael suggested they ride ahead and find a good camp spot for the night, they rode for another couple of hours in silence, save for the incessant squawking of their two tag-alongs. They did not spot any game. In fact, there were no sounds at all, no scolding squirrels, no birdsong to be heard.

Late afternoon found them descending into a willow covered meadow with a wide spring-fed creek cutting a winding path through the middle of it. At the far end of the meadow, near the tree line, the land rose to form a small plateau shaded by several large old growth pines. They both thought it was a good spot to set up camp for the night.

A few hours later, when Nathaniel showed him the site, Whitney agreed with their assessment. Silas Davidson and Harold Grant took care of the stock by striping them of saddles, blankets and packs and then tying them to a tether line they set up at the back of the grove. They gathered firewood, of which there was an abundance, and got a fire going in short time. Harold complained he didn't see the point of going to the trouble of maintaining a fire, if there was nothing to cook. Silas told him they would need the fire for warmth later. When Harold continued his badgering by asking why they didn't build the fire later, Silas simply tuned him out and continued on about his business.

Collin Pilkington was tending to Luke Briscoe's wounds with Mathew standing watch over his shoulder. As Collin pulled back the puss filled bandages, he looked up at Mathew and remarked almost smugly how the old Medicine Man was right and the poultices were very effective in drawing out the infection. Collin asked Mathew to find more of the black lichen and moss for new poultices. Mathew gave a great '*hrrummmpf*' as he rose and set about reluctantly on his appointed task.

"How's she lookin', Doc?" asked Luke.

"Unfortunately, it looks like you'll live," Collin uttered before thinking.

Luke turned to Collin with a look of anger and confusion, "You got no call to say that!"

Collin rose to a standing position and said with bitterness, "Oh, don't I? You just beat a kid to death, so excuse me if I don't have a charming bedside manner."

Luke didn't have a clue what he was alluding to, but he knew Collin was unhappy with him because of what he had done to Sean McClaren. In his defence, he retorted, "I didn't kill the kid, the boss done that."

Using Luke's own words, Collin answered, "The *boss* put the kid out of his misery. As far as I'm concerned, you killed him."

Luke couldn't think of anything else to say, so he spat out, "You go to hell!"

Collin replied, "I am convinced that is where we are all headed." He paused and then added, "You can nurse yourself or get your murdering brother to do it. I am done with you."

Collin turned his back to Luke and began walking towards the fire. Luke got to his feet with the intention of charging Collin, but when Oakley said, "Don't even think about it, Hillbilly," he stopped dead in his tracks and turned to face Oakley, who stood a few paces away with both barrels of the shotgun cocked.

The two men stood and stared at each other for the longest time. Luke finally broke the tension when he relaxed and said, "To hell with both of you," as he turned and walked away.

Michael sat down next to Dancing Crow, who had found a comfortable spot to sit with a big log to lean his back against and a panoramic view of the meadow. "How goes it, old one?" Michael asked, meaning no disrespect.

"Not so old I can not put you in your place," replied Dancing Crow. When he saw that Michael felt guilty for the remark, he softened his tone and said with a smile, "It goes well. And for you?"

Michael told Dancing Crow about the strange noises that frightened away the game and the two ravens continuously harassing them. The old man told Michael about the occurrence of the birds pestering the troop all day long.

Michael asked, "What does it mean?"

"There is more to come for these evil ones," was the only explanation Dancing Crow offered.

Michael wasn't finished. "Does this include me?" he asked with a hint of defiance in his tone.

Dancing Crow stared into Michael's eyes for a moment and then answered, "Only you can decide your fate, my son."

Michael was getting frustrated. "Can't you answer my question directly?"

Dancing Crow was growing fond of young Michael, so he relented, "You must show the spirits you are not with these men. You can not stand on the hillside and watch the battle. You must choose a side and I hope for your sake you choose wisely."

Michael's feelings were hurt. He was sure he had shown Dancing Crow he was not the same as these men. He thought Dancing Crow should have seen he'd already made his choice and he expressed these thoughts to the old Medicine Man.

"It is true, you have chosen to be my protector, but should the time come, you must decide for the good of our people, or they will not know you from the others," was Dancing Crow's final word on the subject.

Whitney was in a heated discussion with Brimsby about his failure to come back with any game. Brimsby, contrary to Michael's advice, gave Whitney all the details of their strange day, hoping to pacify Whitney, but the information seemed to irritate him even more.

"Mr. Oakley and Mr. Briscoe didn't have any trouble finding game. I think, tomorrow, they might have better luck," said Whitney with a sense of finality.

Just as Whitney finished his statement, the Briscoe brothers approached. They stopped short, not wanting to be rude. Whitney noticed the gesture and looking at Nathaniel he said, "Mr. Brimsby and I have concluded our business. What can I do for you, Mr. Briscoe?"

Mathew Briscoe came right to the point, "Me and Luke don't like it. No Sir, we don't like it."

"What is it you don't like?" asked Whitney impatiently.

"Oakley is armed and we ain't. We don't trust him. We think he is waiting for a chance to kill us."

"And what do you think the solution might be?" asked Whitney.

Mathew didn't expect Whitney to ask him for any answers and then an idea came to mind. His face lit up and he said with excitement and expectation in his voice, "You still got two pistols and the shotgun. Could you give us one?"

"That is not an option," replied Whitney.

Briscoe thought a moment before answering, "Then, could you take away Oakley's shotgun?"

"I don't see the need to change the status quo," continued Whitney.

Briscoe wasn't sure what he meant, but he was sure it was a refusal. He stood in silence not sure of what to say next when Whitney added, "Oakley keeps the shotgun. Maybe *you* should sleep with one eye open."

As they walked away, Luke asked Mathew, "Doesn't he like us anymore, Mathew?"

Mathew answered, "I don't think he ever did, little brother. I don't think he ever did."

With no anticipation of an evening meal, the men sat scattered about the small plateau in sullen silence. No one talked to anyone else. They each sat wrapped up in their own thoughts, which in every case centered on what was happening to them. What started out as a bold adventure full of excitement and promise of riches beyond their imagination had deteriorated to the trek from hell. Men were dying, if not murdered by their travelling companions, then torn to pieces by the wildlife. Then there were the strange sounds and some dark entity terrorizing them all night and what about the very odd behaviour of the birds all day.

Whitney stood leaning against one of the large pines. He let his eyes drift from man to man. What he saw did not please him. The troop was falling apart and he still needed most of them to get to where he was going. Time for some action. He stepped away from the tree and shouted, "Front and center, all of you. On the double."

The men were all gathered in a matter of minutes, anxious to hear what Whitney was going to say. Whitney spoke softly and slowly for emphasis, "I can see our morale is a little low. Well, snap out of it, all of you. We still have a job to do. Let us stay focused and never mind all this other bullshit. There are no spooks or goblins. Mr. Morgan was always out of his head. Mr. Murdock was a greedy bastard. He went insane with rage when the preacher stole the necklace from him. Later, he felt so guilty about killing the pathetic parson, he snapped and ran off. Nothing supernatural about it.

"Luke Briscoe beat young Mr. McClaren because that's how he is. He didn't mean to hurt the boy so badly and Mr. Oakley only shot him to save the boy's life. Mr. Guetch strayed too far from camp and happened to stumble into the path of a hungry grizzly. That's all!" He made eye contact with Frank Oakley. Something told Oakley it would be very unhealthy to contradict Whitney at this time.

Whitney continued, "The birds today probably have never seen a human being before. That's what birds do. They chatter and squawk with the intent of driving us out of their territory. This thing, disturbing us at night, is nothing more than a lone wolf hanging about looking for scraps. Nothing to fear at all."

With the statement, a deep throated, mocking laughter filled the air. Whitney reacted with lighting speed. Pulling one of his pistols, he turned and charged in the direction of the sound, which seemed to emanate from the thicker trees at the back of the plateau. As Whitney sprinted towards what he surmised was the source of the laughter, the trees became smaller and thicker and interspaced with willow clumps, making it very difficult to manoeuvre. Several feet into the dense brush, the land suddenly dipped, forming a deep gully filled with thick underbrush. Whitney made his way down the sloping embankment and onto the soggy, swamp-like ground covering the bottom of the ravine. He searched for twenty or thirty feet in each direction, assured he would see deep footprints in the muskeg and mud. He didn't see a thing.

He stood with his hands on his hips, desperately trying to find a rational reason that made sense. He believed he should have caught up with whoever had mocked him. He envisioned dragging the culprit beaten and bleeding, back to the men to show them there was nothing to be afraid of, but here he stood empty handed and not a sign anywhere of anything or anyone having come this way.

A rustling of the willows on the top of the embankment drew his attention. He cocked his pistol and took aim. The sight of Frank Oakley sent a wave of relief through him.

"Did you see what it was?" asked Oakley.

"No — uh, yes. I caught a glimpse of him running down the gully. He's long gone," Whitney lied. He wanted to have the men thinking it was something human, probably someone from the village and not some spectre they needed to fear.

Whitney made his way back to the camp area, where the men waited anxiously to hear what he had discovered. "I saw the back end of some heathen running through the brush. Now that we know he is around, I don't believe he will trouble us any more," Whitney stated like it was a matter of fact.

Dancing Crow said to Michael, "He does not tell the truth."

Michael wanted to ask the old man how he could possibly know, but something told him it didn't matter.

As night fell, the temperature dropped rapidly. By midnight it was cool enough, so most of the men gathered closer to the roaring fire, which Silas and Harold kept going. It was a clear night, not a cloud in the sky. As Collin Pilkington lay on his back gazing up at the star filled heavens, he felt very insignificant in the vastness of the universe he saw before him. Here was a study in contradiction; anyone who took the time to look up into the night sky and see the marvel that was the universe had to believe God did exist, but if the same person had witnessed the slaughter in the village and some of the events that had taken place in the troop lately, they would surely conclude God did not exist, or if he did, then he really didn't give a damn.

The snorting and neighing of the horses and the braying of the mules caught Mathew Briscoe's attention. He rose up from his comfortable spot near the fire and letting his eyes adjust, he searched the area for Whitney, who was in the same spot he was hours ago, sitting on a log about ten yards or so to the right of the fire. He usually didn't like to mingle with the men, saying he needed time alone to think. Mathew approached him and mentioned the stock was restless and something might be bothering them.

"Well, Mr. Briscoe, go and have a look then," Whitney suggested.

Mathew hesitated and said sheepishly, "But I don't have no weapon anymore. Run out of bullets."

"We can't have that, now can we?" remarked Whitney snidely, as he tossed Mathew his shotgun.

Mathew thanked him and set off on a run to the rear of the camp, where the horses and mules were tethered. As he approached the animals, he could see they were fussing about something. He walked down one side of the line and back up the other, looking carefully for any signs of cut rope or untied lines. Seeing nothing out of place, he expanded his search to several yards in each direction on each side of the stock. Again, he saw nothing. He was about to conclude the animals had probably caught the odour of some passing deer or something and it was really nothing at all, when a low guttural growl from behind a willow clump told him otherwise. He walked slowly toward the bush, stopped a few feet in front of it, and fired both barrels of the shotgun in the direction of the noise.

A feeling of satisfaction quickly changed to one of fear when Mathew heard the growl again and realized he was unarmed. He was about to turn and run when Frank Oakley and Whitney arrived on the scene. Mathew quickly filled them in on what had happened.

Whitney started towards the willow clump pointed out by Mathew. As he drew one of his pistols, he heard a growl. Unlike Briscoe, he didn't fire. Instead, he approached cautiously. As soon as he was up to the willow clump, he cocked the pistol and pointed it, ready to fire at the slightest movement. With his left hand he slowly parted the willow branches to see what may lie behind. There was nothing! Although he didn't see anything, he fired two shots in rapid succession in the general direction of where one might have suspected the creature to run.

"What was it, boss? What'd ya see?' asked Mathew.

"A big black wolf. He was running pretty fast. I don't think we will see him again," lied Whitney. "But in case there is a slight chance I may be wrong, we will post a guard over the stock."

He took the two remaining shotgun shells from his pants pocket and handed them to Mathew. "Don't waste them. That's all there is. Mr. Briscoe, you take the first two hours. Mr. Oakley will relieve you for two hours and Mr. Brimsby will take the last two hours or until dawn, whichever comes first." He paused to look for any disagreement with his orders and then continued, "For God sake, don't shoot at shadows. Unless the thing is at your throat, hold your fire. Mr. Brimsby, when your turn comes trade the Spencer for Mr. Oakley's shotgun. I am sure you will find it much more effective at close range."

He turned to see most of the other members of the troop gathered around, curious to know what was happening. Whitney addressed them, "Just a wolf bothering the stock. He's gone now. Get some sleep. We head out at dawn."

-2-

While most of the men were finding it difficult to fall asleep, Luke Briscoe didn't let the events of the day trouble him. He didn't dwell on possibilities. He was curious about what had spooked the animals, but when Whitney said it was a wolf they had scared off and when his brother Mathew told him to not to worry about it, he put it out of his mind. The only things bothering him were his sore butt and shoulder and how hungry he was, but he soon forgot his pain and discomfort and drifted off to sleep.

He found himself back in the village, reliving the scene where he savagely molested the young girl. As he did in the waking world, he dragged her into the lodge, beat her into submission, tore her garments off, and prepared to mount her. As he looked down into her face, he gasped in shock, for it was not the face of a young native girl, but Elizabeth, complete with blue eyes, freckles, and rusty red hair.

She was crying and with a bewildered look on her face, she said, "Why are you doing this to me, Luke? Why?"

He leapt to his feet, pulled up his pants, and buttoned his fly, at the same time apologizing to Elizabeth. When he looked back down at her, she had changed back to the native girl, who looked up and spat at him, cursing him all the while. Luke stood, taking it all in. His confusion quickly turned to anger when she called him a dummy. He never stopped to consider how the girl could have possibly cursed him out in English as he bent over and backhanded her hard, then straddled her and pinned her arms with his knees. He was not interested in carnal pleasures this time. He was going to teach this bitch a lesson she would never forget. He pulled back his fist, prepared to deliver a devastating blow. The girl's face changed to Sean McClaren's, who pleaded with him, "Please, Mr. Briscoe, you killed me once. For God's sake, leave me alone. Let me rest in peace."

Luke sprang to his feet, stumbling backwards with his fist still cocked and ready to deliver a blow. He couldn't keep his balance and fell over on his back. Before he could react, he found himself pinned to the ground, with Elizabeth holding down one arm, Sean kneeling on the other, and the native girl sitting on his chest.

No matter how hard he struggled, even with his great strength, he could not move. Luke looked up to see the native girl holding a knife. With her free hand, she pulled back his shirt and exposed his shoulder wound. She stuck the point of the knife deep into the wound and began to twist it. Luke never felt such pain in his life. He woke up screaming.

Chapter 13 – Luke's Pain

The magnificent mountain sunrise was wasted on the troop. Not a soul, with the exception of Dancing Crow, could have cared less about the blend of oranges, pinks, and purples, changing from dark shades to brilliant hues as the rising suns ray's back-lit the clouds in the eastern sky.

The men were all thankful the night was over. The previous day's events had them rattled. While Whitney's explanations seemed to carry a message of sensibility about the birds, the laughter, and the growling noises, there still lingered a small nagging doubt in most of their minds that it could be something else.

Silas Davidson seemed to be lost without a meal to prepare. With Collin's help, he rebuilt a large fire which was unnecessary since it was already quite warm. Like Silas, many of the men needed to be doing something, so they gathered around the fire under the pretence they needed the warmth. No one talked to anyone else and anyone could see they were all on edge, milling about, waiting for something to happen.

Mathew Briscoe didn't sleep a wink all night. His turn on guard duty was the longest two hours of his life. The horses were constantly restless. They sensed the presence of something in the bushes, as did Mathew. Every so often, he could hear the familiar low growl and on several occasions he was convinced he saw something dark whiz past him. It didn't appear to be moving in any conventional sense such as walking or running, but rather it seemed to zip by. He felt extremely relieved when Frank Oakley came to take his turn at guard duty.

Mathew didn't bed down. He sat with his back to a pine tree, listening and thinking. Two hours later when Nathaniel Brimsby replaced Frank Oakley, he was still wide awake and when Oakley walked past, he spoke up, "Hey, you got a minute?"

Oakley stopped, turned, and walked the few steps back to Briscoe's position. "Sure. What can I do for you?" he asked.

Mathew got right to the point, "Did you see or hear anything out there?"

Oakley thought for a moment before answering, "Nothing out of the ordinary. Some animal in the bush growling once in a while."

"Did you see anything?" asked Mathew.

Oakley thought he would have some fun. He raised his arms over his head, walked zombie like, contorted his face, and made wailing sounds. He stopped directly in front of Mathew and said, "You mean like ghosties?" He added one more moan for emphasis and walked away laughing.

Mathew felt the strongest urge to cut Oakley in half with the shotgun, but he settled for a "*go to hell*".

An hour before dawn, Luke Briscoe woke up screaming in agony. Collin Pilkington and Mathew Briscoe came to his aid almost simultaneously. Collin's intent was to check his physical condition and Mathew came out of concern. Luke looked like a frightened little boy, convinced there were monsters in his bedroom closet. Mathew played the role of comforting father and holding his brother around the shoulders, he gave him a firm hug, inducing a painful scream from Luke.

"Let me have a look at his wound," suggested Collin.

Luke insisted it hurt too much and he didn't want anyone touching it. Mathew convinced him Collin wasn't going to make it any worse, but in fact he might know how to make it better. Collin pulled back Luke's shirt and removed the bandage from the front shoulder injury. To Collin the wound looked fine. It was still somewhat inflamed, but greatly improved since yesterday. There was nothing there to indicate why Luke should be in so much pain.

Collin passed on his observations to Mathew. Luke immediately interjected, "But Mathew, it hurts so bad. She stuck a knife in it and twisted."

"Who did?" asked Mathew

"That Indian lady I had pecker fun with. But Mathew that's not all. Elizabeth and the boy I beat up — they was holdin' me down while the Indian lady stuck me with the knife."

Mathew lifted Luke's head, so they were making eye contact and said, "It was a bad dream, Luke. Just a bad dream, is all."

"Then why does it still hurt so much, Mathew? Why?"

Mathew didn't have an answer for his younger brother and his half hearted, "*just try not to think about it*," didn't help.

Luke's cries of anguish woke the entire camp, not that anybody was sleeping too soundly. As soon as Collin Pilkington checked the injury and informed Mathew he didn't see anything wrong, he redressed the wound and left. As Collin walked by, Whitney stopped him and inquired as to what the problem might be. Collin explained he had checked Luke Briscoe's shoulder and it was doing well. He added Luke had a bad dream, but he could see no reason for the intense pain the big man was suffering.

Whitney made his way toward Luke and Mathew through the milling men. He noticed Nathaniel Brimsby at the far edge of the crowd. "Aren't you supposed to be on guard duty?" Whitney asked.

Nathaniel immediately turned and headed back to his post. Whitney confronted Mathew, who was still trying to comfort his brother. "What the hell is wrong with him?" asked Whitney in a demanding tone.

"Says his shoulder hurts some awful," was Mathew's curt answer.

"Mr. Pilkington has informed me he can see no reason for the pain. What do you make of that?" asked Whitney.

"I don't know, boss. He woke up screamin'. Says he had a bad dream about somebody stickin' a knife in the wound," replied Mathew.

The discussion was broken up by a loud wailing noise coming from one of the men who had thrown a blanket over his head and was doing his interpretation of a ghost. While the onlookers began to laugh, Whitney didn't find it so amusing. He had the bullwhip in his hand and snapped it over the ghost's head, barely missing. His second attempt caught the blanketed spectre in the chest. There was a high pitched yelp and the blanket came flying off, revealing Harold Grant.

"What did you do that for? I was just having some fun. Oakley says the hillbillies is seeing spooks. I was just joking," explained Grant.

The expression on Whitney's face was all business. He gave Harold Grant a dirty look and then glared at Frank Oakley, who shrugged his shoulders and said apologetically, "Sorry, Mr. Whitney. Won't happen again."

Luke Briscoe's blood curdling scream brought all the attention back to him. "Make her stop, Mathew! Make her stop! It hurts so much," Luke pleaded through tears of pain.

Whitney closed the distance between himself and the Briscoe brothers in a couple of his long strides. He stood over them in a command position with his legs apart and his hands on his hips. "Mr. Briscoe, what is this fool going on about?"

Mathew took offence and it showed when he said, "My brother is a tough man and if he says he's in pain, then he's in pain."

"I was alluding to his ramblings about some she-male sticking him," said Whitney.

Mathew softened his tone, "He had a real bad dream. He was seein' this girl he knew as a boy and the Sean kid. They was holdin' him down while some Indian squaw was stickin' a knife in his shoulder wound."

Luke started in again. "Awwwwwhhhh, it hurts! It hurts!"

The men, who were amused by the antics a short time ago, were now more sullen and quiet. Silas Davidson spoke up, "There have been some very peculiar events taking place lately." It was a casual, matter-of-fact observation. Silas didn't mean anything by it and he certainly didn't expect the wrath of Whitney, who in a blind rage rushed at Silas and wrapped the bullwhip several times around his throat. He moved his hands down each side of the whip, so his grip was closer to Silas's throat, and then using both hands, he pulled in opposite directions. The result choked Silas and he buckled to his knees, grasping at the whip with both hands, trying desperately to loosen its grip.

Just before Silas passed out, Whitney let go of the whip and turned his wrath to Luke Briscoe. He knocked Mathew aside and grasping a handful of Luke's shirtfront in each hand, he brought Luke's face close to his own. He said with malicious intent, "Pull yourself together, you big baby. There's nothing wrong with your shoulder. It is all in your empty head." He emphasized the last part of the statement with a very hard rap of his knuckles on Luke's forehead.

Whitney was so absorbed in his chiding of Luke Briscoe he didn't notice Mathew get to his feet, take several paces backwards, lift his shotgun, and cock both hammers. Mathew shouted, "You leave him be!"

Whitney took his hands off Luke and stood up to face Mathew. He smiled and said very calmly, in a fatherly tone, "Now, Mr. Briscoe think about what you are doing. Put the hammers down on the scattergun and stop pointing it at me."

"I ain't gonna let you kill Luke," replied Mathew.

"Kill him? What made you think I was going to kill him?"

Mathew couldn't think of a good answer, so he just said, "Well — it sure looked like you was gonna kill him."

Whitney shook his head back and forth several times. With a big grin on his face he said, "Mathew, Mathew, don't you see the pain your brother is experiencing is all in his head? If he realizes it, the pain will stop. I was trying to make him see that."

Whitney waited for Mathew to digest what he'd said and then he continued, "You and your brother are very important to the success of this venture and I need you both in top form."

Mathew bought it. He gently let the hammers down on the shotgun and then lowered the weapon. Whitney drew his pistol, cocked the hammer, and took aim at Mathew's head. He said, "Mr. Briscoe, kindly set the shotgun on the ground, gently. If you show me any indication you have other intentions, I will kill you where you stand and then I will put this whining sibling of yours in your grave to keep you company."

Mathew didn't hesitate. He lowered the shotgun, butt first, onto the ground. Whitney ordered the nearest man to Mathew to pick up the scattergun and bring it to him. With the weapon in his hands, Whitney uncocked his pistol and put it back in his waistband. It was then he noticed Frank Oakley had taken up a position immediately to his left. Oakley's shotgun was cocked and levelled at Mathew Briscoe. Whitney was feeling good about having talked Briscoe into giving up, but when he saw Oakley, he wasn't so sure Briscoe hadn't surrendered because he knew he was outnumbered.

"Thank you for your support, Mr. Oakley. I appreciate the gesture, but I could have handled the situation myself." Whitney was really thankful for Oakley's backing, but he couldn't show any vulnerability.

"Anytime, Boss," was all Oakley said.

Whitney made a crucial decision. He told every one to gather closer, which included a loud shout to Brimsby. Once everyone was in place, he began, "Gentlemen, we have come to a crossroads in our venture. We are about half way to our goal and it appears some bad luck has befallen us. I have not faltered in my desire to push on with my quest to find the gold mine. There have been many obstacles thrown in our path. Life is full of obstacles, real or imagined and we have to fight through them. We cannot let them detract us from our objective or we will never reach it.

"I want each and every one of you to look inside yourself and decide if you want to continue on with me, or go back to civilization and try and make it down to the coast without being apprehended or massacred by heathens.

"If you choose to continue with me, there will be a new resolve, a renewed enthusiasm and any man who feels he isn't up to it should leave now. If you choose to leave, you take only the clothes on your back and the mount you are riding and good luck, because you'll need it with the Constables and a lot of angry heathens looking for us."

Whitney looked at a spot a few paces to his left and said, "Anybody who chooses to bid us adieu and miss out on a fortune, step over there."

Whitney studied the men as they absorbed what he had said. He felt if one man, any one of them, had stepped up, a few others would have joined him. It was clear after a few moments nobody was choosing to leave.

"Well, it's settled then," concluded Whitney and then an idea struck him. "Mr. Briscoe, if you would take the big knife of yours and dispatch the orneriest of the mules, Mr. Davidson and his crew can conjure up a breakfast of mule steaks. Mr. Oakley, could you escort the breed to find some of those onions and horseradish?"

This simple gesture elated the men. The thought of food of any kind lifted their spirits. Mathew Briscoe took a large rock and hit one of the mules in the head several times before it went down. He had enough common sense to move the intended victim away from the other mules and horses so as not to disturb them. Nathaniel Brimsby helped Mathew skin and butcher the mule and cutting a hind quarter into pieces suitable for cooking.

By the time Mathew brought the mule meat to Silas, there was a good fire going again. Harold Grant kept bringing wood and Frank Oakley and Michael returned with some wild onion, but they were unsuccessful in finding any horseradish.

-2-

On the trail, the riding order changed. Luke, Mathew, and Frank Oakley usually led the troop with Brimsby, Michael, and Dancing Crow not far behind. Whitney chose to ride between this group in front of him and Silas, Collin, Harold, and the string of mules behind him. Whitney and Oakley, who seemed to have slid into a position as Whitney's right hand man, led the troop followed by Brimsby, Michael, and Dancing Crow and then Silas, Collin, Harold, and the mule string. The Briscoe brothers were delegated, as if by natural selection, to ride at the back of the cavalcade.

The pain in Luke's shoulder would not go away. Every time his horse missed a step, or slid on a rock, the jolt would produce a scream of pain. Mathew felt empathy for his brother, but he was at a loss as how to help him, so he rode in silence, leaving Luke to deal with his burden alone.

They weren't on the trail more than ten minutes when all the pesky birds returned. If one didn't know better, one would swear every time Luke cried out in pain, the birds would all chirp at once and then go silent until Luke screamed again, when once more they would break into a momentary discordant symphony of squawks and shrieks as if they were answering Luke. So it went for nearly two hours. As they rode, the collection of feathered fiends would fly ahead of the troop waiting for them to catch up and every time Luke wailed, the birds would answer.

Mathew reached his tolerance level. He stopped at a spot on the trail where the bank was eroded, exposing a bed of two-inch gravel. He filled his pockets with egg-sized stones and as they rode past the birds, Mathew began throwing the rocks at them, producing the opposite response to what he expected. Instead of flying off in mass, the birds would simply rise in the air when one of the rocks came too close and then settle right back down on the perch they had just left.

When Mathew actually clipped a magpie's tail feathers with a stone, it rose in the air and dove straight at Mathew's head. He ducked or the bird would have hit him. As if in response, the entire flock rose as one and took turns swooping at Mathew, who was beginning to panic, flailing his arms above his head. Luke was so engrossed in his pain he never noticed the aerial attack going on around him. He never felt the occasional peck on his back from one of the bolder ravens.

Dancing Crow turned back to watch the spectacle and remarked to Michael, "It would seem the bird spirits do not like those men."

"Looks like it," remarked Michael, just as casually.

Whitney could see the men were becoming rattled again. He halted the troop and rode back to the Briscoe brothers' position. The birds included Whitney in their aerobatics. He didn't flinch. He sat very still and when a magpie came too close, he reached up with a lightning quick hand and snagged it by its long tail feathers. Just as quickly, he brought up his other hand and with a quick twist, broke the bird's neck.

He rode to the center of the group and when he had everyone's attention, he pulled the knife he had salvaged during their escape and gutted the bird, the entrails and organs spilling out all over his hands. He held the mutilated carcass high in the air so everyone could see it and said, "You see gentlemen, just guts and feathers and a lot of noise. Nothing to fear. Not spooks, just goddamn birds! Now, pull yourselves together and that is an order, damn it!"

After Whitney's outburst, one could see his tactic worked. The men feared his wrath more than they did the bird's antics. As mysteriously as they arrived, the birds disappeared, which should have brought relief to the men, but instead it added to the list of strange events playing with their minds.

Shortly after noon, the terrain began to change. The once wide valley began to narrow as the troop was flanked on both sides by mountains. The trail veered to the north for a couple of miles, closer to the mountain on their right, before turning back in a northwest direction once more. They climbed several hundred feet in elevation and once they were high enough, it became apparent that the trail had shifted direction to go around a large rocky knoll. Down in the valley, far below, they could see the trail followed a creek, which appeared to have its source somewhere to the southwest.

Once on the valley floor, they found a spot with easy access to the stream. Whitney ordered a rest stop to allow men and animals to drink. Since Whitney did not find it necessary to stop for a noon meal, the men had learned to ask Silas to cook extra meat at breakfast, which was wrapped and kept it in their pockets to ease hunger pangs later in the day. Whitney knew what they were doing and he didn't object, since it didn't slow him down.

As the horses and mules drank their fill, Dancing Crow pointed out the grove of serviceberry bushes along the opposite creek bank, laden with ripened fruit. Michael passed the message on to Silas Davidson, who commandeered Collin and Harold to help him harvest some of the berries.

The bushes were thick with fruit and the three men picked the equivalent of a five gallon pail in very little time, filling several coffee sacks, which Silas kept when the coffee ran out. Silas happened to look back across the creek to see Nathaniel Brimsby frantically waving his arms and shouting. Once Nathaniel saw he had someone's attention, he began frantically pointing to the hill above the berry bushes.

Silas had no idea what Brimsby was so excited about until he saw the back side of the bushes rattle and heard the growling. Harold and Collin were already running across the creek. Silas quickly followed suit and made it to the shore and the protection of Brimsby and the Spencer rifle without dropping a single berry. Looking back, Nathaniel pointed out a mother black bear and two cubs, which had come to the berry patch to feast and they didn't like competition.

The rest of the troop gathered around to see what all the shouting was about. Silas passed out the berries to anyone who wanted them, all the time claiming he risked life and limb to supply this treat for them. Surprisingly, Whitney took a couple of handfuls, remarked how tasty they were, and ordered everyone back in the saddle.

For several miles, the trail was sandwiched between the bluffs of the creek on their left and a steep rising mountain slope on their right. The forest on the slope was thick, dark and foreboding, while the trees on their left, between the trail and the bluff, appeared just as impenetrable. Many of the men felt constricted, like the world was closing in on them.

Mathew Briscoe was thinking how nice it was not to have those annoying birds bothering them anymore, when the scream of a mountain lion quickly destroyed any thoughts of tranquility. The big cat's roar frightened the horses and mules. It was all Harold Grant could do to keep hold of the rope tying the string of mules together. The cat screamed again, agitating the stock even more. Collin Pilkington came to the aid of Harold Grant and they both managed to keep the mules from bolting.

Once the horses were settled, the men began to look around in all directions, trying to ascertain where the sound may have come from. As their eyes searched the trail ahead and behind and as far as they could see into the dense trees on either side, the cat screamed twice in succession. The stock, soothed by the men, showed little reaction. No one seemed to know where the sound was coming from. Some said it was to the left, some to the right, but no one could really pinpoint it.

Dancing Crow, forgetting Nathaniel Brimsby understood his language somewhat, said to Michael, "The spirit of the cat moves very fast."

Nathaniel heard this and asked, as he cocked the hammer on the Spencer, "You know where this thing is? Show me."

Dancing Crow recovered quickly and answered, "I do not know where he is. I said he moves quickly"

Brimsby turned and hollered, "Mr. Whitney, come quick."

Whitney made his way back to Nathaniel and waited while he spoke, "The old man knows something about this cat."

"Pray tell, Mr. Brimsby, what might that be?" asked Whitney.

"I think he knows where the cat is," replied Brimsby.

Michael jumped into the conversation, taking the focus off Dancing Crow, "That's not what the old man said. Brimsby thinks he understands the language, but he only knows a few words and he misinterprets what he hears. Dancing Crow said the sounds of the cat seem to be coming from everywhere and he found it strange, as all of us seem to."

As if to support Michael's statement, the cat roared again. The sound seemed to be somewhere to their right. Several seconds later, another roar seemed to come from their left followed by a third one that seemed to come from behind them.

Harold Grant shouted, "Jesus Christ, how many of them are there?"

Whitney could see the panic in the men and their mounts. "Stay calm! If you panic, your horse will feel it and panic too. Keep it together!" he shouted and then he turned back to Michael. "Dismount and get the old heathen down."

Michael got off his horse and told Dancing Crow to do the same. When they were on the ground, Whitney dismounted and handing his reins to Brimsby, he pulled his pistol and approached Michael and Dancing Crow. When he looked into Michaels eyes, Michael knew Whitney meant business when he said, "Mr. George, I am certain the old heathen knows what is going on here. I am convinced he knows what or who has been plaguing us since we left the goddamn heathen village. In fact, I believe he may be a part of it all."

Whitney stood waiting for Michael to translate. Michael did not show any indication he was about to do so. "What are you waiting for, Breed. Tell him," ordered Whitney.

Hesitantly, Michael told Dancing Crow what Whitney said. He emphasized the part about Whitney thinking he may be a part of it. When Michael was finished, Whitney turned to Brimsby and asked if Michael had translated correctly. Brimsby replied that to the best of his limited knowledge, Michael had.

Dancing Crow said to Michael, "Tell the Evil One the hunters have caught up to us. Tell him it is the hunters doing these things."

Michael translated for Whitney, who spat back in anger, "Horseshit! No goddamn hunters can get inside peoples heads." He realized the men were listening and he greatly regretted what he said.

Whitney took a deep breath and regained his composure. "Luke Briscoe, is seeing things. Now, it could be the fever, but we all are hearing things, too." He turned back to Michael and said, "You tell the heathen bastard I am going to keep a close eye on him and if I think for one moment he is behind this horseshit, it will be his last moment on this earth!"

Michael said to Dancing Crow, "He is very angry and he thinks you have something to do with what has happened to these white men. He is going to watch you closely, so be careful."

Dancing Crow answered almost indignantly, "Does he truly believe a man can scream like a mountain lion? Does he truly believe I have some magical powers? If I had these powers, I would have vanished in a cloud of smoke before his very eyes, long before today."

Michael debated internally whether to tell Whitney exactly what Dancing Crow said and incur further wrath. He decided to translate verbatim.

Whitney seemed to be deep in thought for the longest time before he said, "Makes sense."

Brimsby was taken aback. He said in disbelief, "You're not buying this load of horse manure, are you?"

Whitney sighed and then spoke, "I usually don't explain myself to the likes of you, Mr. Brimsby, but in this case, I'll make an exception. Like everyone else here, I don't know what has precipitated these strange occurrences that have beset us. Unable to explain them in a rational sense, I looked to the irrational, the supernatural, so to speak. The old heathen convinced me he is not involved. He makes sense. He is a very old man. Why would he endure all this hardship if he didn't have to?"

"If you ask me, I think he is the one doing it. I don't know how, but I think he is more than he represents," Brimsby replied.

"Mr. Brimsby, you are labouring under the assumption I would care what you think," said Whitney. He stood looking up at Nathaniel for a reaction before mounting his horse and putting his pistol away.

Whitney took his place at the front. As he approached, Frank Oakley asked, "Trouble, Boss?"

"Nothing we can't handle, Mr. Oakley. Nothing at all."

Frank felt a sense of pride when Whitney said "*we*". It meant Whitney trusted him and he felt he was right where he needed to be.

The valley began to widen out and the mountain on their right began to diminish in size. The cat was still near by and every few minutes it would scream from what appeared to be different spots. Most of the men followed Whitney's advice and ignored it.

The wolf howl, which complimented the lion scream, renewed everyone's anxiety. Not long after, they could hear coyotes yipping to one another across the hills. Instead of birds squawking and screeching, now there was a chorus of cat screams, wolf howls, and coyote calls to serenade them as they rode along. Respect for Whitney, which grew out of his handling of the bird situation, turned to resentment. Thoughts that he had taken them from the frying pan to the fire began to unnerve the men again.

-3-

Early evening found the troop crossing a marsh formed by a myriad of beaver dams that were once intact, but were now in various stages of disrepair. At the far end of the boggy area, the terrain rose to a small level meadow covered in lush grasses, the result of the rich sediments left behind when one of the larger beaver dams washed away.

Whitney saw an opportunity to let the animals graze, so he announced this would the place to stop for the night. The creature chorus stopped almost immediately when it became apparent the troop was done riding for the day. Most of the men hardly noticed it. They had put the sounds in the back of their minds and didn't pay any attention to them. After a time, one gets used to it and you hardly know it is there, not unlike a dripping faucet.

Silas and Collin methodically went through the motions of starting the fire and cooking the evening meal of mule meat and wild onions. The men ate with the same level of interest. It was only necessary food, nourishment essential to satisfy their hunger, not particularly enjoyable under the circumstances.

Luke Briscoe didn't eat anything. He was still in excruciating pain. No amount of positive persuasion from Mathew or Collin Pilkington could convince Luke the pain was all in his mind. He continued to cry out, pleading for Mathew to make it stop.

The rest of the men ignored Luke's outbursts. They put them out of their minds as they had with the animal sounds, with the exception of Harold Grant. He wasn't really bothered by Luke's outcries, but he seldom missed an opportunity to make himself look better in the eyes of others.

Mathew had taken Luke to the back of the immediate camp area and leaned him up against the trunk of a fallen tree. He went down to the water's edge to wet a cloth in the hope the coolness would sooth Luke's pain. Collin Pilkington was engrossed in rewrapping Luke's shoulder wounds and the one on his posterior, when Harold approached. He stood several feet away, with hands on his hips, turned his head slightly back in the direction of the camp, and said loud enough for everyone to hear, "Can't you shut the big baby up?"

Collin looked up and after assessing the situation for what it was, replied, "Oh, go bother someone else. Your bully tactics are not appreciated at the moment. Can't you see this man is suffering?"

"All I see is a big baby annoying the rest of us with his constant whining and we would all be thankful it if you could shut him up," countered Harold, looking around to see if he had attracted an audience. He had not; the men could have cared less.

Harold increased his volume. "If you can't shut him up then take him far enough back so we don't have to listen to him."

Collin continued his work, oblivious to Harold's prodding. Harold was about to start in again when Mathew came up beside him and demanded to know what the problem was.

Harold was taken by surprise. He didn't expect Mathew back so soon. Collin looked up at Mathew and said, "This imbecile thinks we should endeavour to keep Luke quiet. It appears he is bothered by your brother's outbursts."

Mathew stepped in front of Harold, so they were face to face and asked, "Why don't you take your miserable self back with the rest of the washer women and leave real men be."

By this time most of the men were interested in what was transpiring. Harold noticed this and he couldn't back down. "Real men? I never heard no *real* man snivelling about a little bullet hole, like your idiot brother," he said.

Mathew took an angry swing at Harold, who anticipated such a move and ducked back and away from the punch. Missing surprised Mathew, somewhat. He withdrew the big knife from his waistband and began tossing it from hand to hand while circling Harold.

"You can't even fight fair, can you?" Harold said. "You can't beat a little fella like me without a big knife or gun in your hand. You are pathetic. You are a bigger baby than your brother."

Harold was a very good bluffer in a game of five card draw. He won countless pots with absolutely nothing in his hand. He tried to apply the same tactic in this situation, as he turned his back on Mathew and began to walk away.

Briscoe called his bluff. He caught up to Harold, put his hand on Harold's shoulder, spun him around and said, "Don't you walk away from me you coward," as he swung the blade at Harold's face leaving a long but superficial gash down his left cheek.

Harold put his hand to his face to check the damage and said, "I ain't no coward. I'll fight you on the up and up, if you get rid of the knife."

Mathew Briscoe was not an ethical man. He would have just as soon cut Grant to ribbons, but in the gathering crowd he saw Frank Oakley armed with a shotgun and fearing he might get back shot, he relented and threw the knife, so it landed near his brother. "Alright then, you son-of-a-bitch, let's have at 'er," he said to Harold.

Harold Grant was of average build and height. Mathew Briscoe was about the same size but, unlike Harold, he was well muscled and solidly built from years of hard labour. Nonetheless, Harold gave a good accounting of himself. For a short time, he avoided Briscoe's wild swings and lunges with quick reflexes and fast feet, while landing a few good punches of his own. Briscoe surmised he was getting the worst of the fight using this tactic and he would have to close in to be effective. He lowered his head and charged Harold, catching him in the midsection and knocking him to the ground.

Briscoe was on top of Grant and using his superior strength to advantage, he pinned Harold's arms with his legs and began raining blows on Harold's face. Harold got a rush of adrenaline brought on by extreme fear and he managed to throw Briscoe off. As he turned over on his hands and knees, he felt an apple sized rock under his right hand. He picked it up and as Mathew charged again, he threw the rock, catching Mathew square in the forehead, stunning him momentarily.

Using the advantage the rock had given him, Harold knocked Mathew to the ground and this time he reversed the tables on Mathew by pinning him down and pounding him mercilessly. Briscoe's survival instincts came to the forefront and with a burst of rage and energy, he threw Harold aside.

Both men were cut, bruised, bleeding, and gasping for every breath through burning lungs. They stood several feet apart, each one waiting for the other to make a move. In the mean time, Silas Davidson had gone to Whitney and asked him to put a stop to the fight. He was met with the usual policy of non-involvement from Whitney, saying if Silas wanted the fight stopped, he was free to do so. Silas did nothing.

Collin Pilkington decided nobody was going to interfere until one of the two combatants was dead. He took matters into his own hands and stepped between Mathew and Harold, trying to talk some sense into them, "Stop this nonsense! Stop it at once!"

Harold appeared grateful someone had stepped in. He had given a good accounting of himself and now he wanted to escape with his life. Mathew read the weakness and said, "Come on, Washerwoman, let's finish this."

Collin directed Mathew's attention to the group of men gathered to watch the battle, particularly Whitney and Oakley, who stood to one side of the group, each cradling a shotgun, and looks of amusement on their faces. "Take a look at your audience," said Collin. "They want you to kill each other. It's entertainment for them. Is that who you are, court jesters playing the fool for the king and his court? Don't give them the satisfaction."

Collin could see Harold wanted a way out and Mathew was beginning to calm down. He continued, "Mathew, your brother needs you. Mr. Grant, you are a creature of the lowest order, a bully who preys on the misfortune of others. I suggest you beat a hasty retreat before I step away and let Mr. Briscoe beat you to death."

Harold Grant took the opportunity to walk away. Collin put his arm on Briscoe's shoulder and took him back to his brother, who hadn't relented any in his cries of agony.

"Wonder what set them two off?" Silas Davidson asked no one in particular.

Whitney chose to answer Silas, "Nerves, Mr. Davidson. Nerves. Everyone is somewhat tense and a little high strung."

"Why do the two white men fight?" asked Dancing Crow, after the altercation.

"I believe the one called Harold is like a coyote pup who likes to provoke his littermates. When he is about to get hurt the mother will step in and stop it and he has gotten what he wanted, his mother's attention."

"You are very wise for such a young pup, yourself," replied Dancing Crow in a sincere complimentary tone. "The one called Harold was fortunate the one called Collin was here to play the mother coyote."

-4-

Nothing changed from the night before. Growls, snarls, and howls still emanated from the outskirts of the camp area. Whitney assigned a guard rotation schedule that included himself, Frank Oakley, and Nathaniel Brimsby in two hour shifts from dusk until dawn. The rest of the men were warned to stay away from the horses and mules because whoever was standing guard was going to shoot at anything that came near.

The fear of being torn apart in their sleep by some unknown denizen, either of this world or some other, had dissipated. The men now considered the creature clatter more of a nuisance than a threat. Falling asleep and revisiting their personal nightmares concerned them more.

Mathew Briscoe was far too exhausted to care. He finished applying the cold cloth to Luke's shoulder and had convinced his younger brother lying quiet would be the best thing for everybody. He empathised with Luke and told him he knew the pain he was going through, but he needed to keep quiet because everyone was getting angry. Luke didn't like people angry with him, so he consciously converted his loud outcries to low whimpers.

Satisfied, he'd done all he could do for Luke, Mathew lay down beside him, fell asleep instantly and began to dream. He found himself back at the native village at the spot where he'd killed the wounded man, using Sean's shotgun. The native with shot-up legs tried to get up. Mathew shot him square in the chest with both barrels. The force of the blast knocked the man flat on his back.

Feeling a sense of relief that he had dispatched a potential nightmare, Mathew relaxed for a moment, only to have terror return once more when the native rose from the ground, with legs and chest a mass of disfigured flesh, oozing crimson. Mathew reloaded and shot the man again, with the same result. The man shouldn't have been able to get up, but he did, mangled worse than before.

Mathew felt he was in a never ending loop. He would shoot the native, who would get up, hence Mathew would reload and shoot him again. Mathew's thinking was if he kept aiming for different spots, he would shred the body so badly that eventually there would nothing left to get up.

He couldn't remember how many times he shot the man only to have him rise again, when he heard laughter coming from behind him. He turned to see Whitney and Oakley standing together, pointing and laughing hysterically at him. Whitney said, "Good lord, Mr. Briscoe! Can't you even kill a heathen. Mr. Oakley, kindly show him how it is done."

Frank Oakley positioned himself beside Mathew and as the ghoulish creature advanced, Frank formed his right hand into an imaginary pistol and using his forefinger for the barrel and his thumb for the hammer, he aimed at the walking corpse and shouted "*bang*". The mangled monster dropped to the ground, never to rise again.

Mathew sat upright, fully awake. He half expected to see Whitney and Oakley standing over him, laughing.

Silas Davidson finally got to sleep near dawn. He wasn't having his usual nightmare where the men in camp humiliated him in one form or another. In the new nightmare, Silas saw Harold Grant badly beaten and dying. Harold was lying on his back between the night fire and a small woodpile. His arms were outstretched and he was pleading for Silas to help him. Silas began to frantically pick up sticks, branches, and deadwood. When he had all he could carry, he rushed back to the fire area where he proceeded to stack it all on top of Harold. Silas continued to gather firewood until there was an enormous pile, under which he could still hear the pleading Harold.

Still in his dream, Silas felt exhausted and he lay down next to the woodpile and fell asleep. In the dream, he awoke because he felt something on his legs. He looked down to see Harold Grant's arms had come out from under the woodpile. His hands had a firm grip on Silas's trouser legs and he was trying to pull Silas under the woodpile.

Silas woke up from the real dream. He still felt pressure on his legs. Looking down, he saw a small creature, standing with its hind legs on his shins and it was digging in the wood pile with its front paws. Silas jumped to his feet, simultaneously grabbing a large pine branch to serve as a club. Without hesitation, he began to hit the creature with full-force, two-handed swings of the stick. The animal stopped moving, but Silas gave it a couple more solid whacks for good measure. He stood up, pleased with himself and wiped his brow with his sleeve.

Michael was first on the scene. Dancing Crow had become chilled and Michael decided to build the fire up and bring the old man closer for some warmth. Silas spotted Michael and began to explain how he killed one of the fearsome creatures that were plaguing them. Michael knelt down and examined the carcass and then explained to Silas that he had vanquished a dreaded beaver.

Silas told Michael how he awoke to find the creature standing on his legs and how he thought the beast was attacking him. Michael explained a beaver is a strict vegetarian and all he was after was some of the wood from the pile, probably for construction purposes.

Whitney was listening the entire time. He chuckled as he walked to the mashed beaver, picked it up and said to Silas, "I hear tell beaver tail is a delicacy. I'll have some for breakfast."

Chapter 14 – Trouble with Beavers

Whitney understood why beaver tail was considered a delicacy after sampling the piece Silas prepared. It was delicious, with a rich texture and taste. Silas had pleaded with Michael to give him some advice on the preparation and cooking of beaver tail. Michael wasn't forthcoming, telling Silas he had never eaten beaver tail and he didn't know anyone who had. Michael concluded it shouldn't be difficult; skin out the tail and cook it like any other piece of meat.

Dancing Crow, out of curiosity, asked Michael what had transpired. Michael told him what he told Silas. Dancing Crow then suggested Michael was telling an untruth and he was sure Michael had, indeed, eaten beaver tail. He chided Michael for exhibiting the same cruelty as the white men. He went on to say one does not skin a beaver tail. The thick scaly hide adheres too tightly to the flesh for skinning to be a good method. The trick used by most beaver tail connoisseurs is to stick a thick green willow branch into the meaty end of the beaver tail and roast it over a fire. As it heats, the hide puffs up and separates from the flesh. After a few minutes, you can simply pull the hide away, leaving you with a pinkish filet, ready for frying or roasting.

Michael, upon Dancing Crow's insistence, reluctantly passed on the valuable information to Silas. The result was a tasty hors d'oeuvre

Whitney truly enjoyed and in Silas's mind had gotten him into the good graces of their maniacal leader. By the time Whitney ate his fill and gave a small sample to Frank Oakley, there wasn't any left for anyone else to try. Whitney suggested to Oakley and Nathaniel Brimsby to keep their eyes open for more beaver, as he would much prefer beaver tail to mule meat for his supper.

As they rode, Whitney felt somewhat contented. Perhaps it was the beaver tail breakfast or perhaps it was because there was no incessant squawking of a myriad of birds or a creature concerto serenading them as they travelled that gave him a feeling all their misfortune was behind them and they could refocus on their goal.

The others weren't bolstered by the lack of noise from the forest residents. In fact, the silence was eerie. Normally, there was always something to be heard as one travelled in the wilderness; the distant cry of an eagle as it rode the thermals, the guttural croaking of a raven as it sat on a tree top watching from its lofty perch, or the nattering of a startled squirrel, that would squeal and run up a tree to scold you as you passed by. Now, there was only the silence, not even a breeze to flutter the leaves on the aspens, or create a hollow whooshing sound as the wind gushed through the evergreen tree tops.

Yesterday, the men would have done anything for some peace and quiet. Today, most of them wanted the racket back. The silence was much harder to deal with. The cavalcade of birds that had followed them and the denizens of the forest harassing them, had them concentrating on the events happening around them. The silence allowed their minds to focus inward, to dwell on their individual nightmares. There were ten men riding together, but each man, with the exception of Dancing Crow, was on an island, alone with his own thoughts, his own demons.

Luke and Mathew Briscoe rode at the rear of the column, nearly thirty feet behind Collin Pilkington and Harold Grant. Mathew could see Luke's infernal whimpering was annoying most of the men. Not that Mathew Briscoe would ever back down from any man, but he felt it best not to antagonize them any further. He did not know how to help his younger brother. In the past he always protected Luke from life's challenges, but the largest part of the job was saving Luke from himself and the trouble he could get into because he didn't have an understanding of the way the world really worked.

Mathew felt helpless, like the time Luke brought home the neighbour's dog. It had run into a pack of coyotes and was considerably torn up. It would have been an act of mercy to put a bullet in the poor thing's head and end it's suffering, but Luke would not have any part of it. He held the bleeding, dying creature in his arms for half the night, until if finally succumbed to its injuries and died.

As they rode, Luke would moan for a few seconds and look up into Mathew's eyes and say, "It hurts, Mathew." He was looking to his older brother to do something about his pain the same way he had expected Mathew to save the dying dog. No amount of coaxing could dissuade young Luke into give up the dog, just as no amount of talk was going to convince him his pain was all in his head and he possessed the power to make it go away.

After a couple of hours on the trail, Collin Pilkington dropped back to ride with Mathew and Luke. He observed Luke was not any better. If anything, it seemed he was getting worse. Collin said, "He's not looking very good. I think we should stop and have a look at him."

Mathew reined up and said, "Look at what? You already said his wounds is fine. You said his hurtin' is all in his head and I believe you. So, what is it you think we can do for poor ole Luke?"

Collin was speechless. He never expected a reaction such as this. "Well, I — we —we could make sure his wounds are alright and at the same time, maybe talk to him and see if we can convince him the pain is in his mind and not real."

Mathew fixed his eyes on Collin's and there was a long pause before he spoke again, "Mister, I don't know what you want from us or why you want to help. My brother may not be the sharpest knife in the drawer, but I can figure things out pretty good. You run around like a mother duck lookin' for her little ones. You're a goddamn goodie two-shoes tryin' to help every one. Why in hell do you do that? — I'll tell you why. You think by helpin' other folks you can wash the blood off your hands from what we done to them heathens? Where was you when they needed help? I didn't see you tryin' to stop anybody from killin' or rapin' 'em. How about that Mr. Do-gooder? Is that about right?"

The outburst was so unexpected and the content was too close to the truth for Collin to listen any further. Consequently, he gave Mathew a dirty look, spurred his horse, and took up his position with Silas and Harold again, turning his head around every once in a while to check on Luke because regardless of what Mathew said, he did genuinely care about Luke's welfare.

Mathew felt a twinge of regret from having blasted Collin. The storekeeper, turned arsonist, really meant no harm at all. He was nice enough and he probably did care about Luke, but Mathew was in a place where he didn't trust anyone or anything. Mathew always had fears and anxieties, but he always confronted them and dealt with the problems life threw at him without hesitation or fear of consequence, but how do you deal with an adversary when you don't know who or what it might be?

Mathew's thoughts were interrupted by a loud moan from Luke; at least he thought it came from his brother. He pulled up his horse and stopped Luke's mount by taking hold of the reins. He looked at his younger brother closely and he saw Luke wasn't suffering any worse than before, when he heard the moan again. He looked up and recognized one of the village men he'd killed, standing a few feet off the trail, beside a large spruce tree. When their eyes met, the man lifted his right arm and pointed an accusing finger at Mathew and let out a mournful groan.

Mathew let go of Luke's reins, pulled his knife, and rode headlong for the villager. When he was within a few feet of the spectre, it shimmered like a heat wave rising from a tarmac road on a very hot summer day and vanished.

Mathew didn't have time to digest what happened, for two other wailing figures appeared on the other side of the trail, a short distance ahead. Mathew recognized them as the two women he and Luke had molested and butchered. There they stood, their garments soaked red by the oozing blood from their wounds, arms raised with accusing fingers pointed directly at him. Again, Mathew charged the pair, only to have them shimmer and disappear.

The man Mathew cut down at the knees and then finished off with Sean McClaren's shotgun, stood on the other side of the trail, a short distance from where the women had been. He was also covered in blood and gore, pointing and moaning. Mathew didn't charge the man, or whatever it was. This time he simply spread his arms and shouted at the apparition, "Here, I am in all my glory. Come and get me you heathen devil! Come and get me, if you want me!"

The phantom did not respond to Mathew's challenge. It stood with extended arm and pointed finger and continued to moan. Mathew took hold of Luke's reins and ignoring the figure, rode past it with head down, not wanting to make eye contact. Mathew hoped the apparitions would disappear, if he ignored them. He looked up every few minutes and to his dismay they were still there, pointing at him and moaning as he rode past and vanishing only to reappear a short distance further down the trail.

Mathew concluded no one else was seeing these things because he didn't see anybody else reacting as if they were. Luke continued his whimpering with an occasional pain induced yelp. In one lucid moment, Luke asked, "Mathew, who are all these people pointing at me?"

"Nobody, Luke. It's nobody. A bad dream, is all," he replied firmly, as if he were trying to convince himself as well as Luke.

Frank Oakley noticed Mathew Briscoe charging from one side of the trail to the other with his knife drawn and he relayed his observations to Whitney, who simply shrugged his shoulders and said Briscoe wasn't bothering him, but if he was troubled by the man's actions then he could ride back and do something about it. "After all," he added, "you are armed and he is not."

Frank Oakley wasn't sure what Whitney was expecting to happen by telling him this. A lot of questions went through his mind. Did Whitney want him to kill Mathew Briscoe? Did he want Mathew Briscoe to kill him? Did he want them to kill each other? That would suit Whitney's purposes, wouldn't it? Two less people to share the gold with. Well, he wasn't going to give Whitney the satisfaction. No sir, he was much too smart for that.

Silas Davidson was having different thoughts. He was feeling sorry for himself. He thought Whitney's attack on him when he casually expressed his opinion about the strange goings on, was completely unjustified. He was angry at himself for not stopping the ruckus between Briscoe and Harold Grant and letting Collin Pilkington do it. In both instances, he felt he lost any respect he had gained with the rest of the men. Collin Pilkington seemed to command more good will from everyone than he did. If he couldn't hold his position, he might as well associate with the heathen and the half breed. "*That's what my status will be reduced to,*" he thought. "*Collin Pilkington will have to be put in his place.*"

Unbeknownst to each other, Silas Davidson and Harold Grant were looking for the same thing, but they were going about achieving their goals by different methods. Silas was trying to gain respect through a display of authority and strength while Harold thought that putting down others, especially those weaker than himself, was the road to approval. He had tried these tactics on several occasions since they escaped custody and in all cases it backfired, especially when he picked on that pathetic creature, Josiah Morgan. He not only took a couple of good physical beatings, but his ranking in the pack was declining, if he'd ever had any status to begin with.

Harold re-evaluated his position. He decided he would keep his mouth shut and try to get back in Whitney's good books somehow. He would watch and listen and when the opportunity came, he would be ready for it.

Nathaniel Brimsby was not feeling on top of the world, either. He heard some of the others saying they were having very frightening dreams. No one wanted to go into any detail, but Silas Davidson mentioned he could not recall the last time he remembered a dream and for the last three nights he had very vivid recollection. When pressed for more details by Harold Grant, Silas clammed up and wouldn't discuss the subject any further.

Nathaniel Brimsby recalled his dreams of late and he did not want to admit the visions he saw were anything more than images with no substance or reality to them. His mind mercifully blocked out the details of the gruesome double murder he committed when he killed his wife and her lover and most recently the native woman in the encampment. It was as if there was a secret vault in the back of his mind where he put all the memories that could cause him pain or emotional discomfort and locked them away.

Nathaniel had always been a loner. It was a lonely existence when you didn't get close to anyone or didn't let anyone get close to you, but he preferred it that way. The conversation with Whitney on the river bank, which seemed like an eternity ago, assured him if he minded his own business and didn't cause Whitney any trouble, he in turn would be left alone. Lately, Whitney was reneging on that understanding, as he was ordering Nathaniel around like any other of his flunkies and Nathaniel thought he deserved better.

About noon, the troop stopped at a small pond created by a spring-fed brook. Whitney ordered a rest and a drink for the mounts and mules. While the stock drank their fill, most of the men ate a bite or two of cold mule meat. It was very greasy and barely palatable, but hungry men are not very fussy.

Michael found a shady spot under a large tree for Dancing Crow to rest. He made the old man comfortable and took their mounts down to the water. Nathaniel Brimsby was never far away. He was given the responsibility of babysitting them and although he was quite confident neither one of them was going to try anything, he was not going to give them an opportunity.

A short time later, Collin Pilkington made his way to their location, where he found Michael and Dancing Crow sitting with their backs against a large fir tree and Nathaniel Brimsby a few feet away laying on his back in the grass looking up at the cloudless sky. As Collin approached, Nathaniel sat up and asked, "What do you want?"

"No offence, Mr. Brimsby, but I just want to talk to the old man, if I could," replied Collin.

Nathaniel looked at Collin, then at Michael and Dancing Crow, back at Collin and then replied, as he lay back down on the grass, "Suit yourself."

Collin sat on the ground facing Michael and Dancing Crow. Michael heard the exchange between Collin and Nathaniel, but he asked the same question, "What do you want?"

"I would like to talk to the old man, if that is alright with you," Collin replied.

"Talk about what?" Michael was being short and curt, because he still didn't trust the man, even though Dancing Crow liked him.

Collin turned very diplomatic, "I think he is a very wise man with an enormous amount of knowledge. You would have to have your head in the sand if you didn't think there weren't some strange things going on around here and I wondered if the old man might have any ideas on what might be behind it."

"Who sent you? Whitney?" asked Michael, still distrustful.

"No one!" replied Collin, indignant. "Look, maybe this was a bad idea. I'll leave you two be," he said as he rose to go.

Nathaniel Brimsby, who was listening to the entire dialogue, sat up and said, "No, don't go, Mr. Pilkington. I, myself, am a bit curious myself as to what the old man might have to say."

By this time Dancing Crow knew something was afoot and he asked Michael what was happening. Michael thought for a moment and then he told Dancing Crow that Collin wanted to speak to him about the unusual happenings. He also cautioned Dancing Crow to be careful about what he said; too much information could get them in a lot of trouble.

"Tell him I will be glad to speak to him of such matters," said Dancing Crow.

Michael said to Collin, "He says he will try and answer your questions, but he also says he may not know much more than you do."

Nathaniel jumped in immediately, "That is not the truth. The old man said he would be glad to talk to you."

Collin looked confused. "How would you know that?" he asked Brimsby.

Before Nathaniel could answer Michael spoke up, "Nate thinks he understands our language. He understands very little."

Brimsby rose to his feet as did Michael, "My name is Nathaniel, not Nate. I know you're lying, you goddamn half breed." He turned to Collin and added, "Don't trust this son-of-a-bitch. He only tells you what you think you should hear."

Collin asked Michael, "Is this true?"

Michael was honest with Collin. "The old man says whatever he thinks. He doesn't know how his words can sometimes bring anger or fear from others, so I change his words to keep him from being hurt by these men. Yes, if he says something I think will bring him suffering at your hands, I will leave it out or change it. That's the truth."

Collin thought for a moment and then said, "That is fine with me. Now, can we continue?"

Michael looked at Brimsby and then proceeded to sit. Brimsby, realizing he had said his peace and he wasn't going to get any further, sat back down, as well, adding a sarcastic comment, "This ought to be interesting."

Michael turned to Collin and instructed him to ask his questions.

Collin didn't know where to begin. "What made all the birds act so strangely?" he asked, as a starting point.

Michael translated and he felt a knot building in his stomach, but it quickly dissipated when Dancing Crow said, "Birds are birds. They do what birds will do. They were angry with us for disturbing them and they were letting us know how they felt. That is all"

Michael relayed the information to Colin and he could see the storekeeper was disappointed. It obviously wasn't the answer he was looking for.

"Then, can he shed some light on what is making the animal sounds all around us?" asked Collin.

Dancing Crow's reply was simply, "Animals. What else could it be?"

Again, Collin appeared unsatisfied. Brimsby said, "I told you, you can't trust these bastards."

Ignoring Brimsby, Collin tried once more, "What does he think of all the strange dreams everyone has been having? Where are they coming from?"

Dancing Crow replied, "Dreams are dreams. Our spirit guides often try to give us messages in dreams. It is best to listen to our spirit guides."

After Michael translated Dancing Crow's reply, Collin's body language showed even more frustration. Brimsby rose and walked away, muttering something about not listening to this gibberish any longer.

"Is there anything else?" Michael asked Collin, finding it very difficult to keep from smiling.

Collin rose and said, "No, that will be all. Thank him for his time." He turned sharply and walked away quickly, feeling he'd been made a fool of.

Dancing Crow asked Michael, "How did I do?"

"You did well," Michael replied, but he couldn't help thinking they might have lost a potential ally in Collin.

Collin's questions were the same ones Michael wanted to ask, but they were seldom out of ear shot of Nathaniel Brimsby. Since they were alone, Michael said, "The one named Collin asked some good questions. Why did you not answer him truthfully?"

"I did not speak any untruths," was Dancing Crow's answer.

"But you didn't tell him all you know," countered Michael.

"He would not have understood," said Dancing Crow.

"Then tell me, or won't I understand, either?" replied Michael.

Dancing crow turned his head to look directly at Michael before speaking. "I do not know you. Although we are of the same blood, we are not of the same family. I do not know what you believe." He paused momentarily so Michael could digest what he said and then continued, "I believe the world in which we spend our waking time and the spirit world are connected and we are free to travel between them, if we learn how. Most of us can and have travelled in the spirit world in our sleep, but some have the ability to travel between the worlds any time they choose and they can use all the power of that world to their advantage and for the good of their people."

"It is you who is doing this to these white men!" Michael interjected, as if he just made a relevant discovery.

"Not I," said Dancing Crow.

"Who then?" asked Michael, the disappointment showing in his voice.

"Someone with many times the power I possess. He is truly all powerful and one to fear," said Dancing Crow.

"Do you mean your grandson?" Michael asked.

Dancing Crow turned his head away, an indication he was done talking. He had said nothing to enlighten Michael, but what he did say confirmed Michael's suspicions that the events of the past week were not random, natural, occurrences, but were, indeed, being orchestrated by some unknown force.

As a boy growing up, Michael was exposed to the world of the Shaman for several years, so he was not completely in the dark about spiritual matters and the realm of what Blue Elk, his mentor, called the shadow world.

His memory took him back to the time he had left that life behind. When he was still in his teens, some young men his own age assaulted him. Michael never was accepted because of his white side. Once he began to meditate and study things spiritual, he found contentment for the first time in his life and it showed. He was smiling and happy and treated the elders with respect.

This did not sit well with his peer group and several of them decided it would be a good idea if they put Michael in his place. Three of them pinned him down while a fourth cut him twice, leaving Michael with the permanent scars that ran diagonally across his face from left to right and along his jaw line from ear to ear. After they let him up, the boys stood laughing and jeering. Michael charged the group with his head lowered and he hit them full force, knocking them all down. Before they could react, Michael took the carver's knife away from him and slashed him twice across his face. He learned later he had blinded the boy in his right eye.

Michael panicked and with the knife still in his hand, ran through the village, screaming in anguish with the blood pouring down his mutilated face. Blue Elk eventually found him in one of his favourite meditation spots, deep in the forest. He tended the boy's cuts, but he could do nothing for his wounded soul.

Several days later, when Michael returned, the elders, including his own father, confronted him and banished him from the village. It was the saddest day of Michael's young life and he vowed he would never trust anyone again, white man or native, alike. He never again practised any form of meditation or any spiritual rites he had learned. From then on, it was as if he denounced any connection with either his mother's side or his father's. He tried to make his own path, but unfortunately, the world would not let him. Whites scorned him because of his native blood and the people of his village shunned him because of his white blood.

Michael did not know enough about the shadow world to be positively sure of anything, but he was convinced the events of the past few days were not by accident or random circumstance and he told Dancing Crow how he felt, just as Whitney called for everyone to saddle up.

-2-

Evening found the troop beside a long narrow lake. The body of water was shallow and marsh-like for twenty feet or so out from the shoreline and then dropped off quickly to a considerable depth. Spaced evenly, approximately seventy five feet apart, were huge beaver lodges, some quite new and some very old and likely not used any more.

As Silas Davidson was preparing the evening meal, Harold Grant approached and wanted to talk. Silas was wary, but Harold convinced him he was sincere and he had thought of a good way to get into Whitney's good books. Beaver! They would capture several of the animals and Whitney could have all the beaver tail he wanted. Who knew, he might even share with the rest of the men, if they caught enough.

Pleasing Whitney appealed to Silas, but his enthusiasm waned when he couldn't think of how they might catch these elusive creatures. Harold wasn't sure, either, but he suggested they go and study the beaver houses and maybe they could break through or force the beavers out of the lodge. They didn't know what to do if their makeshift plan was successful and they managed to break into a lodge or force the beaver into the lake.

Silas asked Collin to tend to the fire while he and Harold went on their quest. The first lodge they came upon seemed as if it was constructed recently. The gnawed ends of the branches and small tree trunks were not yet faded with the weather and the mud used as a filler and bonding agent was not completely hardened. Harold waded through the thigh deep water about fifteen feet out to the lodge and scrambled his way to the top. He kept losing his footing on the wet branches and slick mud. When Silas saw the water wasn't very deep and Harold had made it with no great difficulty, he ventured out and joined Harold atop the beaver house.

Harold bent over and began pulling on an embedded branch. He manoeuvred his body so his back was to the lake. He used much more force than was required to pull the stick out. Consequently, when he gave a hearty tug, the stick came out so easily it surprised him. He lost his balance, landed on his back, and slid headlong down the slippery slope of the lodge and into the lake.

The water on the lakeside of the lodge was far deeper than on the shore side. Harold's momentum carried him the twenty feet or so to the bottom very rapidly. He instinctively closed his mouth and held his breath as he went under. He gathered his wits and began to make his way to the surface, when two beavers came out of the underwater entrance to the lodge and swan directly towards him.

Harold did not see two beavers. What he saw were two very large creatures with gaping mouths full of huge razor sharp teeth and vampire like fangs, coming to tear him to pieces. He gasped, a big mistake when one is under water. He panicked when his mouth filled up with water and for some unexplainable reason, he swam down instead of up and out into the lake instead of back in the direction of the lodge. Even though he was drowning, he realized his mistake and began to head for the surface. Something exerted a strong hold on his shirt front and dragged him down. He kicked with his legs and punched with his arms to break free, but he had no air left and he suddenly went limp and sank into the cold, dark water.

It all happened so quickly, Silas didn't have time to react. By the time he was able to focus and locate Harold, he was disappearing into the deep waters with his arms flailing and his legs kicking. It was as if the lake itself had grabbed Harold with a huge watery fist and was pulling him into the cold depths, while Harold struggled frantically to break free.

Silas turned and faced the camp. He began to holler at the top of his lungs while waving his arms to get someone's attention. Collin Pilkington, who had come to the lakeshore with the hope of perhaps finding some drift wood, heard Silas hollering and ran to see what the commotion was all about. As he approached the beaver lodge, he could see Silas was near hysteria. He kept pointing to the lake and saying, "It took him! For God's sake, it took him!"

Collin waded out and climbed to the top of the beaver house. Silas was frantically pointing to the lake and shouting, "It took him!" over and over again. Collin touched Silas on the shoulder to let him know there was someone else with him. Silas stopped his ranting and looked at Collin with despair and deep sadness in his eyes.

Collin inquired, "Who, Silas? Who got taken?"

"Mister — Mister — uh — Grant. Didn't you see him?" replied Silas.

"No, I didn't — Silas, who took him?" asked Collin.

"The Lake! The water reached out and took hold of him and pulled him down!" Silas shrieked.

Collin put his arm around Silas's shoulder and suggested they head back to camp, sit by the nice warm fire, and talk about this in detail. Collin wasn't sure if Silas was hallucinating, so he was uncertain as to the supposed demise of Harold Grant. For all he knew, Harold was sitting on his lazy butt near the blazing fire, waiting for his supper.

As they entered the camp area, Whitney walked towards them and demanded to know what was going on. Collin explained he wasn't exactly sure, but he thought perhaps Harold Grant had drowned and Silas witnessed the tragedy.

Whitney called every one front and center and took a head count. Harold Grant was unaccounted for. "Does anyone know the whereabouts of Mr. Grant?" Whitney asked.

No one had seen him in the last half hour or so. Frank Oakley commented how this was unusual because Grant was always underfoot, needling somebody about something.

Whitney turned his attention to Silas Davidson. "Mr. Davidson, tell me what happened, if you would please."

Silas looked up, eyes wide and stated, "The lake took him!"

"What do you mean, '*the lake took him*'?" asked Whitney, with agitation in his voice.

Collin tried to interject, but Whitney told him he wanted to hear it from Silas and he should stay out of it unless asked for his input. Collin addressed Silas, "Silas, you need to calm down and tell Mr. Whitney exactly what happened out there."

Collin's words of encouragement seemed to bring Silas out of his hysteria. He faced Whitney and said, "Mr. Grant thought it would be a good idea to see if he could somehow manage to catch a beaver or two so you could partake of another meal of beaver tail, seeing as how you enjoyed it so much this morning. He was trying to do something nice for you," and then he added with emphasis, "for you!"

Whitney held his hand over his heart and with a mocking smile and deep sarcasm in his voice, he said, "Ah, I am touched. Please continue, Mr. Davidson."

Silas could feel the anger swelling up inside himself, "He died trying to please you, you heartless bastard!"

"Mr. Davidson, I suggest you curb your tongue and continue on with your narrative," answered Whitney.

Silas continued, "We had not yet devised a method of capturing the beaver, but we decided to try breaking into one of the lodges from the top. Mr. Grant was on the lakeside of the lodge when he slipped and fell into the water. By the time I walked the few feet to the side of the beaver house where he had been standing and looked into the water, he was already being pulled into the depths. There was nothing I could have done!"

Collin said, "No one is blaming you, Silas."

A stern look from Whitney stopped Collin from indulging in any further words of consolation. "Pulled into the depths by what?" asked Whitney with increased irritability.

Silas continued, "It appeared to me — just momentarily, mind you — it appeared as if the water itself formed into a huge hand, grasped Mr. Grant by the shirtfront, and pulled him towards the bottom of the lake."

Silas looked at the men's faces. He expected not to be believed; he hardly believed what he was saying himself. What he didn't expect was Whitney's reaction. Whitney went into a tirade and began to strike Silas with his bullwhip. Luckily for Silas, Whitney did not know how to use the whip and only one of four strikes usually found their mark. Whitney did not know how to crack the whip, either. Consequently, the leather fringes at the end of the whip did little damage. In the hands of an expert, they would cut deep into a man's skin and take pieces of flesh with them as the whip snapped back.

After a dozen or so lashes, Whitney's anger abated. Thinking he inflicted serious damage to Silas, seemed to satisfy his need to punish him. As he wound the whip back up in a tight coil, he said slowly and deliberately, "Hear me gentlemen and hear me well. I will not tolerate any more talk of things supernatural. I shall hear no more of ghosts and goblins, damn it! We are a large contingent of men travelling through the wilderness. We are going to attract attention! The multitude of feathered and fur covered inhabitants of this infernal land are naturally curious and they were doing the things they do because they feel threatened by us.

"Sure, we've lost some of our fellow travellers, but it is all either accident or circumstance. People do get attacked by bears or drown in lakes. It happens. There was nothing supernatural about it. Of the other incidents, one was a misfortunate tragedy, a simple disagreement that escalated into a fatal beating. The other was simply two men who were not well in the head, shall we say — both driven to madness by guilt."

Whitney paused and waited for any response to his speech. Not one of the men dared say anything, but most of them were not dissuaded from their belief that supernatural forces were against them. Some of them thought about the dreams they were having. Whitney hadn't explained them away.

Whitney could sense the men were still uneasy and there was an undercurrent of discontentment. He felt they weren't totally convinced, but he didn't care. All he wanted from them was to refocus on their goal. He hoped they were more afraid of him than the things that may go bump in the night.

Chapter 15 – Collin Makes Enemies

Whitney didn't eat breakfast. He watched as the troop leisurely went about the morning business of feeding themselves and preparing for the day's ride. He lost his temper and in a demanding tone, told the men they were leaving in half an hour and everyone damn well better be ready. He also added, "Put the old heathen on the recently departed Mr. Grant's horse. I don't imagine he will have any further use for it."

As he rode at the front of the troop, Whitney remained silent and sullen. His world was beginning to unravel. Outwardly, he showed no signs of weakening. To the men, he was still as strong as ever, but inside he felt he was losing control, causing him a great deal of anxiety. In fact, a small dose of fear tried to creep into his thoughts, which he dismissed at once. When he had given the 'nothing supernatural' speech to the men the night before, his argument was so well thought out, he even convinced himself.

Last night, he found it difficult to get to sleep. He didn't believe Silas Davidson was a man prone to hallucinations. Yet, here he was, raving about the lake coming alive and taking Harold Grant. "Nonsense," he told himself, "we've been out in the bush too long. If the men continue to behave irrationally, I'll beat the old heathen half to death to convince them it is all in their heads and there is nothing to fear from him or his dead relatives."

He was still having the recurring nightmare where he was in a long line waiting for his share of the gold and when he arrived at the front of the line, there was nothing left. More details seemed to get added to the nightmare every night.

In last night's dream there were over a dozen natives ahead of him in line. They were covered in gaping wounds from knives, shotguns and pistol shots and their clothing was covered in blood and gore. When Whitney reached the distribution table, he already knew there was no gold left for him. He didn't, however, expect the natives to be gathered around and all laughing hysterically at him. He drew his pistol and fired at them. In his nightmare, his pistol didn't need reloading, so he continued to pull the trigger. He must have put a hundred shots into them, with no effect.

Whitney stopped shooting and lowered his pistol in despair. One of the natives stopped laughing, came forward and laid a solid gold bar at his feet. Whitney was totally surprised. He didn't know what to say. He raised his head and looked into the man's face with gratitude. The native said, "I have no use for this gold. You can have mine."

Whitney was even more amazed when each of them, in turn, came to him and set their gold bar at his feet. By the time they were done, there was a king's ransom. Whitney was delighted until he tried to pick up one of the bars. They had all fused together into one huge ingot, weighing close to a ton. Whitney couldn't budge the boulder an inch. He looked all about to see if he could get some help, but to his dismay, everything and everyone was gone — vanished, leaving no sign they were ever there in the first place. Whitney was left all alone with a fortune in gold and no way to move it.

Whitney reflected on what the dream might mean. Was it an omen? Was the dream trying to tell him something? Would he get to the gold and have no way of bringing it out?

Frank Oakley's voice brought Whitney back to reality. Oakley had ridden up beside him and said something Whitney didn't hear. "I'm sorry, Mr. Oakley, but my thoughts were elsewhere. What did you say?" he asked.

"You alright, Boss? You seem a little distracted," said Oakley.

Whitney thought quickly, "No — no, I'm performing some mental calculations, about how far we've come and how far we've got to go."

"So what do you figure?" asked Oakley.

It was such a general question, it caught Whitney off guard. "What do you mean?" he asked.

Oakley explained, "You know, how far have we got to go?"

Whitney answered, "Oh, yes. Well, according to my calculations and based on what the old prospector told me, we should be well beyond the halfway mark. Tonight, we should hit the headwaters of a fairly large river system that we will follow for a week or so and then we should be there."

Oakley mumbled under his breath, "Don't know if this band of misfits will make it."

"What did you say?" inquired Whitney.

"I was commenting on the shape the men are in. I'm not sure if most of them could go another week."

"The men will be fine. You need not concern yourself with such matters, Mr. Oakley," Whitney replied curtly and then spurred his horse to put some distance between them.

As soon as he did it, Whitney regretted his action. Oakley was probably the only true ally he had left and it would be to his advantage to nurture the relationship rather than destroy it. He reined in, let Oakley catch up, and said, "I apologize, Mr. Oakley. It was rather rude of me. I have faith in this group. Men need a goal, some objective they are struggling to reach and all they need is a good leader to keep them focused and motivated."

Oakley asked, "Boss, what sort of thing motivates men?"

"Lots of things, Mr. Oakley. In times of war, fear of dying or hatred of the enemy will drive a man beyond his self perceived limits. In our little scenario, greed will drive these men further than they think they can go."

"You sound like you were an officer in the army or something," commented Oakley.

"The great American Civil War, Mr. Oakley," Whitney replied. He paused briefly and than added as an afterthought, "On the side of right and justice, of course."

Whitney didn't want to get into his days in the war, so he changed the subject and he asked, "How about you, Mr. Oakley? Who are you? What motivates you to keep going? The gold perhaps?"

Frank thought for a long time before answering. "Yes, you're right. What fella isn't interested in getting rich, but you know something, Mr. Whitney, there's something else. All my life I've always wanted to belong to something, to have a real family of my own or even a close friend who would do anything for me and I would do anything for him. I want to be a part of something. Does that sound silly?"

Whitney smiled and for the first time since they started out on this trek, he spoke without the authoritative tone he always used. "Mr. Oakley, if all men actually spoke the truth when you asked them that question, you'd find most of them want the same things, respect and someone to love them. I imagine a lot of them would sacrifice the possibility of wealth if there was a guarantee of contentment without it."

"Would you, Mr. Whitney?"

Whitney sighed heavily before answering, "No, Mr. Oakley, I'm afraid I wouldn't. I have spent too much of my life focused on my own survival to ever get close to anyone or let anyone get close to me. As you have seen, I am capable of killing a man who disrespects me, not the way to win true respect, Mr. Oakley. It is intimidation by fear. They say riches cannot buy happiness. Most likely a statement from a poor man. The gold will go a long way toward a blissful existence for me."

Oakley was at a loss for words. His hard boiled boss just opened up to him and he didn't know how to respond. He came out with, "Well Boss, I hope you find what you're lookin' for." He said it with sincerity and he felt foolish for having said it, thinking it showed a sign of weakness.

Whitney was taken by surprise and he fumbled for an answer, as well. "Thank you, Mr. Oakley. I'm convinced I will."

There was an eerie silence between them and neither one of them could think of anything else to say. Whitney broke the awkward moment by suggesting Oakley should check on the rest of the men.

The day's journey was nothing out of the ordinary. Each man rode with his own thoughts for company. Yesterday, the troop descended onto the vast Interior Plateau of west central British Columbia. Whitney told them the difficult part of the ride was over and it was all relatively flat from this point on. He was hoping to brighten their spirits, to find some positive thing they could grab hold of to encourage them.

Mid afternoon found them at the head waters of another small stream, just one of dozens they had come across. After conferring with Dancing Crow, through Michael, Whitney told them this was the beginning of the river system they would follow to their destination. This tidbit of news seemed to spark a renewed energy amongst the men.

Late evening found them at the junction of the stream they were following and another much larger creek coming from the northeast. Silas Davidson's mind was not on the daily routine of setting up camp for the evening. He had to be reminded twice to get a meal started. "The men are hungry," barked Frank Oakley, who had assumed the role of second in command. Since no one objected, he took the position to be his.

Collin Pilkington came to Silas's defence. "Can't you see he's still in shock over Mr. Grant's drowning? You just toddle along and lick your master's boots and you'll get fed like you always do."

Oakley almost reacted to Collin's condescending attitude, but he wasn't sure if making trouble would sit well with the boss. "It'll be dark soon, so I suggest you get started," he said, intending it as a final warning, although as he walked away, he had the discouraging feeling no one was taking him very seriously.

Collin sat down next to Silas and put his hands on the distraught man's shoulders. He gave Silas a slight shake, bringing him out of the trance. Silas looked into Collin's eyes and said with a quiver in his voice, "The lake came alive, Mr. Pilkington. It came alive and took him away."

Collin tried to divert Silas's focus when he said with encouragement, "You have to let it go, Silas. We have some daily business needing our attention. Why don't we get some supper ready for the men and then we can talk after the meal. Would that be alright with you?"

Silas seemed to give the suggestion some thought and then replied, "Yes, yes. You are right, my friend. Duty first."

Collin caught site of Nathaniel Brimsby and Michael engaged in conversation. He made his way to them and when he was within earshot he said, "Gentlemen, please don't get me wrong. I am not giving orders, but simply asking. Do you think you could help Silas and myself get a fire going and some food cooked up? Silas is in a bad way and I think he could use our help."

Nathaniel gave Collin a cold stare, turned and walked away without saying a word. Michael was about to do the same when he saw Dancing Crow looking at him. When their eyes met, the old man asked, "What does the mother hen want?" To Dancing Crow, that is how Collin appeared, like a mother hen tending to her chicks.

Michael found it difficult to lie about or even cover up anything when it came to the old man. "He wants some help with the fire and meal."

"I am very hungry. I wish to eat soon. We shall help this man," answered Dancing Crow.

Michael turned back to Collin, "We'll help. What do you want us to do? "You could unpack the mules and then set up a picket line for the stock. Silas and I will gather wood and get a fire going. We also need a pot of water from the creek and if you see anymore of those wild onions, we could use some more."

Michael and Dancing Crow set about their appointed tasks. Collin approached Silas with the intent of getting him up and moving. Silas's thoughts went back to remorse and self blame. He remembered the day they started this trip to hell. Every time an opportunity had come up for him to stand up and do the right thing, he either ignored it and buried his head in the sand or didn't have the courage to get involved. He could not have stopped the slaughter in the village, but he didn't even express the outrage he felt at the atrocities being committed. When Whitney shot Sean McClaren, he wanted to rip Whitney's throat out with his bare hands, but again he said nothing.

In his mind, he blamed himself for Harold Grant's death. There wasn't a thing he could have done to save Harold, but he didn't even try. He could at least have berated Whitney for his casual attitude about the death of a fellow human being.

Collin's hand on his shoulder redirected his attention. Collin said, "Come along Silas, you and I need to gather some firewood. Collin went to one of the mules Michael and Dancing Crow were unpacking, picked up one of the axes and with Silas in tow, he headed for a growth of very old and very large spruce trees that usually provided an abundance of dead branches, which could be hacked off the trunk and chopped up very easily.

Daylight was starting to slip away. As Collin and Silas entered the woods, where the light was even dimmer, Silas stopped and stared into the trees. Collin peered at the spot where Silas seemed to focus and didn't see anything out of the ordinary. He asked, "What is it Silas? What do you see?"

Silas began to run forward, shouting as he ran, "Mr. Grant! Harold, you're alive. Thank God! I could have sworn I saw the lake take you."

Collin stood and watched as Silas stopped and extended his right arm and began moving it up and down as if he was shaking hands with someone. He saw Silas fall to his knees and begin to sob uncontrollably. He hurried over and knelt beside Silas and put his arms around the distraught man.

"I thought — he was there — Now he's gone —" Silas said through his sobs.

"Take some deep breaths and calm down, Silas," instructed Collin.

After several minutes of deep breathing, Silas regained some medium of composure and he said, "Mr. Grant was standing right here! Didn't you see him, Mr. Pilkington?"

"No Silas, I did not."

"He was right here. I shook his hand and then he opened his mouth and water poured out of it. He told me I let him drown. I tried to tell him I couldn't do anything. He kept saying I let him drown and then he vanished. Am I going insane, Mr. Pilkington?"

"No Silas, you are not going insane. You've had a very upsetting experience and I am sure it is bound to affect your mind," answered Collin, only half believing the words coming out of his own mouth. He began loping dead branches off a nearby spruce tree and when he had enough, he loaded Silas up with an armful, picked up a bundle himself, and they both headed back to the camp area to start a fire.

A little more than an hour later, there was a hearty helping of mule meat ready to eat. There was a small quantity of wild onion and Michael had found some wild horseradish plants and dug out several roots, making dinner a little more palatable.

With the evening meal and the cleanup completed, the men went about their established routines. Whitney usually found an elevated spot to sit and watch the camp. It was as if he was overseeing his little empire. Frank Oakley was never far from Whitney. He was taking his role as bodyguard and second in command seriously, although, Whitney didn't need either.

Silas and Collin, their work done for the evening, found comfortable spots near the fire where they could sit and chat and feed the fire without having to get up. Nathaniel Brimsby, unable to sit for long and wanting to keep his mind off his terrible visions, liked to wander back and forth across the camp and circle the perimeter with the Spencer loaded and the hammer cocked. The men had learned to let Nathaniel know when they were headed to the privacy of the trees to answer nature's call, lest they be mistaken for someone or something Nathaniel was looking to shoot.

Michael and Dancing Crow could usually be found a short distance from the fire. They would find a piece of ground, either covered with layers of soft moss or overgrown with meadow grass or a combination of both, where Dancing Crow would sit cross-legged with his forearms resting comfortably on his knees. He would bow his head, close his eyes, and began to chant a rhythmic stream of one syllable expressions. Michael would watch him for a few minutes then lie on his back and stare at up the evening sky, often losing himself in his own thoughts that most times turned into revised versions of significant events that occurred in his life. Michael enjoyed altering his past in his mind. He would often change his failures into victories. He would exact sweet revenge upon those who wronged him, emerging as a hero with his enemies vanquished, cowering, and begging for mercy.

His favourite fantasy was the one in which he was accepted by people in both worlds, native and white alike. He imagined himself the owner of a very successful freight line, respected by his employees, customers, and business associates. He would envision himself returning to his village with gifts for everyone, where he was welcomed with open arms and invited to sit in on the council of elders as an honorary member. His favourite part of this daydream was when he asked the council to punish the young men who had cut him up and orchestrated his exile. He took delight in beating the four of them unconscious with his bare hands and then carving up each of their faces in turn. The coup de grace was the banishment of the four boys while he was reinstated.

Michael was deep in one of these musings when he heard someone calling his voice. Reality returned and he opened his eyes to see Collin Pilkington standing over him. He raised himself up on his elbows and asked, "What do you want?"

"I would very much like to speak to the Medicine Man, if I could," Collin answered.

Michael looked in Dancing Crow's direction. He was still in his meditation posture. Michael turned his gaze back to Collin and said, "He can't be disturbed right now. He's busy."

Dancing Crow spoke, "What does the mother hen want?"

"He says he needs to speak to you," answered Michael.

"Then let him speak."

Collin spoke directly to Dancing Crow, who didn't open his eyes or move a muscle. "I don't mean to bother you — but, well you see — my friend, Mr. Davidson, is in a bad way. Mr. Grant's unfortunate death has left him quite shaken. He is unable to deal with the event. In fact, he has taken on the responsibility for Mr. Grant's demise."

Michael loosely translated, "He says the white man who looks like a stork is his friend and he wants you to help him. His friend is blaming himself for the death of the one who died in the lake."

Dancing Crow opened his eyes and spoke to Collin. "I am not sure what it is you think I can do?"

Michael translated. Collin was stumped for an answer. "Perhaps, you could cast a spell or perform some sort of ceremony?"

"He wants you to perform a ceremony," said Michael.

"What does he think will happen?" asked Dancing Crow.

"He says he doesn't know what it is you expect to happen?" Michael said to Collin.

"I don't know what I expect. All I know is that a good man is suffering badly and he needs someone's help. If this old man can help him, then I am begging him to do so," answered Collin with elevated emotion.

"He really cares about his friend. He wants you to do anything you can to help ease the man's pain," translated Michael.

"I will look at the man," answered Dancing Crow.

Michael's news that Dancing Crow would try to help Silas, excited Collin. He was practically doing a jig as he led the old man to Silas. As they approached, Dancing Crow could see Silas was distraught. He sat cross-legged, his elbows on his knees and his chin in his hands. He rocked back and forth as a small child might do and stared wide-eyed into the fire. At regular intervals and in a voice barely audible, he kept uttering, "The lake took him. I saw it. The lake took him."

Collin went down on one knee beside Silas and placed his arm around his shoulders. Silas turned his head and looked up into Collin's face. Collin said, "Silas, the Medicine Man thinks he can help you."

A look of sheer terror came across Silas's face and he begged, "No please, no more demons. I am so sorry I did nothing. I am so sorry."

Collin looked up at Dancing Crow and said, "He's afraid of you." After Michael translated, Dancing Crow replied, "He believes I am the cause of his troubles. Until he trusts me, I cannot help him."

Nathaniel Brimsby approached unnoticed and said, "Should he be afraid of you?" He directed the remark at Dancing Crow, who in turn looked to Michael for a translation.

Michael didn't bother translating. He stepped between Dancing Crow and Brimsby. As he did so Brimsby took two steps towards him. He looked down at the rifle cradled in his arms and then into Michael's eyes. Michael challenged him, "Why don't you go somewhere and shoot something."

"Plenty to shoot right here," was Brimsby's snide reply. "What are you two up to?"

Collin Pilkington stepped in between the two potential combatants, pushing Michael back with one hand, while facing Brimsby. "I asked the Medicine Man to help Silas if he could. He agreed. So, if you don't mind, could you please keep out of our business and let us get on with it."

Nathaniel stood thinking for the longest time, uttered a condescending harrumph, and slowly made his way toward the other side of the camp. Using Michael as a translator, Dancing Crow had Collin move Silas to the edge of the camp, out of sight of prying eyes. He had Silas lay prone with his arms at his sides, close his eyes, and relax. He told Silas he was going to perform three ceremonies — two very short ones and a third one, somewhat longer.

Dancing Crow asked Collin to get a handful of hot coals from the fire. While Collin was getting the coals, using a pot lid to carry them, Dancing Crow had pulled out a tuft of sweet grass out of his medicine bag. No one had bothered to search him back at the encampment except Con Murdock. He tried to take the old man's medicine pouch, but when he looked inside and saw grass, bones, stones, and some feathers, he threw it back at Dancing Crow in disgust.

Dancing Crow built a very small fire bed with some twigs and dry tree lichens stacked next to it. He asked Collin to set the hot coals in the bed while he piled on the twigs and lichen and began to blow. Instantaneously, there was a small blaze going and Dancing Crow stuck the ends of the sweet grass into it. The grass caught on fire and Dancing Crow put the flames out with his bare hand, leaving only smoking grass stalks.

He knelt beside Silas, closed his eyes, and began to chant as he passed the smouldering sweet grass up and down the entire length of Silas's body several times and then back and forth across his body from Silas's left side to his right, again covering the entire length of the body. He repeated this procedure three times, stopping only to reignite the grass.

Dancing Crow reached into his medicine bag and drew out a bundle of different feathers bound to one end of a thick short piece of polished wood with a piece of rawhide string. The feathers were evenly spaced, encircling the piece of wood. The rawhide string was tightly wrapped around the quill ends and continued up the length of the piece of wood to serve as a handle. The whole thing looked like a miniature version of a feather duster a maid might use to clean the library in some big mansion.

Dancing Crow, with Michael's help, got Silas into a sitting position then Dancing Crow closed his eyes and began the rhythmic chanting again. Using a flick of the wrist, he flipped the feather bundle in sweeping motions away from Silas's body, as if he were shooing away mosquitoes, or brushing away loose bread crumbs. He continued this process as he had with the sweet grass ceremony, covering Silas's body from top to bottom three times.

Dancing Crow opened his eyes and told Michael to lay Silas down again on his back. He put the little feather duster back in his medicine pouch and withdrew a solitary shiny-black raven feather and placed it on Silas's forehead. He cupped his hands around the feather and exhaled a slow continuous breath directly onto it. He would stop, take a deep breath, and exhale onto the feather again. The purpose of the exercise was to activate the healing power of the feather with a combination of the breathing and a visualization of the afflicted area receiving the energy and being healed.

Suddenly, Dancing Crow leaped to his feet and gasped. There was a look of terror on his face and before Michael could get to his side, Dancing Crow's knees buckled and he slumped to the ground. He was repeating, "No! No! Go away!" in his native tongue and swatting at some invisible antagonist with both hands.

Collin was stunned by Dancing Crow's sudden reaction. He joined Michael at

Dancing Crow's side and began asking Michael what was wrong. Michael simply said the ceremony was over and he needed to tend to the old man. Helping Dancing Crow to his feet and supporting his weight by putting the old man's left arm around his own shoulders, Michael moved him to a mossy spot under a nearby tree.

Dancing Crow closed his eyes and it appeared as if he'd gone to sleep or passed out. Michael gently shook him by the shoulders to assure himself the old man was still alive. Dancing Crow opened his eyes and recognizing Michael, he smiled. Michael asked with concern, "Are you alright? What happened?"

Dancing Crow replied, "The power is not with me, today. I could do nothing for the man."

Realizing Dancing Crow said all he was going to say on the subject, Michael got angry. "You are not telling me everything you old fool! Something scared you half to death during the ceremony and you are going to tell me what it was! I'm tired of your bullshit!"

He paused long enough to let his words sink in and then continued with less emotion, "You and me! — We! The two of us are in this together and we are going to get out of it together, but not if you don't trust me. Now, again, what happened?"

Dancing Crow was surprised by Michael's outburst. He had taken the young man for granted. From his perspective, he was in this predicament alone. He didn't think of Michael as an ally, but simply as another convict looking after his own skin. He suddenly realized Michael was very sincere. Dancing Crow sat up into a cross-legged position and with a hand gesture, bade Michael to sit across from him. He waited for Michael to get into position and then he began speaking in a solemn, almost reverent tone. "I am the Medicine Man of my village. I know of the things that make people ill and of the things that make them well. This is my power."

Dancing Crow paused briefly. This gave Michael an opportunity to interrupt, "I, too, was studying the path of healing before — before I left my village."

Dancing Crow noted the hesitation and the change of thought in Michael's statement and how he ran his finger along the scars on his jaw line as he spoke, but decided against pursuing it. He continued, "I have learned to travel to the spirit world and once there, to invoke the aid of the spirits in my healings. I have always known this is a very powerful place and I must be careful not to do something to offend the spirits. I would not want to unknowingly do something to make them angry." He paused, let out a heavy sigh and continued, "I am afraid that is what I have done."

It seemed to Michael, Dancing Crow was done speaking and if he wanted to hear more, it was going to take some prodding on his part. "What happened? What did you see, old man?" he asked, pleadingly.

Dancing Crow trusted Michael, now. He looked all about as if he was looking for someone watching, leaned in toward Michael, and continued his narrative, "I was breathing the healing power through the raven feather. I saw the energy going into the thin man's head and driving out his fear. I felt as if the spirits were with me and it was beginning to work, when I was struck with a very powerful force. It felt as if a heavy wet blanket had been thrown over me. I felt very, very afraid and I had an overwhelming feeling this power was very angry, almost hateful."

"Who was it?" asked Michael, trying to coax more information out of Dancing Crow.

The old man continued, "In the spirit world, I looked up and the whole sky was filled with the face of a red fox, with angry yellow eyes. It barred its teeth and snarled at me. The spirit of the fox spoke and told me not to tend to the white man, unless I wanted to have his vengeance take me, too."

Michael, still probing, asked, "Have you seen this spirit before?"

"Oh yes, I have seen him before, but never so powerful or so angry."

Dancing Crow looked at Michael, who was anxiously awaiting the answer. All Dancing Crow left him with was, "My Grandson's name is Little Fox."

Collin Pilkington's approach ended any further discussion. "How is he?" asked Collin.

"He's doing fine. Those ceremonies take a lot of energy and he is an old man. He needs to rest," replied Michael. To change the subject, he asked, "How is Silas?"

"He's much better, thank you. Much better," replied Collin. There was an awkward pause, which Collin broke by saying, "Well, thank the old man for me and I hope he feels better."

As Collin was making his way back to the fire, he was met by Mathew Briscoe. "What do you want?" Collin asked in a rather unfriendly tone.

Mathew was about to react to Collin's malevolent attitude, but he swallowed his pride and said, "It's Luke. He ain't gettin' any better and I don't know what to do."

Collin softened and said, "Well, let's have a look."

As they approached the camp fire, Collin caught sight of Nathaniel Brimsby adding the last of the firewood to the fire. Brimsby saw Collin and hollered, "Hey, Washerwoman, we need more fire wood."

Collin pointed to a grove of trees and said, "Lots over there," and continued on.

Brimsby stood quickly with full intentions of teaching Collin a lesson in manners, but his intuition told him now might not be the best time. It could wait until later when they were alone.

Luke Briscoe lay on a small knoll above the campfire area. Mathew had propped him up against a large deadfall log, and had built a small campfire for some warmth. Collin approached Luke and knelt beside him. His chin rested on his chest and with his arms at his side, he appeared dead. Collin gently lifted his head with his right hand. Luke offered no resistance and he moaned when Collin let his head back down.

Collin asked for Mathew's assistance and they lowered Luke on his back and covered him with a blanket. "He seems to suffer less if he is sittin' up," stated Mathew.

"Let's get him nice and warm and then we can sit him up again if that is what you think best," replied Collin.

Mathew did not like to be contradicted, but he accepted the suggestion, mostly because of Collin's compromising demeanour. Moving Luke was like working with a huge rag doll. Luke was barely conscious and offered no assistance.

"Could you go get the old injun?" Mathew asked.

Collin replied, "I don't think the old man can be of any use just now. He was trying to help Mr. Davidson and wore himself out completely. We could try in the morning."

Mathew was beginning to get angry, "You mean he don't mind helpin' the likes of Davidson, but me an' Luke, we ain't good enough, is that it?"

Collin stood his ground, "No! It is just like I said. The old man is dead tired and couldn't do anything if he wanted to."

Mathew shouted, "Then what are we supposed to do?"

Collin rose and put his hands on Mathew's shoulders. "I suggest —"

Mathew knocked Collin's hands from his shoulders and said, "Don't touch me. Don't you ever touch me."

"I was trying to say, we should see if we can get some food into him," explained Collin.

"How? He won't eat nothin'," snarled Mathew.

"We can make a strong broth from the meat and some onions and get him to drink it," said Collin.

This suggestion seemed to anger Mathew even more and he said with a vicious tone, "I should have known better than to count on some old injun and a washerwoman. Jesus, what was I thinkin'."

Collin saw red, "Fine! As far as I am concerned, you and your brother can both go to hell!" and he stomped down the hill to the campfire.

Mathew Briscoe watched him leave and muttered under his breath, "You'll get yours, Washerwoman. You'll get yours."

Silas Davidson arrived at the campfire at the same time as Collin. Silas was carrying an armful of large branches, which he dropped near the fire, and then said to Collin, "Where have you been? You are slacking on your job, Mr. Pilkington. Let us focus on our responsibilities."

Collin was so shocked, he could barely speak, "You ungrateful son-of-a-bitch! What do you think I've been — never mind. You can go to hell, too!" He turned and stomped off in the direction of the stream.

Silas followed Collin with his eyes. Gone were the fear and confusion and look of desperation, replaced by a cold, maniacal stare. He said to himself, "We shall see, Mr. Pilkington. Yes, we shall see who goes to hell."

Chapter 16 – Collin's Fall

It wasn't quite daylight and Whitney was already walking among the array of sleeping bodies, giving each one a kick and shouting, "Rise and shine gentleman. We march in one hour — be ready!" Whitney fully intended to get a good start and put in a full day's travel. He was anxious to finish the trip. By his calculations, there was about a week to go and he was going to try and shave a day or two off the time, but life has a funny way of ruining the best of intentions.

Silas Davidson hadn't slept at all. He saw very brightly lit, full colour images every time he closed his eyes and drifted off toward sleep. In his dream, he was standing on a beaver lodge watching a huge hand of water pulling Harold Grant to the depths of the lake. Suddenly, the scene changed and he found himself running through a dense growth of trees and when he emerged on the other side of the grove into a large meadow, the old Medicine Man stopped him and asked him what was wrong and why he was running.

While Silas talked, Dancing Crow listened and then totally unexpectedly, he blew some powder into Silas's face. Silas found himself flat on his back on the ground. He saw Dancing Crow doing a strange dance where he hopped on both legs, ran a few feet, and then hopped again, like a crow after something on the ground. Throughout the dance, the old man circled Silas, but he always had his back to him. Silas was trying to rise up, but found he couldn't move. The old man stopped dancing abruptly and slowly turned to face Silas. Instead of the face of the Medicine Man, Silas saw the face of a crow or a raven; he wasn't sure which, because he could never tell them apart. The crow-like being brought its face close to Silas's and said, not in the raspy crow voice one would expect, but with the voice of the old Medicine Man, "There is nothing to fear from the water. There is nothing to fear, at all. The only way the spirits can do you harm is if you let them. Do not let them." Then the crow man cawed like the crow he was and began to dance again.

Without warning an enormous red fox appeared and took the Medicine Man in its huge teeth, shook him like a rag doll, dropped him to the ground, and stood over him with one huge paw holding him to the ground. The fox appeared to be saying something to the old man and when it was done, it raised its paw and the old man got up and ran away. The fox turned towards Silas and its head grew so large it filled the sky. The immense fox face snarled and said, "You have fear, white man, and your fear will kill you!"

Still in the dream, Silas managed to get to his feet and run for the cover of the trees. He crawled under the ground level canopy of a huge spruce tree, where he lay cowering. The first time, Silas stayed in the dream state for the whole sequence of events. Now, every time he drifted off to sleep, the vision would start all over again. Finally, in desperation, he decided the best thing to do was to stay awake. He prided himself on his ability to control his emotions and if what the fox said was true, that his own fear would kill him, then he would shut off his mind to any emotion, especially fear.

As Silas started the cooking fire, Whitney approached and asked how much mule meat was left and commented that it might be time to send Brimsby and the breed out to do some hunting.

Silas usually gave Whitney his full attention, but this time he merely glanced up from his work and said, "I am not afraid of you. I am not afraid of anything."

Whitney paused, momentarily taken aback by Silas's strange behaviour and then said sternly, "I could give a good goddamn what you may or may not be afraid of, Mr. Davidson. I asked you how much meat we have left."

Silas stopped what he was doing and stood erect. To Whitney, he appeared very different. He no longer looked like a friendly business man waiting to cheat you out of your last dollar. His permanent little smirk was gone, replaced by a sinister sneer. The ashen color of his face gave him the appearance of a mortician who hadn't seen daylight in a long while, but it was the man's change in attitude Whitney noticed the most.

Silas looked right into Whitney's eyes, sneered, and said in a voice, reeking of sarcasm and condescension, "Why don't you look for yourself?" as he pointed to the elk hide in which the mule meat was wrapped. "It's right there."

Whitney wasn't sure what to make of Silas's insubordination, but he knew, in order to maintain discipline, he would have to deal with the situation. He unravelled the whip from his belt.

Silas saw the action and said, "You can beat me all you want, I'm still not afraid of you." He said the words, but a small crack of doubt appeared. He really didn't want to get whipped. He was afraid of pain. "If you would just treat me with some measure of respect, we would get along a lot better. Would it put you out any to ask me politely how much meat we have? Perhaps something like, '*Mr. Davidson, could you please inform me on the current status of our meat supply*' would get better results."

Some of the men had gathered to watch the confrontation. Whitney, always the shrewd tactician, saw an opportunity to get in good with them. "Very well, Mr. Davidson, what is the status of our meat supply?" he asked, politely.

"We have enough for today's meals and then we will need some more," Silas replied, still with an undertone of condescension.

"Thank you, Mr. Davidson," Whitney said. He started to leave, stopped, turned back to face Silas, and added, "I suggest, Mr. Davidson, in future you conduct your business with me in a more civil manner, or fearless or not, I will give you a good taste of the whip."

Nathaniel Brimsby stood a few feet away. Whitney saw him and changed his course. Frank Oakley was not far behind. It seemed over the last couple of days Whitney had acquired a new shadow. Whenever one saw Whitney, Frank Oakley was always on his coat tails. At first Whitney liked the idea of someone covering his back, but lately it was becoming bothersome.

Whitney stopped in front of Brimsby and said, "Mr. Brimsby, once we are on the trail, take the breed and get us some fresh meat. I do not fancy mule meat for another meal."

Whitney did not wait for a response. He simply turned and walked away, with Oakley right behind him. Whitney did not witness the dirty look Brimsby gave him, but Frank Oakley did. He paused in front of Brimsby and returned his hateful stare. The two men glared at each other and then Oakley asked, "Is there a problem?"

Whitney heard the question. He did an about face and returned to his original position directly in front of Brimsby and said, "Well, Mr. Brimsby, answer the man."

Brimsby took in a deep breath and looked skyward. As he lowered his head, he let the breath out and said to Whitney, "Not a problem with you, Sir, just your lap dog."

Frank Oakley reacted immediately. He cocked the hammers of the double barrel shotgun, but just as he looked up, the butt end of Brimsby's Spencer rifle caught him full in the forehead, with enough force to knock him flat on his back. Nathaniel Brimsby glanced at Whitney for his reaction. Whitney's hand was on his pistol. Brimsby cradled the rifle back in his arms and said, "Now, Mr. Whitney, where were we?"

Whitney took his hand off the pistol butt, thought for a moment, and replied, "Perhaps, I am mistaken, Mr. Brimsby, but I believe our business was concluded. You have your orders."

By this time, Oakley was on his feet. He was too angry to think clearly and he would have gotten himself killed, if Whitney hadn't shouted, "Mr. Oakley!" Once he had Oakley's attention, Whitney continued, "That will be all, Mr. Oakley!"

"But, the bastard hit — " Before Oakley could finish his protest, Whitney took a long stride towards him and backhanded him across the face, not hard enough to knock him down, but hard enough to get his undivided attention.

Whitney said, "Mr. Oakley, I fail to see why you find it so difficult to understand that it is I who decides who is to be reprimanded for their behaviour and not you."

Without a second thought, Whitney turned and walked away. Oakley picked up his shotgun and after a quick glance at a smirking Brimsby, he ran at top speed into the grove of aspens at the back of the camp. He muttered to himself as he ran. "I'm gonna kill you both. I'm gonna kill you both, if it's the last thing I ever do."

A few feet into the grove, he sat down with his back to a large tree, put his face in his hands, and began to cry, uncontrollably. As he sobbed, he felt a swell of anger growing inside him. It was so intense, he shook his head violently and screamed at the top of his lungs, "I hate you! I hate you! I hate you!"

After the outburst, his anger subsided and after a short time he was able to control the sobbing. Whenever Frank was feeling angry or persecuted, he would fantasize. The daydream usually involved Frank and his antagonist(s) in a gunfight. Frank would disable each of his opponents and casually walk up to each wounded man, where he would listen to their pitiful pleas for mercy. Then slowly and deliberately he would cock the hammer on his pistol and shoot each one through the heart, taking delightful pleasure in the surprised look on the dying man's face.

In his current illusion, he stood on a dusty deserted street, in a dusty deserted town. Several yards down the street stood Nathaniel Brimsby and Clarence Whitney, ready for the fight. Sweat was pouring down their foreheads and into their eyes, their hands were trembling and you could see a dark spot in the crotch of their pants where they had just wet themselves.

Frank smiled and nonchalantly drew his pistol, knowing he would win the fight. His heart jumped into his throat, when to his surprise, both Brimsby and Whitney outdrew him and two bullets tore into his flesh; one into his left leg just above the knee and the other into his right hand, knocking his pistol to the ground. In an instant, the men were on him. He began to plead for his life. Whitney cocked his pistol and shot him in the chest. He could feel the bullet shred his heart. He saw the blood spurting from the hole in his chest, but it didn't hurt.

He shook his head and the daydream disappeared. He jumped to his feet, cocked the two hammers of the shotgun, crouched down, and looked all around. Twice, he completed a full circle sweep with his eyes before he stood erect and waited, watching and listening for the longest time, completely bewildered. He needed time to think. He was supposed to be in complete control of his own daydreams, wasn't he? He decided a face wash in the ice cold stream would clear his head.

The troop had made camp atop of an embankment in a small meadow, overlooking the confluence of a creek and the headwaters of the river they would be following for the better part of the rest of their journey. To reach the meadow, they followed a game trail that began several yards downstream and ran diagonally up the steep embankment of loose gravel and broken shale, back in an upstream direction to the meadow.

When Frank reached the creek, he propped the shotgun against a big rock, lay down on his belly, and submerged his head into the stream, taking a couple of big gulps of the cool water. He sat up and wiped the loose water from his eyes with his shirttail and scooped his wet hair out of his face. He took several deep breaths and let out a heavy sigh. The anger was gone, but not his resolve that Whitney and Brimsby were somehow going to pay.

As he sat quietly, he thought he could hear a muffled voice. He listened more intently. It seemed to be coming from upstream and as far as Frank could tell, someone was shouting, "Go away!" repeatedly and then calling for help. Frank stood up, collected the shotgun, and proceeded upstream through the thick willows.

He'd gone about forty or fifty feet through the brush, pushing the willow branches aside as he went. The willow clump ended and opened into a large gravel area, strewn with landslide debris. Part of the fifty foot high embankment had given way and brought tons of sand, gravel, huge boulders, and several trees cascading down into the water, diverting the stream and creating a new beach area under the embankment.

Frank heard the call for help and he tried to focus on the location of the sound. Directly ahead, there was a very large, round boulder with a fallen spruce tree lying across the top of it. Collin Pilkington lay with part of his body across the tree and the rest of it flat on the top of the boulder. In the dim light, Frank could see three coyotes. Oblivious to his approach, they were leaping in the air, trying desperately to catch hold of Collin's dangling right leg, which protruded over the edge of the boulder, just out of their reach. Their intent was to drag him off the big rock and onto the ground where they could finish the meal they started.

They were excited by the blood they found dripping down the face of the boulder. They had lapped it up greedily as high as they could reach and now they were determined to get at the source. Several ravens were perched in a tall, thin pine tree that clung to the top edge of the embankment. They squawked and complained at the coyotes for taking a meal they thought was theirs, exclusively.

Not wanting to waste one of the two shells he had left, Frank picked up several apple sized rocks and began to hurl them at the coyotes, shouting at them as he threw. For a moment, it didn't appear as if they were going to pay any attention to him, but then one of his rocks found its mark, catching one of the coyotes square in the head. It gave a surprised yelp and took off running across the shallow stream with its two compatriots in close pursuit. The ravens' squawking grew in intensity, as if they were cheering Frank's efforts at getting rid of the coyotes.

"Who's there?" called Collin.

"It's Frank Oakley. You can come down now. The coyotes have run off." He assumed Collin was injured and had climbed on top of the boulder to get away from them.

"I can't move. I'm paralyzed. I think my back is broken. Frank, please help me," pleaded Collin.

Frank thought for a moment and then said, "Yeah, just give me a minute, 'til I can figure out how to get up there." He made his way to the rear of the boulder and discovered there was no way to climb up the huge rock. In fact, the only way onto it, was to walk very gingerly or crawl along the tree that lay across the top of the boulder.

Frank was confused. In order to use the tree to get to the boulder top, Collin would have had to climb two thirds of the way up a very steep slope to even reach the base of the fallen tree. Why would he do that? If he made it that far up the embankment, why didn't he continue to the top? And why go up the embankment in the first place? The instinctive thing to do would have been to run for cover over easier ground. One other thing, Frank thought to himself, the coyotes wouldn't have followed him up the embankment. Or would they?

Frank decided he was going to need help to get to the top of the boulder. With a boost, he could reach the branches of the spruce tree and then pull himself up. He ran as quickly as he could back to the camp. The first person he saw was Michael. Stopping long enough to catch his breath, he said through gasps for air. "Goody-two-shoes is hurt bad. I need some help."

Michael wasn't sure whom Oakley was referring to and his puzzled looked told Frank exactly that.

"You know, the storekeeper, Pilk something," added Frank.

"Do you mean Mr. Pilkington?" Frank and Michael both turned at the sound of Whitney's voice.

"Yes, that's him. He's hurt bad, but I can't reach him," answered Frank. "What do mean, you can't reach him?"

"He's on top of this great big rock and I can't get to him. I need someone to lift me up."

"Well, let us go and see what we can do," suggested Whitney.

Oakley led the way while Whitney followed with Michael and Dancing Crow in tow. Nathaniel Brimsby didn't hear the conversation clearly, but he knew something was afoot. His curiosity got the better of him and he decided to follow.

It took them less than five minutes to get to the spot where Collin lay, still calling out for help. His shouts were much weaker and further apart. As they entered the clearing, Oakley pointed to the top of the boulder and shouted, "He's up there! He's up there!"

A feeble, "Is somebody there?" came from the top of the rock.

Whitney spoke up, "Yes, Mr. Pilkington, we are here to help. We shall be with you, shortly."

Oakley, pointing to the boulder, said, "I can get up on the other side. If someone could give me a boost, I can grab the tree and pull myself up on top."

Michael didn't have to be asked. He liked Collin and was genuinely willing to help. He led the way to the back of the rock and his hands were cupped and ready for Frank Oakley's foot by the time Frank got there. Frank wasn't sure what was supposed to happen, so Michael explained that Frank should stick one foot in his cupped hands. On the count of three, Michael would then catapult Frank in the air and he could grab the branches of the tree. Michael explained it was the way young Indian boys would help each other onto big horses.

It worked well. Michael lifted with all his might, easily sending Frank into the air the extra three feet or so he needed. Frank, after uttering several curses because of scratches he received from dried branches, was atop the boulder, assessing the situation.

Now, he could see where all the blood had come from. Collin was impaled through his left shoulder by a thick broken branch. The wound was still seeping a lot of blood. Frank made his way to the edge of the boulder and described to Whitney what he'd found. He stood waiting for someone to tell him what to do.

"For God's sake, pull the man off the damn tree and lower him down to us, so we can get a look at him," instructed Whitney and then he added, "Christ, can't any of you people think for yourselves!"

Frank knelt beside Collin and said, "I'm going to get you down off this rock. First, I gotta pull you off this tree branch. It is gonna hurt you something awful, but I gotta do it."

Collin was barely conscious when he opened his eyelids and staring into Frank Oakley's eyes, he said, "Why did you push me off the cliff?"

The question took Oakley completely by surprise. "I never — goddamn it, what the hell are you talking about? I didn't push you!"

Surprise was replaced by anger at having been falsely accused. Frank put his right hand under Collin's shoulder and grabbed a handful of Collin's shirtfront with his left hand. He stood quickly, lifting Collin's limp body from the branch as he rose. Collin's eyes rolled to the back of his head and then he passed out. Frank moved the inert body to the edge of the boulder. He sat down and grasping Collin under his arms, he slowly slid the body down to the waiting Michael, who took a good grip on each of Collins legs, just above the ankles. It was as far as he could reach. In the sitting position, Frank couldn't lower the body any further. Michael hollered up and told him if he lay on his belly and by holding onto Collin's shirt collar and extending his arm, he could lower Collin another foot or so.

Oakley did as Michael suggested and got Collin down far enough to where Michael could secure him around the waist, put him over his shoulder, and take the unconscious man a few feet to the creek side.

Oakley made his way to the front of the boulder, slid himself part way down, and then jumped. As he hit the ground, he stumbled and nearly fell into Nathaniel Brimsby, who put out his right arm and stopped Frank's momentum. They exchanged nasty glances and Frank hurried around to the back of the boulder, where he'd left his shotgun leaning against a small pile of rocks.

Michael lay Collin on his back and scooped some loose gravel and dirt into a small pile to use as a pillow to rest the injured man's head. Whitney knelt down to get a closer look. Collin opened his eyes again and staring wide-eyed at Whitney, he said, as he did to Oakley, "Why did you push me off the cliff?"

Whitney stood and said, "The man is delirious. I did no such thing."

Oakley added, "He said the same thing to me on up on the rock. He accused me of pushing him."

"And did you?" asked Whitney.

The question hit Oakley like a punch in the stomach. He replied, "No, no — I didn't. I'm just saying he said the same thing to me, is all."

"Then how do you account for him being on top of the boulder, impaled on a tree? The only way he could of gotten there is if he was pushed from the cliff above," continued Whitney.

"Or fell." said Brimsby.

Brimsby's interjection caught Whitney off guard. He stared at Brimsby momentarily and added, sarcastically, "Or fell." He paused briefly and continued, "Mr. Oakley, tell me exactly what happened when you discovered Mr. Pilkington?"

Oakley summarized, "Well Sir, I come down to the water to wash up and to get a drink when I heard someone yelling '*go away*' and then hollering for help. I figured out where the voice come from and I went upstream to have a look. I broke through the willows here and saw three coyotes jumping up trying to grab his leg. I chased the coyotes away and tried to figure a way up the boulder. Well Sir, I couldn't, so that's when I come and got you."

He stood silent, thinking he was done when Whitney asked, "Did Mr. Pilkington say anything to you when you acknowledged your presence."

Oakley thought for a moment, then answered, "Yeah, he said he was hurt and he needed help."

"His exact words, if you please, Mr. Oakley," said Whitney with a touch of impatience in his tone.

"He said he thought his back was broke and he needed help. That's all, I swear, Mr. Whitney," replied Frank, not sure of where the interrogation was headed.

"And what exactly did he say when you were on top of the rock with him?" continued Whitney.

"He looked me right in the eyes and he said, '*why did you push me off the cliff?*' But I didn't, Mr. Whitney. I swear, I didn't have nothin' to do with it."

"Breed, have the old man look at Mr. Pilkington and see if he can tell if the unfortunate soul has a broken back," Whitney commanded.

Michael translated Whitney's request to Dancing Crow, who immediately knelt beside Collin, put his hand under his back, and gently ran his fingers up the spine from his tailbone to his shoulder blades. He then took out the raven feather from his medicine bag and placed it on Collin's forehead. Putting his right hand on the feather, he closed his eyes and began a slow rhythmic chant.

After about a minute, he stopped chanting, put the feather away, and told Michael his findings. "The mother hen has broken his back in two places; one between the shoulder blades and the other just above the hips. He has also lost much blood. I do not think he has much time left in the land of the living."

Michael told Whitney what Dancing Crow had found. Whitney took it all in and then he said to no one in particular, "He was laying there a long time to lose so much blood. I would guess most of the night. Interesting."

"Which means he went off the cliff early last night," commented Nathaniel Brimsby.

"Very astute, Mr. Brimsby. Sometimes you surprise me," Whitney answered, sarcastically.

Whitney ordered Oakley and Michael to carry Collin up to the warmth of the camp fire. Michael protested, claiming that because of his broken back, if they moved Collin, they could very well kill him.

"He's as good as dead, anyhow. Isn't that what the old heathen said?" Whitney argued.

Oakley helped lift Collin's inert body onto Michael's shoulder and they all headed back to the camp. Michael, with Oakley's help, gently laid Collin down by the fire. Silas Davidson stood nearby. He appeared very indifferent, almost nonchalant to the discovery that a supposed good friend of his was seriously hurt.

Whitney found Silas's behaviour puzzling. He said, "Mr. Davidson, you seem to have a rather callous indifference to your friend's misfortune and eminent demise."

"It is unfortunate Mr. Pilkington has met his end, but what business is it of mine?" Silas paused long enough for emphasis and then added, "I am not afraid! I'm not!" He walked a few paces to the wood pile, gathered a few sticks, added them to the fire, and asked, "Who is going to help me prepare breakfast, now?"

Whitney was enraged. He had no idea what Silas was eluding to when he said he wasn't afraid, but he'd reached his tolerance level with the man. He spat on the ground and then said very slowly and deliberately, "The hell with breakfast. We have a dying man here who needs our immediate attention!"

Silas stopped poking at the fire, slowly stood erect, and looked directly at Whitney. With his sunken eyes and snide little grin, Silas looked like a ghoul from one of the ghost stories Whitney's drunken father used to tell him when he was a child, just to see the look of terror on his young son's face. Silas said, "My, my, Mr. Whitney. Where did you suddenly find some compassion in your dark soul? You expect me to believe you are truly concerned about poor Mr. Pilkington's welfare."

Inside, Whitney was seething. He wanted to take the three steps between himself and Silas, grab the man by the throat, and choke the life out of him, but he took control of his emotions and kept a calm demeanour as he addressed Silas's question. "You are right, Mr. Davidson. I don't give a tinker's damn about this lot of scoundrels and riff-raff. Mr. Pilkington was, without doubt, the best of a bad lot and deserves a little more consideration than any of the rest of you, but you are correct in your assessment. What I am truly concerned about is, who pushed him off the cliff? Any thoughts on the subject, Mr. Davidson?"

Silas looked like a young boy who had just been caught taking a fresh baked cookie off the counter when he wasn't supposed to. He quickly caught his composure and answered Whitney. "I thought as much."

Whitney crossed the short distant to Silas, put his face near Silas's ear and said in a whisper no one else could hear, "Don't presume to know me or understand me, Mr. Davidson. If you push me any further I will have Mathew Briscoe demonstrate to the rest of the men the quickest way to cut a man's throat, using you as a test subject. Do I make myself clear?"

Whitney stepped back far enough so he could watch Silas's face for a reaction. Silas wore a blank stare, not unlike a deer caught in lamplight. Silas had come to a crossroads in his mind. He convinced himself, if he showed no fear, the fox's prophecy could not possibly come true. However, he did feel afraid, but his dilemma was that he wasn't sure whom or what he feared more; Whitney or some Indian witch doctor. He lifted his bowed head and looked at Whitney and said, "You've made yourself very clear, Mr. Whitney. Very clear, indeed!"

Whitney was still not sure of Silas's state of mind, so he chose not to pursue the issue any further. He turned to face the rest of the men and commanded, "I want every man front and center, on the double!"

-2-

The Briscoe brothers were the only ones out of ear shot. Frank Oakley volunteered to fetch them. As he approached their small camp, the sun was just breaking over the eastern horizon. In the dim light of dawn, Oakley could see Luke Briscoe lying on the ground near the dying fire, but Mathew was nowhere to be seen. "Hey, Hillbilly! Where are you? Boss wants everybody front and center," Frank shouted.

Mathew Briscoe stepped out from behind a large tree to the right of the small camp. He eyed Oakley up and down and then asked, "What's he want?"

"Wants to talk to everybody, be my guess."

"Tell him I'm busy with Luke."

"Might not be the time to do that, Hillbilly. He's madder than a wet hornet. I's you, I'd see what he wants, but that's just me. You suit yourself," Oakley said and then turned and headed back toward the rest of the group.

Mathew hesitated a moment and then said after Oakley, "Tell the Boss we're on our way."

Luke was alternating between states of complete coherence, in which he would sit up and hold a conversation with Mathew and semi-consciousness, where it appeared he had a grasp of things happening around him, but he seemed incapable of responding to them. Mathew knelt down and with his hand on Luke's chest, he gave his younger brother a shake. To Mathew's delight, Luke was in the coherent state. He opened his eyes and smiled when he saw his older brother. "How's the shoulder?" asked Mathew. He regretted having posed the question as soon as he said it. The last thing he wanted to do was remind Luke of the pain he was going through.

Sure enough, it appeared as though Luke wasn't hurting until Mathew brought it up. "Oh, it hurts somethin' awful, Mathew. Why are they doin' this to me?"

"Who?" Mathew asked again and then he remembered Luke had mentioned Elizabeth and young Sean McClaren were holding him down while the young Indian girl jabbed the knife point into his shoulder wound.

"You know, Mathew. I told you. It was — "

Mathew cut him off, "Yeah, I remember, little brother. I remember. The boss has called a meetin' and he wants everybody there, pronto"

"Tell him I'm too sick to come. I don't like him, Mathew. He is a very mean man!"

Mathew Briscoe snapped. He grabbed his brother's shirtfront with his left hand, lifted him up a few inches and then backhanded him as hard as he could with his right hand. Luke rolled with the slap, sat upright and easily threw his much smaller brother to the side. He stood up and wiping at the trickle of blood oozing out of his left nostril, he asked, "Now, what did you do that for?"

"Because you dumb ox, if you don't smarten up, the miserable bastard is gonna kill you or leave you out here for the coyotes and the ravens to pick at your sorry bones and there won't be a damn thing I can do to help you," answered Mathew, in angry desperation.

"Why would he do that, Mathew?" asked a surprised Luke.

Mathew thought for a moment before answering. His anger had subsided and he put on a teaching hat, using past experiences to help his young brother understand. "Luke, you remember when Pa caught us at the swimmin' hole when we was supposed to be workin'? Remember what he said? He said if we didn't work, we didn't eat and if we kept foolin' 'round and not workin', then we could go make a livin' somewhere else, 'cause he didn't want no lazy youngin's on his farm."

He waited for some sign of acknowledgement from Luke that he remembered and when Luke got it, he continued, "You remember how scared we was? We buckled down and did our chores after that. Well Luke, Mr. Whitney is just like Pa. He needs us to help him find the gold and just like Pa, he don't like no slackers. Only thing is, when he gets mad, he's a lot more dangerous than Pa ever was. You understand me, Luke?"

Luke hesitated before replying, "Yeah, I understand Mathew, but I don't know what it is you want me to do?"

Mathew approached his brother, put his hands on his shoulders, and gently pushed Luke to a sitting position on the ground. He then sat directly across from Luke and said in a soft, almost pleading tone, "Luke, there is nothin' wrong with your shoulder that it should hurt so bad. It's all in your head. You keep dreamin' and seein' this injun squaw stickin' the knife in your wound. I know you think what you see is real and you think the pain is real, but they ain't, Luke. They ain't.

"Listen, I heard some of the other men talkin' and they have been havin' strange, scary dreams, too and a lot of them is sayin' it's some injun Medicine Man, what's makin' us see these things and feel things like the pain in your shoulder."

Luke interjected, "You mean that old man, Breed's friend?"

"No, this is a very powerful Medicine Man who can make you see and do things. I think he is from the village where we kilt all those injuns."

Mathew could see this was beyond Luke's grasp, so he tried a different approach. "Luke, you remember when Ma would read to us from the Bible most evenin's after supper? You remember the story of Noah. You remember how God told him he was gonna destroy the world and Noah should build a big boat and save his family and all the animals?"

There was a big smile on Luke's face and he was shaking his head in affirmation. Mathew continued, "Well, God lives in a world we can't see, right? Even though you can't see him you believe God is there, don't ya?"

Luke indicated by his body language that he did. Mathew went on, "This Medicine Man can live in the world we can't see, just like God and he can make us do things and see things. He's makin' you think your shoulder hurts, but you can beat him by not listenin' to him."

Mathew explained further, "When you see the injun squaw and Elizabeth and the kid, you say to them '*You're not real. Go away*'. And when your shoulder hurts, you gotta tell yourself the pain is not real."

"I'll try, Mathew. I'll try," said Luke, in all sincerity.

"You have to do more than try, Luke. I got a feelin' if the Boss don't think you're up to it, he's gonna leave you behind or something worse. So you gotta convince him you're fine. Your life and maybe mine could depend on it! You got that, little brother?" pleaded Mathew.

Luke looked frightened when he said, "Sure, Mathew, sure."

Whitney looked impatient as the Briscoe brothers approached. He scowled at Mathew and said, "Now, since we are all here in body and I assume in mind," as he glanced at Luke for a moment and then continued, "you all can see, Mr. Pilkington isn't doing so well. He went off the steep embankment down from the camp, landed on a huge boulder and consequently suffered a broken back and other injuries. The only reason this would concern me in the least, is he claims someone pushed him."

Whitney looked around the circle of men, making eye contact with each of them. When he tried to look into Luke Briscoe's eyes, Luke lowered his head. Whitney caught the gesture and addressed him, "Mr. Briscoe — uh — the big one."

Mathew intervened, "His name is Luke, Boss."

Whitney thanked Mathew and then continued, "Luke, why are you hiding your eyes? Are you afraid of me? Do you have something to tell me?"

Luke kept his head down and merely shook it to indicate a '*no*' answer.

"I'm talking to you, Luke Briscoe and I would appreciate it if you would look at me when I am speaking to you."

Luke lifted his head and said, "Yes Sir."

"Did you have anything to do with pushing Mr. Pilkington off the embankment?"

"Oh, no. Not me. No. No. No," said Luke, shaking his head, vigorously.

"Then why are you acting so nervous? What is troubling you?" continued Whitney.

"Brother Mathew said you was mad and you might leave me behind if I didn't tell my shoulder to stop hurtin'," Luke replied.

Whitney looked to Mathew for further explanation. Mathew said, "I told him he'd better knuckle down and get hisself together if'n he wants to continue on the ride, that's all."

Whitney knew there was more to it, but it was of no matter because he was sure Luke had nothing to do with Collin Pilkington's plight. Whitney concluded Luke was wrapped up completely in his delusional pain and Mathew was attending to him the entire time. He said to Luke, "Your brother speaks the truth. By my calculations we have about a week to our destination and it is time we upped the pace to reach our objective in as little time as possible."

Whitney saw a confused look on Luke's face, so he put it in simpler terms. "You need to pull your weight, Mr. Briscoe, or as your brother told you, I will leave you to the ravens and coyotes and whatever demons are plaguing you."

Whitney began a process of elimination in his mind. Nathaniel Brimsby and the old heathen never left the camp, but Frank Oakley did. He couldn't account for the movement of either Silas Davidson or the breed. He concluded it wasn't Frank Oakley's style to push a man off a cliff in the dark, which left the breed and Silas Davidson, or as Nathaniel Brimsby stated earlier, maybe Pilkington simply fell.

Another option was slowly creeping into Whitney's mind, but he quickly shooed it away like a bothersome fly. The thought that something supernatural could be behind Pilkington's fall, was not an idea Whitney was prepared to entertain.

He looked over the assembled men once more before speaking. "Well gentlemen, I have given this matter some serious thought and I have concluded our poor unfortunate Mr. Pilkington most likely fell over the embankment edge, but there is a question needed to be answered — what was he doing out there in the first place?"

Whitney paused for effect and then with a dramatic shift, he asked Silas in a most accusatory tone, "And what were you doing by the embankment, Mr. Davidson?"

The question hit Silas like a splash of ice cold water. He sucked in a lung full of air, his eyes went wide, and he stammered as he answered, "I — uh — that is — I thought I heard something. That's it. I thought I heard something and I went to see what it might be. I didn't see anything, but it must have been the noise of Mr. Pilkington falling that I heard."

Whitney smiled. His trap had worked. He tried again, "You, Breed, what were you doing there?"

Michael answered without emotion, "Wasn't anywhere near the cliff last night."

Whitney didn't show any signs of disappointment as he said, "Well then, the conclusion I have come to is Mr. Pilkington fell or one of these two pushed him." He paused long enough to point to Silas and Michael and continued, "Saddle up and let us be on our way. We have wasted enough time."

Silas spoke up, "Wait, what are we to do about poor Mr. Pilkington, here?"

Whitney replied, without breaking his stride or turning around, "Not my problem. Whoever started it can finish it."

Silas Davidson looked at each man with pleading in his eyes. He wanted someone to have the courage he lacked, the wherewithal to put Collin Pilkington out of his misery; a mercy killing, not unlike shooting a lame horse or an old crippled dog. Frank Oakley turned and followed Whitney, spitting at Silas's feet as he walked by.

"Please, Mr. Brimsby, you have the rifle. Don't let Mr. Pilkington suffer any longer," Silas begged Nathaniel, who merely shook his head and walked away.

Mathew Briscoe approached Silas. He took out the big knife and tried to hand it to Silas, silently indicating he should be the one to do the deed. Silas simply lowered his eyes in humility. Mathew put the knife back in his waistband and he and Luke headed in the direction of their small camp.

Michael knew what was coming, so before Silas could ask, he said. "It's not for me to end the man's life. If you don't have the guts to do it, then leave him to die on his own." He turned his back on Silas and he and Dancing Crow set about gathering their things and headed to the picket line to saddle up.

Silas was left alone with his fear and the dying man at his feet and all he could say was, "What about breakfast? Who is going to help me with breakfast?"

-3-

While the rest of the troop rode an easy, relatively flat trail all day, Collin Pilkington lay dying where he had been dumped earlier in the morning. Whitney expected to gain some time with the easy going. He remembered what the old prospector told him about this part of the journey. "You'll be followin' the river on top of the east bank. The river'll be below ya and there will be a pretty flat plateau on your right. It'll be easy goin' for three days or so."

There was no conversation amongst the men with the exception of Michael and Dancing Crow, who were exchanging thoughts on the events of the morning. Whitney led the troop with Frank Oakley not far behind. As he rode, Oakley ran various scenarios through his imagination in which he got his revenge against Brimsby and Whitney.

Nathaniel Brimsby rode a few feet behind Oakley. His mind was focused on his status in the group. He was beginning to feel isolated, like he was alone against the rest of the men. He wasn't afraid of them, but he didn't trust any of them, particularly Frank Oakley. He thought, *I'll have to keep an eye on that little bastard.* He didn't trust that goddamn Whitney, either, but he thought he would let sleeping dogs lie, for now.

Silas Davidson was next in line, at least his body was. His mind was in another reality, where he kept seeing Harold Grant standing on the surface of a lake, pointing an accusatory finger at him. This image was replaced by a red fox with a wicked smile, who kept asking, "Are you afraid Silas? Are you afraid, yet?"

Silas would scream "No! No!" out loud, which would cause Brimsby to turn in the saddle to see what the problem was.

Michael and Dancing Crow were next in line with the Briscoe brothers bringing up the rear. Mathew was leading the string of five mules and the spare horse, about thirty to forty feet behind Michael and Dancing Crow. Luke was still having his delusional bouts where he would cry out in agony from his painful shoulder. Mathew would chide him and remind him it was all in his head. Luke would give a look as if he remembered something he had forgotten and the pain disappeared for a few minutes and then the whole cycle would repeat itself. Mathew was becoming paranoid. His sense of duty to protect Luke was growing into an obsession. In the daylight, he sensed Whitney would not hesitate to get rid of Luke if his brother slowed down the procession. At night, in restless sleep, he dreamt Sean McClaren came to extract his revenge on Luke and there was nothing he could do to stop him.

"We should have helped the mother hen," commented Dancing Crow, referring to Collin Pilkington.

"What do you think we could have done for him? He is a dead man," replied Michael. "You bandaged his wound. What more could you do?"

"Dying men need someone to be with them as they pass to the land of the spirits. No one should make the journey alone," answered Dancing Crow.

Michael was surprised by the old man's response. He posed a question, "These killers, they deserve to have someone comfort them as they die?"

Dancing Crow paused and thought before he answered, "I do believe this to be true, but I do not know as I could do it. I know I would have liked to help the mother hen. He was a good man, a very good man."

There was a long pause and then Dancing Crow spoke again. "What are you called by The People?" He was asking Michael what his Salish name was.

Michael thought of lying to the old man, telling him he did not have a Salish name, but he knew Dancing Crow would see right through him. "The People call me Angry Crane."

Dancing Crow didn't show any signs of surprise. He merely said, "Ah, the Crane, symbol of solitude and independence. Yes, I see it fits. Tell me Angry Crane, why was the mother hen with these evil men?"

"He owned a place where he traded goods for the white man's money. They say he burned the place down and so he was sent to jail."

"I do not understand," said Dancing Crow. "If it was his place, then why could he not burn it down, if he wanted to?"

"It is against the white man's law," replied Michael.

"If I live to be as old as the trees, I shall never understand the white man and his laws." Dancing Crow reined in and said, "If you will lead my horse, Angry Crane, I will travel to the land of the spirits and see if I can be of comfort to Mother Hen's spirit.

Michael felt uncomfortable when Dancing Crow called him Angry Crane and he felt like telling the old man he preferred to be called Michael, but he thought better of it. He took the old man's reins and led the horse while Dancing Crow bowed his head, closed his eyes, and began a low rhythmic chant.

-4-

The mid morning sun shone on Collin Pilkington's face as he regained consciousness. It took him several minutes to piece together what had happened and where he was. His last clear memory was leaving the camp. He was angry, very angry at Silas Davidson, the ungrateful wretch. His intent was to go down to the edge of the creek and cool off, but in his angry state he'd cut into the woods too far upstream and ended up on the cliff overlooking the creek. He decided to make his way along the bluff edge until he found the deer trail down to the water.

As he started to feel his way through the darkness, he heard someone or something close behind him. As he turned to see what it might be, he felt a push on his back and he shuddered as he recalled the sickening thud when he landed on the boulder some thirty feet below.

From that point, his memory was a blur. He recalled going in and out of consciousness and there were flashes of recollection; coyotes trying to reach him, Frank Oakley tugging and pulling at him, Whitney and the others standing around him arguing about something, the sound of horses and men riding off. He tried to lift his head so he could see someone. He didn't have the strength, so he began to call out instead. "Mr. Davidson? Silas? Anyone? Is there anybody there?" He waited several minutes and then tried again, "Silas? Silas? Where are you, for God's sake?"

He remembered vaguely hearing the noise of the men and horses leaving and then it hit him. They had left him behind! The bastards left him to die! Panic overtook him. Using all his strength, he tried to lift himself upon his left elbow. He couldn't move his legs. In fact he couldn't even feel them. He lifted his head up high enough so he could see his feet and tried to wiggle his toes on his right foot and then tried the left foot. Nothing!

Collin lay his head back down and slowly slid his good arm under himself to feel his lower back. He gasped for air when his hand touched a protrusion of bone. His broken spine had pushed through the skin. A swell of emotion caused him to sob uncontrollably. He quickly pulled his hand out and felt his shoulder, which brought a hazy recollection of Frank Oakley pulling him off the tree branch on which he was impaled. He stuck his fingers under a crude bandage that someone had put on the wound. He felt a sticky mixture of moss and some other plant material that had mixed with his blood and filled a hole the size of a shot glass, just below his collar bone. Whoever worked on the wound knew what they were doing because it had stemmed the bleeding.

Suddenly, he felt an unbearable thirst. The creek was a good two hundred feet away, but his survival instinct told him he needed to get to the water. Using all the strength he could muster, he tried desperately to turn himself on his belly. The exertion was too much and he lost consciousness.

Collin found himself standing in complete darkness, a blackness so dense it left him with an overpowering feeling of complete isolation. It was as if the entire world had disappeared and left him alone in this ebony void. He dared not move. He felt he was standing on a very small island and if he stepped off, he would fall and tumble endlessly into the dark nothingness.

His back and shoulder were somehow miraculously healed and he felt no physical discomfort. He began to turn slowly and carefully, looking about and as he did so, he saw a faint light in the distance. It flickered, becoming smaller and then larger at times. Collin recognized it as a campfire and decided to head toward it. He stuck one foot out gingerly and let it down. It hit solid ground. He brought the other foot forward and it also ended on good old dirt. He began to move his feet faster, although carefully, one ahead of the other and before long, the campfire was growing in size as he got nearer.

As he inched closer and closer, he could see a figure standing near the fire. He wished he could get to the fire more rapidly and before he could take his next step, he found himself standing beside Dancing Crow, who must have seen the astonished look on his face, because he said, "Do not seemed so surprised. You are in the land of dreams where anything is possible."

Collin was completely bewildered. "Where am I? Did I die or something? I don't understand."

"You have not died, or you would be in the land of the spirits. I have called to you in this dream world and you have come," offered Dancing Crow as an explanation.

"Why is it so dark?" was Collin's next question.

"It is your dream. It is as you feel or want it to be," said Dancing Crow.

"Alright, I want it to be a bright sunny day and I am in a high alpine meadow full of flowers," replied Collin, only half-heartedly believing it would happen. For a very brief moment, he was in that meadow and then everything reverted to the complete darkness with only the old man and a campfire for company.

"What happened? Why didn't it last?" Collin asked.

"It would have. I brought us back to the darkness," explained Dancing Crow.

"For God's sake, why?" pleaded Collin.

"Others can come into our dreams. Unwanted others," explained Dancing Crow.

Collin took a moment to gather his wits and then asked, "What do you want with me?"

"I came to help you as you passed into the land of the spirits, to be with you as you leave the world of the living."

"Help me die? What are you talking about?" Then Collin realized like many dreamers do that it was, indeed, just a dream. He remember his broken back and his seeping shoulder, but no matter how hard he tried to wake up, he couldn't.

Collin thought long and hard and then said to Dancing Crow, "I know I'm a dead man back in the — the — well, you know, the land of the living, I guess you'd call it. So, I can stay here by this campfire and have a pleasant fireside chat with you until the time comes. Is this what you are telling me?"

"If you wish," said Dancing Crow.

"If I wish? Jesus, can't you give me a straight answer?"

"This is the land of dreams. You can spend your time here in any manner you choose."

"Then why did you make it so dark?"

Dancing Crow sighed and spoke as he were addressing a small child, "We are taking a chance with the campfire. In the land of dreams there are Dreamwalkers, who can do you great harm and I am making it difficult for him to find us."

"Him! You said *him*! You know who this Dreamwalker thing is, don't you?"

"There are many Dreamwalkers. I believe there is one who is tormenting the Evil One and the men who follow him," replied Dancing Crow.

Collin didn't understand at first and then caught the inference. "You mean Whitney and the rest of us!"

"That is what I believe."

"So, who is this spirit? Talk to him. Tell him I had nothing to with the killing of those people. In fact, tell him I helped a woman escape from them! Tell him!"

Before Dancing Crow could answer, the darkness itself formed a huge hand and extinguished the fire. Dancing Crow felt himself being lifted in the air and then tossed through the void a great distance before hitting the ground with a thump. As he landed, he woke from his trance so suddenly he nearly toppled from the saddle.

Michael was still leading the old man's horse when he felt a tug on the reins and turned in time to see the look of terror on Dancing Crow's face.

Michael rode back to him and asked what was wrong. Dancing Crow looked up. A calmness came over his face and he said with an undertone of defeat in his voice, "I can be of no help to the mother hen. I am not strong enough."

Michael wanted to push the issue further, but something told him not to. Whatever happened in the old man's trance had frightened him and he was not going to talk about it, in any event.

Collin returned to the physical world, regaining consciousness momentarily. He felt himself drifting into oblivion again. He knew something horrific was waiting for him if he passed out and he fought with all his might to keep himself conscious. He felt as if he was walking a tightrope where one side was the blackness and the other side, consciousness and as he made his way, he was swaying from one side to the other; temporary consciousness and then a brief period of blackness.

He kept this up for hours. Each time he dipped into the darkness, it seemed for a longer period of time. He could see the campfire again with a figure next to it, but this time it was not the old man, but a strange looking creature with the body of a man and the head of a fox.

During his most recent stints of consciousness, he thought he could see some coyotes advancing towards him. He felt trapped with nowhere to go; eternal darkness and a demon on one side and coyotes intent on having him for dinner, on the other. Then it came to him, didn't the old man say it was his dream and he could make it anything he wanted it to be? He let himself slip into unconsciousness and he thought of a spot he visited once; a beautiful alpine lake surrounded on three sides by towering peaks. It was the most peaceful spot he could imagine.

He found himself sitting on a small boulder by the lakeshore, soaking in the warm sunshine. He looked up and saw an osprey riding the thermal waves high above. A herd of mountain sheep came down to the water's edge to drink, not at all bothered by his presence. He was beginning to feel at peace when it all went pitch black. He wasn't afraid. He was angry. "Stop this, you son-of-a-bitch!

I've never done anything to hurt you or your people, so bugger off and leave me alone!"

His beautiful scene did not return, but an envelope of light extended several feet in every direction around him, forming a dome. On the edge between the darkness and where the light began, stood a red fox. It stood half in the dark and half in the light, not moving, just staring at Collin as if it wasn't sure what to do.

Collin and the fox stared at each other for what seemed a very long time and then Collin broke the stalemate by saying, "What do you want? You know what? I don't give a damn. Do whatever you want. God will be my judge, not you!"

The fox didn't say or do anything. It simply disappeared as Collin came back into the conscious world only to find one of the coyotes licking his oozing shoulder. As they made eye contact, the coyote snarled and tore out Collin's throat.

-5-

It was late afternoon, about the same time Collin Pilkington left this world, when the darkest, most ominous looking thunder clouds appeared over the mountain tops to Whitney's right. He knew within the hour they were going to be in the middle of a nasty one, but he did not even think about looking for some possible shelter. His mind was set on making time and he wasn't about to let man or nature slow him down.

Nathaniel Brimsby had been scouting ahead, looking for any sign of game. He pulled up alongside Whitney and reported that he didn't see a thing. He voiced his concerns about the impending weather and the possibility of looking for some cover. Whitney didn't say anything for the longest time. He turned in the saddle and glanced at the line of men behind him, took a quick peek at the purple clouds approaching, then looking back at Nathaniel, he said, "Keep it moving, Mr. Brimsby."

Nathaniel took it upon himself to pass the word along to the others. The news didn't seem to bother anyone except Michael and Dancing Crow. Michael said something about it being very foolish and Brimsby said, "Tell it to the Boss."

As the northwest wind blew the storm rapidly closer, the men could feel the temperature drop significantly and as the wind increased in velocity, it brought with it a wet, earthy odour. An eerie, expectant stillness was in the air. The mounts grew uneasy and began to fight the rein, as if they knew something was about to happen. Silas Davidson's horse was especially skittish. It began to snort and shake its head, which brought Silas back from wherever his mind had been. He yanked as hard as he could on the reins and gave the horse a good stiff kick in the side, which only made it more agitated. It reared up on its hind legs and almost threw Silas off. Michael, who was riding close behind, handed the reins of his horse to Dancing Crow and dismounted. As Silas's horse was about to rear up for the second time, Michael grabbed hold of the left rein where it met the bit ring and kept the horse from rising up. He talked gently to the animal, stroking its head and neck and as he did so and the horse settled down.

"You need to pay more attention to what you are doing," he told Silas as he remounted his own horse. Silas didn't say anything audible. He merely muttered something under his breath.

The first streak of lightning ran vertically from one side of the massive thunderhead to the other. The thunder hadn't reached their ears yet, when another bolt ran the same path as the first one, across the plum coloured sky, followed immediately by a third. The three thunder claps hit them in rapid succession. It reminded Whitney of cannon barrages and he felt a momentary déjà vu, where he found himself back on the battle field.

There was barely enough time to catch their collective breaths, when another light and noise show began and then without warning the skies opened up as if someone burst a balloon and hail the size of marbles pelted man and beast, alike. Whitney hollered for them to dismount, hold tight to their horses, and wait out the worst of the storm. Mathew Briscoe found it difficult to control the string of five mules and the spare horse, as well as his brother's mount. He stopped and prodded at a semiconscious Luke. "Wake up, Brother Luke. Come on you moron. I could use a little help, here."

Luke snapped to attention as if he was jabbed with a cattle prod. "What's happening, Mathew? What's wrong?" As he spoke, an excruciating pain ran through his injured shoulder. He screamed and grabbed for it and as he did so, his horse reared up and Luke went sliding backwards off his mount, right into the feet of the first mule in the string. The mule instinctively, jumped out of the way, not wanting to step on the man. Kicking and jumping, it broke free of the lead reins from Mathew's grip, turned back in the direction they had come, and took off in a fear driven gallop, taking the other four mules and the spare mount with it. Luckily, Mathew was still holding onto Luke's horse so it couldn't join the runaways. Before Mathew had time to think, the mules and the spare horse were out of sight and still running.

Hanging on tightly to his and Luke's horses' reins, he knelt down beside his brother to see how he was. When Luke fell and the mule began kicking, he brought his hands up over his face to protect himself. A powerful kick broke three fingers on his right hand. He was screaming in agony and Mathew mistakenly assumed Luke was bellyaching about his shoulder again and grabbed his right hand, intending to get Luke off the wet ground. Luke let out another scream and then Mathew realized his brother's hand was crushed.

"Luke, Luke listen to me!" pleaded Mathew. "I gotta go after those mules. I need you to stay here and hold on tight to your own horse. You got that?"

"I can't, Mathew. I can't! Everything hurts so much," cried Luke.

There was a small embankment, about a foot high, paralleling the trail on the right side. Mathew manoeuvred Luke so he was half sitting and half lying on the path, propped up slightly by the embankment. He tried getting Luke to hold onto his own horse's reins but Luke was in too much pain, so he tied the reins around Luke's waist and mounted his own horse to go after the loose stock. He was about to put boot to flank, when he suddenly felt he could not ride off and leave his brother alone to deal with, what would certainly be, an enraged Whitney.

After the initial surge, the hail became much smaller, pea sized. However, it grew in intensity and was mixed with heavy pelting rain. Everyone and everything was totally drenched in a matter of minutes. Michael could feel the temperature dropping rapidly. He could see Dancing Crow begin to shiver and his first thought was to find some shelter for him.

Two hours previous, the trail had veered away from the river in order to get around a small canyon. It rose rapidly until they were atop the canyon wall, looking down onto the river. They had begun their descent back down to the river valley when the storm hit. Forty feet up the hillside from the trail was a grove of Silver Spruce trees. Michael knew, from experience, they would find shelter under the trees. He told Dancing Crow his intentions, helped the old man to his feet, and with the horses and the Medicine Man in tow, Michael made his way to the tree line.

Whitney saw the movement. He stood and watched Michael and Dancing Crow make their way to the trees. It was obvious what Michael was up to. It was a good idea. He shouted as loud as he could, hoping to be heard over the driving wind and rain, giving orders to follow Michael into the trees and find some cover. Whitney, Oakley, and Brimsby, all leading their horses, followed Michael up the hillside.

Part way up the hill, Whitney looked back and saw that neither Silas Davidson nor the Briscoe brothers had moved. "Jesus!" he cursed, as he handed his reins to Oakley and started back down the hill. He was beside Silas in a matter of seconds, who was seated on the trail, his horse's reins clenched in his fist. Whitney kicked him hard on the thigh, expecting Davidson to leap to his feet from surprise. He didn't. He simply raised his head very slowly and looked at Whitney with hollow, sunken eyes. As he methodically rose to his feet, he said, "I'm not afraid, you know. You think this storm scares me? Well, it doesn't."

Whitney was at a loss for words. All he managed to get out was, "Get your sorry self under some shelter or you can stay here and drown, for all I care, you silly old fool!" and he proceeded down the trail in the direction of the Briscoe brothers.

He couldn't see three feet in front of his face through the downpour, so he was nearly upon the Briscoes before he could clearly make them out. His mind told him something was not quite right and then it struck him that the mules were gone. Mathew was bent over, tending to Luke. Whitney reached down and grabbed him by the shoulder to get his attention. As Mathew rose and turned to face Whitney, he took out the big knife. Whitney reacted quickly, drawing his pistol and cocking the hammer.

Mathew saw who it was and relaxed his stance, "Sorry, Mr. Whitney. I didn't know it was you."

Mathew hadn't put the knife away, yet. As a result, Whitney kept his pistol cocked and pointed at him when he said, "Where the hell are the mules? Did you let them get away? Christ almighty, you let the mules get away, you stupid hillbilly!"

Whitney extended his pistol arm and took aim at Mathew's forehead. Mathew put the knife back in his waistband and then said with a sneer, "You ain't gonna shoot me, Mr. Whitney. I know as sure I'm standin' here. You need me. You need all of us. Who's gonna help you carry all the gold if we all die before we get there? Who, Mr. Whitney?"

Whitney was flabbergasted. It was as if Mathew looked inside his mind and had a front row seat to his nightmare. Gaining his composure, he shifted the pistol so it was aimed squarely at Luke. "How about, I shoot Brother Luke, instead. He's of no goddamn use to me, now is he?"

"Then you'll still have to kill me before I cut your sorry throat, which brings us back to where we was, don't it?" replied Mathew, with a maniacal grim on his face.

Whitney lowered the pistol and said, "It seems, Mr. Briscoe, you have me at a stalemate, but the question still remains, what are we going to do about the runaway livestock?"

"Well now, that's a different kettle of fish, ain't it Mr. Whitney. Luke ain't fit to go after 'em and I sure as hell ain't doin' it and leave Luke here to the likes of you and the goddamn gunslinger."

Whitney sighed heavily, uncocked the pistol and put it away. "Get your brother up into the tree line and for God's sake don't lose them horses or so help me I will shoot the both of you." Whitney started to walk away, stopped and turned back to Mathew and added, "Just so you know, this isn't over."

-6-

Nathaniel Brimsby could not remember ever feeling this cold. Even when he worked his gold claim in the dead of winter with the temperature well below freezing, he had never been this uncomfortable. He was soaked to the skin and he couldn't stop shivering. Like the rest of the men, he found a big spruce tree with long spreading branches that reached to the ground. He tied his horse securely to the leeward side, if one could call it that, for the pelting rain seemed to be swirling in the wind and was coming in from all directions. He fought his way under the limbs of the tree and close to the trunk, breaking off dried branches with his bare hands, as he fashioned himself a body sized nook in which he could sit up. There wasn't any rain coming into his little shelter, but the damage was already done. He was drenched and only a blazing fire would warm him up, but he wasn't about to go back out into the weather to try and find Silas Davidson, the keeper of the matches.

He guessed it to be late afternoon, perhaps early evening, although he couldn't tell by the amount of daylight. It was as dark as if it was late evening and had been that way since the rain started. The hunger pangs in his belly told him it was near meal time. Nathaniel shook his head and sighed — not only cold and wet, but hungry, too.

He wrapped a musty smelling blanket around himself as tight as he could and closed his eyes, trying to think of other things and not how cold and hungry he was. He imagined himself seated at his kitchen table. He had put in a hard day at the claim and had come home to a nice warm cabin, a smiling wife, and the odour of a venison stew, simmering on the back of the stove. Anna was all smiles as she came over to him and gave him a hug.

The cabin, although very spacious, was just one big room. They had set up a line with a couple of blankets draped over it to separate the living area from the sleeping quarters. Nathaniel could hear some noise behind the barrier. He broke Anna's embrace, stood up, walked to the makeshift curtain, and pulled back one of the blankets. A man sat on the bed looking up at Nathaniel. His face was covered in blood and bits of skull bone and pieces of brain tissue were seeping out of a gaping hole in the man's forehead. The gory figure pointed an accusatory finger at him and said, "You say you can't remember what you did? Well, take a good look. This is what you did to me with a pick axe."

Nathaniel turned away in disgust and fear, only to see Anna covered in blood and gore. She was unrecognizable, as was the native woman standing next to her. The women raised their arms simultaneously and pointed at Nathaniel. Anna spoke, "This is what you did to us. Now do you remember?"

Nathaniel was trying to make sense of it all, when a strange figure stepped out from behind the native woman. The body was a human being dressed in native garb, but it had the head of a fox. The creature put its arm around the native woman and said, "An unfaithful wife and her lover, perhaps you can justify them, but how do you explain what you did to this innocent woman?" As soon as the creature finished the last word, it seemed to glide across the floor and was standing with its face in Nathaniel's, when it added, "How?"

Nathaniel fell backwards in his daydream. He jolted awake, having physically hit his head on the tree behind him. His eyes went wide and a cascade of emotion came from deep within him and he sobbed in mortal anguish. He tried desperately to make the vision go away, but all he could see were the three gory figures pointing their accusing fingers at him, whether his eyes were open or closed. When he committed these atrocities, his mind had protected him by hiding away any memory of the details. Now, it was all he could think about. He curled up into a fetal position and cried well into the night.

Chapter 17 – Chicken and Rabbit

The morning light, which usually brought the hope of a new day and the thought of a hot meal, only illuminated the troop's misery. They had spent the night under the canopies created by the spreading branches of large fir and spruce trees. The rain was still falling and although it had ebbed to a light drizzle, it was still cold and wet. A thick mist had fallen to ground level, which limited visibility to about twenty yards in any direction.

At the start of the trip, Whitney had conscripted the only piece of canvas available, so he found some semblance of comfort under its protection. Whitney was the first one to crawl out from under his makeshift shelter. He hollered as loud as he could, "Listen up, men. Listen up!" He pause for effect and then added, "Front and center on the double!" which he repeated twice more for emphasis. He waited a full five minutes before a couple of shadows emerged from the mist, namely Brimsby and Oakley.

"What can we do for you, Boss?" inquired Brimsby.

"Do for me? What do you mean do for me? It's time to move out! Where the hell are the rest of them?" Whitney asked in an irritated tone.

Brimsby didn't answer and it didn't look like he was going to, when Oakley spoke up, "We got pretty scattered in the storm. Most likely, they didn't hear you calling. I'll go round them up."

It was a nearly a half hour before the men were gathered about Whitney, each one with his mount in tow, including Luke Briscoe, which mildly surprised everyone. Whitney looked at each man in the group and then began, "Gentlemen, we've had a minor set back. It appears our mules and spare horse have galloped off into the night, along with our gear and the little food we had left." He paused, gave the Briscoes each a dirty look. Changing the subject, he said, "Mr. Brimsby and Mr. Oakley, join me over here, if you please."

Brimsby and Oakley flanked Whitney, one on either side of him, while Whitney continued, "Mr. Briscoe, you and the breed go find our runaway stock and supplies."

Michael didn't say anything, but Mathew Briscoe began to object vehemently, citing the same old excuse that he wouldn't leave, Luke. Whitney shrugged his shoulders, threw his head back, sighed heavily, and then shook his head back and forth, all in one continuous motion. He pulled his pistol and cocked the hammer, aiming it at Luke Briscoe. To Mathew he said, "Mr. Briscoe, we have to come to an understanding and this seems like as good as a time as any. You see Mathew, Brother Luke, here, cannot even pull his own weight, but what annoys me more — he is keeping you from doing your duty."

Mathew interrupted, "Duty? What goddamn duty? I don't work for you!"

Whitney shook his head again, "Mathew, Mathew, what am I going to do with you? Of course, you work for me. I know where the gold is and if you and Luke want a share, I suggest, as of this moment, both of you, and I do mean *both*, start earning it."

"Well, Mr. Whitney, you can shove the goddamn gold up your ass. I could give two hoots about it or about you. Me and Luke is leavin'. You can keep our share," retorted Mathew.

"Mr. Briscoe, I was hoping it wouldn't come to this, but you don't seem to have a complete grasp of the situation you find yourself in. Mr. Brimsby, Mr. Oakley, and myself are the only ones armed here." He stopped and looked at Brimsby and Oakley and then continued, "Oh, which reminds me, it is time for promotions. Mr. Brimsby is now a Sergeant and Mr. Oakley is a Corporal, and both entitled to a bigger share of the gold. You men can call me Captain Whitney. Mr. Briscoe, you can continue to be a problem, which of course will entail some sort of punishment, or you can strive harder and who knows, maybe, just maybe, you can have a bigger slice of the pie."

Mathew still didn't understand and Whitney could see he wasn't getting through to the man. "Mr. Briscoe, you do exactly what I tell you from here on in or I will have my Sergeant or my Corporal put a bullet between old Luke's eyes. Is that a little clearer for you?" Whitney turned his attention to Michael and said, "Same goes for you, Breed. You step out of line and the old man pays for it. Do we understand each other?"

Michael smiled and said, "Yes Sir, I understand you very well." The way he said it caused Whitney to wonder if there was a deeper meaning, but he passed it off as the breed's way of talking.

Whitney continued, "Now that we have that out of the way, where were we? Ah yes, Mr. Briscoe and the breed will go see if they can find our stock. Don't search too long. Hopefully, they didn't run too far. I believe our trail is going to head away from the river and take a shortcut across a large plain. Our track should be easy to pick up. If you're not back by nightfall, I'm not sure who will protect Brother Luke or the old heathen from the trials and tribulations that can befall a man out here."

"Sergeant Brimsby and Corporal Oakley, you will ride ahead and see if you can't scare up some game and I will play nurse maid to these three," Whitney said, referring to Dancing Crow, Luke Briscoe, and Silas Davidson.

Michael explained to Dancing Crow what had transpired. The old man seemed like he didn't care. In fact, he didn't say anything at all, which worried Michael. "Are you alright, old man?" he asked with genuine concern.

"I do not fear these white men. They cannot harm me. It is the one of the dream world who brings fear to my heart," said Dancing Crow.

Michael wanted to talk longer, but he was getting nasty looks from Whitney and his two newly appointed henchmen. Further discussion would have to wait. Mathew Briscoe explained to Luke how he needed to go away for a little while and Mr. Whitney would look after him until he got back. Luke didn't like the idea and started whining. Mathew said very sternly, "Look, you big baby, this is the way it's got to be. I'll be back in a little while. You behave yourself and don't do anything stupid."

Mathew mounted his horse and joined the waiting Michael, but before they rode off, Mathew turned back to Whitney and said, "I know you think I'm a dumb fella, Mr. Whitney, but what I know, I know for sure and I can tell you as sure as I am sittin' here if anything happens to Luke while I am gone, you won't have no threat to hold over me anymore and all the goddamn gold in the world won't save your sorry ass."

Michael and Mathew rode at a slow trot. They hadn't spoken a word since they set out. Mathew led the way while Michael lagged behind, searching the ground from side to side, looking for any sign. The rain and the number of horses and mules that passed in the other direction on the narrow trail, made it nearly impossible to distinguish any definitive tracks.

About an hour out, they caught a break. Michael noticed a pattern of downed grasses off to his right, heading towards the river. Thirty yards away, the meadow gave way to heavy trees. Michael followed the path through the grass and as he entered the edge of the tree line he could hear the river. It sounded much louder than when they crossed the day before. The heavy rain from the storm made the gentle stream a raging torrent. Freshly broken tree branches told Michael something big had come through the trees recently.

Mathew turned off the main trail and followed Michael. When he was close enough, he asked Michael what he had found. Michael told him he was sure the animals had come through here, but he didn't know why because the canyon edge was twenty feet ahead of them through the trees. It just didn't fit.

Michael dismounted, tied his horse securely to a nearby tree and headed on foot to the edge of the cliff. Mathew did the same, catching up to Michael, who stood looking into the canyon.

"There's our stock," said Michael, pointing to the five mules whose broken bodies lay strewn over the rocks at the water's edge, a hundred feet below.

"Jesus, what a waste," remarked Mathew. After a momentary pause he added, "I don't see the horse. Where's the horse?"

Michael considered the question before answering. "If he hit the river, he would have been washed downstream, but I don't think he would have made it to the water, if he went over."

As they made their way back to their mounts, Mathew remarked. "That don't make any sense. Why would those mules run over the cliff? I know mules is stupid critters, but they ain't dumb enough to do that."

Michael untied his horse and walked it slowly, while he scrutinized the ground. Once he got back to the main trail, he continued on foot for a hundred yards or so, carefully looking for any sign of something that may have frightened the mules.

Mathew mounted and rode slowly close behind Michael. Curiosity got the better of him and he asked, "What ya lookin' for?"

Michael stopped and looked back at Mathew, "Something frightened the mules so badly they ran over the cliff in blind fear. I think they were so afraid they didn't even see the canyon edge. What made them panic?"

Mathew shook his head and replied, "Jesus, you seein' spooks, too?"

"What do you think happened?" asked Michael.

"A goddamn lightnin' bolt, a grizzly, I don't know — a Jesus cougar. Don't have to be some spook," answered Mathew, with a hint of apprehension in his voice.

"I don't see any tracks," replied Michael. "You are probably right. It was the lightning. We better get back." Michael didn't believe what he told Mathew, but he thought it was the best thing to say for now.

They rode slowly, neither one in any particular hurry to get back to Whitney and what he might have to say about them finding the animals all dead. Mathew broke the silence when he asked, "You sure it was lightnin' what scared them mules?"

Michael replied after a slight hesitation, "You looking for an honest answer or something that will make sense to you?"

"I want an honest answer," replied Mathew.

"Alright, I'm sure a bolt of lightning must have hit near or right in the middle of those mules to scare them so bad. I mean what else could it be?" Michael studied Mathew's face for any sign of disbelief.

Mathew gave a positive nod and said, "Ya, you're right. What else could have scared the bejesus out of them?" He paused momentarily and then added, "Ya know, for a breed, ya ain't half bad."

Michael started to get angry for what he thought was a slur, but then he realized it was really an attempt at a compliment. Instead of showing irritation, he smiled and replied, "Well, thank you, Mathew."

This seemed to open a door for Mathew. He asked, "Answer me honest. You think there is anythin' to this spook business?"

Michael deflected the question, "Why do you ask me?"

Mathew seemed comfortable talking to Michael. An hour ago, he had no use for him and now it was like they were close drinking buddies. "It's just my younger brother Luke, he has these dreams, see, and he thinks he sees some ghosts. There's a girl he know'd once and that young fella what he beat up, and the Injun woman from the village. He swears all of them is makin' his shoulder hurt and makin' him sick. I tell him it's all in his head, but he don't listen to me. I'm scared Whitney is gonna shoot him if he don't start pullin' his weight."

"I'm still not sure what you want from me," said Michael.

"I was thinkin', you seem pretty close to the old injun. Do you think you could ask him if Luke is being haunted or somethin'?"

Michael grinned and replied, "Yes. Yes, I'll do that for you."

Mathew actually smiled when he said, "Thank you."

Michael's horse snorted and an answering whinny came from their left, near the tree line. The trail dipped below an embankment, so neither of them could see anything between themselves and the trees. Mathew forced his mount off the trail and up the knoll. When he reached the top, he stopped and shouted back at Michael, "It's the horse! It's the goddamn horse! Don't that beat all!"

By the time Michael made his way up the knoll, Mathew was already on his way back with the horse in tow. It had found a nice patch of sweetgrass in a small ravine just below the embankment. It was easy enough to miss seeing the horse if one was focused on searching the trail for tracks.

"Well, a least we're not comin' back empty handed," remarked a grinning Mathew.

Michael wondered about Mathew's sudden friendliness. Did he have some sort of angle or did he just need a friend? Michael wasn't above being friendly in return, but he decided he would play it cautiously until he could be sure of Briscoe's intentions.

-2-

Frank Oakley was seething internally, but as he rode with Nathaniel Brimsby, he was determined he wasn't going to let Brimsby know how he felt. *A Corporal? A Corporal? And Brimsby gets to be a Sergeant? That's not fair. After all I have done for the son-of-a-bitch.* Frank let these and a myriad of other negative thoughts run through his mind.

Frank tried to make small talk with Nathaniel, who wasn't in a talkative mood. Nathaniel tried to ignore Oakley's overtures at conversation, but it finally annoyed him to the point where he had enough and he said, "Why don't you keep quiet for a spell and let's pay more attention to finding something to eat."

Frank's quick temper took over and he said, "You ain't telling me what to do! Just 'cause the Captain says you're a Sergeant don't hold no water with me. No Sir!"

Brimsby reined in his horse and turned in the saddle to face Oakley. Frank had the twelve-gauge loosely cradled in his arms and pointed in Brimsby's general direction. His thumb was on one of the hammers, ready to cock it. Brimsby saw the pose and said, "Let's you and me settle what you think may be between us, boy. For some reason, you got a hate on for me and I really don't know why. How about you explain it to me."

All along Oakley thought Brimsby was competing with him for Whitney's favour. "You got no right being the top hand. I worked hard for the job and I figure you stole it from me."

Brimsby seemed surprised Oakley was so passionate about his place in the pecking order of the group. He didn't take this "Sergeant" thing with any seriousness at all and he assumed Oakley felt the same. As far as he was concerned, Whitney was losing it with all this army talk. "Look boy, I don't know what's stuck in your craw. I could give a damn about Whitney and his big ideas and least of all his goddamn chain of command. I got one thing in mind and that is getting rich and living long enough to spend it."

Oakley was just as surprised by Brimsby's perspective of the situation as Brimsby was of his. The only thing he could think to say was," Don't call me *boy*! I hate it." He kicked his horse in the ribs and rode ahead of Brimsby which, to Oakley, felt like a gesture of defiance to the new established order.

-3-

Whitney was the one man in the group who could easily rationalize the cause of his nightmares. He had horrible dreams as far back as he could remember. If he wasn't having a nightmare about life on the streets of London or the buggery he endured on board the ship that took him to America, then it was vivid dreams about the two years he spent in the war. It was always the same — he was either hurting or killing someone or someone was trying to hurt or kill him.

As he rode, he reflected on some of the peculiar things happening to the group since they embarked on their mission. He did not believe in ghosts or spirits. He was one of those who believed when you died that was the end of it — into the ground, no heaven or hell, just a small patch of dirt you called home until there is nothing left of you but the dust of your bones.

He heard the murmurings and comments about spectres and things unseen. In order to instil some discipline, he twice gave lectures that there were no such things as ghosts or goblins haunting them, but there was still a small nagging element of doubt tucked away in a corner of his own mind. What did Silas Davidson actually see when Harold Grant drowned — a huge hand of water or was Silas already losing his mind before Grant met his demise in the cold lake waters? Were there some unseen phantoms digging at Luke Briscoe's shoulder, or was he just having fever dreams? Whitney had seen something similar hundreds of times with wounded soldiers in the war. He firmly believed Collin Pilkington went off the cliff with the aid of a human hand and not an invisible one.

His own private nightmare didn't faze him. As far as he was concerned, it was just another dream. He did, however, recognize that the dream could very well represent reality. If the old prospector was telling the truth about the amount of gold he had dug out and left behind, Whitney would need some of the men to load it and carry it all out of the wilderness. Not that he couldn't load up a string of horses himself and get back to civilization, but time was of the essence. He did not want to be caught in the wilderness when winter hit and in the high country that could be soon. By his calculations, they were already into the month of September.

He was starting to feel uneasy about losing his tight control over the men. Silas Davidson had gone off into a realm of insanity, the Briscoes could care less about any gold, and Whitney didn't know why the breed and the old heathen hadn't slipped away before now. There was plenty of opportunity. Maybe the white half of the breed showed the white man's propensity for wealth and the power it could bring and he wasn't going anywhere until he got his share.

Whitney chuckled as he congratulated himself for the brilliant plan he'd devised; divide and conquer. He would use military discipline to restore order and control. Military discipline would keep their minds off spooks, goblins, and other things going bump in the night. With his promotion scheme, he thought he'd bought the loyalty of Brimsby and Oakley and at the same time had drawn a line in the sand where he, Brimsby, and Oakley held the power and Davidson, the Briscoes, the breed, and the old heathen were on the other side of the line, expendable when the time came.

Silas Davidson's ability to distinguish the difference between the physical realm and the world he created in his imagination had vanished. He was barely aware he was on a horse, riding to God-knows-where. A portion of his brain maintained enough coherence to keep his mount under control and on the trail.

Silas had, in essence, hidden away his ego, his personality, any emotion or memories. It was as if he had taken all the things that drove Silas Davidson to think, talk or react in the physical world and shut them up in a small broom closet deep in the recesses of his brain. In his mind's eye, he was merely an observer, someone who stood on the sidelines and watched as a kaleidoscope of images marched by in precision; a giant watery hand pulling Harold Grant to an icy death followed by a dying Collin Pilkington, pitifully pleading for someone, anyone to help him as they all walked away. Next in the procession came Whitney accusing him of pushing Collin over the cliff. Silas could not recall whether he had pushed Collin or not. He remembered being very angry with Collin and following him through the trees to the edge of the embankment. There was a hazy image of him startling Collin, who then lost his balance and went over. Yes, that was it! That's what had happened! It wasn't his fault at all, just a silly accident.

A very large fox followed by native villagers covered in blood and gore from their wounds came next in the procession. The fox turned its head and looked Silas in the eye and said, "Don't forget, your fear will destroy you," while a multitude of gruesome spectres pointed accusatory fingers and asked Silas why he hadn't done something to stop the slaughter in the village.

At this point, Silas said in his mind, "You are wrong, Sir. I am not afraid of you, or anyone else for that matter. What could I possibly have done to stop those fiends?" As if in response, a seemingly prophetic vision showed Silas on his knees begging for his life, as Whitney stood over him with a cocked pistol aimed squarely at his forehead. Silas concluded this was a warning to help him and not an image of things to come, so he would use the information to his advantage by not saying anything to Whitney to provoke him. In fact, he decided not to interact with anybody. In this way, he felt he had nothing to fear from anyone.

-4-

Michael and Mathew hadn't ridden very far down the trail, when a trio of spruce grouse ran across their path and into a large grove of alder bushes. Michael reined in and gave a halt signal to Mathew. He dismounted, handed his reins to Mathew, and began to search the path. He picked up three fist sized rocks and slowly and very quietly made his way to the spot where the birds had entered the bushes. He knelt down and began making a guttural cooing sound.

Mathew seemed enthralled as he watched. Michael continued cooing and it wasn't long before one of the birds poked its head out of the alder bush. Michael remained motionless even though the bird was looking directly at him. Thinking it was safe, the bird stepped out about three feet from Michael. He threw a rock with the flick of his wrist, catching the bird square in the head. He snatched up the grouse and snapped its neck before it had time to gain its senses. He used the same procedure to call out the other two birds, with the same result.

-5-

For nearly three hours, Brimsby and Oakley had been riding along the tree line, about a hundred yards upslope from the trail, and they hadn't seen a hint of any living thing. They had been hoping to flush a deer or two that were usually a short distance into the trees. Every so often, the deer would leave the safety of cover and warily venture out into the open to nibble at the sweet grass and young willow shoots.

Frank was so focused on the tree line he didn't notice the two rabbits scurrying across his path, but Nathaniel did. The rabbits ran a dozen feet or so and then stood still, to see if the horses were potential predators or not. This gave Nathaniel an opportunity to bring the Spencer up and fire, hitting the closest rabbit. The other one dashed down the path, cutting in front of Oakley's horse. Nathaniel couldn't shoot because Frank was directly in his line of fire, so he hollered, "Shoot him! Shoot the little bugger!"

Oakley had seen the rabbit run by and could have easily stopped it with one of the barrels of the 12 gauge, but as he cocked back one of the hammers and raised the shotgun, he changed his mind about shooting. He was thinking that he had only two shells between him and whoever would do him harm and he wasn't about to waste one on a rabbit.

Brimsby reined up beside him and asked, "Why the hell didn't you shoot?"

"He was moving too fast. I couldn't get a clear shot. Didn't want to waste ammunition," answered Oakley in a casual tone.

Brimsby hesitated momentarily and then accepted Oakley's response as the truth. He dismounted and picked up the rabbit he had shot. There usually wouldn't be very much usable meat left on the rabbit after being hit by a .52 calibre round, but Brimsby was either a very good shot or had gotten plain lucky, because his shot hit the rabbit in the head, decapitating it while still leaving the body intact.

-6-

"One rabbit and three chickens! That's all you people could come up?" snarled Whitney.

Mathew Briscoe and Michael had caught up to the troop around mid afternoon. Whitney was enraged at the news of the loss of the mules, but his ire seemed to dissipate somewhat when Michael told him they had found the horse and then showed him the three spruce hens he had bagged.

Brimsby and Oakley had ridden a couple of miles ahead of the troop for most of the day. The two rabbits and a pair of coyotes that seemed to be following them, at a safe distance, were the only living things they saw. In the late afternoon Brimsby and Oakley doubled back to the troop with their bounty of one scrawny, headless hare.

Everyone was famished, including Whitney. He ordered a halt so they could cook their bounty and abate their gnawing hunger, somewhat. He approached Silas, who was still sitting on his horse seemingly oblivious that they had stopped. "Mr. Davidson, if you would be kind enough to dismount and instruct the breed and the heathen as to their duties, I would very much like something to eat and soon," he commanded.

Silas slowly dismounted, reached inside his pants pocket, and took out a saturated, pink coloured mush that had once been a box of matches. He stared at the mess in his hand for a few seconds and then showed it to Whitney and said, "No fire today, Sir." He tied his horse to a bush and then sat down on a small protruding rock ledge, upslope a few feet from the trail.

Whitney was on him in two strides, grabbed him by the shirtfront and lifted him to his feet. He put his face right into Silas's and said, "Do what I tell you, soldier or I will gut shoot you and leave you here for the coyotes to gnaw at while you're still breathing."

A knowing smile appeared on Silas's face as he said, "You need me, Mr. Whitney. If you kill me, who is going to carry your gold."

Whitney felt like he had been stomach-punched. The wind came out of him as he let go his grip on Silas and he took two steps backwards. He wasn't surprised so much by what Silas had said, but that he had the knowledge to say it. '*How does he know what I am dreaming about?*' Whitney thought as he tried to regain his self control. He drew his pistol with full intentions of killing Silas. *The fool is right,* he thought. He needed Silas's help to get the gold out, but he needed to keep control of the troop more. The only solution was to follow through with his threat.

As he cocked the pistol and began to raise it, Mathew Briscoe stepped in front of Silas and said, "Gonna shoot me too, Boss?"

Before Whitney could respond, Michael stepped up beside Mathew and grinned at Whitney without saying anything. Mathew looked somewhat surprised to see Michael there. He smiled to show appreciation for Michael's support and then turned to Whitney and said, "Looks like we got us a situation here, don't it, Boss?"

Whitney laughed, uncocked his pistol, put it back in his waistband and still chuckling he said, "Alright men, you win this time, but be assured this matter is not settled." He paused and then said in a much gentler tone, "We still need to eat, so let's all pitch in and get these birds and what's left of this rabbit cleaned up. Breed, see if you and the old heathen can get a fire going by whatever means you people use. I would really prefer my meat cooked and not raw." He stood momentarily and then turned and walked away, fully expecting his orders to be carried out.

Michael translated for Dancing Crow, but the old man didn't seem interested. He seated himself, cross-legged, on a dry clump of grass and he seemed distant, preoccupied about something. Michael asked him three times if he had the means to start a fire. Finally, Dancing Crow handed him one of several deer hide pouches attached to a leather sash tied around his waist.

Michael opened the pouch and found everything needed to start a fire from scratch; a two foot thin strip of fire-dried rawhide, a cylindrical piece of wood, the thickness of a man's thumb and about eight inches long, tapered to a point at both ends, which were both charred black. There was also a second piece of flat wood, rectangular in shape, approximately four inches by three inches and two inches thick. This piece had a half inch indentation on one side, also blackened like it had been burnt.

Michael recognized the contents. He had started many a fire with similar apparatus. He convinced Mathew Briscoe he needed to use his knife for a moment. Mathew gave it up reluctantly, using the excuse he needed the knife to clean the hens and rabbit. Michael looked around and spotted a fir tree with thick branches. He wiggled his way past the limbs to the inside of the tree near the trunk, where he selected one of the thickest dead branches, cut it down, and dragged out into the open, being careful not to put in on the still wet ground.

He cut two pieces from the branch; one about a foot long and the other about eighteen inches. The shorter piece, he whittled down until he had a stick that was flat on both sides. He shaved the longer piece at one end to a thick rounded point and then two inches from the end, he cut a circular notch around it. The other end of the stick, he shaved flat on both sides and then using the point of the knife, he drilled a hole through it about two inches up from the end. He handed the knife back to Mathew and collected a handful of very small, dry twigs from the unused portion of the dead branch. He added some of the lime green, thin, stringy lichen, which was commonly referred to as "*witch's hair*", to his collection.

Mathew followed Michael back to where Dancing Crow sat. He was fascinated by what Michael was doing and he wanted to see how all this was going to be useful in starting a fire. Michael took the witch's hair and formed it into a small, loose bundle which he then wrapped around the handful of twigs. Next, he took the rawhide strip and tied a loop in one end which he slipped over the thick pointed end of the longer stick and into the groove he'd carved. He picked up the wooden cylinder and wrapped the loose end of the rawhide string around it four times and then shoved the loose end of the string through the drilled hole at the other end of the longer stick. He pulled the string taut and tied a knot in the loose end to prevent it from slipping. It looked like a small bow with a stick caught in the middle of the bow string. Borrowing Mathew's knife again, Michael dug out a small hole on the flat piece he had made. Then he inserted one end of the cylinder in the hole and turned the bow sideways parallel to the ground. He put the charred rectangular piece on the other end of the cylinder and held it in place with his left hand. Using his right hand, he moved the bow back and forth in a sawing motion, thus spinning the cylinder back and forth, creating the friction needed to generate heat.

Mathew watched in fascination, as smoke began to appear in the hole where the cylinder made contact with the flat piece of wood. Michael sped up the sawing motion and the amount of smoke increased. He began to blow gently at the contact point. After several minutes of bowing and blowing, he stopped to check his progress and there was a tiny glowing coal. Using a twig, Michael lifted the small ember onto his prepared bundle and cupping his hands around it, he began to blow very gently. It took only a couple of puffs and the bundle burst into flame. Michael quickly began adding small twigs and dry grass to the tiny fire until there was a small blaze going. Now, it was simply a matter of adding larger fuel to make the fire bigger.

Mathew shook his head and said, "Well, I'll be damned! If that don't beat all! I heard 'bout somethin' like this, but this is the first time I ever seen it for myself."

Mathew, with Michael's help, skinned and cleaned what was left of the rabbit and plucked and eviscerated the hens. Mathew cut four thick green willow sticks on which they skewered the rabbit and hens, stuck the other end into the ground and dangled them over the blazing fire.

Unknown to both of them, Whitney was watching from a discrete distance. Genuinely pleased, he slowly approached Michael and Mathew and said, "Nice work, gentlemen. Very nice." He turned his attention to Silas Davidson, who hadn't moved from the rock ledge. "Mr. Davidson, what was your participation in the preparation of the meal?" he said, knowing full well Silas hadn't moved from his perch.

Silas didn't answer. In fact, he didn't respond in any manner. He simply continued to stare straight ahead with vacant eyes and a blank expression.

"Not going to talk to me, Mr. Davidson?" asked Whitney, not expecting an answer. "I gave you specific orders and you refused to carry them out. Well, Mr. Davidson, since you can't be bothered to do your duty, I guess you don't eat." He turned back to Mathew and Michael and said, "No food for Mr. Davidson."

Three scrawny Spruce Hens and a bush rabbit didn't go far among seven hungry men, but everyone got enough to quell the gnawing hunger in their stomachs, with the exception of Silas Davidson. When he was sure Whitney was occupied, Michael offered Silas some of his share, but Silas just sat there unresponsive in his catatonic state.

Michael sat down next to Dancing Crow and made himself comfortable. He offered a share of the meat to Dancing Crow, who took a tiny bite and handed the rest of it back to Michael. He put it and his own share of the meat in his coat pocket, for future use. He sat for several moments in silence before speaking. "What's the matter?"

Dancing Crow turned his gaze toward Michael and replied, "Nothing you would understand."

"I understand a lot more than you think I do," replied Michael.

Dancing Crow looked into Michael's face for a moment and then turning his gaze skyward, he said, "Yes. Yes, I believe you do."

"Then talk to me."

"I believe a very powerful Dreamwalker is among us! I believe he intends to destroy us all and it puzzles me."

"Why does it puzzle you," asked Michael, prodding the old man to continue.

Dancing Crow thought for a long while as if he were formulating an explanation before he spoke. "Do you know what a Dreamwalker is?"

Michael had heard the term before and he thought dream walking was a technique where a Medicine Man could enter the dream state while in a trance and seek information from spirits on healing and other personal or tribal matters. He said as much to Dancing Crow.

Dancing Crow spoke softly and slowly, "You are correct. That is what a Medicine Man does when he dream walks. He may visit with spirits of ancestors, or animal spirits or talk to mother earth or father sky. He must meditate long and hard to acquire enough skill to be able to do this with any success." He turned his face directly to look at Michael and continued, "It is said, every ten generations there will come one so powerful, he has merely to close his eyes and he walks among the spirits."

Michael took advantage of the pause and asked, "And you think one of these powerful ones is among us?"

"Yes, I do. He is the one causing these men to see their visions. He is the one turning the birds and animals against us. I believe he is tormenting the big one," referring to Luke Briscoe, "and the one who looks like a stork," referring to Silas Davidson. "It seems impossible, but I also believe he caused the lake to swallow the one called Grant."

Dancing Crow stopped talking, but Michael was convinced there was something the old man wasn't telling. He tried a stab in the dark when he asked, "What is this Dreamwalker doing to you?"

Dancing Crow was taken by surprise with the question. He thought about ignoring it then decided he'd better finish the narrative. He was growing to like this young man and along with that, came trust. "I went to the land of the spirits to help the one called Silas. While I was there I was confronted by a very powerful spirit who told me I was not to help these men. It took the form of a fox, but I do believe it was of human origin." He paused, took a deep breath and sighed and then concluded, "I think, but I am not sure, this powerful Shaman is my grandson, Little Fox."

"That's really interesting," interjected Brimsby, who was listening from a position several feet behind them. "Wonder what Mr. Whitney will have to say about this."

Chapter 18 – Brimsby and the Bear

Two hours before dawn, Whitney screamed, "Get up, you lazy bastards. We are going to make up some time today." Everyone was wide awake, for no one, including Whitney, had slept at all the previous night. It was very late in the afternoon when they finished their meagre meal of rabbit and hen, so Whitney called it a day, with full intentions of starting very early in the morning. He waited impatiently for about ten minutes and then started making the rounds again, accompanied by Frank Oakley.

Luke Briscoe was up and his horse was saddled and ready to go. Mathew Briscoe, on the other hand had just risen, relieved himself, and was shaking off as Whitney approached. "Get a move on soldier. I won't be saying it a third time," commanded Whitney. He seemed mildly surprised when he saw Luke fully conscious and not bent over in pain.

Nathaniel Brimsby heard Whitney addressing the Briscoes. He jumped to his feet and began to saddle up. It didn't fool Whitney and he gave Nathaniel a scowl as he walked by. Brimsby knew he wasn't pleased.

"Have you sat there all night?" Whitney asked Silas Davidson. Silas hadn't moved from the spot he had taken when he dismounted the previous evening. He had his knees drawn up with his arms encircling them and his hands clasped in front. He rocked back and forth every so slightly and he showed no signs of awareness. "I am talking to you soldier," Whitney said sternly. "Do you hear me?" he asked, as he gave Silas a swift kick, catching him in the right thigh.

Silas didn't move or even acknowledge Whitney's presence. Whitney kicked him a second time, with all his might. The force of the blow knocked Silas over on his side. The kick served its purpose. Silas sat back up, turned his head toward Whitney, and said, "I am not one of your soldiers. I am not afraid of you. I am not afraid." He kept repeating the phrase as he assumed the sitting position again and began rocking back and forth.

Whitney turned to Brimsby and said, "If he's not on his mount in five minutes, leave him, but the horse comes with us."

Frank Oakley interjected, "I'll look after it, Boss."

"Thank you, Mr. Oakley, but it's Captain and I would prefer Sergeant Brimsby did it," Whitney answered.

Frank looked like he'd been slapped in the face. He glared at Whitney and then at Brimsby. Whitney caught the look and he realized Oakley was just trying to be useful. He felt he needed to do some damage control, so he put his arm around Frank's shoulder and said, "My boy, in any good unit you have to follow the chain of command or discipline falls apart. The chain of command in our unit is I, Sergeant Brimsby, you, and then the rest of the riff-raff. Son, men like you don't ever question orders. They do what they are told and they like it. Am I making myself clear, soldier?"

"Yes Sir," replied Oakley. He looked at Brimsby, who seemed puzzled. They were both wondering why Whitney was referring to everyone as soldiers and why he had gone "*military*" on them.

Michael took the chicken meat he'd stashed in his pocket the night before and was sharing it with Dancing Crow as Whitney approached. Before Whitney could ask any questions, Michael said, "This meat is our share from last night. We saved it."

"That's fine, Mr. George," said Whitney. Michael knew something was different. Whitney was never formal with him. It was always "*Breed*" or "*Heathen*", never his given name. Whitney continued, "Mr. Brimsby tells me he overheard a conversation between you and this elderly gentleman. He tells me you have an explanation for some of the strange events that have beset us lately. Is this true?"

Michael looked up at Whitney and then at Brimsby before he spoke, "Mr. Whitney, I have said once before, Mr. Brimsby has a very limited understanding of our language and he usually misinterprets what he hears."

Brimsby stepped forward so he was between Michael and Whitney. Michael stood up as he approached and the two of them stood face to face, barely a foot apart. Brimsby said, "You're a goddamn liar, Breed."

Michael smiled and said, "*Loot stim ks'meis tul nak'wa t'uul ktl k'laux!*"

Brimsby looked at Michael with a puzzled look and then at Whitney. Michael asked, "What did I just say?"

Brimsby turned to Whitney and stammering, said, "He says he can see in the dark— or something."

Michael, smiling, said to Whitney, "It's an old saying elders tell to children to warn them about spirits in the dark. It translates to, '*Nothing's for sure because there's dangerous things you can't see in the dark!*' Not even close to what Mr. Brimsby thought he heard."

Whitney believed Michael and was all set to walk away when Dancing Crow said, "*Loot swit ks'meis ixi nak'wem k'im i Whitney.*"

Having heard his name, Whitney asked, "What did he say?" Turning to Michael he added, "And don't bullshit me, Mr. George!"

Michael translated, "He said, '*Nobody knows it better than Whitney*'." Michael could see Dancing Crow had crossed into territory he maybe shouldn't have and he added "Before you get mad, Mr. Whitney let me ask him what he meant, please."

Whitney sighed and didn't say anything, which Michael took as a sign to go ahead. He asked Dancing Crow what he meant by his remark. Dancing Crow wouldn't answer. Michael told him Whitney was angry and he needed an explanation or he may do something rash. Dancing Crow said to Michael, "The one called Whitney knows of what I speak, but he would have us think he knows not of such things. He may not know who or what is tormenting these men, but he knows something is. That is all I meant."

Michael felt there was more to it and he hoped Whitney wouldn't detect the concern in his voice when he said. "He says he knows you believe the strange things happening to us may come from the spirit world. He didn't mean anything by it. He's a crazy old man, don't punish him for that."

Whitney stood quiet for what seemed an excruciatingly long time. He looked at Michael and then stared at Dancing Crow. Michael couldn't decide if Whitney was trying to understand what Dancing Crow meant, or if he was deciding what to do about it. Finally, Whitney took a deep breath and said, "Tell him he doesn't know me, for if he truly did, he wouldn't have been so foolish to say what he did. He should keep his ideas to himself." Whitney then turned to face the rest of the troop and shouted, "We ride in five minutes!"

Michael felt as if they had dodged a bullet, but he also felt the old man hit a nerve and Whitney, for all his façade, really was bothered by things that go bump in the night.

On the trail, the troop rode in two groups with about twenty yards distance between them. Whitney, Brimsby and Oakley were in the lead, with Frank leading the two spare horses and the Briscoe brothers, Michael, and Dancing Crow made up the other group.

Looking at the riderless horses in front of him, Michael thought of Silas Davidson and the strong urge he had felt to help him mount, but an even stronger feeling overpowered the first one, which told him it would not be a good idea. He felt some compassion for Silas and he chided himself for not acting and then something in his mind said, "Just a crazy white man. You don't owe him anything." He dismissed his feelings of guilt and turned his attention to Dancing Crow.

"Tell me more of this Dreamwalker."

Dancing Crow replied, "You know what I know. There is no more to tell."

"You're not telling the truth. There's more to it. You're afraid to speak of him," Michael said, hoping to get a rise out of the old man. Dancing Crow didn't answer and it looked like he wasn't going to, so Michael pressed on, "If this demon is your grandson, he won't harm you. Why are you afraid of him?"

This brought a rise out of Dancing Crow, "He is not a demon! He is overpowered by his need for vengeance. He has stepped off the path of light and walks upon the path of darkness."

Michael interrupted, "Good for him. I hope he gets all these bastards."

Dancing Crow looked at Michael with sympathetic eyes. He shook his head and continued, "You truly do not understand, my son. Once a soul is on the path of darkness, it is very, very difficult to step off. The longer Little Fox is on the dark path, the harder it will to be to get him to step back on to the path of light." He paused to reflect on what he'd said and then added, "I'm not afraid for myself, but for him — and for you."

Michael was surprised, "Me? Why would you be afraid for me?"

"You are not free from his wrath, because you have the blood of The People. I believe he means to destroy you as well. He sees you as no different from the others."

Michael became defiant and said, "Next time you are talking to your grandson tell him I haven't done anything to anger him and if he wants a fight he'll get one."

"You cannot fight him, my son."

"Why not?"

Dancing Crow used his mentor's tone, "You need to set aside your anger and listen to me." He paused long enough for Michael to settle down and then continued, "One legend of my people says a powerful Medicine Man such as this one has many powers. He can command the animals, the birds, the rocks, the trees, the water, and the weather to do his bidding. While he can do these things in the world of the living, his true power lies in the world of thought and dreams. Here, he can make men see, hear, and feel things that can bring them great joy, or great fear. Whatever he creates in the dream world, he can bring to the world of the living."

Michael asked, "Like the hand of the lake that took Grant?"

"Yes," said Dancing Crow.

Michael processed the information and said, "We need to talk more about this."

Clarence Whitney was deep in thought. He never let what somebody else had to say bother him, but the old man had gotten under his skin. "Did the old heathen have some insight into his thoughts or was it a lucky guess?" he asked himself.

The subject of spectres and hauntings was not new to Whitney. He decided a long time ago they were nothing to fear. He remembered the day he deserted the Union Army. He'd bayoneted a young comrade in arms through the heart because the boy, who couldn't have been more than fifteen, caught him killing wounded Confederate soldiers. He panicked and ran as fast as his legs could carry him away from the scene of the battle. He remembered running and running until he collapsed from sheer exhaustion.

He found shelter in an old barn that night. As tired as he was, he could not go to sleep. Every time he closed his eyes he saw the young boy's face, the eyes wide open from surprise. He saw the crimson gush when he pulled his bayonet out of the young man's chest. He heard the lad say, "Why? Why did you kill me? Why?" as he slumped to his knees and then fell face first into his own blood and died.

Whitney could not understand why he would be haunted by this memory. It wasn't like he hadn't killed before. He recalled how, several years before the war, in New York City, he stabbed a young man for his purse. As the man lay bleeding, he begged Whitney to send for help. He said he didn't care about the money, but he didn't want to die. His wife and two small children needed him. Whitney, of course, didn't send for help. In fact, he never gave the man a second thought. He never knew if he had lived or died.

As Whitney made his way westward, living off what he could steal, the same image of the bayoneted boy filled his head constantly for days. A week after he deserted, he'd just finished a meal of smoked ham and a jar of peaches he stole from a root cellar on a nearby farm. He lay down and closed his eyes and the image of the young, dying soldier appeared again. This time, instead of fearing the image, Whitney confronted it. In his imagination, after the young soldier fell face first into the ground, Whitney kicked the body over on its back. He knelt down beside the corpse and using both hands, he picked the body up by the shirt front so its face was close to his and said, "I am not afraid of you. You are not real. You are a figment of my imagination and my own guilt created you. I no longer feel any guilt. No guilt, no ghost." That night signified the death of what little conscience Whitney had left, and from that day forth, he felt no remorse for anything he did. To him, his murderous deeds were either for self preservation or a means to an end.

I t was the better part of an hour after the troop started out, before Silas Davidson raised his head and looked around. He was entirely alone. There were vague recollections of the men leaving and Whitney telling him he was being left behind for some reason. The mental wall against fear he'd put up, suddenly came crashing down. His mind was clear for the first time in days. He was trying to deal with the shock that his so called comrades had left him behind, left him to survive with nothing, not even his horse.

He had been riding through this godforsaken country for over two weeks and this was the first time he noticed it. He became aware of the vastness and how insignificant one can feel when surrounded by an endless sea of green in every direction. He looked to the east and saw the mid morning sun trying to break through the cloudy sky.

He stood silent and listened. He could hear not a sound, except when the wind picked up slightly, there was a deep rustling noise as moving air whooshed through the tree tops. This was the first time in his life he truly knew what "*alone*" meant, and he could feel the fear creeping in.

Surprising himself, Silas didn't panic. He began to reason out his situation and his options. He could go back or he could try and catch up with the troop. Which one to choose? Going back seemed a formidable task. He hadn't paid attention to the trail, leaving it to others in the troop. He would most likely get himself lost. What if he did make it out? What would be waiting? Perhaps vengeful natives or the Constables? How could he survive another two or three weeks without food or a fire to keep himself warm?

What would happen if he caught up with Whitney? He could beg forgiveness and hope to be accepted back into the fold if he promised to pull his weight. They would take him back, wouldn't they?

Silas was imagining himself back with the men, cooking them a meal when a voice filled his head. "YOUR FEAR WILL KILL YOU!" the voice screamed.

Silas, as if in answer, said aloud, "No. No, it won't. I'm not listening to you. I told you I am not afraid of you."

The voice continued, "It is not me you need to fear. You have wronged The People. It is their anguished spirits who will destroy you."

"I did nothing to your people! I did nothing," Silas said frantically.

"You speak the truth when you say you did nothing!" the voice said with a hint of sarcasm.

Silas's mind carried him back to the village and the atrocities he witnessed and he felt very, very ashamed for his fellow men who had committed these acts and for himself because he'd done nothing about it. "But what could I have done?" he said more to himself than the voice in his head. "They would have killed me, too."

Silas was expecting an answer, but none came. The voice was gone. He decided the only way he was going to survive, was to catch up to Whitney and make amends. He began to run, which for Silas was really a slow jog at best. It didn't take a lot of concentration to follow the trail the troop had left. Consequently, Silas let his mind wander as he trotted along.

It is ironic how the mind can work against one at times. You block out bad memories of a certain person or event and for some reason the mind seems to think you are reviewing all negative experiences and it brings up another person or occasion for your viewing pleasure. This is what Silas's mind was doing to him. He blocked out the gruesome scenes from the village only to have them replaced by a shameful memory of his beating of Harold Grant. He closed the door on that memory only to have it replaced with one of a dying Collin Pilkington begging for help. And so it went, hour after excruciating hour, vision after painful vision, each one showing Silas committing a brutal or cruel act on some person or standing by with indifference while some poor soul was being set upon. Finally, Silas stopped and fell to his knees. He held his arms out towards the sky and pleaded, "Please, please make it stop! I am sorry! So sorry! I am a coward. I should have tried to stop the killing in the village. I am so sorry!"

He lowered his arms to his sides, bowed his head, and began to sob, uncontrollably. As if in answer to his pleas, a soft, gentle, feminine voice called out, "Silas — Silas."

He stopped his blubbering and with eyes still closed, he listened. Again the angel's voice said, "Silas — Silas." He opened his eyes and there seated on a small rock outcrop was a young woman, perhaps in her early to mid twenties. She wore a long yellow flowered dress, soiled from soot or dirt in several places. Her hands appeared to be dirty, which complimented the smudge on her right cheek. Her long auburn hair was tied back in a pony tail and it, too, looked like it could do with a wash. Silas's eyes were drawn to the woman's wrists which both sported a deep gash that gushed blood in rhythmic spurts, in tune with the woman's heart beat.

Silas stood and approached her and as he got nearer with each step, recognition set in. He said, "Margaret? Margaret is that you?"

"Yes it is, Silas," the woman answered.

"But — but how is this possible? You are in England. The last I heard you —you were dead," stammered Silas.

"Thanks to you," she said with a cutting tone.

Silas was beginning to get indignant, "You killed yourself, my dear. What did I have to do with it?"

Margaret softened and said, "Oh, poor Silas, you really don't have any idea, do you?"

"No. No, I do not!" was the curt reply.

"Darling Silas, I was with child and all alone. I did not have a roof over my head or a crust of bread to eat. Would it have been so hard for you to have given me a little money or even a place to stay for a few days?"

"With child? I didn't know — I uh — Well, it was none of my business. You took up with that scoundrel against our parents' and my wishes. Besides, I was saving every penny I could for my passage to Canada."

Margaret looked into Silas's face with sympathetic eyes and said, "No Silas, you are wrong. The welfare of others is everyone's business."

"Not in my book," snarled Silas.

Suddenly, Margaret became engulfed in a cloud of white smoke with a blue tinge to it. As the smoke dissipated, the figure of a drenched Harold Grant appeared in her place. Harold raised both of his arms, palms facing upward and with pleading eyes said, "Why didn't you help me, Silas?"

Silas was dumbfounded. "Margaret? Where is Margaret? I need to — I — uh —"

Harold interrupted and said in the same condescending manner he used on Silas before, "You what, Mr. Davidson? You need to apologize? You need to ask you sister for forgiveness? Oh my, you know, I believe it is too late." Just as Margaret did, he disappeared in a veil of smoke and Silas was left alone again with only the gentle breeze for company.

He sat down on the ground and remorse filled his soul. "Margaret, I am so sorry," he said aloud. A woman's mocking laughter filled the air, leaving Silas with a feeling of hopelessness. He slowly got to his feet and started out again, following the trail. To an observer, it would have appeared Silas was very drunk, as he staggered from side to side on the path, sobbing and uttering "I am sorry," repeatedly.

He continued in this manner for what seemed like hours. The trail cut across the middle of a huge flat meadow that eventually gave way to a line of trees flanked by a small gully that housed a tiny, shallow creek. Silas didn't realize how thirsty he was until he saw the water. He lay flat on his belly and drank his full. As he drank, he saw some depressions of horses' hooves in the mud on the creek bottom. If he had any tracking skills at all, he would have seen the water in the depressions was still murky from being disturbed and the slow moving stream didn't have time to clean out the disrupted silt, yet. This meant the horses that left the tracks couldn't be far ahead, perhaps a half an hour or so.

Forty yards from the gully, the trail broke into another huge grassy meadow, which appeared to disappear into the trees in the far distance. If Silas had taken the time to stop and look up, he would have seen the back end of the troop disappear into the trees. As he staggered on, a large wisp of the bluish white smoke appeared in front of him again. Silas wasn't frightened. In fact, he was quite unaffected as he had crawled back behind his wall of safety in his mind. He simply said to himself, "What now?"

A s on the previous day, Whitney sent Nathaniel Brimsby and Frank ahead of the troop to look for game. As they rode, neither one said anything to the other. The eerie silence made them both feel very uneasy. Usually, there was always a jay or a squirrel squawking in the trees or several ravens flying overhead, cawing to one another, and once in a while, one could hear a distant screech of a bald eagle riding the thermal waves overhead. The two of them didn't hear so much as a chickadee's chirp, all day long.

The thought of Whitney ranting, should they return empty handed, kept them at their mission for the majority of the day. Oakley finally broke the interminable silence when he said, "This is really strange."

"What is?" snorted Brimsby. The silence bothered him, but having to talk to Oakley annoyed him more.

"There ain't no noise, no birds, no nothin', or didn't you notice?" retorted Oakley.

Brimsby didn't answer. "You don't say much, do you?" said Oakley, not wanting to let the issue drop.

Brimsby stopped his horse, compelling Oakley to do the same. Brimsby turned sideways so he could face Oakley and said through clenched teeth, "Look, I don't like you. If I thought for one minute Whitney wouldn't mind, I'd beat you within an inch of your sorry, miserable life."

The outburst took Oakley by complete surprise. He knew Brimsby didn't care much for him, but he didn't think it was this severe. He wasn't going to back down. He swung the shotgun so it faced Brimsby, cocked both hammers, and said with a wide grin, "You could try."

Brimsby looked down at the shotgun and then lifted his gaze so he was looking into Oakley's eyes and said, "There's gonna come a time, real soon, when you are gonna have to pull those triggers. Best you don't miss." He turned back in the saddle, gave his horse a gentle kick in the ribs, and trotted ahead.

Oakley said loud enough for him to hear, "Believe me, I won't."

Nathaniel Brimsby wanted nothing more than to choke the life out of the little weasel, Oakley. As far back as he could remember, injustice in any form caused anger to swell up in him and he always got a strong urge to do something to set things right. He had a genuine dislike for anyone who used their station or strength to abuse others beneath them. Case in point, he felt the hair rise on the back of his neck when Con Murdoch was badgering Josiah Morgan and when Silas Davidson took a club to Harold Grant. After Luke Briscoe beat Sean McClaren, he would have caved Briscoe's head in if Oakley hadn't shot him first. Now, this ass-kissing little twerp was getting under his skin.

Brimsby believed Oakley would use the shotgun if he truly thought his life was in danger. He had no quarrel with that, but what got his goat was the way Oakley hung around Whitney and pushed his weight around, sort of like a dog that only growls when it knows its master is watching. He was getting tired of the long journey, but he trusted Whitney and he believed there was a fortune in gold waiting for them. It never occurred to him Whitney would not keep his word about sharing the wealth, but he didn't trust the others, especially the two heathens.

He didn't always think ill of the native people, but sometimes it only takes one bad incident to prejudice a man. For Nathaniel Brimsby that occasion took place about a hundred miles west of Fort Edmonton. He was part of a group of travellers, Overlanders as they were called by many. They were trying to get to the gold fields overland by crossing the prairies.

They set up camp for the night along the McLeod River, the evening meal was over, and the men were standing around the campfire smoking pipes and trading lies while the women cleaned up the camp for the night. Their quiet evening repose was interrupted by five mounted local natives, who came to trade. Among Nathaniel's group was a man who had guided and scouted on the prairies for years and because he knew most of the native dialects, he acted as the interpreter. The natives wanted to trade some buckskin, pemmican, and berry biscuits for a live ox. Apparently, game was scarce and they were in need of some fresh meat. They were told the ox was needed to pull a wagon and it was not for eating and certainly not for trading.

The natives rode away somewhat disgruntled and everyone thought it was the end of the matter. However, come morning, the ox was gone. The wagon master told the young couple who owned it there was nothing he could do about it. Without the ox, there was no way of pulling their wagon and they would have to leave behind anything they could not carry.

Nathaniel was enraged. He wanted to go find the natives and if the ox was not alive, he would demand a couple of horses in payment. The scout assured him he would spend a week trying to find the natives and by the time he did, the ox would have been eaten and there would be no way to prove they had taken it in the first place. Nathaniel let the issue drop, but he never forgot the incident and he did not trust anyone of native blood after that.

An hour or so after his confrontation with Oakley, Brimsby pulled up his horse. They had come over a small rise in the meadow and were starting down the other side when Brimsby noticed a large brownish coloured shape a short distance down from the left side of the trail. It appeared to be a large deer or even an elk, but it wasn't moving. Brimsby waited for Oakley to catch up and then pointed out his find.

They rode to within a few feet of the remains and Oakley dismounted. The stench was so strong Brimsby dry heaved and if there had been any food in his stomach, he would have vomited. Oakley put his hand over his nose to stifle the odour and began poking the body with the tip of his shotgun. As he lifted the hide to see inside, the rotting carcass caved in on itself and a white wiggling mass of maggots spilled out on the ground.

"Think we can save any of the meat?" asked Oakley.

Nathaniel thought it was probably one of the dumbest questions he ever heard in his entire life, but after a moment's consideration, he realized it was probably Oakley's hunger talking and he said, "I ain't hungry enough just yet, but you go ahead and help yourself."

Oakley was about to remount, when a fierce roar came from the willows not more than twenty feet away. The enormous grizzly bear was downwind so the horses didn't react, but both of them went into a wide-eyed frenzy at the sight of the huge bear. Brimsby was between the bear and Oakley and when his horse reared up and threw him to the ground, the bear charged. Brimsby saw him coming and rolled on his stomach and clasped his arms behind his head to protect his neck. The bear took a powerful swipe with its claws across Brimsby's back, trying to turn him over.

Oakley hollered at the bear and distracted it away from Brimsby. It focused its attention on Frank and his horse. Frank was hanging on as tight as he could to his horse's bridal, all the while talking gently to his mount. He put the elk carcass between himself and the bear. As the bruin approached Frank, it was attracted by the wiggling mass of maggots, a delicacy in grizzly bear circles. The bear stuck its nose right into the middle of the creepy crawlers and began licking up mouthfuls of them, all the while keeping a close eye on Oakley, who very slowly and deliberately raised the shotgun and very carefully pulled the hammers back. He was about to fire when a loud report rang out from behind the bear. Brimsby was on his feet and had fired the Spencer, catching the bear in the middle of the back.

He levered another shell into the chamber of the rifle and approached the bear cautiously. It was still very much alive and trying frantically to get to its feet, but Brimsby's shot had broken the creature's spine, paralyzing the lower half of its body. It was a pathetic, yet, intriguing thing to watch. The bear was so determined to get at Brimsby it somehow managed to turn itself in Brimsby's direction and began dragging its inert body towards him, all the while snarling viciously, oblivious to the pain it must be enduring.

Brimsby took careful aim and shot the bear in the head, putting the poor creature out of its misery. To Frank Oakley's amazement, Brimsby reloaded and shot the bear a third time. He was about to fire a fourth shot, when Frank yelled at him, "Brimsby! Brimsby!"

Nathaniel vaguely heard his name being called and looked up, pointing the Spencer at Oakley. "What the hell are you doing? The goddamn bear is dead. You are wasting ammunition," shouted Oakley.

Brimsby looked at the dead bear and then up at Oakley and said, "I don't know what happened. I must have blacked out for a minute, there." Changing his tone he said with a grin, "Bear meat ain't exactly good eatin', but it'll fill a hungry belly!"

Whitney and the rest of the troop heard the rifle reports and stepped up their pace. They hadn't ridden very far when they saw a riderless horse trotting towards them. Whitney caught the horse, which slowed to a walk when it saw the troop. "Mr. Briscoe, if you would be so kind as to take care of this mount, I will ride ahead and see what has happened," he shouted and then rode off at a gallop.

Five minutes later he came over the small rise and saw Oakley and Brimsby in the distance. He spurred his horse and was at the scene in a matter of minutes. He quickly looked around and then addressed Brimsby, "Looks like we have lots of meat." Noticing Brimsby's shredded coat and shirt with some telltale red underneath, he added, "And it looks like one of them put up a fight."

Oakley quickly interjected, "The elk has been dead a long time. It's not fit to eat, but we got ourselves a load of bear meat."

Brimsby spoke up, "What do you mean *we?*"

Oakley turned indignant, "If I hadn't distracted the bear, he would have had you for lunch." Then as an after thought he added, "Maybe I should've kept my mouth shut."

Whitney defused the situation when he said, "Good work, boys. We have your horse, Mr. Brimsby. Luckily, he ran in our direction."

A few minutes later, the rest of the troop arrived. Michael and the Briscoe brothers skinned and quartered the bear, wrapped the hind quarters of meat in the deer skins, and packed it all onto the spare horses. There was no sense packing all the meat, simply because they could not possibly eat it all before it started to go bad. Nathaniel Brimsby insisted on keeping the bear hide, so Michael cleaned it of all fat and blood as best he could with Mathew Briscoe's knife, rolled it up, handed it to Brimsby, and said, "If you don't dry this out good, it is really going to start to stink in a few days."

A mile beyond the meadow, the trail came out of the trees and onto the top of a canyon wall overlooking the river. The troop had cut across country and arrived exactly where the old prospector told Whitney he would, which gave him a renewed sense of purpose and confidence that they were on the right track. They saved a day's travel by going directly across the high plain instead of following the river. From the top of the cliff, the trail gradually descended back down into the river valley.

The trail narrowed considerably as they descended and Whitney ordered the men to dismount and lead their animals. He could have cared less if one of the men went tumbling down the embankment to the collection of boulders below, but he couldn't afford to lose another horse, not if he wanted to get all the gold out. Once down on the valley floor, the trail took them through a small aspen grove, a barrier of willows and then they emerged onto a rock table, perhaps forty feet wide and three hundred feet long, just like the old prospector had described.

Whitney dismounted and handed his reins to Oakley. He made his way carefully to the edge of the rock table and took a quick look over the rim. Fifty feet below, the river converged into a narrow gap no more than twenty feet wide. Beyond the gap, the river bed was strewn with boulders and the rushing water broke up into a collage of white crested waves, sprays, and splashes.

"Gentlemen, these are the rapids we expected to find." Whitney shared this news with the rest of the men, hoping it would give them a sense of excitement, but to his dismay, Frank Oakley was the only one who showed any signs of enthusiasm. The old prospector told Whitney when he reached the river again, there would be a set of rapids, but not to be dismayed because a mile below them, the river widened out and was very shallow. He also went on to say, at this point, the river would turn sharply to the east. Whitney was not to follow it, but cross at the shallows and continue in the same northerly direction they had been travelling. Another three miles would bring them to the south shore of another west to east flowing stream. The old prospector told Whitney to follow this river upstream until he saw a rather striking embankment of red rock on the other shore. This would be the place to cross for the final leg of their journey.

The brilliant orange and fuchsia coloured clouds on a dark grey background in the western sky indicated darkness was not far off. "Another mile and we will come to a safe place to navigate the river. We'll make camp there and cross in the morning," Whitney said with an air of confidence, hoping to install some of it in the rest of the troop.

They picked up the trail again at the end of the rock table and as predicted, a short, steep downhill ride through some scrub spruce and juniper brought them to the shore of the river. The terrain was quite level and provided a good spot to camp. Whitney barked out orders and before long, Michael had a roaring fire going, as once more Mathew Briscoe watched in fascination. Luke Briscoe and Frank Oakley cut up some of the bear meat into chunks, skewered them on green willow sticks, and had them roasting over the fire.

Whitney told Dancing Crow, through Michael, to see if he could patch up Brimsby's wounds. Nathaniel refused at first, but relented when Whitney said it wasn't an option but an order. He removed his coat and shirt and exposed his raked back to Dancing Crow. There were four gashes running from the top of his right shoulder, down and across his back to his left side. The middle two slashes were the deepest and were still seeping some blood, while the outside cuts were more superficial and were already crusted over. Whitney came closer to inspect the wounds and said, "He got you pretty good, Mr. Brimsby. Looks like the bleeding has pretty well stopped. Let the heathen doctor you up. It'll keep them from festering."

Dancing Crow disappeared into the trees and seemed to be gone a long time. Just as Michael was beginning to get concerned, the old man emerged carrying some moss and other greenery, with healing properties. Dancing Crow appeared ashen and he kept looking over his shoulder, back at the trees he'd just come from, as he almost ran to the vicinity of the fire. He tugged on Michael's shirt and brought him to where Brimsby sat patiently waiting. Dancing Crow spoke while he applied the lichens, strips of bark, and some leaves to the wounds and tied them down with several strips Mathew Briscoe had cut for him from one of the deer hides.

Michael translated for Brimsby, who kept muttering he knew what the old man was saying, but Michael ignored him and told him he was to leave the dressings on for a couple of days. It would get very itchy, but he was not to remove it or Dancing Crow could not guarantee his wounds would not get infected.

-4-

At about the same time the troop was ravenously stuffing themselves with half cooked, greasy bear meat, Silas Davidson emerged onto the table rock. Since nightfall, Silas had slowed his pace somewhat after he tripped and fell flat on his face several times. Finding even a clearly marked trail in the dark was difficult, but when Silas found himself on solid rock, he knew it was impossible to follow the troop until daylight.

He lowered himself down to a sitting position, caught his breathe and began to think about his dilemma. As he sat in silence, he suddenly felt very thirsty. Thoughts of crystal clear, cold running water filled his head. He could see himself belly down with his face in a tiny, icy brook, sucking in the life giving liquid. He saw himself splashing his face with the invigorating water and running it through his hair. It felt so good.

The desire for water became intense. He was totally obsessed, like a junkie desperately needing a fix. The only thing he could think about was getting a drink of water. He wasn't sure if it was in his mind or real but he could hear the sound of rushing water coming from directly in front of him. He looked up and there, to his amazement, stood Harold Grant. He was surrounded by a glowing bluish aura and was beckoning Silas to come forward. If Silas would have really paid attention he would have seen Harold Grant was not standing directly on the rock bed, but seemed to be suspended several feet above it.

Silas rose and walked towards Harold. His need for water overshadowed any reservations he might have about a dead man standing over a canyon calling him forth in the dark. As he went headlong over the rim and into the raging waters below, he realized his error in judgement.

-5-

Michael asked Dancing Crow as he wiped his mouth on his sleeve, "What frightened you in the forest earlier?"

Dancing Crow seemed irritated when he said, "It is nothing that concerns you."

"Come on, we've had this conversation before. I only want to help you."

Dancing Crow hesitated and then replied, "I was gathering the lichens and bark when a fox appeared before me. It looked up at me and asked me why I was helping the killers of The People. At first I was afraid, but then I told it that it is not the way of my people to seek revenge. I told it the man was hurt and I was going to help him. It stood and looked at me for the longest time. Then it growled at me, turned, and trotted away."

"Do you think it was your grandson?" asked Michael.

"I do not know, my son. I do not know." He paused briefly and then started in again as if he remembered something important, "The fox did the strangest thing. He trotted a little ways, stopped and turned his head to look back at me. I could see directly into those dark eyes and I believe those were the saddest eyes I have ever seen. Call me a foolish old man, but I believe I saw tears in those dark eyes."

The two men looked at each other for the longest time and then simultaneously turned their heads away. After an awkward silence, Michael said, "Have you had enough to eat, Grandfather? Can I get you some more?"

Dancing Crow looked surprised when Michael called him "Grandfather". It was used a term of endearment amongst The People. He smiled and said, "No, my belly is full, thank you."

"This here bear meat ain't half bad, Brother Mathew," Luke Briscoe said through a mouthful.

"Fella will eat just about anythin' if he is hungry enough," replied Mathew. He paused and then said, "Your shoulder ain't botherin' you much now, eh?"

"Nope. I stopped it. I chased those people away like you said."

"How did you do that?"

"Well Sir, I told Elizabeth and the young fella and the injun squaw they wasn't real and they couldn't hurt me no more, so they should go away and they did, Mathew. They did!"

No sooner were the words out of Luke's mouth when a huge timber wolf, leapt out of the darkness knocking Luke onto his back. Luke tried to fight it off, but it was very powerful and it clamped its jaws into Luke's shoulder wound and began to shake its head back and forth like it was tearing a piece of meat from a deer it had downed. Luke let out a blood curdling scream.

"Luke? Luke, for Christ sake, what's wrong?" yelled Mathew.

"Get it off! Get it off!" screamed Luke.

By this time all the men had come running. They stood witness as Luke Briscoe writhed on the ground, screaming as if in mortal agony and punching wildly with both fists into the air. Mathew Briscoe knelt down beside him and grabbed Luke's flaying arms, all the while shouting "Stop it, Luke! Stop it, goddamn it. There's nothin' there."

Luke relaxed and opened his eyes. "There was this big wolf, Mathew. He was bitin' my shoulder."

"There ain't no wolf, Luke! It was all in you head," said Mathew. His eyes went to Luke's shoulder and he gasped. Luke's shirt was torn to shreds. Mathew pulled aside the tattered garment and looked at the wound. It was gaping and torn as if some animal, a wolf perhaps, had taken a large bite.

Chapter 19 – Maggots Galore

The first light of morning chased away the shadows of the night, only to reveal a white, churning mist, covering the ground. It swirled about at the slightest breeze and it danced around Clarence Whitney's lower legs as he made his way to the campfire. As he approached, he saw Michael and Dancing Crow sitting next to a cozy little blaze. "You gentlemen are up pretty early. Can't sleep?" he asked.

"The old man had a bit of a chill, so we thought we'd get the fire going," replied Michael.

"Good," said Whitney, "get some of that horseshit you call meat cooking and I'll roust the —"

Nathaniel Brimsby's hysterical screams cut him off in mid sentence. Whitney made it to Brimsby's location in four or five long strides with Michael and Dancing Crow right behind. Brimsby was in a sitting position and he was clawing at his back with both hands. It appeared as if Brimsby was snatching up handfuls of something from his back and throwing it to the ground.

Whitney stood over him and said, "Sergeant Brimsby, get a hold of yourself!" When Brimsby didn't respond, Whitney kicked him hard on the side of the leg and tried again, "Sergeant Brimsby, come to your senses!"

Brimsby stopped his frantic grasping motion and looked up. Whitney asked, "What seems to be the trouble, Sergeant?"

In response, Nathaniel reached back with his right arm and made a scooping motion with his hand, which he brought forward, opened and showed to Whitney. "This is what has me spooked," he replied.

Whitney could see Brimsby's hand was empty and Whitney's bewildered look suggested exactly that to Brimsby. He asked, "What? Are you blind? Can't you see them?"

Whitney kept his composure and said, "Sergeant, there is nothing in your hand."

"Maggots! Hundreds of goddamn maggots! They're eating me alive!" screamed Brimsby.

Whitney thought fast and said, "Let the old heathen take a look."

Brimsby became enraged, "You keep the son-of-a-bitch away from me. He did this to me in the first place."

Whitney knelt down to Brimsby's level and grabbed him by both shoulders, looked him in the eyes, and said very slowly and emphatically, "Sergeant, there are no maggots. They are all in your head. The old heathen put some lichen and bark on your wound. I have observed the procedure before. He didn't do anything but try to help you. Now, let him take a look!"

Whitney turned to Michael and asked him to instruct the old man to look at Brimsby's wound. Michael translated and Dancing Crow began to move himself in position behind Brimsby. After he looked down at the ground, he lifted his head and made eye contact with Michael, who saw the strange look on his face and asked, "What is it, Grandfather?"

"The maggots, they are everywhere," replied Dancing Crow, as if in awe.

Michael took two steps closer and bent down slightly, so he could see more clearly. His eyes went wide when he saw the crawling mass on the ground.

"What the hell is going on?" demanded Whitney.

"Looks like Brimsby's telling the truth. There are maggots everywhere," replied Michael.

Whitney partially knelt as well, but all he saw was empty ground. He rose quickly, drew his pistol and cocked it. "Alright, alright. What kinda of game are you playing?

The look of distrust on Whitney's face told Michael this could be a dangerous situation, not only for Brimsby but for him and Dancing Crow, as well. He doubted if Whitney was thinking about able bodied men to haul out gold at the moment. He said, "Look, I don't know what's going on anymore than you do, I swear — and neither does the old man." He paused and then continued, "You said it yourself, all the old man did was put some medicine on the wounds and hell, you saw the look on his face. He was as surprised as Brimsby. I don't know why we see the maggots and you don't, Mr. Whitney, but I assure you, we have nothing to do with it."

Because they were discussing the old man, Whitney's attention was drawn to him. Dancing Crow pulled back Brimsby's torn garments and was inspecting his wounds. Dancing Crow turned to face Whitney and Michael and he wore the same look of confusion he had moments before. Brimsby had torn off the make shift bandage and medicinal flora. Dancing Crow expected to see the wounds crawling with larvae, but they were clean and healing nicely. As his gaze dropped to the ground, he could no longer see any of the maggots. He shook his head and said to Michael, "This is powerful magic." Then his face lit up as if he'd discovered a great secret. He didn't notice until now, but Brimsby was using the bear hide for a ground cover.

He told Michael to tell Whitney the pelt still held the spirit of the bear and it was extracting its revenge on Brimsby, but because they had discovered its secret, there shouldn't be anymore trouble.

Michael translated. For a moment Whitney stood like he was deciding whether to believe the story or not. He lowered the hammer on the pistol and tucked it back in his waistband, turned and waked away. All he said was, "Horseshit!"

Whitney was rattled. He was always in control. He never let anything cloud his judgement. He always remained objective. He never doubted his senses. He needed time to think. A refreshing face wash in cold water would clear his head and with the thought in mind, he made his way to the river's edge. He removed his jacket and hat and set them on the bank, rolled up his sleeves, squatted on his haunches, and splashed the icy water on his face. "Ah, but this feels good," he said aloud.

As he scooped up another handful of water, he happened to glance upstream. Forty yards away, on his side of the river, was a small log jam where a large tree had fallen into the river from the eroding bank above. It acted as a catchall for anything coming downstream on that side of the river. A man's body appeared to be hung up in the branches of the tree. Whitney thought the man was dead until he saw him raise one arm and he heard a faint and laboured, "Help me."

He stood up and doubt entered his mind. Was this real, or another goddamn hallucination? He drew his pistol and fired a shot into the air. The report had barely died out when Oakley showed up, with Mathew Briscoe and Michael George not far behind. Whitney pointed to the log jam and asked, "Do any of you gentlemen see anything unusual on the tree in the water?" He was inwardly praying they too would say they saw a body.

Mathew Briscoe spoke up first, "Looks like somebody lyin' on top of it awavin' at us."

Whitney felt relieved. "Go and see who it is," he ordered. While Briscoe and Oakley made their way upstream, Whitney turned to Michael and asked, "You don't seem to follow orders very well, do you?"

"Don't need three of us to see what's what," replied Michael, as a statement of fact.

"The logic of the heathens," commented Whitney and he let the issue drop.

Oakley and Briscoe made their way through the willows, followed the slope of the embankment up to the top and made their way along the edge of the bank until they came to the downed tree. Making his way around the overturned root system of the huge tree, to the upstream side, Oakley saw a prone Silas Davidson lying across the trunk. He was about ten feet out from the shore, at the point where the tree met the water. His upper body was suspended by the tree trunk and his lower half was still in the stream.

"Hey Stork," hollered Oakley, "you alright?"

Silas turned his head in the direction of the voice. "Please, help me. I can't move."

Mathew Briscoe lay on his belly and edged himself, feet first, over the embankment. He let himself slide and using a thick limb of the fallen tree to hang onto, he let himself go until he was suspended in mid air hanging from the branch. From there it was a four foot drop to the ground. Mathew let go and landed with knees bent to cushion the blow. He used the tree limbs for support as he slowly made his way along the trunk to Silas's position.

"The water is awful deep," warned Oakley from the top of the bank. "You be careful."

Concern from the gunfighter. *'Now there's something different,'* thought Briscoe. Mathew was taken aback when he got closer to Silas. There was a deep gash running across the middle of his forehead. It turned sharply down his face, past his right eye, and disappeared into the thick red hair of his lamb chop sideburn. His left arm ran at a strange angle, behind his head, across his neck, and down his back. A person's arm wasn't supposed to be able to bend in such a fashion. Having once seen a farming neighbour of his father's with a dislocated shoulder, Mathew made the assumption the same thing had befallen poor Silas.

Mathew turned, facing Oakley, and said, "You go back downstream to the crossin'. I'll get him free and float him down to you fellas."

Oakley hurried back to Whitney and Michael and by the time he got there, Briscoe had already freed Silas and made his way to the downstream side of the tree. He was wading waist deep near the shore, with Silas in tow.

Oakley and Michael helped Briscoe pull Silas ashore and lay him on the sandy bank. Mathew turned Silas on his right side. He asked Michael to hold Silas's head down to keep it from moving. With Michael in position, he planted his foot in Silas's left armpit, took a good hold of the dislocated arm, looked down at Michael and asked, "Ready?" Michael gave a go-ahead nod. All in one motion, Mathew straightened Silas's arm, pulled as hard as he could and then shoved the arm back towards Silas's body with all his might. There was a sickening crunch and a shriek of agony from Silas, but the end of his humerus was back in his shoulder socket where it belonged.

"That was a waste of time," chided Whitney.

The three men around Silas looked stunned. They were looking for more from Whitney, but he simply turned and started the short walk back to the camp. Michael caught up to him and by quickening his pace, he stepped in front of Whitney, blocking his way. "You going to let him die, or are you going to shoot him?" asked Michael, demanding to know.

Whitney replied with complete indifference, "I'm not wasting a bullet on him. My ammunition is somewhat limited, but you can do what you feel is necessary to ease your conscience, Mr. George. You can leave him to die, or bash his head in with a rock. Personally, I don't care one way or the other." He stepped around Michael and started toward the fire. Remembering something else, he turned back and shouted loud enough for everyone to hear, "We leave in an hour!"

This time Mathew Briscoe spoke up, "We ain't goin' nowheres, Boss. River's too damn high."

"We're going, Mr. Briscoe. Best you see my horses don't drown," replied Whitney.

There wasn't much conversation among the men as they hurriedly wolfed down some seared bear meat before saddling up. Again, Dancing Crow found some chives in a little bog not far from camp, which made the meat a little more palatable, but not much. Mathew Briscoe kept complaining about the river being too deep to cross. Michael guessed he was hoping to get everybody to see his point of view and maybe they could approach Whitney en masse and voice their concerns.

Frank Oakley separated himself from the rest of the group. He didn't hang around Whitney like a little lost puppy anymore, but he didn't associate with anyone else in the troop, either. He walked around, his arms folded with the double barrel 12-gauge, resting in the nook of his bent left arm. To Mathew Briscoe, he looked like one of the much hated guards at the prison work camp.

"Why don't you take a break from your guard duty and get a bite to eat?" teased Mathew.

"Why don't you shut your mouth, Hillbilly, 'fore I close it for you?" was Oakley's testy reply.

Briscoe pulled his big skinning knife and headed for Oakley with anger in his eyes and purpose in his mind. Oakley anticipated the move and was ready for it. He levelled the shotgun and drew back the hammers, thinking the action would be enough to deter Briscoe.

It wasn't. His finger was starting to squeeze the front trigger when Mathew Briscoe dropped like he'd been hit with a sledge hammer. Nathaniel Brimsby stood over him with the Spencer in his hands. He'd driven the butt end of the rifle into the middle of Briscoe's back, right between his shoulder blades. Later, Mathew Briscoe's thinking would be that Brimsby had sided with Oakley in subduing him, but if he thought about it a little, he would see that Brimsby had saved his life.

"You keep out of this, you son-of-a-bitch! This is between me and the hillbilly," snorted Oakley.

Brimsby smirked when he said, "Well, I didn't want the hillbilly to kill you, boy. I want the privilege."

Oakley raised the cocked shotgun to eye level, aimed it directly at Brimsby, and said with conviction, "Then let's get to it."

Brimsby wasn't concerned that he was close to getting his brains blown out. His mind had retreated to the place where it went when he killed his wife and her lover and the native woman in the village. Mathew Briscoe, unknowingly, saved him from certain death when he tackled him from behind. Mathew had recovered from the dazed state he was in after the blow from the rifle butt. He picked up his knife and now with his anger directed at Brimsby, he charged at him, hit him from behind, and knocked him to the ground.

The two men were about the same size and strength, but the element of surprise gave Briscoe the edge and he was on top of Brimsby with the big knife at his throat before Brimsby could react. Oakley was surprised by the suddenness of the attack, but he quickly recovered and he saw an opportunity. Brimsby's Spencer was lying on the ground within easy reach. Oakley lowered his shotgun and stepped forward, bending at the waist to reach for the rifle. He was startled back into a standing position when Whitney's dirty boot came down on the barrel of the weapon.

Whitney shouted, "Alright Gentlemen, break it up!" as he stooped over and picked up the Spencer and levered the breech open slightly to check if there was a shell in the firing chamber and then closed it again, satisfied there was.

Mathew Briscoe looked up and Whitney could see he was thinking about taking his chances and cutting Brimsby's throat although he'd been ordered to stop. "If you kill him, Mr. Briscoe, I'll have to shoot you. Not that I care so much for Sergeant Brimsby, but I will shoot you for disobeying a direct order. Now, put the knife down." He turned to Oakley and continued, "Explain yourself, Corporal. What is your involvement in this?"

Oakley felt Whitney already knew, so he didn't offer any lame excuses or alibis. "I guess I started it all, Mr. Whitney — uhh — Captain, I mean — but someone has to teach the goddamn hillbilly some manners."

Whitney took several deep breaths and he turned his body to his left and to his right so he could look every man in the face and then said as if he were a preacher giving a Sunday sermon to his flock, "Look Gentlemen, this is the last time I give this speech." He paused as if gathering his thoughts then continued, "I need able bodied men to help me carry a king's ransom in gold out of this godforsaken wilderness. You all know this. Make no mistake about my sincerity, I will not put up with anymore bullshit from you people. If anybody else gets hurt in a fight or squabble and you can't travel, I will personally tie you to the nearest goddamn tree and let the coyotes have you. Do I make myself clear?"

Mathew eased up on the knife at Brimsby's throat and cautiously stood up. Brimsby slowly made his way to his feet and said to Mathew, "We're not done."

Mathew grinned and said, "Anytime, Maggot Man."

Brimsby caught sight of Oakley. He didn't say a thing, but gave him the most hateful stare and then walked off.

"Mathew, what's going on? What's all the commotion?" asked a bewildered Luke Briscoe.

Mathew looked at Luke and decided rather than give a long winded explanation, which Luke wouldn't have understood anyway, he simply said, "Nothin' Brother Luke, nothin' at all."

Whitney was in the saddle, looking out over the swollen river. Normally, the water would have been knee deep at the crossing, but because of the deluge two days ago, it was at least chest deep in the middle, not necessarily bad for crossing on horse back. Whitney knew the horses would do fine; it was the men who concerned him. That fool Luke Briscoe and the half comatose Silas Davidson could cause a problem if their horses panicked from lack of rein control.

Michael and Dancing Crow brought Silas's horse to the river bank and loaded him on it. Whitney didn't object. He simply reminded

Michael there would be the devil to pay if anything happened to the horse. Silas was conscious and fully aware as Michael wrapped a rawhide strap around his wrists and tied his hands to the saddle horn. "What's this for?" asked an uneasy Silas.

"So you don't fall off and drown. I'll lead your horse myself," said Michael.

Silas smiled. In over two weeks of riding, no one had seen Silas smile, but there it was, like the grin of a drunk who has realized that he just shit himself. He said with an air of smugness, "You don't have to worry about me, Sonny. I ain't afraid. They keep trying, but they can't kill ole Silas. No Sir, they can't. That miserable bastard Harold Grant led me over the edge and into the gorge, but I'm still here." Nobody understood what Silas meant.

Whitney gave the same warning to Mathew Briscoe as he did to Michael, "I don't give a damn about your lunatic brother, but you better not lose my horse."

Luke turned to Mathew and asked, "What's a lunatic, Mathew?" Mathew said without hesitation, "A crazy man, Luke."

"What's he wanna go and say a thing like that, Mathew? I ain't crazy! I don't like him very much," replied Luke as he scowled in Whitney's direction.

The crossing went smoothly except for a minor mishap. Silas lost consciousness and slumped sideways in the saddle. With his wrists tied, he wasn't going anywhere, but his horse, which wasn't used to the strange shift in weight, began to act up. Michael handed the reins of his horse to Dancing Crow and hanging onto the reins of Silas's horse, he jumped into the chest deep water. He shortened the lead on the reins until he was holding them tightly under the horse's neck. He gently stroked the horse's nose, all the while talking to it. The horse calmed down and Michael led it to the opposite shore and out onto the bank.

Once everyone was out of the water, Whitney said, "Men, don't get too comfortable. There's another wider and deeper stream to cross in a couple of miles."

He was referring to what the old prospector had told him. "You'll cross a fairly shallow river, but a couple o' miles further, you'll come to a wider deeper river, and she's a beaut. The trail is on the other side.

You might think about stayin' on this side, but don't do it. There's no trail and you'll most likely get yourself lost."

It was exactly as Whitney had described. After about two and a half miles of trail that led them up a row of low hills and down the other side, they came to another stream. It was wider, looked much deeper, and was a lot muddier than the stream they had crossed a short time ago.

Whitney dismounted and was pensively looking across the water. Michael approached him cautiously, cleared his throat and then spoke. "I'm not going against you, Mr. Whitney, but the river isn't safe to cross. I know you don't care about the men, but we could lose some of the horses."

Whitney turned his gaze to Michael. As he had seen his officers do in the army, he wanted Michael to give him possible solutions, not point out the obvious. He asked, "So what do you think we should do about it, Private?"

Michael pointed to a hat sized boulder, about four feet out from shore. The top three inches of the rock were dry. There was a band of wet stone about six inches between the dry part of the rock and the surface of the water. "See the wet part of the rock? That is how much the water has gone down since the rain. If we were to rest up here a day or two, I'm sure the river would be down to normal," Michael explained.

"No, Private, we will press on," countered Whitney.

Michael didn't mean to say it, but he did. "I thought you were a lot smarter." He expected to be punched or gun butted and he braced for it. Whitney completely surprised him by saying, "Perhaps, the horses could use a good rest. We'll camp for the day, but come first light we cross, high water or not. Pass it on to the rest of the men, Private."

Private, thought Michael. *Did Whitney think he was commanding a group of soldiers?* Michael shrugged and headed back to the rest of the men to announce the news to those who didn't hear Whitney say it.

-2-

The bear meat was a little more palatable thanks to Dancing Crow, who wandered through the forest for several hours before returning with some wild sage and chives to sprinkle on the meat and some wild mint to chew on to clean the greasy taste out of the mouth. After a noonday meal, something they never had on the trail, Michael sat down on the ground close to Dancing Crow. "Grandfather, may we talk?" he asked.

"What is it you wish to talk about," asked the old man.

"I want you to tell me more about this Dreamwalker."

"I told you all I know last time we talked."

Ignoring him, Michael said, "This spirit troubles all the men, yet he has done nothing to me. Why is that?"

Dancing Crow paused to think before replying. "I believe it is because you have looked after me. You could have escaped many times, but you chose to stay for my sake. I thank you and I think the spirit knows it also."

Michael seemed confused when he said, "But I don't understand. Hasn't he entered your dreams and threatened you?"

"I believe he would not harm me, but he has become very angry with me because I have helped the white men with my medicine."

Michael remained silent for several minutes before speaking again. "Then why don't we go looking for some more chives and sage and keep going? They won't miss us for most of the day and we could get a good head start. Whitney won't waste any time coming after us."

"I believe it is time, to do so," said a smiling Dancing Crow. He started to get up and abruptly sat back down again. There was a very sharp pain in his lower back and his legs felt like rubber.

He closed his eyes to alleviate the pain and a fox appeared in his inner vision. "You will stay. You and the half-blood must help me avenge The People," it said and then disappeared.

"Are you alright?" asked Michael.

"I am fine, but I do not think the spirit wants us to leave. He told me so."

"Don't listen to him. If we don't leave now, Whitney and his foolishness will be the death of us," pleaded Michael.

As if in answer, Whitney interrupted them, "I don't know what you two are talking about, but this little voice in my head keeps telling me you two want to leave our little troop here. That's desertion soldier and deserters get the firing squad."

Michael seemed stunned that Whitney would understand what they were talking about. He'd only got the idea himself a few minutes ago. When Whitney was out of earshot he said to Dancing Crow, "He knew we were planning to leave. How?"

All Dancing Crow said was, "I think a sly fox told him."

Luke Briscoe ate enough bear meat to feed a regiment. He was stuffed and contented and he found a soft moss covered spot to lay down for an afternoon nap. He no sooner closed his eyes, when he heard a growling noise nearby. He snapped open his eyelids and standing no more than five feet away were three coyotes, all with heads lowered and snarling, with lips pulled back, exposing a mouth full of fangs. They would growl and then take a step closer. The minute Luke moved, the three coyotes charged him and began tearing at his already ravaged shoulder.

Luke screamed in terror. Mathew, who wasn't very far away, raced over, grabbed Luke, and shook him. He wasn't getting any response, so he backhanded Luke as hard as he could, twice. Luke opened his eyes and seeing Mathew he pleaded, "Mathew, help me! They're tearin' me apart!"

There's nothin' there, Luke. I've told you a thousand times, boy. It's all in your head."

"But the coyotes, Mathew. They're eatin' me alive."

Mathew was getting angry. "Yesterday a wolf and today coyotes. Look around you, Luke. You see any coyotes? No! Nobody does, but you. They're all in your goddamn head, for Christ sake!"

Luke's expression changed from one of pain and anguish to one of defiance. He pulled back his jacket to reveal the wound. To Mathew's complete and utter surprise, the wound was larger than the day before. It looked like something had taken another bite out of the muscle below the clavicle. Something was eating its way down Luke's right side, one bite at a time.

"If there ain't no coyotes, than what is doin' this to me, Mathew? — What?" asked Luke, not expecting an answer.

Mathew slumped to the ground as if his legs could no longer hold him. He ran his fingers through his hair to get it out of his eyes. He hid his face in his hands for several seconds, lifted his head, took a deep breath, and said to Luke, "I don't know, Brother Luke. I ain't never seen anythin' like it all my born days." He jumped up quickly as if he was bee-stung. "The heathen might know. He's some kinda Medicine Man or somethin'. I'll go get him."

Whitney was planning the next day's itinerary when Luke Briscoe let out his latest scream. Whitney thought, *that pain-in-the-ass Luke Briscoe is at it again. I'm going to put an end to this. It is interfering with the discipline in this troop. I can't have a soldier screaming the night away in enemy territory. Every Reb for a mile can hear him.*

Whitney's long determined strides had him standing over Luke in short order. "What is the problem, soldier?" he asked.

Luke wasn't sure what was happening. Why was Whitney calling him a soldier and what was he going to do with the coiled bullwhip in his hand.

"I asked you a question, Private," emphasized Whitney.

"It's my shoulder, Mr. Whitney — the — "

Whitney uncoiled the whip and said, "That's Captain Whitney to you, soldier." He meant to crack the whip over Luke's head, but he wasn't very proficient with it and as a result, caught Luke across the top of the forehead.

Luke stood up at the same time that Whitney cracked the whip again. This time he hit Luke's left shoulder. Luke reacted instinctively, by reaching up and grabbing the whip. He yanked it out of Whitney's hand before Whitney knew what happened. Neither man knew what to do next. They stood looking at each other momentarily and then Luke threw the whip to the ground and took three long strides towards Whitney, at the same time pulling aside his torn clothing to expose the fresh wound.

"I know you think I'm crazy. Then tell me how his is happenin'?" asked Luke.

Whitney never saw Luke Briscoe this animated. He stepped closer and carefully examined the gaping wound. It certainly appeared fresh and it sure looked like something had taken a bite. Whitney did not know what to make of it, so he changed the subject and said, "Alright soldier, you get it looked after, but you have to keep the screaming down. There are Confederates all around us and we don't want them to hear us, do we?"

Luke did not know how to respond, so he simply said, "Yes, Sir."

A loud, "What's goin' on?" from Mathew Briscoe, disrupted the scene.

"Private Briscoe and I were discussing the merits of silence in enemy country," replied Whitney, as he picked up the bullwhip and left.

Not understanding a thing Whitney said, Mathew addressed his brother, "You alright, Luke?"

"Yeah, fine," said Luke.

"The old Injun told me what to do to keep the wound from getting' infected. You relax and I'll go fetch some things that'll help," instructed Mathew. He took a glance in Whitney's direction to make sure he didn't have any intentions of coming back.

As he made his way into the denser growth of trees to collect some resinous bark and lichens as per Dancing Crow, Mathew began to feel a stronger and stronger hatred towards Whitney. *What was all this soldier garbage, anyway?'* he thought. *Whitney is as loony as Luke, for Christ's sake.* As he walked, his inner voice kept saying Whitney was dangerous and his protective instinct for his younger brother roused defensive feelings in him. He came to the conclusion that if Captain Whitney, or whatever the hell he was calling himself, bothered Luke again, he would kill him and gold be damned.

-3-

It was early evening, when the troop finished their last meal of the day. Most of them were sick of the greasy bear meat, but it satisfied their hunger. Silas Davidson joined them for the repast, and every one could see there was something definitely not right with the man. He moved cautiously to the fire and snatched a willow stick with a sizzling hunk of meat on the end, furtively looked all around him as if his head was on a swivel, scurried to a spot some distance away from the rest of the men, and took little bites out of his meat. After every nibble, he would cradle the uneaten portion to his chest and look all around before taking the next bite. It reminded one of a robin eating a freshly caught dew worm, the way it takes a few bites, looks all around for danger, and then takes a few more pecks.

Frank Oakley was watching Silas and driven by boredom, he decided to have some fun. He circled around the back of the rest of the men, took a wide berth, and went into the thicker trees, behind Silas. He made his way to a tree about four feet directly behind him.

He timed it so when Silas bent his head to take another bite, he jumped out from behind the tree. He covered the distance between them in two long strides and was a foot directly behind Silas when he yelled, 'BOO!' in his ear.

Silas leapt up, dropping his half eaten piece of meat on the ground. Oakley continued his assault. He pulled the back of his jacket up over his head to appear headless, and advanced toward Silas, making moaning and groaning sounds.

"Stop acting like a child, you buffoon. I am not afraid of you, you silly fool," said Silas.

Oakley stuck his head back out from underneath his jacket. He was somewhat annoyed. Nobody laughed at his little prank and he expected Silas to run screaming into the woods, but it never happened. There was one more little tidbit up his sleeve. "Ooh, big, brave, Silas. Not afraid of anything, eh?" He raised his right arm and formed his hand into a claw and said, "Look out, Silas here comes the hand of the lake to take you away — watch out."

Silas Davidson snapped. He was tottering on the fine edge between plain delusion and complete insanity and Oakley's mention of the hand in the lake pushed him over the edge. He stripped off all of his clothes and ran stark naked the short distance to the river. He waded out to the deepest point which was just over his head and sank under the water. He stayed under for a very long time and then he surfaced, gasping for air.

At the crossing, the river bed was spread out, twice as wide as in most places. Although, earlier in the day the water was much deeper and faster, the run-off from the rain was nearly gone. Consequently, the water level was down considerably and the current was a lot slower. Silas went under for the second time, only to come splashing to the surface, sucking for air, again. He waded back to shore and bowed to Oakley, Whitney, Michael, and Mathew Briscoe, who had all come to the river bank to watch the side show. He looked directly at Oakley when he said, "See, I'm not afraid. Silas Davidson is invincible!"

Oakley began to laugh as did Mathew Briscoe. Silas cocked his head sideways at them and said, "Still not convinced, eh?"

Forty feet downstream was a tall stand of pine with one particular very tall, very wide, and very old tree with thick branches for easy climbing. Silas ran to the tree and climbed up about thirty feet in a matter of minutes, in spite of his throbbing shoulder and almost useless arm. He turned his body to face the men and shouted, "I am not afraid!" He bent his knees and pushed off with all his might. He went sailing through the air in a swan dive position and stayed in form until he hit the ground with a sickening thud.

The men stood in disbelief for a moment. Michael rushed over with Mathew Briscoe close behind. When Silas hit the ground, he fractured most of his ribs and the inward thrust of broken bones punctured most of his internal organs. Michael and Mathew got to him in a matter of seconds, but Silas had only enough strength left to say, "I told you I wasn't afraid," before he died.

Clarence Whitney made his way to the scene, looked at Silas and said, "No room in this man's army for a lunatic coward. Good riddance."

Nathaniel Brimsby didn't go down to watch the demise of Silas Davidson. He was trying to cope with his own delusions. He lay down on the bear hide and fell asleep from sheer exhaustion. He wasn't asleep very long when he had a very vivid dream, in which he found it difficult to breathe. It was totally dark and he was confined in a tight space. It felt like a long rectangular box. He panicked. He was in a coffin! He began to claw at the roof of the coffin and dirt was falling in his face. At least he thought it was dirt until it began to move. He reached up to brush the dirt away and felt crawly things. Maggots! He frantically felt the walls on either side of him and the floor. They were all alive and moving. He was buried in a coffin made of maggots.

Nathaniel forced himself awake. He sat upright and breathed deeply until he caught his breath. He'd never had a dream so vivid. He couldn't remember ever having experienced such a high level of fear. "Thank God, it was a dream," he told himself.

Suddenly, his dead wife and her equally dead lover materialized ten feet in front of him. They pointed accusatory fingers at him, both screaming, "Murderer" over and over again.

Nathaniel gathered his wits and chuckled at the spectres, "Huh, you are both dead. I killed you. Yes, I see it now, but you know what? I don't feel at all guilty because you deserved what you got, you cheating whore."

Another figure materialized next to Nathaniel's wife. It was the young woman he had slaughtered in the native encampment. "Did I deserve it, Nathaniel?" she asked in perfect English.

Nathaniel didn't have to think for an answer. "Women are all whores. They all want something and they'll open their legs wide to anybody they think will give it to them."

There was a momentary silence and then the three figures dissolved from the bottom up, getting shorter and shorter as they melted into the ground. Nathaniel heard the rustling sound. The figures weren't melting— they were turning into maggots and they were crawling en masse toward him. His first thought was to get up and run, but he couldn't move. He watched in horror as the maggots reached his feet and began crawling up his legs.

In seconds, he was covered in the dank smelling, gag inducing, white horde. They got into his ears, nostrils, and mouth. He frantically tried to pick them out of his nose and he bit down on the ones in his mouth, making him retch. More and more maggots crowded into his mouth and nostrils and started down his throat, choking off his air.

Just as he felt he was going to suffocate, he forced out a voluminous "NO!" Instantly, all the maggots vanished including the foul odour accompanying them. Nathaniel felt triumphant. He told himself he knew all along they weren't real. He felt something on his hand and he saw a solitary maggot crawling across his knuckles. He picked it up with his other hand and squished it between his thumb and forefinger. His new found confidence disappeared as quickly as it came. The maggot certainly felt real enough!

Chapter 20 – Sibling Rivalry

For the first time in recent memory, Clarence Whitney felt unsure of himself. Even as a stowaway, when he was being passed from one rum smelling, pork belly eating, sailor to another for their sexual amusement, he endure the buggery, telling himself it was the price he had to pay to get to America.

He hadn't slept all night because his restless mind wouldn't let him. If he wasn't rerunning all the strange events that had taken place on their journey to date, it was a highlighted review of the life of Clarence Whitney. Thoughts such as; what could possible have driven a man to climb a tree and leap to his death? What made Briscoe and Nathaniel Brimsby see things that weren't there, and yet he'd seen Luke's wound and others had seen Nathaniel's maggots, didn't they? Why weren't Oakley, or Mathew Briscoe, or the two heathens showing any symptoms? Yes, why did the breed and the old man seem immune? He would have to look into it.

Daylight was slowly making its presence felt. Whitney rose with intentions of rousting all the men. As he made his way to the campfire, he was surprised to see them already up and about and hunks of breakfast sizzling over the fire.

"Good morning, Captain," said Oakley, as he actually stood at attention and saluted.

For a split second, Whitney thought Oakley might be mocking him and then he realized the man was sincere. Whitney returned the salute and said, "At ease, Corporal." He found a place near the fire and sat down. He looked around at all the men and then at the roasting bear meat and asked, "Is there a piece there for me?"

Without saying a word, Mathew Briscoe got up and cut a sizeable piece of meat from the supply, stuck it on a green willow stick and handed it to Michael, who was closest to the fire. Michael stuck the other end of the stick into the ground at an angle, so the meat dangled over the flames.

No one was saying anything, nor had anyone spoken for the longest time. Whitney tried to make small talk, but when no one answered, he started to take it personally. His gaze centered on Nathaniel Brimsby, several feet down and away from the rest of the men. He sat cross-legged, with the Spencer cradled in his arms and he seemed to be staring at something beyond the camp.

Whitney was becoming irritated. He took the men's solemn mood for personal disrespect at his attempts to be friendly and he picked Brimsby as his whipping boy. He stood and walked over to Nathaniel's position and began to speak, "Sergeant, I —"

Brimsby rose so quickly, Whitney didn't have a chance to react. As Brimsby came up, he used the rifle to shove Whitney away from him, so there was some distance between them. Then he swung the rifle up into a shooting position and levered a shell into the chamber, all in one motion.

"What is the meaning of this insubordination, Sergeant?" asked Whitney.

"Don't you '*Sergeant*' me, you son-of-a-bitch. I'm not in your goddamn army, you sick bastard," spat Brimsby. He had the look of a cornered dog that was defending a bone it had found.

Whitney's mind was racing. He could handle most men in a similar situation, but it was clear Brimsby wasn't in his right mind. He decided talking Brimsby down would be the best approach, when he heard the double click of a pair of hammers being pulled back. Oakley stepped up beside him and levelled the cocked shotgun at Brimsby.

"You shoot the Captain and I shoot you," Oakley said with the sly smirk on his face that everyone had come to despise.

Brimsby turned the Spencer, so it was centered on Oakley. "You know I've had about all of you, I can stand," he said. "I can blow a hole right through you and still have time to reload and finish the '*Captain*' off."

Whitney said calmly, "Kill me and you won't find the gold, Mr. Brimsby. I'm sure it won't sit well with the rest of the men. In fact, I'm convinced they will tear you apart, if you kill me."

Whitney's threat was ineffective. There was no hesitation from Brimsby when he said, "I could give two hoots about your goddamn gold, anymore. Ain't none of us going to get there alive to see it, anyway. You brought this on us. You — you blood thirsty bastard! You had to slaughter those heathens in the village, didn't you? Did you ever ask yourself why, '*Captain*'? Did you?" Every time he said the word '*Captain*' it dripped of mockery and sarcasm.

Whitney saw an opening. "What did I have to do with you carving up the heathen woman?"

The enraged Brimsby couldn't think of an answer, so he just shouted out, "Shut up! You shut your mouth!"

The troop would never know if Nathaniel Brimsby was going to shoot at that instant or not, because he never got the chance. During the heated exchange all eyes were on Whitney and Brimsby. No one noticed Mathew Briscoe sneaking up behind Nathaniel with his big knife drawn. A quick upward thrust just below the ribcage dropped Brimsby to his knees and before he could even blink, Briscoe grabbed him by the hair, pulled his head back, and cut his throat with such force it almost decapitated him.

Everyone stood completely shocked and awed by the suddenness of the attack. Briscoe let go of Brimsby's hair and the body slumped to the ground in a bloody heap. He took two steps back and crouched slightly with the knife poised in his hand as if he was expecting retaliation from Whitney. He stood for a few seconds and then bent down to pick up the Spencer.

"I wouldn't do that, Private Briscoe. Give him both barrels, Corporal Oakley, if he gets any nearer to the rifle," said Whitney.

Oakley grinned and said, "Come on, Hillbilly, pick it up. Pick it up, if you've got the guts."

"That's enough, Corporal," commanded Whitney. Addressing Briscoe he said, "Why did you do it, Mr. Briscoe? I believe I had the situation under control."

Briscoe didn't back down. "From where I was standin', it sure looked like he was about to put a big hole in you. You was right when you said the rest of us still want the gold and I for one, sure as hell, don't want you dead," Briscoe smiled and added very sarcastically, "unless you want to tell us where it is and then I don't think I'll care as much about you dyin', Captain Sir." He turned his gaze in Oakley's direction and said, "Ain't nothin' holdin' me back from slicin' this little scum suckin' pig, though."

Whitney could feel the tension growing in Oakley and he was afraid he was about to pull the triggers on the shotgun and cut Briscoe in half. He extended his arm and gently took the shotgun by the barrel and carefully lifted it out of Oakley's hands and aimed it at Briscoe. Mathew instinctively braced himself for the blast, which didn't come. Instead Whitney said to Oakley, "Pick up the rifle Corporal. You have just inherited it."

Once the Spencer was in Oakley's hand, Whitney broke the breech of the shotgun, took out the two shells and put them in his pocket. Since he still had his own shotgun, he took Oakley's by the barrel and tossed it as hard as he could into the bush.

It looked like the situation was over. Briscoe straightened up and put his knife away while Oakley was fondling the Spencer like he just got it for Christmas. Whitney started barking orders. "Get some food in your bellies and be quick about it. We head out in half an hour."

"What about burying the two dead men?" asked Michael?

"If you can do it in the next half hour, fine. If not leave them for the coyotes and maybe they will leave the big dumb hillbilly alone," replied Whitney.

Michael enlisted Mathew Briscoe's help and the two of them hoisted Nathaniel Brimsby into the thick branches of a nearby silver spruce. Michael climbed up a few feet and Mathew lifted the body up to him. Michael pulled the corpse up to his position and laid it out flat across the branches. He covered it with the bear hide and climbed back down.

They had intentions of doing the same for Silas Davidson, but when they got to the spot where the body should be, it was nowhere in sight. They searched the area in a circular pattern looking for any sign, such as drag marks that might indicate what happened, but they didn't find a thing.

Michael saw the bewildered look on Mathew's face and said, "I've heard of some big cats that can carry a deer off in their jaws and not leave any drag sign. That's probably what happened. Maybe, we shouldn't say anything to the rest of them about the body being gone? What do you think?"

"Yeah, yeah. Don't say anythin'. Yeah, that's good," replied Mathew, still somewhat perplexed.

-2-

The crossing was entirely uneventful. The water had dropped nearly a foot and a half, back to its usual early September level. Whitney insisted Michael and Dancing Crow lead the way. He told them from this point on he wanted them where he could see them. He felt as they got nearer to the gold, he would need Dancing Crow to point out landmarks and he needed Michael as a translator. He felt he could control them provided he didn't let them both out of his sight at the same time. Michael already knew if he ran, he was signing the old man's death warrant. Whitney felt strongly the old man wouldn't go anywhere without Michael.

Oakley was a pain in the neck, but loyalty served a purpose. He'd have to sleep with one eye open while Mathew Briscoe was still around. Earlier in the morning, for a brief moment, he contemplated giving Oakley the go ahead to let go with the shotgun, but common sense had taken over. He still needed the Briscoes. Mathew would be worth his weight in gold if they ran into any hostiles. If he killed Mathew, he'd still have Luke to deal with.

Whitney put the Briscoe brothers next in line, followed by Oakley, to whom he'd given the task of leading the spare horses. Whitney brought up the rear with his shotgun in one hand and reins in the other. He wasn't taking any chances from here on in.

They were nearly two thirds of the way across the river when Whitney heard, "Captain, oh Captain," coming from behind him. He turned in the saddle and looked at the far shore. There was a row of soldiers all in Yankee Blue, standing at attention and saluting.

Whitney sensed there was something familiar about them, but he couldn't quite put his finger on it. Had he been closer, he would have recognized all the ill fated members of the troop. They all looked as they did when they died, with bullet holes, torn flesh and broken bones. Nathaniel Brimsby's head kept falling backwards, exposing the huge gap, which once was his throat. He kept reaching back and putting his head back in its proper place, only to have it fall backwards the minute he let go.

Silas Davidson was the spokesman for the ghoulish group. "Lieutenant Davidson here, Sir. Can we come too?" he asked, as they all entered the water and began to wade across.

Whitney turned to face the men ahead of him. "Let's get a move on up there," he shouted. "This water is cold." He didn't dare look back until he was completely across the river and safely up on the other shore. He turned his horse back around to face the water and at the same time, he brought up the shotgun and pulled back the hammers. As he looked up, all he saw was the flowing water and nothing of anyone or anything coming across.

"Something wrong, Captain?" asked Oakley.

Whitney took a deep breath and said "No. No, Corporal, nothing at all. I thought I heard something."

Whitney thought if he focused on finding the next landmark he would forget about what he'd seen or thought he'd seen at the river crossing. The dying prospector indicated once they crossed the two rivers, it would about a half day's ride to where the trail would split. The next sign to look for would be a large wall of red rock that formed the north shore of the river. The south branch of the trail followed the river to its headwaters to the southwest and the other branch went to the northwest, the direction they needed to go. He also mentioned at almost a day's travel there was a very large swampy area they would have to skirt around.

Frank Oakley was in a state of confusion. His emotions kept changing from moment to moment. He was elated Brimsby was out of the picture and he was Whitney's right hand man, but at the same time he shuddered when he recalled the brutal way in which Brimsby died. A gunfight was much more civilized, well maybe not civilized, impersonal would be more like it; your opponent was fifteen maybe twenty feet away, you drew your gun faster than him, and you shot him. If upon immediate observation, you saw you didn't hit him in a vital spot, you took better aim and finished him off and then you walked away, satisfied with a job well done.

As his horse plodded along beneath him, he let his mind wander into his daydream world. He hated Nathaniel Brimsby and he wished he'd been the one to kill him. He hadn't in real life, so Frank imagined doing the deed in his fantasy world.

As in all his fantasies, he saw himself at a bar surrounded by well wishers buying him drinks and bosomy dance hall girls jostling for position to get next to him. Then, from out in the street was heard the all too familiar call, "Gunfighter, I'm calling you out." He would knock back one more drink, kiss a couple of the closest girls, strut to the swinging bar room doors, open them, and stand in a dramatic pose before letting them swing back. He would walk slowly into the street and when he was within easy shooting distance, he would draw and fire, hitting his opponent in the knee, knocking him down. Then he would walk over, stand above his victim, and shoot the poor devil through the heart.

Frank Oakley forgot the last time he retreated into an imaginary gunfight with Whitney and Brimsby, it didn't quite turn out the way it was supposed to and he was the one who ended up getting shot. But here he was, out on the street ready to dispose of the hated Nathaniel Brimsby.

As usual, he drew and fired, the bullet hitting Brimsby square on the knee, sending a spray of blood and bone upon impact. Frank expected Brimsby to drop, but he didn't fall. In fact, he barely moved. Frank fired again, this time aiming for the heart. As before, the bullet made impact and Brimsby's shirt began to turn crimson, but he didn't go down.

Frank panicked. He emptied the revolver, with all the bullets hitting their mark. Still no effect. Frank kept shooting and shooting (he didn't have to stop to reload in his fantasy world) but Brimsby kept coming towards him until he was right upon Frank. Brimsby took the pistol by the barrel and ripped it from Frank's hand and threw it to the ground. Mathew Briscoe's huge knife was in his hand and in a lightning quick motion, he slashed Frank's throat from ear to ear.

Frank didn't feel any pain, but he instinctively put his hand up to his throat. He could definitely feel his own warm blood seeping through his fingers and down his shirtfront. "No! No! It's not supposed to happen like this," he shouted.

Reality returned. Mathew Briscoe turned backwards in his saddle and was talking to him. "You alright, boy? Who the hell are you talkin' to?"

"Nobody. I fell asleep. Had a bad dream," Frank replied.

Briscoe didn't question Oakley's reply because he could relate. Mathew used the same escape mechanism Frank Oakley did. Whenever he was stressed by someone, he would fantasize that he slowly beat his antagonist to death, enjoying every single punch. Other times, he imagined himself stabbing and slicing with a knife or whatever was handy until his victim lay dying, a bloodied mess at his feet. In fact, earlier in the journey he remembered fantasizing how he sliced Oakley up. Later, he relived the rape and murder of the two native women. Lately, the fantasy was about Luke lying on the ground, encircled by dozens of coyotes that were eating him alive, bite by bite. Mathew leapt into the middle of the circle with a pistol in one hand and his large knife in the other and began to rip coyotes away from him. Luke wasn't even fighting back. He continually screamed, "Help me."

Mathew shot and stabbed coyotes as fast as he could, but it didn't seem to do any good. There were dozens of dead or dying animals stacked all around him, and yet they kept coming as if there were an endless supply of them. Mathew stood still for a moment to catch his breath and heard mocking laughter and a voice that said, "You can not save him, Brother Mathew. His fear will drive him to his death and your passion to protect him will be your demise."

That was the part bothering Mathew. He had always been Luke's protector since they were kids. Mathew never considered it a burden. In fact, it came natural to him and he enjoyed the good feelings it gave him, feelings of self worth and accomplishment. Lately, however, he was having strange thoughts like *why me* and *if he's not going to listen to me, to hell with him*. He was starting to think of how Luke might actually be holding him back from getting his share of the gold. The big dumb lummox might actually ruin their chances of becoming rich for life.

And so it went for the rest of the day, everyone alone with their own thoughts. Nobody said much to anyone else, including Michael and Dancing Crow. Michael glanced over at Dancing Crow several times, but each time it seemed his eyes were glazed over and he was gazing at something in the distance. Michael called out to him several times, to no avail.

Shortly after high noon, the trail began a steep incline, which brought them out of the river valley. When the terrain flattened out again, they found themselves on the top of a ridge with a panoramic view. Straight ahead, they could see that the river they were following, took a sharp turn to the west and then another turn to the southwest. There was a long stretch of brownish red rock that replaced the usual sandy-grey color of the sandstone cliffs following the course of the river.

Whitney seemed genuinely excited when he saw the red wall. "Men, the red rock means we are going the right way. Be careful, the trail splits somewhere close to here. We need to keep to the right and head in that direction." He pointed to a row of hills heading to the northwest. "The trail we want should be down below those hills somewhere."

Five minutes later Michael shouted for Whitney to come to the front. There was the split in the trail, as Whitney had described. Whitney dismounted and went to the far side of the right branch of the trail and began to inspect the trees closely. A short while later he shouted a joyous "Yes!" He had found a diamond shape with a '*J*' right behind it, carved on a tree. Diamond Jack was the old prospector's name. He told Whitney the trail was hard to follow for the next dozen miles or so, giving boggy terrain as the main reason. So, about every mile, he'd left a blaze on the north side of the trail; the diamond with the '*J*' next to it.

Diamond Jack was right on the money. The trail down was steep and muddy from the myriad of springs emerging from the hillside, which used the path as a conduit. When they reached the bottom of the slope, the trail headed at a right angle up the hillside adjacent to the trail. This caused Whitney some concern, but he was relieved when he searched for and found the reassuring Diamond '*J*' on a nearby tree. It appeared the pathway headed some distance up the hill and then veered back down again. The idea was to go up high enough to avoid the marshy lowland that seemed to stretch to the horizon.

For most of the afternoon, it was a hard ride along a narrow path that cut through heavy timber and scattered deadfall. Several times, when there was no trail to follow, they fanned out to look for the blaze mark. Luke Briscoe's periodic screams, added to the tension. Even Mathew was wishing he would be quiet.

It was near nightfall when the trail took them back down into the valley. They came out of the timber at the far end of the huge marsh. Men and horses were tired and Whitney called a halt for the night. While the men were grateful for the rest, they weren't especially looking forward to another meal of greasy bear roast.

With the horses all watered at a small rill and then tethered in a grassy patch between two pine groves and with supper washed down, the men began to settle in for the night. Mathew Briscoe made sure Luke ate something and took him back away from the main camp about a hundred yards. Using the embers from the main fire, he built another smaller fire and made Luke comfortable. He was all set to leave when Luke started screaming in pain again. Mathew had reached his limit. He bent over the prone Luke and lifted him up by his shirt front. Their faces were no more than inches apart when Mathew said with as much seriousness as he could muster, "Brother Luke, listen to me! For the last goddamn time, this is all in your thick skull. You stupid lummox, I keep tellin' you are doin' this to yourself."

Calling him stupid or dumb always got Luke's attention. For a moment he forgot all about his pain, sat up, and pushed Mathew aside. He got to his feet quickly and stood over his prone brother. For the first time in his life, he felt hatred toward Mathew and he kicked him in the midsection as hard as he could, knocking the wind out of him. He gave him another vicious kick for good measure and then knelt down on his haunches and watched over Mathew until he got his breath back. "Don't you ever call me stupid again. You know I don't like it," he said when he thought Mathew was recovered enough to hear him.

Mathew coughed twice, gasped for air, and then asked, "How's the shoulder? Don't seem to be botherin' you much now, do it?"

There was a stunned expression on Luke's face. He didn't know what to say. Mathew continued, "I keep tellin' you over and over, it's all in your head, Luke, but you don't listen."

In answer, Luke showed Mathew his wound. It was larger, as if another couple of bites had been taken from his flesh. "This ain't in my head! You go ahead and tell me this is in my head!"

Mathew sighed and then spoke softly, "Luke, you say there's dozens of coyotes eatin' at you all the time —"

Luke interrupted, "I don't just say it. There is, damn it, Mathew. Why won't you listen?"

Mathew continued with his train of thought, "If all these coyotes was eatin' at you all this time there'd be nothin' left of you but some teeth and hair. How do you explain that?"

Luke thought for a moment and then went into a childlike tantrum. "You don't care 'bout me. You never cared 'bout me. All you care 'bout's the gold."

Mathew saw red. He was almost shouting when he said, "You ungrateful dumb shit. My whole life, I been lookin' out for you. I coulda done a hell of a lot better if'n I didn't have you always hangin' on my shirt tail."

All Luke heard was '*dumb*' and he was about to go at Mathew again, but his older brother pulled out his big knife and was ready for him. Luke stopped and then in a pseudo act of surprise, said "You pullin' a pig sticker on me, big brother?" He turned his back on Mathew and said, "Well, go ahead. Stick it in my back." He gave it a few seconds and then turned back to face Mathew. "I'm thinkin' no man worth his salt would pull a knife on his own brother. You go to hell, you ain't my brother no more!"

Mathew retorted in anger, "Good riddance," and then stomped back to the main camp area, leaving Luke to stew in his own anger, a decision he would deeply regret later.

Dancing Crow, who was usually quite talkative during the evening quiet time, wasn't saying anything. He seemed distant, with a look of sadness in his eyes. Michael watched in silence for the longest time and then began to prod the old man to see if he could get him out of his funk.

Dancing Crow was not responding to anything until Michael got on the subject of trying to escape and leaving the company of Clarence Whitney.

"I must stay," said Dancing Crow.

Michael didn't know which approach to use next. He never tried scare tactics, but he thought he would give it a go. He said, "You heard the one called Brimsby. He may be right, not one of us will be left alive by the time we get to where this mad man is taking us."

"The spirit of the fox will not hurt you or me," answered Dancing Crow.

"Then why don't we leave?" continued Michael.

"I can not. I believe the spirit wants us to remain. It is like a young one dancing for us and he does not want us to leave until he has finished his dance. I must try and convince him that the way of vengeance is not the right path for him to walk."

"But you said it yourself, Grandfather. He isn't listening to you."

"I must keep trying. Don't you understand, I must keep trying."

"You are right. I don't understand," said Michael.

Dancing Crow spoke very softly and solemnly, "It is a test of my own beliefs, a test of my own faith. I have often felt hatred and vengeance in my heart, but I have always known it was not the true path. I am an old man and I believe that forgiveness is the only way to lead the fox spirit away from his path of destruction."

Michael wanted to press on, but the approaching figure of Whitney diverted his attention. Clarence Whitney was the epitome of a loner. He never needed anybody or anything in his life and yet he found himself on this cool, early fall evening in the middle of God-knows-where, wanting the company of his fellow travelers. He came into the light of the fire and looked all around at the men. The entire troop was there with the exception of Luke Briscoe. Mathew Briscoe sat upward and behind the fire, Oakley sat to the right of it, and Michael and Dancing Crow sat together to the left of the fire from Whitney's perspective. Whitney sat down in the gap, thus completing the circle.

They were all somewhat apprehensive about Whitney's presence. It usually meant someone was going to catch it or there was a rant coming about something that didn't please him. Uneasiness turned to mild surprise when Whitney said, "At ease men. I thought I would come down and share your fire with you."

Whitney expected a cordial reception and he anticipated someone else starting the conversation, but when no one was forthcoming, he began by addressing Mathew Briscoe. "Private Briscoe, what is your background?"

The *'friendly'* Whitney surprised Mathew. He became tongue tied and began to stutter. Whitney rescued him. "I apologize, Private. I seem to have put you on the spot. I simply wanted to get to know the men in the troop a little better. It's the sign of a good commanding officer when he takes the time to get to know his men."

Mathew wanted to inform Whitney, in no uncertain terms, he was not one of his soldiers in whatever army was in his head, but something inside told him to bite the bullet and play along. "Well Sir, me and Luke was born in Tennessee and we moved to Oregon when we was youngin's. We worked on my pappy's farm 'till he kicked us off and then we been doin' odd jobs here and there to earn a livin' ever since.

"How did you end up in jail?" Whitney asked.

"That there's a funny story. Just another calamity by Brother Luke. We took up bounty huntin' for awhile. Thought we was gonna make a fortune. Cornered this here fella what was wanted for a killin' in Victoria. Luke thought he was goin' for a pistol and he shot him. We took him in for the reward and they arrested us. Appears Luke killed a storekeeper, who coulda passed for the wanted man." He paused and then added under his breath, "That goddamn Luke is always gettin' us in trouble."

Whitney was beginning to regret he had asked and didn't press for more information. Mathew interpreted the silence as Whitney becoming upset at the mention of Luke. He said, "You don't need to worry, Mr. Whitney. Luke won't be causin' anymore trouble, I swear."

"That's good to know soldier," replied Whitney, "but it's *Captain* Whitney."

"Sorry Captain, just forgot," was what Mathew said, but what he was thinking was, *here we go with this army horseshit, again.*

Whitney turned his attention to Frank Oakley "And you Corporal Oakley, what is your story?"

Oakley was torn between bragging himself up or staying humble so as not to annoy Whitney. He chose the latter. "Been a cowpuncher most of my life. Left home in Texas when I was sixteen and worked my up north through Kansas, Arizona, and into Montana. Heard about folks finding gold all over the Caribou country. Came up to try my luck. That's about it. Not much to tell."

Whitney wasn't done with him. "It is my understanding, Corporal, that you were in the process of beating a man to death with your pistol when the Constables arrested you?"

"Son-of-a-bitch didn't have a gun. Where I come from, you keep your mouth shut unless you are prepared to back it up with a pistol. He insulted me. I told him to draw, but he wasn't armed, so I hit him a couple of times with my pistol butt," answered Oakley with a proud tone.

"Have you shot many men in a gunfight?" asked Whitney.

"A few," replied Oakley.

"I am sure they were all fair fights," concluded Whitney with a somewhat condescending tone.

Before Oakley could dig himself any deeper, Whitney rose and said, "Time to call it a night. I'll take the first watch, Corporal. You take the second and Private Briscoe will take the third. Since the demise of Sergeant Brimsby, Mr. Briscoe, you will have to fill in." He turned to Frank and said, "Corporal Oakley, don't pass on your weapon at the end of your watch. Private Briscoe will do fine with his big knife, I'm sure."

Frank responded with a "Yes Sir!" and a salute.

As Whitney passed Michael's position, Michael looked up and asked sarcastically, "Want to hear my life story, Captain?"

Whitney answered without breaking stride, "Not particularly."

Chapter 21 – Talk of Destiny

Mathew Briscoe opened his eyes when he felt someone poking his shoulder. In the darkness, he squinted to see who it was. When Frank Oakley said, "Come on Hillbilly, it's your turn," Mathew remembered he was assigned sentry duty.

"Christ, what time is it?" Mathew asked.

"Don't know. Nobody owns a pocket watch in this outfit. I figure it's a couple of hours before daylight," said Oakley.

Mathew sat up and rubbed the sleep out of his eyes. He looked over at the spot where Luke had bedded down. It was too dark to see and he didn't hear anything. He was relieved Luke was quiet because it meant the big lug finally listened to him, had put the pain out of his mind, and was getting some much needed sleep. Mathew tried to make as little noise as possible as he made his way to the picket line.

He talked gently to the animals as he came near, so they would not become agitated. He checked each tie line carefully to make sure they were all still tight. When he got to the end of the line, he saw a large figure standing near a tall, half dead pine tree, about forty feet away. "Luke? Luke is that you? What are you doing up, little brother?" he asked.

"I heard you," Luke replied.

"Heard me what?" asked Mathew.

"You told me good riddance and you told the Captain fella I was the one always gettin' us in trouble. You thinkin' it's my fault we got sent to jail?"

"Luke, I'm sorry. I was just mad, is all. I'm over it now," replied Mathew, then he wondered how Luke knew about his part of the conversation around the campfire. *'Must have been listenin', I guess,'* he told himself.

To change the subject, Mathew said, "Shoulder seems not to be botherin' you, anymore. See, I told you it was all in your head."

Luke said, "Nope! No more pain, Mathew. All gone." And then he disappeared. Mathew didn't see him leave, but it was pretty dark. Still, he expected to see some movement.

Mathew put it out of his mind and found a comfortable spot under a wide tree to sit and wait for the dawn. He didn't have to wait long. It seemed like he barely sat down when the eastern horizon began to lighten up. There wasn't a cloud in the sky and as the sun slowly crept up over the eastern edge of the world, everything was bathed in the soft golden texture of morning light that made a person feel good and excited about the new day.

Mathew got up, stretched, yawned, and began to survey the world around him. He saw the horses, snorting and shaking their heads. Their leads were long enough, so they could feed on the grass near them, but they had eaten all they could reach and were wanting more. He looked at the surrounding hills as the golden rays of the morning sun ate up the darker night colors. He glanced into the tree tops and then his eyes focused on the tree under which he had seen Luke a short time ago.

At first he didn't see Luke swaying rhythmically back and forth about fifteen feet up the tree. It was the sound of the creaking from the strain of Luke's weight on the short piece of rope connecting his neck to a thick branch of the knotty old pine that attracted his attention. Then it hit him. The dumb ox had hung himself!

"Oh God, Luke, what have you done," he shouted as he ran to the tree. The old tree's branches were pretty thick and widely spaced, which made the climb to Luke's position relatively easy. Mathew used his knife to cut the rope and Luke dropped to the ground like a sack of rocks. By the time Mathew climbed down out of the tree, Michael had arrived on the scene.

"What happened?" asked Michael.

"He hung himself! The stupid bastard hung himself!" shouted Mathew.

When Whitney, Oakley, and Dancing Crow arrived, Michael turned to them and informed them of what happened.

Whitney walked to Luke, who sat on the ground next to his brother, trying to cut the rope from his neck, tears streaming down his cheeks. "Are you sure he hung himself?" Whitney asked.

Mathew didn't understand the meaning of the question. To him it was obvious what Luke had done. "What do you mean?" he asked Whitney.

Whitney realized he shouldn't have said anything, but the door was opened, so he continued, "I didn't mean anything by it. Things are not what they seem lately and I was trying to ascertain whether your brother met his demise by his own hand, or if he had some unseen help."

Mathew was despondent at the thought of his brother killing himself. Actually, he was feeling sorry for himself because he thought he was the cause of Luke's apparent suicide. Whitney's suggestion that some unseen force, either hung Luke or made him do it, took him off the hook and he felt relieved.

"Corporal Oakley and Private George, you men find some rocks or sticks or whatever you can and bury this soldier. Let's get a move on. We are wasting daylight," commanded Whitney. To Mathew he said, "Your brother was a good soldier."

Mathew wanted to say something derogatory, but he thought better of it, not because he was afraid of Whitney, but he came to the conclusion Whitney was going a little loco with all this military talk. So he just said, "Thank you, Sir," and left it there.

No one was interested in breakfast, whether it was the unexpected demise of Luke Briscoe, or they were just plain tired of greasy bear meat. As the men gathered, Whitney gave some last minute instructions. He assigned Michael the task of leading the four spare horses and he put Mathew Briscoe on point, partly to keep his mind off the death of his brother and partly because he wanted him up front where he could keep an eye on him.

They were about to head out when Frank Oakley asked Whitney politely, "Sir, can you tell us how much further it is?"

"By my calculations, Corporal Oakley, you will be a rich man the day after tomorrow," Whitney said with a smile.

"That's good news, Sir," replied Oakley. "I'll take the horses. I don't trust the goddamn half breed."

"Corporal Oakley! You are now Private Oakley! If you try to countermand my orders again, I will have you put in the stockade. Is that clear, Private?" shouted Whitney in fit of rage.

Two thoughts were trying to go through Oakley's mind at the same time. He was quite confused about the stockade business, but it was quickly swept out of the way by the surging anger towards Whitney. How many times did he have to go through this scenario, where he was doing his best to be helpful and all Whitney did was shoot him down? "This is the last time," he said quietly to himself.

-2-

The day's ride took the troop along a relatively flat trail that meandered around and above marshy areas and between stretches of towering fir trees and patches of pine divided by areas of grassy meadow. Whitney called several halts in some of the meadows to let the horses browse, as they didn't have much to eat the last few days.

As the horses grazed, the men were alone with their thoughts. There was no conversation, not even so much as a nod of acknowledgement as the men passed by each other. Each one of them felt there was something odd, something unnatural in the air, but no one wanted to be the first to bring it up for fear of ridicule, with the exception of Michael, who kept after Dancing Crow for more information. It was as if he'd become an audience member watching some bizarre play unfold in front of him. He watched as the characters changed and each one seemed to be sliding into their own private insanity. Not understanding what he was seeing, he looked to Dancing Crow for answers, but the old man either didn't know anymore than he did or was not willing to share his knowledge or opinions on the subject.

"Did the big one hang himself, or did he have help?" Michael asked. Dancing Crow shrugged his shoulders and looked away. Michael kept pestering him with, "Why don't we leave, Grandfather? What is keeping us here?"

The old man would always give vague answers. He indicated he had a purpose in sticking around. The fox spirit needed him for something.

Michael tried a new tactic, "You stay then, Grandfather, but I am leaving."

The old man became very serious and he spoke very solemnly when he said, "You are free to choose your own destiny, but your path lies at the end of this journey."

"So, you're saying I should continue on and get my share of the gold?" Michael thought for a moment and then continued, "Yeah, I'm going to start my own freight line. I'll be rich and well respected. I'll wear fancy clothes like all the white men and I'll go back to my father's village with gifts for everyone and show them how successful I've become."

"I am not saying that, at all!" replied Dancing Crow.

Irritated with the old man, Michael said, "Think of all the things you could buy to make life easier for The People in your village."

"Wealth is not your destiny and it certainly is not mine," rebuked Dancing Crow.

"Michael ended the conversation with, "Ah, you don't know what the hell you're talking about."

Frank Oakley would not take his eyes off Whitney. Wherever Whitney went, as he made his rounds, Oakley's gaze followed him. Whitney could feel the hairs on the back of his neck stand up and he sensed someone was watching him. When you are staring at someone and they feel you looking at them, they usually turn and make eye contact. Most people, when found out, will lower their head or look away at someone or something else. Frank didn't do that. When Whitney made eye contact, he continued to stare at him with the most hateful look on his face.

Whitney didn't have the energy to waste on vile looks from Oakley. There were other things to deal with, much more pressing things. His invisible army was showing up more frequently, demanding their share of the gold and the group seemed to be growing larger with every appearance.

On one of the brief stops in one of the grassy meadows, Whitney dropped the reins and walked a few steps to his right to sit on an old log. As he lowered himself down, he turned back to look at his horse. Silas Davidson, naked as the day he was born, with cuts and contusions all over his body and caved in rib cage, sat upon Whitney's mount. "Nice horse, Captain," Silas said. "Can I take him for a ride?"

When Silas kicked the horse in the ribs, it raised its head while still chewing a mouth full of grass and looked around. It couldn't feel anyone on its back or the kick in the side and yet there was something there the horse could sense. It began to fret and become nervous, ready to bolt. Whitney got to the reins in time to prevent it from running away. Silas was still in the saddle and Whitney said loud enough for everyone to hear, "Get off my horse, you despicable abomination."

Silas didn't move. As Silas didn't have his foot in the stirrup, Whitney put his boot in it and began to pull himself into the saddle. With his left hand on the reins, he led with his right forearm with full intentions of knocking Silas off his horse. He wasn't sure what would happen. His own concept of reality told him Silas should go flying off the other side, but his elbow hit only air and Silas simply disappeared.

As he swung fully into the saddle, his eyes fell on the rest of his ethereal entourage, who were all chanting in unison, "We want our gold! We want our gold!"

Whitney said, "Go to hell, where you belong." Most men would have run screaming into the woods by now, but not Clarence Whitney. He was in control enough to use his superior power of analysis and assessment. He believed he was seeing something, but he gave them neither value nor respect. He knew some outside force may be causing these hallucinations, but again it did not frighten him. It merely annoyed him because the goddamn things were detracting him from achieving his objective.

Michael was observing Whitney throughout his confrontation with his demons. He walked within earshot and asked, "Everything alright?" There was the start of a smile on the corners of his mouth as he waited for an answer. He didn't know what Whitney saw, but he knew Whitney had seen something and he wanted to twist the knife a little.

"Goddamn horseflies, they are everywhere. Drive a man crazy if you let them," replied Whitney without the slightest indication he was lying.

Michael smiled and said, "Yes, they can."

Whitney stared at Michael a moment before he turned his horse and trotted away. He noticed the attitude change in Michael. He was coming across as smug and disrespectful. Whitney stored the information away for future use. When the time was right, he would wipe the damn grin off his ugly face.

As Whitney rode away, Dancing Crow said to Michael, "It is best not to aggravate the evil one. He is a dangerous man."

"Ah, the old one speaks," Michael said, his words dripping with sarcasm.

"I don't believe your destiny is to let your anger get you killed before you can fulfill it," said Dancing Crow, ignoring Michael's cynicism.

"Destiny, destiny, destiny. What destiny? I really hate it when you do this!" said Michael with an undertone of annoyance in his voice.

"I do not understand. What is it I do to make you so angry?" asked a surprised Dancing Crow.

Michael thought for a moment before he spoke. He put his hands on Dancing Crow's shoulders and looked into his wrinkled and weathered face and said, "Grandfather, I like you very much, but you keep saying my destiny. What destiny? What in hell are you talking about? Give me more."

Dancing Crow spoke as if he were disappointed, "My son, I had hoped that you would find that path for yourself. Are you still having the vision where you are guarding the meadow and the deer and the coyote want in, but you can only let one enter?"

"Yes, every night," replied Michael.

"The dream shows that you will have to choose between two things and your choice will determine your fate. It is your destiny to make the choice," said Dancing Crow and then concluded with, "Now, help an old man onto his horse."

Frank Oakley's eyes were fixated on Clarence Whitney, while the motion picture projector in his mind kept showing the same movie over and over again. However, each time it ran, Frank's imagination added a few embellishments. It started with Whitney standing in the middle of a street calling Frank out, who would emerge from a saloon where he'd had a drink and a kiss from a cute dancehall girl. He would pause on the wooden sidewalk, roll and light a cigarette, and step out into the street. He would take slow deliberate steps toward Whitney and as he got closer he could see the sweat running down Whitney's forehead and into his eyes. Whitney would remove his hat and wipe his brow with the back of his trembling hand. As he was putting his hat back on his head, he went for his gun and on every occasion Oakley saw it coming and outdrew him, shooting him in the right knee. Oakley would casually saunter over to Whitney and raise his pistol and while tears rolled down Whitney's cheek and he begged for his life, Oakley would draw back the hammer on his pistol and shoot him in the heart, chuckling all the while.

Lately, he was adding a few things to the daydream. In one version, Whitney was standing in a huge pile of gold pokes. After he shot Whitney through the heart, he would empty the sacks of gold onto the dead man until he was covered in gold dust and nuggets. In another version, Mathew Briscoe stood with Whitney and he shot them both. In a third version, after he finished with Whitney and Briscoe, he heard a noise behind him and there were the breed and the old Indian charging at him on horseback. Frank got off two miraculous shots, catching each one between the eyes and knocking them off the back of their horses, end over end in spectacular fashion.

To Mathew Briscoe, it was as if his brother Luke had never left, the only difference being, instead of having to listen to Luke's constant complaining about his painful shoulder wound and the coyotes eating at it, now Mathew was forced to listen to Luke go on and on incessantly about his suicide. Mathew was constantly reminded that he had driven Luke to kill himself, that it was all his fault. He kept on about how Mathew broke his promise to their mother about always looking after him.

Whereas, at one time Mathew would get frustrated with Luke and try desperately to convince him the pain and the coyotes were all in his head, now he was fighting a losing battle trying to convince Luke he was not real and he should move on to heaven or hell or wherever he should be going and stop bothering him. The trouble was Mathew was constantly gesturing and shouting at the unseen Luke in front of the other men, as if they could see Luke as well.

-3-

Dusk found them entering another meadow with a foot wide creek, spawned by a spring higher in the hill, running through it. Whitney ordered a halt for the night and assigned the duties. Michael and Mathew were to water and picket the horses. Whitney told Dancing Crow, through Michael's translation, to get a fire going and cook up some of the god-awful bear meat, if there was any left. Dancing Crow uttered some remark about not being a squaw and Michael told him jokingly he sure whined like one.

Michael tied one end of the picket line to a sturdy pine and the other end securely around and under a large boulder. After the horses had their fill of water, he and Mathew tied them all on alternate sides of the picket line, with enough lead rope so they could feed on the grass around them. In a few hours, they would come and move the one end of the picket line so the horses were standing over new grass to eat.

While they were tending to the horses, Mathew kept up a running conversation with the dear departed Luke. At times it was very animated, with Mathew waving his arms and shaking an admonishing finger at someone unseen to Michael.

Michael got closer to Mathew and asked, "Who are you talking to?"

Mathew pointed with a hand gesture to where he perceived Luke to be standing and said, "It's Luke! He's right —" Having Luke's image around aided Mathew in his denial about Luke's suicide, but Michael shattered his world with his question. Mathew realized the situation he put himself in and he tried to talk his way out of it. "— right here in my head with me. I ain't crazy. I like to talk out loud is all, even though I'm just talkin' in my head. You know what I mean?"

Michael smiled sardonically and said, "Sure," and then finished up with the horses.

Like the past several meals, the men ate only because they needed to, not because they wanted to. There was no gathering about the campfire on this night. Michael and Dancing Crow were the only ones who took up permanent residence by the fire. Whitney, Oakley, and Briscoe would wander by, cut a small piece of meat from the chunk Michael was roasting over the fire and wander off again into the darkness.

Later on in the night, they would come by one at a time, like a moth drawn to the lantern, on the pretence of warming their hands, but it seemed to Michael they were checking to make sure the fire was still there, as if it were a haven, a beacon in the darkness.

Michael observed them closely as they came and went and commented to Dancing Crow on the men's odd behaviour. It seemed as if Dancing Crow wasn't listening. Michael said, "I think the one called Mathew sees his dead brother. He talks to him all the time. What do make of that, Grandfather?" Dancing Crow still did not answer.

Michael said, "The one called Whitney thinks he is a Captain and we're all his soldiers and the one called Oakley stares at Whitney with the eyes of a hungry cougar."

Dancing Crow showed no signs of having heard Michael.

Frustrated, Michael said, "Ah, you're as crazy as the rest of them."

This got dancing Crow's attention and he replied, "The end of the journey is very near and I see great danger."

Chapter 22 – Swamp

Michael had slept very soundly the night before. In fact, Dancing Crow had to shake him vigorously several times before he woke up. He rose, stretched, and half stumbled to the tiny spring-fed stream, plunged his head into an icy pool, and drank. He washed his face and wet down his hair with several handfuls of the cold water.

The night fire was out and the bear meat that still hung over the ashes had lost its heat. Michael didn't care. He used the sharp, flat piece of slate they were using as a slicer and hacked off a thick piece.

Whitney came up as he was eating and said, "Soldier, when you are through filling your belly, you and Private Briscoe get them horses saddled and be quick about it."

Michael gave him a sarcastic, "Yes Sir!" and went off to find Mathew. He thought of saluting as he left, but his intuition told him not to push it too far.

Mathew was already working with the horses when he saw Michael approaching. Michael heard him say, "Quiet, here comes somebody. You go away now."

"Horses giving you a rough time?" Michael asked, knowing full well Mathew was talking to his dead brother again.

"Uh, yeah — yeah they are," replied Mathew. Seeing Michael gnawing on the cold greasy bear meat, he asked, "Jesus, how can you eat that shit?"

Michael answered him honestly, "I try not to think about it."

With five of the horses saddled and the other four on a string, Michael and Mathew led them out to the staging area. As they were walking, Mathew remarked that if this thing went on any longer, he was through eating bear and a good change in the menu might be horse meat.

Unfortunately for him, Whitney was within earshot. He stomped over and stuck his face into Mathew's, so their noses were only inches apart. Mathew could feel Whitney's hot breath as he spoke, "Private Briscoe, we will be dining on steaks cut from your sorry carcass long before we eat one of these horses. Are we clear on that?"

Mathew, who'd only said it as a casual comment, was surprised by Whitney's reaction. When Whitney was out of earshot Michael said, "You would probably taste better than horse meat, anyway," and then he laughed.

Mathew retorted, "Ah, just shut up, funny man."

Michael was still smiling because Mathew spoke without anger, as if he didn't take Michael's remark personally, but when Mathew turned and looked up at one of the unsaddled horses and said, "And you can stop laughin', too," Michael changed his expression. He wanted to make another joke about how he didn't think the horse was laughing, but he knew Mathew wasn't talking to the horse.

-2-

A two hour ride brought them down from the slope and out into a wide marshy flat, about a half mile across. His instincts told Whitney to go around, but he didn't listen and drove straight ahead. At first it was easy going, the water was just over the horse's ankles. A hundred feet further, the bottom was much softer and the water a lot deeper, well over the horse's knees.

Whitney spurred his mount, but it didn't have the strength to pull its legs out of the sucking mud. He decided to back out and go around the slough, but his horse couldn't make that manoeuvre either. He dismounted and tried to pull the horse around, a critical error in judgement, because the minute he stepped off, he was up to his hips in mud, planted firmly, unable to move. He began to wiggle his body sideways and then back and forth, frantically hoping to loosen the mud's grip, but it seemed the more he struggled, the harder it was to move.

"Some help would be appreciated," he called out.

Nobody was quite sure what to do until Frank Oakley spoke up. He still had the non-blinking gaze as he looked at Whitney and said, "I dragged many a steer out of bog holes like this. We need to get a rope around the Captain's waist and pull him out and then we'll worry about the horse."

Michael came forward with the rope used for the picket line and handed it to Oakley, who began giving directions to Whitney. He suggested they should first get Whitney's gear to shore. He told Whitney to remove the saddle and bedroll from the horse and secure the rope around them, as well as the shotgun he was holding.

"Never mind the goddamn gear. Get me and my horse out of here!" barked Whitney.

"Think about it, Captain," replied Oakley, "if we pull you out first and we can't get back to the horse, you'll lose the saddle and your bedroll."

Whitney took a few seconds to mull over Oakley's suggestion. Oakley caught the pause and said, "Don't worry, Captain. We won't leave you to rot in this swamp. We still need you to show us where to find the gold."

Whitney seemed embarrassed that Oakley had read his very thoughts. When Whitney dismounted, he simultaneously turned back to face the way he had come, which made it much easier to undo the cinch and get his gear off the horse. Oakley tossed the rope right to him on the first try. Whitney tied the saddle, bedroll and shotgun together and Oakley hauled it out. He told Michael to carry the whole bundle out of the marsh and set it on dry ground.

Oakley tossed the rope back to Whitney and said "Tie this on and hang on tight, Captain. You best take a deep breath and close your mouth unless you want to drink a gallon of this here swamp water."

Whitney secured the rope around his waist and took a deep breath. Oakley tied the other end of the rope tight around his saddle horn and gave his horse a good hard heel in the ribs. It took off like it had been slapped, ploughing its way through the water and muck. The sudden yank pulled Whitney out of his trap and onto his belly, face first into the brackish water.

Oakley could have stopped a lot sooner than he did. Michael and Mathew both thought Whitney got a little extra ride. Whitney crawled out onto dry land, shakily got to his feet, bent over with his hands on his knees, and went into a coughing spell, trying to clear the brackish liquid out of his throat.

Oakley didn't wait for Whitney to recover. He reeled in the loose rope and went back out after the horse, suggesting Michael should come along and assist him. Oakley deftly threw the loop around the horse's neck on the first try. He tossed Michael the rope and told him to wind it around his saddle horn several times, leaving enough rope so he could wrap it around his own saddle horn. Now they had two horses pulling on the one that was stuck. It couldn't help but come out.

As Oakley and Michael pulled, Whitney's horse began to turn. Its front legs were pulled free, but its hind legs remained staunchly entrenched and the horse fell over on its side. The sheer force of the other two horses dragged Whitney's mount sideways out of the deep muck and into the shallow water at the edge of marsh.

Oakley dismounted quickly and removed the rope from Whitney's horse. Holding its long neck in both hands and using all his strength, he tried to push the horse onto a standing position, but it wouldn't budge and whinnied in pain. Oakley let go of the horse's neck and walked around the animal inspecting it. He saw the problem right away. The horse's left hind leg was twisted like a broken branch. When they turned the horse around and it fell, its entire weight was on the immovable leg and it snapped like a dry twig.

Oakley untied the Spencer from the back of his saddle, aimed and fired at the horse with no effect. He'd forgotten to chamber a shell. He quickly levered a shell into the firing chamber and put the poor creature out of it's misery. Whitney, covered in mud and slime, was beside Oakley in a half dozen strides with a cocked, mud covered pistol in his hand. "Corporal Oakley, you better be able to explain why you shot my horse!" he shouted.

"If you'll take a look, Sir, the horse's back leg is busted in half," explained Oakley.

Whitney moved to where he could see the broken hind leg. "You should have been more careful pulling him out, Corporal! I could have you court marshalled for this."

Oakley was through playing the soldier game and retorted, "We did the best we could, Sir. I don't know as you could've done much better. Hell, it was a dumb idea to try and cross the swamp in the first place, so don't go blaming me for your stupidity."

Whitney raised the pistol and fired, there was a muted thud as the hammer came down on a mud packed cartridge cylinder. Whitney cocked the pistol, aimed and fired again, with the same result. He put the pistol back in his waistband and went for his shotgun, which was still with his saddle and bedroll.

"Captain Whitney! The only thing keeping you alive right now is we don't know where the gold is, but it don't mean I can't put a nice big hole in your leg to slow you down," Oakley said as he raised the rifle and took direct aim at Whitney.

Michael stepped between the two men and acted as a mediator, "The horse was done for. He needed to be put down. Now, let's saddle another one and be on our way." It was a good thing for Oakley because, again, he forgot to put another shell into the chamber of the Spencer and Whitney would have surely killed him with the shotgun.

Whitney sighed, bowed his head, and then lifted it again as he spoke, "I guess when we get to the gold, we should all keep an eye on our backs."

Oakley wasn't put off by the veiled threat. He said as a reminder, "That includes you, Captain."

Michael and Mathew put Whitney's gear on another horse and brought it over to him. Mathew handed Whitney the reins and then pulled out his knife. Whitney's eyes went wide and he instinctively reached for his pistol.

"Easy there, Captain. I was just going to ask you if it would be alright if we ate horse for a few days instead of bear?" said Mathew.

Whitney hated to see a good mount desecrated, but he was getting tired of bear meat himself. "That will be fine, Private Briscoe," he replied.

The rest of them waited while Briscoe expertly cut out one of the horse's hind quarters, leaving the hide on to protect the meat.

He dumped the bear meat out of the buckskin it was wrapped in and replaced it with the fresh horse meat, rewrapped it and tied it securely to the pack horse. "We eat good tonight, boys!" he said as he mounted and motioned to the rest that he was ready to go.

Clarence Whitney felt very uncomfortable for two reasons; one, he was covered in stinking mud and grime and two, he knew he no longer maintained any control over the remaining troop. He would have to wait for the opportune moment to disarm Frank Oakley and take the knife away from Briscoe. The only ones he would really need after he found the old prospector's treasure were the breed and the old heathen, to help him get past any hostiles he might encounter on his way back down to the lower mainland.

He'd already formulated a plan in his mind. Once the gold was loaded on the horses, he would double back to the hardly used Old Wagon Road and take it down to the coast. By the time he arrived in New Westminster, he would just be another gold miner who'd struck it rich. The authorities may still be on the lookout for a large group of men travelling together, or they may have given up the hunt, thinking the prisoners had made their way out of the territory. There might even be some questions about some of the horses having Provincial Police brands on them, but the Service bought and sold horses all the time, so it wouldn't be a far stretch to say he bought them and misplaced the bill of sale. Besides, people don't pay much attention to the horse you're riding when you are tipping them with gold nuggets.

About an hour in the saddle brought them to another small spring-fed stream running down the hillside. Whitney called a halt, telling the troop to water the horses and that he needed time to clean himself up. He stripped down to his filthy long johns and washed the half dried mud from his pants, shirt and jacket. He took off the long underwear and washed them out after he put his trousers back on. He hung everything, except the pants he was wearing, over several low bushes to dry. He quickly brushed the dried mud from the shotgun and removed the two shells, replacing them with two clean ones. He laid the shotgun down close to himself with both the hammers drawn back and then he began to meticulously clean the mud and slime from the pistol and shells.

He never looked at what he was doing for any length of time. His gaze was always wandering from man to man as he cleaned the pistol. He was grinning slightly as if he was saying to them, "Come on, try me. I'm ready for you."

Whitney put his still damp, but clean clothes back on and ordered the men back in the saddle. Around noon the trail began a slow ascent and then an hour or so later the grade got considerably steeper. Even though they were high up and still climbing, the trail was wet and soggy because of the dozens of springs emerging from the hillside. Whitney thought a man might get hungry in this country, but he sure as hell wouldn't have a problem with thirst.

By mid afternoon, the trail levelled off and then began a steep descent into a valley below. Early evening found the troop on an embankment that overlooked a level gravel plain with a small stream winding its way through the middle. Whitney told the men this was a good place to camp for the night. He rode back and forth along the top of the embankment until he found a trail that the deer and other animals used to get down to the water. Once down on the flat, he ordered Mathew and Michael to get the horses watered and secured for the night. Then he and Oakley gathered wood while Dancing Crow got a fire started.

Horse meat wasn't a great improvement over bear meat, but at least it was a change. With their bellies full, they gathered around the warmth of the fire. There was a chill in the air and it felt like it was going to be a cold night. No one talked. They had all eaten in silence and now they were sitting or lying in various postures just staring into the flames.

Dancing Crow sat cross-legged with his palms open and facing upward, one on each knee. His medicine bag sat in his lap. His eyes were closed, his head tilted backwards, and his face pointed skyward. He began a low rhythmic chant that increased in pitch and volume as he sang.

At first the rest of the men looked at him out of curiosity, but it wasn't long before Oakley was becoming agitated. "Hey Breed, what's he doing? Get him to shut the noise off, will ya?" he said to Michael.

"He's talking to the Great Spirit. He knows something is coming soon, maybe even tomorrow and he is singing a song of praise," answered Michael.

Whitney seemed genuinely interested when he asked, "To what purpose?"

Michael didn't understand the question. Whitney, sensing it, expanded, "Why does he praise his God, when he thinks he might be in peril?"

"It's hard to put into terms a white man could understand, but he is asking for strength and wisdom and a brave heart to do the right thing when the time comes, so if he should die, the Great Spirit will give him a place of honour in the other world," explained Michael.

Whitney paused to digest what Michael had said and then rising, he asked, "The right thing?" He was flushed and angry as he continued, "What are you two heathens up to? I want to know what you two are planning and I want to know now!"

Michael stood as well, which was not the right thing to do. As soon as he was erect, Whitney swung the shotgun in an arc, the butt end catching Michael squarely on the chin, knocking him out cold. Dancing Crow hadn't changed positions and was still chanting when Whitney planted the sole of his boot in the middle of Dancing Crow's chest, knocking him onto his back.

"What are you up to, you old heathen?" he almost screamed. Of course, Dancing Crow didn't have the faintest idea of what he was saying. Whitney realized he wasn't going to get anywhere questioning the old man since he had put Michael under.

He looked at Oakley and shouted, "Throw some water on him. Do anything, but wake him up," indicating the prone Michael.

Oakley retrieved some water and it took several handfuls thrown into Michael's face, before he showed any signs of recovery. Whitney did not hit him hard enough to break his jaw or cause any other serious damage. It took several minutes and a few more handfuls of cold water to bring him to a state of consciousness. When Whitney felt Michael was coherent, he told him to stand. Michael rose on wobbly legs and faced Whitney with a hateful stare. He glanced at Dancing Crow, who was lying on his back, and asked, "Are you alright?"

"Do not worry about me. It is Whitney we need to be careful with. It does not look like he needs us as much as he did earlier," replied Dancing Crow, as he sat up.

"What did he say?" snapped Whitney. "I heard my name! What did he say?"

"He said, you are angry with him, but he doesn't understand why?" answered Michael.

"Oh horseshit," scoffed Whitney, "he is hiding something. He thinks something is going to happen soon, even tomorrow. Didn't you say it yourself, a few minutes ago? I want to know what this something is so I can deal with it."

Michael paused to look at Dancing Crow before speaking. He knew Whitney could not understand the words, but he was very perceptive when it came to body language and he needed to have a conversation with the old man without him giving anything away either through his body movements or facial expressions.

Michael chose his words carefully. "Grandfather, the evil one is very clever. He does not understand our language, but he can tell of how we speak. You must be careful. Nod, if you understand." Dancing Crow nodded and Michael continued, "We have to tell him something that will satisfy him. He knows that you know more about what has been happening to the men, than you are saying and he is convinced you know something is going to happen. He wants to know how you know and what it is you think might occur. He needs to feel he is still in control."

"What do you think we should do, then?" asked Dancing Crow.

"You keep talking about anything you like and leave the rest to me."

"What shall I talk about?"

"I don't know. Think of something. How many grandchildren you have or how many beautiful young women you've bedded. Just talk."

"Your mention of bedding young women reminds me of a story. There were two bull elk; one was an older, wiser elk and one was a rash young buck. They met on the top of a grassy hillside. Down below a dozen females were grazing. The young one said to the older one, '*Let us run down and get one of those beauties.*' The old one stopped him and said, '*Let us walk down and enjoy them all.*' Do you want to hear another story?" Dancing Crow smirked as he could see Michael was having a hard time keeping himself from laughing.

Whitney was growing impatient. He put his arm on Michael's shoulder and spun him around. "Let's have it!" was all he said.

"Look, he said a lot. Give me a minute to sort it all out." Michael paused and then continued, "You have to know how a Medicine Man works in order to understand how he thinks."

"Try me. I'm sure I'll understand just fine," said Whitney with a scornful tone.

"The old man does not *see* things, he *feels* them. That's why he can't put his finger on anything specific." Michael could see either Whitney wasn't understanding or he wasn't buying it, so he tried another approach. "I'm sure in all the things you've done and places you've been, you've had a feeling something was about to happen. You didn't know what, exactly, but the knot in your gut told you something was."

Michael paused long enough for Whitney to think about it. Whitney shook his head in agreement and said, "Yes, there have been a few times."

"Well, this is how he works. He gets those feelings and he acts on them." Michael stopped speaking to indicate that was all there was.

Whitney stood waiting, expecting more. When Michael didn't say anything, Whitney said, "That's it? — I don't believe you. What else?"

Michael took a deep breath and sighed, "Are you sure you won't hurt the old man if I tell you what he said?"

"I give you my word that I will not shoot the messenger," replied Whitney.

Michael looked at Oakley and Briscoe to make sure they were listening and then he spoke, "He says he had a vision in which we all die tomorrow."

Oakley and Briscoe both gasped at the same time and the same stunned looked appeared simultaneously on both their faces. "How does he know?" asked a defiant Frank Oakley.

"This is what he does when he chants. He asks for visions on the feelings he is having," Michael explained.

Whitney interjected, "You lying bastard. I watched you two talking and the old heathen had a smirk on his face like this was some kind of joke." Whitney levelled his shotgun at Dancing Crow and continued, "You tell me the truth or so help me God, I'll blow the old heathen's head off, right now!"

Without hesitation Michael said, "I have told you the truth. The old man smiled because he is at peace. He knows he is going to die tomorrow, but it doesn't frighten him. Because he knows he is going to die, he can prepare. He smiled when he told me he knows you won't believe him and won't make peace with your own death."

Whitney stared hard at Michael and then said, "What about you, Breed? You don't seem to be shaking in your boots?"

Again, Michael answered without hesitation, "Must be the white blood in me. I'm like you. I don't believe him either."

Michael could see Whitney wasn't entirely satisfied, but he wasn't going to say anything more. Whitney said, "You are nothing like me, Breed, and I don't think the old man is far from wrong. Some of us may die soon," and he walked away.

Dancing Crow asked, "What did you tell him?"

"I told him we were all going to die tomorrow."

"Why did you do that?"

Michael smiled when he answered, "To give them something to think about"

Chapter 23 – Gold

Daybreak found Whitney still thinking about the old Medicine Man's prediction of eminent death for them all. He kept telling himself there was no truth to it, yet, the damn breed was right. There were times when he had an uneasy feeling, a premonition that something was about to happen and it did. He felt that tightness in his gut, now.

Mathew Briscoe didn't give the ominous prophecy a second thought. He was too busy trying to deal with his annoying brother. Frank Oakley kept wondering how the old man knew he was going to kill Whitney and anyone else who got in his way.

"Be very careful today, my son," Dancing Crow told Michael over a piece of seared horse meat. "I feel this is not a good day."

Michael put his arm around the old man and said, "Do not worry, Grandfather. I have a feeling this is going to be a very good day."

Whitney gave them a half hour to get ready to ride, which included breakfast. He did not know exactly how much further they had to go, but he knew they were close and he was anxious to get started.

They broke camp, saddled up, and crossed the creek and up the far bank, where they saw the gravel flat continue on up the valley. There was no vegetation other than the occasional scrawny pine or spruce that somehow managed to gain a foothold and survive. Half an hour later, they came to a thick grove of tall willows about a hundred yards wide, fed by seeping spring water. They followed a narrow animal path through the dense willows and emerged to a spectacular view. It seemed as if the thicket was a gateway to another world. The valley widened out, as the mountains themselves had been set back a half a mile or so, on both sides.

This was the first time in nearly three weeks that the rest of the men saw Whitney display any joy. He was like a young boy on a Christmas morning after getting the gift he wanted. "We've found it! By God, we've found it!" he shouted in his exhilaration.

Oakley and Briscoe flanked him on either side and Oakley asked, "Are we here, Captain?"

"Almost, Corporal Oakley. Almost. How does it feel to be a very rich man?"

For a moment, Oakley's murderous visions and his hatred for Whitney were forgotten as his thoughts changed to images of what he would do with his new found wealth. He was excited, as well and wore a big grin that stretched from ear to ear. He'd forgotten himself for a moment, but as soon as he realized it, he regained his nasty demeanour.

Whitney was too wrapped up in his own excitement to notice. He pointed to his left, in the direction of some sandstone hoodoos a short distance ahead. The wind and rain had sculptured and shaped the sandstone into a dozen separate columns. They looked like the spires one might see on a magnificent cathedral in St. Petersburg or Rome. One, in particular, stood out from the rest. A huge boulder, once embedded in the sandstone, now lay atop one of the hoodoos. From a distance it looked like a giant turtle, as Diamond Jack had described. It was only when you were right up close that the image disappeared and it looked like any other ordinary rock.

Whitney spurred his mount into action. The trail was wide and flat, which made it easy and safe to travel at a good gallop. He reached the hoodoos in a matter of minutes with Briscoe and Oakley close behind. Leading the spare horses, Michael was taking his sweet time catching up, much to the dismay of Whitney, Oakley, and Briscoe, who all stood waiting impatiently.

Whitney pointed to a small creek flowing out from between two hoodoos about fifty yards ahead of their position. He rode to the embankment overlooking the shallow brook. He motioned for the rest of them to follow as he spurred his horse into the water and rode upstream, following the creek bed until it disappeared into a steep moraine, made up of loose shale, coarse gravel, and fist-sized stones mixed with occasional boulders of different sizes. He veered to the right when he saw a distinct pathway that had been carved out by centuries of mountain sheep making their way up and over the rock pile. Whitney dismounted and gave orders that they were going to follow the sheep path and to take it slow and easy, leading their horses.

With Whitney in the lead, they walked single file, zigzagging around house-sized boulders, gradually making their way up and over the immense rockslide and down the other side. As they came down the backside of the rock pile, they could see the creek again at the bottom, but it quickly disappeared around a sharp corner about a hundred yards upstream. They remounted and followed the creek around the bend, where they were treated to another spectacular natural sight. A short distance away, there was a magnificent waterfall about forty feet high. The canyon closed in on them to the point that it was only about fifty feet across. As they approached the waterfall, they could see the canyon walls had been scooped out into the shape of a bowl by eons of flowing water.

"This must be it, eh Captain?" asked an excited Mathew Briscoe.

Oakley was somewhat more practical when he remarked, "It better be, Hillbilly. We can't go any further."

Whitney said, "The horses can't, but we still have some distance to go on foot. He made his way to the left side of the falls where on a scraggly spruce he found the Diamond 'J' blaze. From a distance, anyone looking at the falls would think there was no way to climb up and around them. Yet, close to the canyon wall, one could see the rock formation ran at about a sixty five degree angle and the mountain sheep had found a way up and around the falls.

Whitney started giving orders, "Private Briscoe, you stay with the horses and keep your mind on the job. I'll get back and let you know what we find. I will lead and Corporal Oakley you will bring up the rear with the breed and the old heathen between us. If the breed tries anything, shoot the old man."

Whitney started up. The sheep trail was easy to follow, a virtual highway through the moss and rock protrusions. The climb was very difficult, however. The ground was slippery from the spray of the waterfall and they couldn't make any headway climbing upright. The best method was to make sure you had a good hold of a sapling or a root and pull yourself up a few feet and then repeat the process.

Once he was on top of the outcrop overlooking the waterfall, Whitney realized he was standing on part of a sandstone and slate wall that ran perpendicular to the canyon. The water, over the centuries, had cut the wall down to the present height of the falls. He looked upstream and saw it was simply a continuation of the same canyon as below the falls, with vertical walls over a hundred feet high on either side and a creek at the bottom, winding its way down the mountain.

He couldn't see very far up the canyon because of his low elevation and the canyon didn't run straight, but zigzagged like the coils of a snake. From where he stood, Whitney could see that the steep, but climbable pathway continued its way up the slope to the top of the canyon wall. The climb was somewhat steeper than the piece up to the outcrop on which he stood, but considerably drier.

By the time the four men got to the top, they were spent and winded, breathing rapidly to get some air into their burning lungs. "Jesus, how much more of this is there?" complained Frank Oakley.

Whitney said between gasps for air, "It should be fairly level from here." He was bent over with his hands on his knees and he stood and started out again. Dancing Crow was having difficulty getting his wind and needed a few more minutes. Michael was standing over him, encouraging him to relax and breathe deeply. Whitney wasn't about to wait, so he ordered Oakley to get the old man to his feet and bring him along.

The sheep trail followed the edge of the canyon a few feet back from the rim. It was very narrow in places where it passed through groves of stunted spruce that grew very close together. It was like making your way through a hedge in places. Whitney would peer ahead whenever they came to a clear spot that allowed him to see upstream. Although he was convinced they were on the right track, he could feel a tiny bit of doubt creeping in. Old Diamond Jack had said, "When ya gets to the top, a short walk along the canyon edge and you'll see where I dug."

Whitney burst through another hedgy grove of scrawny spruce and all doubt flew from his mind. He made it! There it was, as Diamond Jack described. They emerged onto an enormous flat table of sandstone measuring thirty feet wide and perhaps two hundred feet long, void of any vegetation. Here, the canyon was very narrow, twenty five feet across, at best. The opposite canyon wall was another fifty or sixty feet higher than the side they were on.

In the middle of the opposite wall, running parallel with the top of the side the men occupied, was a horizontal ledge about three to four feet wide. There was a small cave like structure at the back of the ledge. A crude bridge spanned the narrow gap between the canyon walls. It looked like a ladder with the rungs spaced close together. Diamond Jack cut down and laboriously dragged two large pines up the gruelling climb. Whitney found a new respect for the old prospector. Diamond Jack used the two pines for the main frame and then used smaller trees for the rungs that he lashed to the long pieces with rawhide, rope, and odd pieces of leather that once were reins.

Diamond Jack was beaming with pride when he told Whitney this part of the story. He had found some colour where the creek came out of the rock pile and he decided to follow the creek upstream. He left his two mules where Whitney had left their horses and following the sheep path, made his way to the top of the canyon wall. His intent was to see if he could find another way down to the creek above the falls, perhaps from the other end of the canyon.

He emerged on the rock table and sat down to catch his breath. The afternoon sun bathed the opposite canyon wall and a glint caught his eye. He jumped up and ran to the edge of the canyon on his side and squinted at the other wall. Gold! It was gold! The exposed vein was almost a foot wide and at least ten feet long and God-only-knows how deep.

Diamond Jack spent nearly a week, hauling his tools and gear up to the table rock, setting up a camp and finding trees big enough to make his crude bridge. Once he built it, the hardest task was standing the whole thing up and dropping it just right so it landed on the ledge. He made it long enough, so there was plenty of overlap and he was smart enough to tie a safety rope to one end of the ladder and the other end around a big rock. It was good thinking on his part because on his first two tries, he miscalculated and his contraption went over the edge into the canyon. He painstakingly pulled his ladder back up, stood it on end, and tried again.

The third time he was lucky. The end of the make-shift bridge landed on the ledge with its ends squarely against the wall. Diamond Jack crawled on his hands and knees across his bridge. It was sturdy and would easily hold his weight. He spent the next two months digging out the vein.

"Clarence," he would say at night in their cell, "there is enough gold, so's a man would never want for anything. There's enough gold there so's a dozen men would never be able to spend it in a life time."

"Could I have your attention, gentlemen?" said Whitney. "Here's how this is going to work. Across the ladder bridge you can see a small cave. Our friend, Diamond Jack, dug out the hole in the wall and it contains the gold we have been seeking. It is all in gunny sacks and ready for the taking. Hell, he did all the work for us. We just have to haul it out of here and on down to the coast. Breed, you and Corporal Oakley will take turns hauling the sacks over to this side. Breed, you go first."

Michael gave him a hateful stare and made his way to the ladder bridge. He stepped out onto the first rung. The bridge began to sway ever so slightly. He brought his back foot onto the bridge and it began to sway a little bit more. When he took the next step, he began to lose his balance, so he dropped down on all fours and made his way across the ladder bridge in a bent over position, using his hands and feet, not unlike a chimpanzee.

When he reached the other side, he saw the wide ledge and he felt greatly relieved. He stepped off the bridge and onto the ledge just to the right of the hole in the wall. Stooped over, he went inside the cave and let his eyes adjust. At the back of the small cavern there were at least two dozen bundles. About ten were gunny sacks and the rest was a collection of some flour sacks, one coffee sack and some crude pouches made out of deer hide. Michael picked up one of the gunny sacks. It had to weigh thirty to forty pounds. He untied the top and poured out some of the contents out onto the floor. Fist size chunks of almost pure gold spilled out. He picked up a piece and brought it out into the sunlight.

"What's the hold up, Breed?" shouted Whitney.

Michael didn't answer him. He put the gold back in the sack and headed for the cave mouth. The way back would be more difficult with the bag of gold to carry. He stood upright and took careful agonizing step after step until he reached the other side. When he was a few feet from the edge, he swung the sack and threw it at Whitney's feet and then almost ran the last few steps to safety.

Whitney turned the bag upright, opened it and took out a large nugget.

He was overcome with sheer joy and he began to dance around in circles in a kind of a fast waltz, holding the nugget out in front of him like it might have been a beautiful lady at a fine southern ball in the Governor's mansion. He stopped his waltz after several turns around the dance floor and handed the stone to Oakley, who stared at it with the same lust in his eyes as Whitney's. "We're rich, Captain! We're rich!" Oakley shouted.

Whitney regained his composure and asked Michael, "How many sacks are there?"

"I'd say two dozen, maybe," replied Michael.

Whitney seemed almost disappointed, as if he expected a lot more. "Alright then, let's get them all over to this side," he ordered.

As Whitney turned and looked at the far wall, he saw a tall, well dressed man, including a top hat, standing on the ledge. It was Silas Davidson. He removed his top hat, bowed at the waist and said, "I have come to collect my gold, Mr. Whitney. If anybody has earned the right to it, I believe that it would be me."

Whitney's eyes went wide. He drew his pistol and fired off two shots in Silas's direction, without taking good aim. The bullets seemed to go through him and ricochet off the canyon wall.

Seeing the pistol was ineffective, Whitney reached towards Oakley and demanded the Spencer. This was the moment of truth for Frank Oakley. He would not get a better opportunity than this. He levelled the rifle at Whitney and said, "You want this? Well Captain, you can have it," and he pulled the trigger. Frank Oakley made a fatal error. Again, he forgot there wasn't a shell in the firing chamber. He quickly levered a shell in place and was bringing the rifle up again as Whitney fired the remaining three shots in his pistol in rapid succession, placing all three shots in and around Oakley's heart.

Oakley was positioned between Whitney and the edge of the canyon. The force of the shots drove him backwards. He lost his balance and went over. He was fatally wounded, but his dying act was to squeeze the trigger of the Spencer rifle as he fell. The shot clipped Whitney's hip, not deep enough to cause any serious damage, but enough to knock him down.

Michael and Whitney had the same idea, at the same instant — the shotgun! Whitney was the closest to it, but he was on the ground. He rose part way and half scrambling on all fours, he reached the shotgun a split second before Michael. He cocked both hammers and fired at precisely the same time that Michael put his hand on the barrel end of the shotgun. Michael turned the shotgun upwards in the nick of time and the pellets went harmlessly into the air. He pulled the shotgun from Whitney's grasp and stood over him. He raised the empty weapon to butt end Whitney with it, but Whitney was too quick. He kicked upwards with all his might, catching Michael in the groin. Michael slumped over in mortal agony. As he fell, the shot gun dropped several feet to the side.

Whitney scrambled to the shotgun and picking it up, he took the last two shells out of his pocket, broke the breech and began inserting them. Although in excruciating pain, Michael didn't lose sight of Whitney. He knew it meant his life, if he didn't get up quickly. He tackled Whitney in the midsection just as he was trying to put the shells in. Whitney was entirely focused on reloading the weapon and he didn't expect Michael to get up from the vicious kick, so the tackle took him by complete surprise. It knocked the wind out of him and he ended up flat on his back.

Whitney did not quite get the breech closed on the shotgun. When he was hit by Michael, it bounced and hit the ground with the shells rolling harmless away. Michael acted quickly. He picked up the shotgun and his thought was to get the shells and load it. He could see Whitney was already rising and he knew he wouldn't have time to pick up the shells and load the weapon before Whitney was on top of him, so he took the shotgun by the barrels and using a full swing, he threw the shotgun as far as he could. It was enough. The shotgun landed about a foot from the edge of the canyon and on the first bounce, went over and into the water and boulders below.

Michael didn't have time to react. He had taken his eyes off Whitney long enough to throw the shotgun and as he looked back, Whitney was on top of him and clubbed him across the side of the head with his pistol butt. He knew all the shells in the pistol were spent, but he cocked the hammer back and fired anyway. His assessment was correct; the pistol was empty, so he grabbed the barrel end of the revolver and was going to use it as a club and beat the meddlesome half breed to death.

"That's too easy, Captain. Why don't you try a live body?" said Mathew Briscoe, standing ten feet away with his big knife in his hand. He had decided he wasn't going to wait in the canyon, so he tied all the horses securely and as soon as Whitney and company were partway up the slope, he scrambled up the sheep trail as quickly as he could, emerging at the top a few minutes behind the rest. While he was climbing, he convinced himself, with the help of his ever present brother, that since Whitney found what he was looking for, he no longer needed anyone else. He was going to surprise Whitney and take care of business before Whitney came for him.

Whitney rose slowly and put the butt end of the pistol back in his hand and cocked the hammer. Aiming the gun at Briscoe he said, "Drop the knife, Hillbilly or I'll shoot you where you stand."

The bluff worked momentarily. Mathew believed him and was about to turn and run when Luke appeared beside Whitney. He stuck his face within inches of the cocked pistol and withdrew it. He said to Mathew, "He's out of bullets. Why do you think he was gonna club the breed, 'stead of shootin' him?"

"Go ahead and shoot then, Captain," said Mathew. "I think you're empty."

Whitney turned the pistol in his hand and charged Mathew, who saw it coming and sided-stepped Whitney's lunge. As Whitney went by him, Mathew turned quickly and came down with the knife in a huge arc aimed at the middle of Whitney's back, but wounded hip and all, Whitney was too quick for him. He ducked down and pirouetted away from Mathew, so he ended up to Mathew's right and slightly behind him. As Mathew's momentum carried him by, Whitney reached around with his left arm, put him in a choke hold, and squeezed with all his might. As Mathew was gasping for air, Whitney loosened the grip of his right arm, swung the pistol in one quick motion and buried the butt end in Mathew's skull. As he lifted the pistol for a second devastating blow, Mathew, in desperation, swung upwards with his knife, embedding it just below Whitney's collar bone. Whitney instinctively reacted and swung down with all his might, caving Mathew's skull in. He released his grip on Mathew and let him slide to the ground. There was just enough time to look around and the last thing he saw before he passed out was Michael getting to his feet.

Michael regained consciousness just as Whitney was clubbing Mathew for the second time. He rose on wobbly legs and stood for a moment to get his bearings. He saw Mathew's body on the ground and watched as Whitney lost consciousness. Michael walked to the prone Whitney, straddled him, and sat down on his chest. Whitney was barely conscious when Michael yanked Mathew Briscoe's knife out of his shoulder, causing Whitney to cry out in pain. He lifted the knife very slowly over his head and held it with both hands, ready to plunge it through the white man's vile heart. He nudged Whitney with his right knee several times trying to get him to open his eyes. Michael wanted Whitney to see who it was that put an end to his miserable life. Whitney opened his eyes momentarily. Michael was all set to drive the knife home when a voice behind him said, "It is not for you to do."

Michael rose, stood to the side of Whitney, and turned to see who had spoken. There stood seven natives. The speaker was a smallish man, not much over five feet tall. Michael said to him, "Who are you to tell me I should not kill this piece of shit?"

Dancing Crow stood beside Michael and gesturing to the little man, he said, "This is my grandson. He is called Little Fox." As soon as he spoke, the other members of the group gathered around Dancing Crow and began hugging him and patting him on the back, expressing their joy at finding him alive and well.

Michael's anger subsided. He moved closer to where Little Fox stood. Turning the knife, so the handle faced outward, he offered it to Little Fox and then gestured toward Whitney as if to say, "He's all yours."

Michael stepped back in complete surprise when Little Fox took the knife and slammed it to the ground at Michael's feet. He didn't understand. Their enemy was down and out and Little Fox didn't want to finish him? Instead, Little Fox smiled and stepped forward. He reached up and put his arm on Michael's shoulder and said, "Sometimes the greater vengeance is to let a man live with his demons."

While the hunters were greeting Dancing Crow and Michael and Little Fox were conversing, Clarence Whitney was looking across the canyon. Joining Silas Davidson on the ledge, were Frank Oakley and the Briscoe brothers. Frank Oakley said to Whitney, "Come on over, Captain. There is lots for everybody."

Whitney was shouting, No! No! No! It's mine. It's all mine," as he scrambled across the make shift ladder to the ledge. Whitney's mind had finally snapped. Once on the ledge, he reached down and using his good arm and all the strength he could muster, he lifted the ladder and pushed it sideways hard enough, so that it went toppling into the canyon. Then he began jumping up and down and pointing at Michael and the rest. He was laughing and shouting, "You bastards can't get my gold, now. It's all mine!"

Ignoring Whitney, Dancing Crow gave Little Fox a passionate embrace. He then turned to Michael and said to Little Fox, "This man has the blood of The People. He saved me from the evil one and from my own stubbornness several times. I don't want you to —"

Little Fox interrupted him and said, "I know, Grandfather. I know."

Michael walked to the sack of gold he had brought across the bridge. He knelt down beside it and opened it, taking out a large nugget. He moved it closer to his face and stared at. He could see himself as the owner of his own freight line and all his imagined respect that would come with it.

Whitney was still dancing and hollering, as Michael put the nugget back in the sack and picked it up. Whitney, noticing him, stopped his antics and said, "You're a rich man, Breed. Don't spend it all in one place," and then he began to laugh, hysterically.

Michael looked back at Dancing Crow, Little Fox, and the hunters and it seemed everyone stood still with their eyes focused on him, waiting for him to do something. Little Fox's head was cocked to one side, as if he was fascinated by what he expected to happen next, while Dancing Crow had a pleading look on his face.

Michael picked up the sack of gold, walked to the edge of the canyon, calling Whitney's name as he went. Whitney looked in Michael's direction and when he was sure Whitney was watching, Michael smiled and dropped the sack of gold into the canyon.

The End

CPSIA information can be obtained at www.ICGtesting.com
Printed in the USA
LVOW12s0601190215

427260LV00002B/61/P